No Easy Deeds

Book 1 in The Echo Lane Series
Keith A Pearson

Inchgate Publishing

For more information about the author and to receive updates on his new releases, visit:

www.keithapearson.co.uk

Copyright © 2024 by Keith A Pearson. All rights reserved. This book, or any portion thereof, may not be reproduced or used in any manner whatsoever without the express, written permission of the author, except for the use of brief quotations in a book review.

Chapter 1
Friday 21st July, 1989

During my years at infant school, I recall having vague thoughts about the difference between adulthood and childhood. Principally, being a grown-up seemed like a better deal. No school, no set bedtime, and free rein over confectionery consumption. If an adult fancied a Curly Wurly for breakfast, it was their choice to make.

My assumption evolved as I stepped up to junior school, and I focused on the benefits of being a male grown-up — my dad, really. He could drive a car, use power tools, and watch whatever he liked on TV. He had to occasionally kiss my mother, though, and I considered that a significant downside.

When I reached secondary school, my envy of grown-ups centred on material possessions. I spent countless hours poring over the Argos catalogue — 1975 Autumn/Winter edition — wishing I had the money to buy an ever-expanding list of items. Top of that list was a Pye 14" portable colour television set with push-button channel selector: £199.50. Second, a Waltham music centre with an auto-changer record deck and cassette player: £115.00. The third spot on my list went to an

Edward O'Brien racing bicycle with derailleur gears and whitewall tyres: a snip at £42.66.

At the age of fifteen, I lost interest in the Argos catalogue after I experienced arguably the two best features of being a grown-up, namely alcohol and sex. Both delivered equal amounts of joy, shame, and deep regret.

Then, without truly realising the implications, I left school. I had become, in some sense, a grown-up, although I don't ever remember feeling like one.

I got a job via a youth training scheme, working forty hours a week for a company that produced reproduction furniture. They paid me the princely sum of £25 a week, and I, in turn, paid my parents £5 a week towards housekeeping. However, despite transitioning from burden to contributor, I still had to adhere to my parents' rules. I definitely didn't feel like a grown-up, particularly as I couldn't vote, legally drink in a pub, or drive a car. I became temporarily trapped in the no man's land between adolescence and adulthood.

Even as I passed through my teenage years to my early twenties, I still couldn't shake off the feeling that I wasn't a proper grown-up. Eventually, I met Zoe Carter in a nightclub, and six months later we moved in together. Having a rent book and a long-term girlfriend still didn't scratch the grown-up itch, so I proposed.

We were about to set a date for the wedding, but then, nine weeks ago, a twist of fate changed the course of our lives.

On the Saturday in question, I promised Zoe we could have lunch in town and then watch *Licence to Kill* at the cinema, but my piece-of-shit car had other ideas and refused to start. Resigned to a mile-long walk, we set off. I don't know how it happened, but we took a wrong turn and ended up on an unfamiliar road. Halfway along that road, we passed a new development of luxury flats and a sign positioned to the front of the landscaped grounds: *Last few remaining — Move in for just £99.*

As it happens, our landlord had just raised the rent on the pokey one-bedroom dump we were living in, so, more in naive curiosity than expectation, we ventured into the sales office.

Two hours later, we emerged from the sales office almost a hundred quid worse off, but with the promise that we could move into our very own luxury flat within eight weeks. Dad had always told me that mortgages were hard to get and banks weren't keen on lending to people our age, but he was way off the mark. We spent forty minutes chatting to a mortgage broker, and she confirmed we could obtain a 110% mortgage at a heavily discounted fixed rate for the first year.

We signed the forms, and within a few days, the Alliance & Leicester Building Society agreed to lend us £60,000 to buy the flat, plus an additional £6,000 we could spend however we saw fit. That six grand will go towards new furniture, a state-of-the-art TV and video system, plus a decent second-hand car.

The weeks have dragged on, but today is the day. We just received a call to confirm that the legal process is complete. Flat 55, Sefton Court, is now ours.

Today, I am officially a homeowner. Today, I feel like a proper grown-up.

I pull into the parking bay marked 55 — *our* parking bay for *our* luxury flat.

"I'm so excited," Zoe squeals from the passenger seat. "Who'd have ever thought that we might own a flat in Sefton Court?"

"Not my parents," I snort. "That's for sure."

"They're jealous, I reckon. Remember, they had to scrimp and save for years to buy their first place, as your dad tells us at every given opportunity."

"Well, as I keep telling him, it's nearly the nineties, not the seventies. The world is a different place."

"Too right," Zoe replies while removing her seat belt. "Anyway, shall we go get the keys to our lovely new home?"

"Let's do it."

We hurry into the sales office, where a middle-aged woman, Susan, presents us with an information pack and four keys on a Tennison Homes-branded fob.

"Would you like me to conduct a walk-through?" Susan asks. "Most of what you need to know is detailed in the owner's information pack, but I'm happy to show you around if you'd prefer."

"We'll be fine on our own, thanks," Zoe replies.

"If you need anything or you have any questions, the sales office will be open for a few weeks, or at least until the last buyer moves in."

With all the excitement of kids on Christmas Day morning, we thank Susan and hurry out of the sales office.

"What time is your dad getting here?" I ask as we hurry through the landscaped gardens towards the communal entrance.

"Not until two," Zoe replies, glancing at her watch. "So, we've got just over an hour to ourselves."

Her confirmation is delivered with a flirtatious grin, ramping up my eagerness to step through the front door of our new home. Whilst I'm no Casanova — I'd enjoyed a few dozen dalliances with members of the opposite sex before I met Zoe — I've never quite connected with another girl in the way I connect with Zoe, from our shared sense of humour to our sexual appetites. She is my soul mate, which is just as well as we're now tied into a twenty-five-year mortgage together.

We virtually sprint up the stairs to the second floor and the door to flat 55.

"Are you going to carry me over the threshold?" Zoe asks, slightly out of breath.

"We're not married yet, and I don't want to risk putting my back out ... not until we've christened our new home, anyway."

"Hey! Are you suggesting I'm too heavy?"

I ignore Zoe's mock indignation and slip the key into the lock.

Having never opened the door to my own home before, and despite the fast-developing bulge in my jeans, I mark the occasion by pushing the front door open with a theatrical sweep of my left arm.

"Ta-da!"

"Ooh, we've got mail already," Zoe says, bending down and snatching up two envelopes lying on the doormat.

We step inside and, as I close the door, Zoe examines the first of the envelopes.

"It's to the homeowner," she says. "That's disappointing."

"Probably junk mail."

She hands the letters to me and then dashes up the hallway, flinging open the door to the lounge. I thought we'd agreed not to wear shoes in the flat, but I don't want to spoil the moment.

The lounge is an empty shell of a room: the walls are a buttery shade of cream, and the brand-new carpets are kind of beige in tone. I wouldn't dare say it to my deliriously happy fiancée, but it reminds me of a custard cream biscuit.

Zoe spins around excitedly in the centre of the room, her golden locks flowing in rhythm with the hem of a summer dress that errs dangerously close to too short.

She is a stunning woman, and I am a lucky man.

"This is all ours," she coos, her arms outstretched. "I can't believe it!"

Zoe then grabs my hand and drags me towards the feature she loves most about the flat — a small balcony behind a set of sliding double-glazed doors.

"Let's check out the view," she says excitedly.

Once I've mastered the locking mechanism, I slide the door open, and we step outside. The view isn't much to admire — a row of semi-detached houses and a bus stop — but, on a sultry summer's day, the slight breeze is welcome.

"Can we pop out and buy a bistro set later?" Zoe asks. "I'd love to eat our first meal out here."

"Yeah, why not," I reply as we lean up against the balustrade and survey the scene.

While my fiancée drinks in the view, I turn my attention to the letters. The first is in a brown envelope and marked for the attention of the homeowners. That's us, I guess.

I tear it open and pull out a letter. Instantly recognising the logo at the top of the page, I inwardly groan. It's a legal notice that we must register for the community charge, or poll tax as it's colloquially known, within seven days of occupation. Tucking the council's poll tax demand into my pocket, I open the second letter, addressed to Mr Daniel Monk and Miss Zoe Carter.

Another recognisable logo features at the top — the Alliance & Leicester Building Society.

"Anything interesting?" Zoe asks.

"It's from the building society, confirming our mortgage terms."

"Boring."

"Yeah. Very."

Boring as it might be, I should probably check everything is in order.

It only takes a cursory scan to undermine my good mood. I knew home ownership would come with certain responsibilities, but seeing those responsibilities outlined in black and white proves quite the passion killer. Our mortgage is set for a twenty-five-year term, and for the first year, the fixed rate discount represents a monthly mortgage payment of £560 — significantly more than we were paying in rent.

Zoe sidles up next to me, presumably to see what I'm frowning at.

"We'll be fine," she declares, sensing my unease. "We might have to tighten our belts for the first year but the mortgage broker did say that interest rates will likely be a lot lower by the time our fixed rate ends."

"I know. It's just ... it's such a massive commitment and a bit scary, don't you think?"

"No, not at all. This is just the start for us."

"You reckon?"

"Now you're assistant manager, it's only a matter of time before they offer you a manager's position at another store, and you'll be raking it in."

"Hmm, maybe."

"And Debbie has plans to open a second salon next year, and who do you think she'll ask to manage it?"

"Gaynor?"

"Oi!" Zoe chides, playfully slapping my arm. "She'll give the job to her best stylist — me, of course."

"I'm only kidding. I know you'll do well."

"We both will, and in a few years, we'll sell this place, make a huge profit, and buy a lovely house with a garden."

"And then?"

"Then, Mr Monk, we can put all that baby-making practice to good use."

Zoe read in some glossy magazine that the ideal age for the modern woman to have her first child is twenty-eight. I can't remember why, but Zoe wholeheartedly bought into the idea. She's just turned twenty-five, so we've got three years to enjoy ourselves before the responsibility of parenthood.

"How many should we have?" I ask, pulling Zoe into my arms. "Two? Three? Four?"

"Two, I think — a boy and a girl."

"I'm not sure you get to decide."

"No, but that's what I'd like … in an ideal world."

"Well," I say, leaning in so our lips are only inches apart. "I'd say that the world is already close to ideal."

We share a slow, lingering kiss, and in that moment, it hits me. I don't care about being a grown-up — all I care about is sharing the rest of my life with this amazing woman.

409 Days Later...

Chapter 2

Monday 3rd September, 1990

Standing in a portacabin on the dreariest of Monday mornings, the guy behind the desk sits back in his chair and folds his arms.

"Best I can do, mate," he reiterates. "The Volvo plus three hundred quid."

"You've got the Volvo up for £899," I protest. "My car has got to be worth more than twelve hundred quid, surely?"

"Ain't you heard? We're in a recession."

"I know, but I paid two grand for that car just over a year ago. It can't have lost almost half its value in that time."

"I've got overheads to cover, mate. Take it or leave it."

The deal sucks, but I'm already at my overdraft limit, and the bills are mounting up. Three hundred quid doesn't come close to solving my financial problems but it'll buy some time.

"Fine," I sigh. "I'll take it."

Half an hour later, once the paperwork is complete, I swap the keys to my cherry-red Peugeot 205 GTi for those of a dark-blue Volvo 340. It's akin to trading a pair of Nike trainers for wooden clogs. The car dealer then counts out the only reason I've entered into such a shitty transaction — thirty ten-pound notes.

"Nice doing business with you," he says once I've tucked the wad of notes into my jacket pocket.

"I wish I could say the same."

Outside, I hurry through the drizzle to my new motor and get in. I noticed the slight whiff of pipe tobacco and wet dog on the test drive, but it seems more pungent now I own the car.

"You're twenty-eight years of age and own a Volvo," I mutter under my breath. "You sad bastard."

I then remind myself of the two other options the dealer offered in part-exchange: a Soviet-built Lada in hearing-aid beige, and a rust-stricken Mini Clubman. The Volvo was the least-worst option and, if there's any silver lining, I'm slightly less likely to die in a road traffic accident.

As I pull away from the lot, it crosses my mind that maybe surviving a car crash wouldn't be a silver lining at all. Death's sweet embrace would put a permanent cross through my long list of woes.

I don't want to be pessimistic, but it's hard not to be.

To avoid my mind drifting any further into the darkness, I try to focus on the Volvo's positive attributes. The windscreen wipers are quietly efficient, and there's no denying the seats are more comfortable than those in my Peugeot. Comfortable, like an old armchair — it would explain why Volvos are so popular with pensioners.

I reach a junction and turn right rather than left towards the flat. Of all the many debts I've amassed, there's one I'd rather settle ahead of the others — my parents are more deserving than Southern Electric and British-fucking-Telecom. Saying that, my parents haven't yet resorted to threats of legal action, unlike my other creditors.

After a few more streets, I turn into Alma Place. I could close my eyes and drive the final few hundred yards as I know this road intimately. It's the road where I grew up, where I first kicked a football, first rode a bike, and in the second bedroom of number 29, I broke my virginity — twice, if you were to ask Alison Bennett and Nicky Maynard.

I pull up outside and remove two ten-pound notes from my pocket. Dad's Cortina isn't anywhere to be seen because he's likely at work, which is why I'm here now and not later. It was humiliating enough asking Mum for a loan to buy groceries. I'm sure Dad would have agreed to lend me a score, but it would have come with a lecture I couldn't stomach.

Rather than knock on the front door, I take the same route I've used more times than I remember: through a rickety gate and up a path leading to a door at the side of the house. I rap my knuckle on the glass twice before letting myself in.

"Only me," I call out while untying my trainers.

Mum wanders into the kitchen, a cup and saucer in her right hand. If she's surprised to see her eldest son on a Monday morning, it doesn't show on her face.

"Morning, sweetheart," she says casually while making her way to the sink. "Would you like a cuppa?"

"No thanks. It's only a flying visit."

I withdraw the two tenners from my back pocket and place them on the kitchen table. "Thanks for the loan, Mum."

"Are you sure you can afford to pay me back this week? I said I don't mind waiting."

"No, it's fine. I traded in my car this morning, and I managed to negotiate a deal on a nice Volvo that won't cost so much to run. Plus, I got three hundred quid into the bargain."

Mum nods and carefully places her cup and saucer in the sink.

"How long will that last you?" she then asks.

"I don't know. Depends on how quickly I find a job, I suppose."

"Any luck on that front."

"I'm still waiting on that Dixons job I applied for last week. I don't really want to be a sales assistant in an electrical store, but it's marginally better than being on the dole."

"We were watching the news last night, and one of those financial chaps painted a pretty bleak picture of the economy. He said unemployment might top three million."

"Thanks for the pep talk, Mum."

She wipes her hands on a tea towel and steps over to the table.

"Times are tough, son, and there's no sense in burying your head in the sand."

"I'm not."

"But last week, you didn't even have enough money to feed yourself."

"It was just ... a temporary cashflow problem. I'll be alright."

"Will you?"

Two little words, but Mum adds just enough intonation to get her point across.

"Are you keeping on top of your bills?" she then asks.

"On the whole, yes."

"Daniel?"

For a moment, it could easily be 1977 and rather than standing in this kitchen as a twenty-eight-year-old man, I'm a teenage kid with raging acne and a guilt complex. Mum, however, has not changed one iota. She'd never admit to dying her hair or using face cream, and she might have put on a pound or two, but she's barely changed. Maybe I haven't changed either.

"I'm fine," I mumble while inspecting the pattern on the lino floor.

"Listen to me," Mum responds in a tone which sits perfectly between concerned and authoritative. "I've looked after the household budget since before you were born, and there have been times I've had to make very little money go a very long way. If you need help, that's what I'm here for — not to judge, okay?"

Whilst I'm more than willing to lie to myself, I can't lie to my mother.

"I know," I say quietly. "Truth is, I'm in a bit of a hole."

"Sit down," Mum orders.

I take a seat at the table while Mum retrieves a notepad and a calculator from one of the drawers.

"Let's go through your finances and see what's what, eh?"

"If you think it'll make any difference."

"It usually does, so let's start by listing your current outgoings."

Knowing you're in debt must be like knowing you're overweight. There are constant reminders in every aspect of your life but after a while, you learn how to ignore those reminders. They become issues for another day. *Tomorrow, I'll order the salad. Tomorrow, I'll pluck up the courage to check my bank balance at the cash machine.*

The last financial burden I relay to Mum is, without doubt, the heaviest.

"Our fixed rate ended three months ago, so the monthly mortgage repayment is now £794."

Mum stares back at me, open-mouthed. "£794?"

"The broker sold us on the idea that interest rates would almost certainly go down. We thought we'd be paying eight per cent, not fourteen."

"How on earth are you paying it?"

"Um, I'm not. I'm two months behind."

"Good grief. And what about Zoe?"

The mere mention of her name spikes a physical reaction not too dissimilar to chronic indigestion.

"What about her?"

"The mortgage repayments are just as much her responsibility as yours. Is she paying half?"

"No," I mumble.

"Why not?"

I don't want to lie to Mum, but that doesn't mean I want to tell her the truth.

"Zoe made it clear that she wants nothing more to do with me, and the feeling is mutual."

"That's as maybe, but she can't just flounce off and leave you to manage the mortgage alone. When was the last time you spoke to her?"

"Some time in May."

"Four months ago?"

"Yeah."

"Surely you must have discussed the flat?"

That conversation back in the late spring was as short as it was heated, and we never discussed the practicalities of our split. Zoe wrote to me a few weeks later, but I recognised her handwriting on the envelope and tore it up.

"No, we never discussed the flat."

Mum puffs a tired sigh and then frowns at the long list of debts she's committed to ink.

"You don't have a choice, Daniel. You have to sell the flat."

"I don't want to sell the flat."

"And I don't want to see my son in bankruptcy court, but that's where you're heading if you don't get a grip on your finances."

"I'll find a way out of this mess."

"There's already an obvious way out: to sell the flat."

"And I said I don't want to sell it."

"Give me one good reason why not."

"For starters, where the hell do I live?"

"You can move back here ... temporarily, of course. I know you value your freedom."

How can I tell her that I'd rather share a cell with The Yorkshire Ripper than move back home?

"That's nice of you to offer, but I can't move back here."

"Why not?"

"Because ... because I'd feel like a failure."

"Nonsense," Mum replies, shooing away my objection. "You've just suffered a slight blip, that's all. We all encounter difficulties from time to time, and there's no shame in taking a step back, regrouping, and then moving forward again."

"I dunno, Mum."

"It'd solve most of your problems. I'm sure you'd make a modest profit, and you could use that money to clear your debts. A clean slate. Do you know what the flat is currently worth?"

"No idea."

"Then surely a good place to start is speaking to an estate agent, wouldn't you say? Keith and Moira moved home last year and were very complimentary about their agent. Gibley Smith, if I remember rightly."

"Okay, I'll think about it."

"You do that, but please, Daniel, don't just sit back and hope your problems will fix themselves. Look at what happened to Robbie when he ignored his ... his situation."

"That's a bit different, Mum."

"No, it's not. If he'd been honest with himself, it would have saved everyone a lot of heartache, including his poor fiancée."

My kid brother proposed to Lucy when he was just eighteen, but by the time his nineteenth birthday came around he was two-timing her with a guy he met at work, Stephen. They're still together, and I know they're happy, but the fallout from Robbie denying his sexuality pissed off a lot of people, not least his fiancée and her family. Consequently, Robbie and Stephen now live eighty miles away in Brighton.

"Anyway," Mum continues. "This is about you, not Robbie. If you don't want to sleepwalk into financial ruin, you need to get on top of things."

"Yes, Mum. I hear you."

"So, you'll get the flat valued?"

"As I said, I'll think about it. I promise."

"Fine," she huffs. "Just don't think about it for too long."

"I won't."

Mum then glances up at a clock that has lived on the kitchen wall for as long as I can remember. "Your dad will be home soon for his lunch. I'd better get on."

"Yeah, me too."

I get to my feet and plant a kiss on Mum's cheek. "Thank you."

"Your gratitude only has meaning if you actually take my advice on board."

"I have taken it on board. Just let me do this my way, okay?"

"Fair enough."

Debt settled, advice absorbed, and keen to get away before Dad returns, I depart.

Halfway down the path, I remember the vehicular monstrosity waiting for me on the road. If I do decide to sell the flat, maybe I could trade it in for another 205 GTi, or maybe even a Golf GTi. That would be a positive upside, but a more daunting downside would be dealing with Zoe. We co-signed at least a dozen different forms to purchase the flat, so it stands to reason that we'll likely have a fair number to co-sign if we sell it.

That would mean being in the same room together, and I don't think I'm ready for that yet. I don't know if I ever will be.

Chapter 3

Unlike Alma Place, where everyone seems to know everyone else's business, living in a development of almost one hundred flats does offer a degree of anonymity. I know a few of my neighbours well enough to nod a good morning to, but that's as far as the familiarity goes. Consequently, I doubt anyone will notice the downgrade parked in bay 55 of the residents' car park.

Having passed the postman on the way into the communal hallway, I open the front door to the flat with a sense of foreboding. The postman rarely delivers good news these days, but a tiny part of me is still clinging to the hope that I might receive an unexpected tax rebate.

Four letters: one addressed to me, one to Zoe, and two to both of us.

I head straight for the kitchen, which is my preferred destination for opening mail. There's a bin handy and a drawer where I can stuff unpaid bills — out of sight, out of mind.

Tentatively, I open the first of the two letters addressed to Zoe and me. It's from our life insurance company, confirming that our policy will be terminated in seven days unless the account is brought up to date. If I die tomorrow, there's no way I want Zoe to financially benefit, so I file it straight into the bin. The second is from the building society and is of significantly greater concern. If we don't contact their debt recovery department urgently, they'll start legal proceedings, which may result in our home being repossessed.

"Fuck," I gulp before placing the letter in the drawer of denial.

I then take a closer look at the letter addressed to Zoe. On the back, the return address confirms who sent it: Barclaycard. It could be a final demand or a statement, but it's not my problem. I drop it in the bin.

The final letter is marked private and confidential, but there are no clues on the envelope as to the sender's identity. I rip it open. The letter is from Dixons Retail, and four words immediately leap off the page: *unsuccessful on this occasion.*

I can't even get a job as a poxy sales assistant at Dixons, selling overpriced Taiwanese crap.

Fuelled by indignation and ignominy, I scrunch the letter into a ball and hurl it towards the bin. Unsurprisingly, it misses. That job, undesirable as it might have been, was my last hope. She might have phrased it differently, but Mum was right — I am in deep shit.

Deep down, I knew this moment would arrive. It's no longer a case of choices or options but necessities, and selling the flat now sits firmly in that category. I open another drawer and pull out the Yellow Pages. Fingers crossed, BT hasn't yet disconnected the phone line.

I take the Yellow Pages through to the lounge and pick up the phone. The dial tone has never sounded sweeter.

After flicking through the Yellow Pages, I locate the number for Gibley Smith and dial it. A young-sounding woman answers. "Good morning, Gibley Smith Estate Agents."

"Hi, I'm considering putting my flat on the market. Can I arrange for someone to pop by and do whatever it is you people do?"

"No problem, sir. When would you like one of my colleagues to conduct a valuation?"

"The sooner the better."

"Our branch manager, Lee, has a slot free early afternoon today if that's not too soon?"

I'm slightly taken aback that they're able to come out so quickly, but maybe that's a positive sign. Perhaps they've got a long list of hungry buyers looking for flats and are keen to sign me up before one of their competitors.

"This afternoon would be great," I reply. "Does one o'clock work?"

"Yes, it does. Let me take your details, and we'll book you in."

The young woman, I learn, is called Tina and, after asking her questions, she confirms my appointment. I end the call and return the phone to its base.

Sitting on the sofa purchased from the six grand we should never have borrowed, I try to focus on the positive elements of selling the flat. I know the property market has been crazy because I read it in the newspaper a while back, so it's not beyond the realms of possibility that the value of the flat has gone up dramatically in the relatively short time we've owned it. It could be worth seventy grand. Maybe even seventy-five or eighty. If I can walk away with five grand, I could even look at buying somewhere a bit cheaper once I get a job. Worst case, a few grand would allow me to rent somewhere for six months, thus avoiding a return to my teenage bedroom.

I have to credit Mum for forcing my hand, but selling the flat could turn out to be a blessing in disguise.

Buoyed by a sudden injection of positivity, I return the Yellow Pages to the kitchen drawer and check the cupboards for lunch. The pickings are so slim they're barely pickings at all.

"Toast it is then," I mutter to myself.

Still wearing my positivity hat; at least the coffee and sugar caddies remain well stocked, and there's half a packet of digestive biscuits I can dip into for dessert.

Lunch prepared, I take my plate through to the lounge and switch the TV on.

Being one of the unemployed masses for the last nine weeks, I've become accustomed to watching more daytime TV than any man should have to endure. It's become part of my daily routine, along with a visit to the Job Centre and prolonged spells of self-loathing and existential dread. On Tuesdays and Fridays, I get to mix things up with a visit to the library, where I scour the employment section of the local paper for an hour.

As if my life wasn't grim enough, today is Monday — the worst day of the week for TV options.

The lunchtime news is on BBC One, but I've stopped watching the news because it's just a barrage of depressing data relating to the economy. On BBC Two, there's a programme about the demise of farm horses, presented by two pathologically dull men. The kids' show *Rosie & Jim* is all ITV has to offer, and *Sesame Street* is about to start on Channel 4.

I switch the TV to Channel 4.

Twenty minutes pass, and with my hunger sated and numeracy improved, I decide it might be a good idea to tidy up before the estate agent arrives. I wash up the cup and plate, run the hoover around, and light one of the expensive candles Zoe never returned to collect.

Right on cue, the intercom buzzes just as I'm rearranging the cushions on the sofa. I hurry through to the hallway and grab the handset.

"Hello."

"Mr Monk?"

"Yes."

"It's Lee Ross from Gibley Smith."

His accent isn't local. Yorkshire, I think.

"Come on up. It's the second floor."

"Righto."

I press the button to disengage the lock on the communal door and then return the intercom handset to its cradle. It usually takes half a minute for someone to reach the flat, and I've learned from experience that there's insufficient time to do anything other than pace the hallway carpet. In this instance, the pacing is partly due to impatience but mainly because I'm anxious about what Lee Ross might say. His valuation will determine how easy it is for me to move on — financially, at least.

I hear a door close in the communal hallway, and that's my cue to open the front door. The timing is perfect as a man who couldn't be anything other than an estate agent approaches. Although Lee Ross might dress like a typical estate agent, his side parting and thin moustache give him the air of a wartime spiv. He's also slightly older than I imagined — mid to late thirties, I'd guess.

"Mr Monk, I presume," he says, holding out his hand.

"Yes, but call me Danny. Nice to meet you, Lee."

We shake hands and I invite him through to the lounge.

"I've never sold a property before," I confess, unsure whether to offer the estate agent a seat or not. "How does this work?"

"I'll just have a quick look around if that's okay?"

"Sure. Would you like a guided tour?"

"No, don't worry. I've seen at least a dozen flats in this development, and they're all much of a muchness."

"Right, well, help yourself. Can I get you a tea or coffee?"

"Not for me," Lee replies. "If I drink any more tea today, I'll be pissing like a racehorse all afternoon."

With that, he wanders back across the lounge to the hallway.

I've barely got myself comfortable on the sofa when he returns.

"That was quick," I remark, half-jokingly.

"You've seen one, you've seen them all. Mind if I grab a seat?"

"Yes, of course."

He lowers himself into the nearest armchair and flips open his clipboard.

"How long have you been here?" he then asks.

"We completed in June last year."

"I see."

The estate agent scribbles something down.

"Are you looking to sell the flat, or are you just after a valuation?"

"I'd rather not sell it, but, realistically, I don't have a choice. My circumstances have changed over the last six months, and not for the better."

"I'm sorry to hear that. It's tough out there, no mistake."

"You're telling me," I huff.

"Am I right in presuming you paid around sixty thousand?"

"For the flat, yes. We got one of those 110% mortgages, which I'm beginning to regret."

Lee winces. "Not much consolation, but you weren't the only one."

"Have you sold other flats in this development, then?"

"Aye, but not for the original owners."

"Eh?"

"You're not going to like this one jot, but you strike me as the type of man who prefers blunt honesty over your typical estate agents' bullshit."

"I suppose, yes."

Returning his attention to the clipboard, he extracts two sheets of paper and hands them to me.

"Sales particulars of two flats currently for sale in this development," he says by way of explanation.

I glance at the first of the two. It's for number 18 Sefton Court — a two-bedroom ground-floor flat on the other side of the block. Then I stare in horror at the asking price printed below the photo.

"£52,950," I gasp. "Is that a misprint?"

"Look at the second set of particulars."

My hand suddenly shaking, I flip over the first set of sales particulars and then promptly wish I hadn't.

"£49,950?"

"I'm afraid so. Both flats have been up for a while now, and even at those prices, they're not shifting."

"Are the sellers crazy? Why sell a flat for significantly less than you paid for it?"

"In the case of those two, the original owners are out of the picture. Both flats were repossessed back in the summer, and we've had three more in the last six months. All of them repossessions."

I continue to stare at the sales particulars, utterly gobsmacked.

"I'm sorry, Danny, but if you need to sell this place quickly, you'd be wasting your time if you put it up for anything more than forty-seven grand."

"I ... I, that's nineteen grand less than we owe on the mortgage, and I presume I'd have to pay your company a fee, not to mention a solicitor."

"That's the way it works. You need to allow a couple of grand for fees, and I don't know if you checked, but some mortgages have an early redemption penalty, too. They're crafty bastards."

It's the third time Lee has dropped a swear word into the conversation, but his lack of professionalism is hardly my biggest concern at the moment.

I'd rather avoid breaking down in front of a stranger, so I get up and stare out of the patio doors towards a cheerless grey sky. Long silent seconds pass.

"Fuck sake," I groan, unintentionally out loud.

"Are you okay?" Lee asks.

What a question. I'm a million miles from okay.

"Not really, no," I reply, turning around. "I split with my fiancée in the spring, lost my job in the summer, and now I've just discovered that I'll be twenty grand out of pocket if I sell my home."

"Could be worse."

"You reckon?" I snort. "I don't see how."

"I could take you to watch my team, Rotherham United. Ninety minutes of that shite would shift your perspective, no mistake."

I appreciate his efforts to lighten the mood, but it changes nothing.

"What did you do?" Lee then asks. "For a job?"

"I was an assistant manager with Presto Supermarkets," I reply, returning to the sofa. "They shut a load of branches, including mine."

"No luck finding another job?"

"Not in retail and that's all I really know."

Lee rubs his chin for a moment and then sits forward. "If you worked in retail, I presume you've got half-decent people skills and a bit of common sense about you?"

"I like to think so, yes."

"Listen, I might have an opportunity, but don't get too excited."

"At this point, I'll consider almost anything."

"It's probably below what you're looking for, but we've got a vacancy for a trainee negotiator. The money is crap, and the hours are long, but if you can stick it for a few months, you'll get bumped up to a negotiator. That role comes with a company car and a half-decent salary."

"That sounds interesting. Just how crap is the salary?"

"Seven grand a year, plus commission."

"Ouch."

"I told you it's crap, but it's more than dole money, eh?"

"That's true."

I ponder Lee's suggestion for a moment.

"Tell you what," he says. "Have a think and, if you're interested, give me a bell in the morning. You can pop in and we can have a proper chat about it. How's that sound?"

"Okay, thanks. I will."

"Now, about this place. Do you want to put it on the market?"

"Is there any point trying to sell it for more than fifty grand?"

"Ask another agent, and they'll tell you yes, but only because they have targets to meet. As a Yorkshireman, I'm genetically predisposed to talk straight — you've bugger all chance of selling your flat unless you peg the asking price well below fifty grand."

"I understand, but seeing as it's not just my name on the deeds, I suppose I'd better check with my ex."

"You do that."

Lee closes his clipboard and gets to his feet. I shake his hand.

"I appreciate you being honest, and I'll definitely think about the job."

"No worries, but don't think too long. There's an advert going in the local rag on Thursday, and that'll create a queue of applicants."

Despite the measly salary, I suspect he's not exaggerating.

"I'll call you in the morning, either way."

I see Lee to the front door and thank him again. As he strides off down the communal hallway, I try to imagine what he'd be like as a boss, and if I'm really suited to a career in estate agency. Then, a more damning thought rocks up and blows the other two away — what the hell am I going to do about the flat?

Chapter 4

After Lee Ross left yesterday, I trudged down to the Post Office and handed over three-quarters of the money I made from trading my car. For the time being, I don't have to worry about the electric and phone being cut off, but I only had enough money left over to pay a fraction of the mortgage arrears. Those arrears will significantly increase again next week when my bank declines a third consecutive repayment. Ultimately, if I don't get a job soon, that token payment will be of little consequence.

Of course, selling the flat is still an option, but doing so creates two further problems — I'll have to find somewhere else to live, and I'll need to speak to Zoe. Neither appeal. There's also the not-insignificant issue of plugging a five-figure gap between what the flat is worth and how much we owe the building society.

However, those are tomorrow's problems. Today's problem is getting the Volvo to start.

"Come on, you bastard!" I yell while turning the key for the third time.

Perhaps detecting my stress, the car obliges and splutters into life. When I spoke to Lee at Gibley Smith this morning, he asked if eleven o'clock would be fine for an interview. I thought two hours would be ample time to prepare myself, but that was before I wasted forty minutes trying to find my left shoe and then another fifteen minutes ironing a second shirt after I spilt coffee on the first.

I take a deep breath before pulling out of the parking bay.

I'm not sure why I'm so stressed. I spent most of yesterday evening weighing up the pros and cons of becoming a trainee negotiator for an estate agency chain, and I wasted precious little ink when it came to filling out the pros column. The cons, however, are numerous. The salary is shocking, the prospect of working long hours unappealing, and beyond my experience of buying a flat, I know next to nothing about the property market.

The only reason I'm now burning valuable petrol is because, as crappy as this job might be, I can't live on dole money much longer. My savings account is empty, I've nothing of value left to sell, and my debts are mounting by the day. This is the only opportunity on the horizon, and if I try to be positive about it, at least it'll help stem the tide of debt until a better job opportunity comes along.

That assumes I secure the position, and there's no guarantee of that.

Rather than pay for a spot in a car park, I pull into a side street a few minutes' walk from the Gibley Smith office. I check my reflection in the rear-view mirror and offer a few words of encouragement.

"You've got this, Danny."

He looks less than convinced. Having suffered so much rejection in recent months, my self-belief isn't what it once was. That lack of confidence might explain the sudden fluttering of butterflies in my chest as I lock the Volvo.

With ten minutes to kill, I take a slow amble towards Victoria Road. It was once the main location for the town centre shops up until the new shopping centre opened. Apart from Woolworths, most of the big-name retailers moved into the centre. Hence, Victoria Road is now a mishmash of estate agents, bookmakers, takeaways, and a handful of independent retailers that can't afford the rent in the shopping centre.

I've never had cause to count them before, but there are an awful lot of estate agents. I pass five of them on my way to Gibley Smith, and I'm almost certain there are a few more at the other end of the road. Why does a town of maybe forty thousand residents need so many estate agents? I don't know the answer, but maybe it's something I can ask Lee during the interview. There's typically an opportunity at the end of an interview, and asking a valid question will make a change from staring blankly at the interviewer and shaking my head.

I reach my destination, straighten my shoulders, and open the door to Gibley Smith.

Despite owning a property, for now, anyway, I've never had cause to set foot in an estate agent's office before. I'm not sure what I expected, but the scene before me is fairly corporate and drab. Of the three desks in the main office area, two are occupied: one by Lee and another by a youngish-looking guy in the middle of a phone conversation.

"Danny," Lee booms, getting to his feet. "You're early."

"Oh, sorry."

"It's alright. I was going to have a quick ciggie before you arrived but you don't mind if I smoke during the interview, do you?"

"Um, no."

"Good man. Come this way."

He guides me towards a door behind his desk, which, I presume, leads to another office, maybe a staff room, and whatever other facilities the building houses.

"After you," Lee says, holding the door open for me.

"Thanks."

I step through the doorway and come to an almost abrupt halt.

"It's a bit tight in here," Lee says behind me as he closes the door. "But it serves a purpose."

The word tight doesn't quite do the space justice. Pokey would be a better adjective, or possibly claustrophobic. I can hear a ventilation fan whirring above my head, but there are no windows. There is, however, another door, and it's probably safe to assume it leads to the toilet unless they don't have toilets.

"Let's sort out some chairs," Lee says.

There are two beaten-up office chairs against the wall to my right. Lee steps forward and drags one of them towards the door while inviting me to sit on the other one.

"As you can see," the Yorkshireman then says. "We're a bit tight on space. As well as being our staffroom, it's the only place I can hold interviews in private."

"Let's hope no one needs the loo, eh," I jest, nodding towards the mystery door to my right.

"We won't be long but if you do take the job, bear in mind we have a strict no-dumping policy between 11.00 am and 2.00 pm."

"No dumping policy?"

"Basically, if you need to take a shit between eleven and two, you have to use the bogs in the shopping centre. No one wants to sit and eat their lunch with the stench of shite lingering in the air."

"Right. Makes sense."

"Good, now that's out the way, I guess we'd better get on with the interview. Smoke?"

"I don't, but thanks."

Undeterred by my status as a non-smoker, Lee takes a packet of Benson & Hedges from his jacket pocket and lights up.

"Let's get on with this," he then says before puffing a plume of smoke towards the ceiling. "Do you know much about Gibley Smith?"

"Not really."

"Peter Gibley and Martin Smith opened the first branch in 1949, and we're now the fourth largest estate agency chain in England with just under three hundred branches. The upside is that there are plenty of opportunities to progress if you want a career. The downside is that we have far too many pointless meetings at our regional office."

"Okay."

"Now, I suppose you want to know a bit more about the role, eh?"

"Yes, please."

"It's not exactly rocket science. People call in or ring up to register when they're looking to buy a property. You take down their contact info on a card along with details of what they're looking for, and then it's your job to convince them to view any suitable properties we have available."

"That sounds simple enough."

"It is. Once a punter has agreed to a viewing, you either call the vendor and arrange a convenient time with them or, if the property is vacant, you find a free slot in the office diary. Got it?"

"I think so. A vendor is the homeowner, I presume?"

"Aye."

"And for the vacant properties, will I show people around?"

"Too bloody right you will."

"I presume I'll receive some kind of training first?"

"Training? You open the door, walk them around, and answer their questions. Simple as that, lad."

"But, am I not expected to, you know ... *sell* the property?"

Lee shakes his head and takes another drag from his cigarette.

"What type of women are you into?" he then asks.

"Um, I don't know if I have a type."

"Come on, every bloke does. Think about it."

I adopt a suitably thoughtful expression as if I'm pondering his wholly irrelevant question.

"I suppose I quite like petite women. Feminine."

"So, if I introduced you to a strapping six-foot lass with arms like Popeye, is there anything I could say that would convince you to go on a date with her?"

"Probably not."

"There you have it, and it's the same with properties. The place is either right for them, or it's not. If it is right for them, we just have to negotiate a price everyone's happy with, but if it's not, there's nowt you can say that'll change their minds."

"I understand."

"Good, and bear in mind that although you won't be expected to sell a place on a viewing, there are targets. In fact, this company is bloody obsessed with targets."

"Such as?"

"You need to secure a certain amount of viewings each day — that's your bread and butter. It's worth the effort, though, as it's a numbers game. You get a hundred viewings a week, and you'll likely sell five properties. You earn one per cent commission for every deal that completes."

"One per cent?" I respond, my attention suddenly piqued.

"That's what I said."

I do a quick calculation in my head. If the average property sells for eighty thousand pounds and I earn one per cent, that's eight hundred quid in commission. As much as I'd love that to be the case, it sounds ridiculously generous.

"One per cent of the price the property sells for?" I confirm.

"No, you daft sod. One per cent of the commission the company earns. If we sell a house for a hundred grand, the company earns two per cent, or two grand. You get one per cent of that, so twenty quid."

"Oh."

"I know it doesn't sound a lot, but if you're selling fifteen to twenty properties a month, it adds up."

"Okay."

"And on top of your viewings target, you'll be expected to book at least five valuations a week."

"And how do I do that?"

"Half the folk who contact us looking for a place to buy will have a place to sell. We want as many properties on the books as possible, and it's part of your job to convince anyone with a place to sell that we're the ideal firm for the job and then organise a valuation. Eventually, you'll go out on valuations, but for now, it's either me or Gav, the senior negotiator."

"Right."

"And lastly, there's mortgage leads — the company expect you to book at least ten a month. We have a mortgage advisor who pops in a few times a week and, if you can get a punter in front of her and they sign up, that's an extra twenty quid in your pocket. A lad in the Basingstoke office makes five hundred quid a month in commission from mortgage leads, so it's worth the effort."

I don't know how I feel about working with so many targets, but the prospect of topping up the derisory salary with an additional few hundred quid in monthly commission certainly appeals.

"That all sounds great. What about the hours?"

"There are plenty of those bastards," Lee sneers. "Monday to Friday, it's 8.30 am till 7.00 pm, although we usually close an hour early on a Friday to get a few pints in. On top of that, you'll work Saturdays from 9.00 am till 5.00 pm, but you get one in three off."

Lee's revelation about the hours dampens my optimism for the potential commission earnings, but it's not as if I have anyone at home waiting for me.

"Understood."

"One other question: how well do you know the town?"

"I've lived here all my life, so I know it pretty well."

"Then you'll have no problem getting around. I only ask because we employed a lad last year, and the daft twat couldn't use a map. We sent him on a viewing to a house a mile away, and he was gone for three hours."

"Wow."

"That wasn't my reaction. He didn't last a month."

"Well, I think I know my way around town pretty well."

"Good lad. Any other questions?"

"Um—"

"Excellent," Lee says before stubbing his cigarette into an overflowing ashtray. "Can you start tomorrow?"

"Oh, er, yes. Yes, I can."

"Nice one. If you've got five minutes, I'll introduce you to Junior and Gav."

"Sure."

Lee gets to his feet and as I do the same, he holds out his hand. "Welcome to Gibley Smith, Danny."

"Thank you."

We return the chairs to their original position and then Lee leads me out to the main office.

"Gav," he calls out. "Let me introduce you to our new junior neg, Danny."

The guy who was on the phone when I arrived stands up and steps around his desk. Dressed in a pale-grey suit and roughly five inches shorter than my six foot, I couldn't begin to work out his age. His facial features are almost childlike, with deep dimples, freckles, and bright-blue eyes, but his gingery hair is on the retreat from his forehead.

"Gavin Flint," he says, holding out his hand. "Good to meet you, Danny."

We shake hands, and I return the pleasantry.

"And over in the back," Lee then says. "We have Tina, or Junior as she's more commonly known."

I follow my new boss towards a narrower section of the office dominated by a huge photocopier and a desk with a computer monitor on top.

"Hiya," the young woman behind the desk squeaks. "I'm Tina."

"Yes, we spoke on the phone yesterday. I'm Danny Monk."

I can see why Tina has the nickname Junior. I'd be amazed if she's legally old enough to buy a glass of wine in a pub. She kind of reminds me of a girlfriend I dated briefly at secondary school, Karen, although Tina's mid-brown locks aren't permed and she's a few inches shorter.

"Nice to meet you," she says without the offer of a handshake.

"That's the introductions over," Lee then says, clapping his hands together. "We'll see you bright and early tomorrow morning."

"Yes, you will."

Mere seconds later, I'm striding back down Victoria Road, not entirely sure what just happened. My quest to find a job has involved so much waiting and hoping, and no short measure of disappointment, I didn't expect to walk into an interview and then leave fifteen minutes later with a job.

I am now an estate agent.

Granted, I'm an estate agent saddled with numerous debts, an ex-fiancée I can't bring myself to talk to, and a flat worth significantly less than I owe on the mortgage, but at least I have a job.

Maybe, just maybe, I won't remain at rock bottom much longer.

Chapter 5

Standing in the hallway, I double-check my reflection in the mirror. Lee never specified what I should wear on my first day at Gibley Smith, but as I only own two suits, both of which are dark-grey, it's not as though I had much of a decision to make when I got dressed this morning. I did wrestle with the choice of tie as I own five of those, but I settled on a reddish Paisley design that counters the dullness of the suit.

If nothing else, I at least look competent. I still can't believe that I'm off to work, it's been that long.

After the interview yesterday, I was in two minds how to celebrate. My first thought was to head to my local, The White Horse, and sink a few pints, but I didn't fancy drinking alone. And, as I'll likely have to survive a whole month before my first paycheque, I need to be at my frugal best. In the end, I visited the video store and rented a film as a celebratory treat. I then popped over to Alma Place to share my good news with the parents.

Mum was delighted. Dad, less so.

I love both my parents dearly, but Dad has a habit of giving advice in the most brutally frank fashion. After updating Mum on the situation with the flat and then spinning a modest white lie about it not being the ideal time to sell, Dad delivered his advice. He said I should accept that Zoe is never coming back and it would be prudent to get a lodger. Good advice on the financial front, but his damning statement on my relationship felt like a punch in the gut.

Painful to hear? Yes. Wrong? Almost certainly not.

Dad was equally blunt regarding my new career. True, estate agents aren't generally renowned for their honesty and integrity, but that doesn't mean I have to sacrifice my principles. I have no intention of lying to anyone, and despite his scepticism, I think I convinced Dad that selling properties for a living isn't quite the same as joining a cult and agreeing to sacrifice your firstborn.

I take one final look in the hallway mirror and snatch my car keys up. It's time to go to work.

The early start gives me an advantage over the retail employees who start work at nine, and I manage to bag a parking space in the same side street I parked yesterday. Parking is one of the many questions I should have asked Lee in the interview but, as is often the case, not one of those questions came to mind when it was appropriate to ask.

When I approach my new place of work, Tina is wrestling with the door lock.

"Morning," I chirp.

"Oh, hi ... Danny, isn't it?"

"Yep."

"Sorry. I'm still half asleep and this bloody key won't budge."

"Want me to have a go?"

"Feel free."

Tina stands back and I grasp the key between my thumb and forefinger. It takes a bit of wiggling and jiggling but eventually, it turns. I pull out the key and hand it to Tina.

"Thank God for that," she responds. "I'm gagging for a coffee."

Being the gent I am, and keen to set a good first impression, I grab the door handle and pull hard with the intention of holding the door open for Tina. It doesn't budge so I tug it again with a bit more force but the aluminium frame just rattles defiantly.

"You push it," Tina says flatly.

"Oh. Right."

So much for setting a good first impression. I can't even open a bloody door properly.

I sheepishly follow Tina inside and she heads straight to the pokey back room where Lee interviewed me yesterday. Feeling like a spare part, I pretend to browse the display of properties on the wall.

"You want tea or coffee?" Tina then calls out.

Rather than shout back, I stride over and lean up against the door frame.

"I'd love a coffee, please — milk and two sugars. Is there anything I can do?"

"Like what?"

"I don't know. I've never worked in an office before."

"What did you do before coming here?"

"Retail management."

"Bit of a come down."

"A job's a job."

"I suppose."

Tina takes her coat off and then dumps copious amounts of coffee into two mugs. Both are chipped and the red Gibley Smith logo that once adorned the front of each mug has faded to a shade of muddy-grey.

"How long have you worked here?" I ask, purely to break the awkward silence.

"About eighteen months. I joined straight after I finished my secretarial course at college."

"You like it here?"

"As you said, a job's a job. I did try out for *Page 3* but my tits are too small, apparently. That was my dream job but it wasn't meant to be."

"Oh ... um, sorry," I splutter, my cheeks reddening. "That must be—"

"I'm kidding," Tina sniggers. "You'd better get used to the wind ups — they're part and parcel of working here."

"Okay, you got me. In my defence, it's early."

"Early worms and all that, Danny."

"Noted," I reply with a smile. "So, what's it like working with Lee and Gavin? They seem like decent blokes."

"Yeah, they're alright. Lee can be a bit of a chauvinist but that's probably because he's a bit older. My dad's the same."

"Right. How old is he?"

"My dad?"

"Eh? No, Lee."

"He's thirty-nine, I think. Gavin's only twenty-five so closer to my age. We have a right laugh when Lee ain't around."

The kettle comes to the boil and Tina fills both mugs.

"What's your story at home?" she asks over her shoulder. "Single? Married? Divorced?"

"I split up with my fiancée some months ago."

"Single man, eh? I'd keep that to myself if I were you."

I'm about to ask why when the front door clatters shut.

"I hope that kettle is on," booms a now-distinctive Yorkshire-accented voice from behind me. "I'm fucking parched, me."

I turn around to find Lee taking off his jacket.

"Morning, Danny," he says. "Got your priorities right, I see."

"My priorities?"

"Checking Junior isn't slacking on her tea-making duties."

"No, that's not—"

"I'm pulling your pisser," he snorts, sitting down at his desk. "I'm a firm believer in equal rights, aren't I, Junior?"

"Yes, boss," Tina shouts back with a distinct lack of commitment.

"Anyway," Lee says. "You all set for your first day?"

"I think so."

"We'll run through the basics once I've had a brew but in the meantime, that's your desk there."

He then points to the empty desk opposite, next to Gavin's.

"And you need to complete this," he adds, handing me a form. "It's all the crap that our HR department need. Fill it in when you get five minutes and stick it in my tray."

"Sure."

"Now, make yourself at home. When that lazy shit Gav finally graces us with his presence, we'll crack on with the morning meeting."

I do as instructed and plant myself behind the desk on what is, without question, the most uncomfortable chair my backside has ever met.

The front door then opens and Gavin breezes in. He glances towards the clock on the back wall at the exact same moment Lee does.

"Bang on time," Gavin beams. "Give or take a few seconds."

"Wonders will never cease," Lee huffs. "First time in a while, mind."

Tina then appears with two mugs. She hands one to Lee before bringing the second to my desk.

"Don't get used to the waitress service," she says. "I'm not here to fetch and carry for you three."

"No, of course not. Sorry."

"Where's my coffee?" Gavin asks while transferring his jacket to the back of his chair.

Tina replies by giving him the finger as she walks away.

Gavin turns to me. "First day then, mate. Feeling nervous?"

"A bit."

"You'll be fine," he says with a wide grin. "If they can train northerners to sell houses, you'll have no problem."

"You cheeky bastard," Lee retorts. "Perhaps you should tell Danny where you'd be now without my training and guidance. Stacking bloody shelves in Tesco, that's where."

Gavin rolls his eyes and sits down at his desk just as Tina returns from the back room with her mug of coffee.

"Right," Lee then says. "Let's get on with it."

With nothing to contribute, I sit and observe what I learn is a daily ritual — the morning meeting. It seems to follow a loose format covering yesterday's events before Lee moves on to what's in store for the day ahead. With that, he grabs a dog-eared journal and holds it aloft.

"Danny, this is the office diary. Anything and everything must be noted in here, okay?"

"Understood."

"The first appointment is at half nine; a valuation at 14 Haig Road for Mr and Mrs Lunn. You booked it in, Junior — what's the score?"

"It's a three-bed semi, and they're considering downsizing to a bungalow."

"Have you sent them any details of the bungalows we've got?"

"No, I thought it'd be better for you to take them with you."

"Good girl. Next appointment is at ten, and that's a repo at 56 Nutshell Close. You're on that one, Gav, and take Danny with you."

"Okay."

"Sorry," I interject. "What's a repo?"

"A repossession," Gavin replies. "We turn up with the bailiff and a locksmith, and once we've gained access, we measure the place, take a photo or two, and then report back to the lender. A few days after that, they almost always instruct us to put the property on the market."

"And you'd better get used to attending repos," Lee adds. "Head office has just signed a deal with two more lenders, and with interest rates the way they are, we could be doing four or five repos a week before long."

"Bloody hell," I gasp. "That's awful."

"Not for us, it's not. Every repo is another guaranteed commission cheque, and my missus wants a fortnight in Tenerife next year."

Much as I'd like to say what I really think, I decide to bite my tongue. I'm still within the first hour of my first day, yet I've already established just how callous and cut-throat the estate agency industry really is. While some poor sod is losing their home, my boss is planning how to spend the spoils of that poor sod's misfortune.

Lee finishes running through the diary and then instructs Gavin to show me the ropes while he prepares for his valuation. That preparation, I notice, begins with another cup of tea and a cigarette in the back room.

"Your main role is to get viewings," Gavin begins. "And for that, you need three things."

He then opens the left-hand drawer of my desk and extracts a plastic box roughly half the size of a shoebox.

"Appo cards," he then says by way of an explanation before flipping the lid of the box open. "This is where you keep all your cards for applicants currently looking to buy."

I lean forward and inspect the box. The thick wad of cards is split into tabbed sections based upon price, starting at £40,000 and then increasing in increments of ten grand up to the final, thinnest section of the box: £150,000+.

Gavin rummages around in the drawer, pulls out a blank card, and slaps it on the desk in front of me.

"It's pretty self-explanatory," he says. "Name, address, home and work phone numbers at the top, then their current status."

"Status?"

"Yeah, their position, basically. You've got your *FTB* which is a first-time buyer, then your *PTS/OM* and *PTS/NOM*, which means they've got a property to sell that's either on the market or not on the market, and then *CUO*, which is currently under offer.

"What's NTS?" I ask.

"Nothing to sell — cash buyers and the like, but not first-time buyers."

"That seems simple enough."

"Good. Now, when we take on a new instruction—"

"Sorry, a what?"

"A new instruction is a property that we've just put on the market, basically."

"Right, gotcha."

"When we take on a new instruction, your job is to call all the applicants in your box and encourage them to view the place over the phone. If they're not willing to view without more details, post out a set of particulars and then follow up a few days later."

Gavin then reaches into the second drawer and pulls out an A4-sized book with the word 'Viewings' printed on the front.

"This is your personal viewings book and, as you heard, we go through all the viewings in the morning meeting. Once you've arranged a viewing, make sure you record it in here otherwise it won't count towards your target, and you'll forget to follow it up."

"What happens if I forget to follow it up?"

"You'll have the vendor on the phone moaning that they haven't received any feedback."

"I take it we have to call the viewer first?"

"Exactly. Once you've got the viewer's feedback, let the vendor know."

"Word for word?"

"Depends on what the feedback is. If they tell you that the house was a shithole and they'd rather live in a skip, just make something up."

"Like?"

"Mate, no one cares. Just don't piss off the vendor."

"Understood."

"Come with me and I'll show you where all the property files are kept."

I get up and follow Gavin to the rear section of the office, and what is clearly Tina's domain.

"Are you showing Danny the only part of the office where any actual work happens?" she asks, looking up from her computer monitor.

"Excuse me," Gavin responds with fake indignation. "Remember you're talking to runner up in the Negotiator of The Year Awards 1988."

"Yeah, for our region," Tina scoffs. "You came second out of sixteen negotiators."

Point made, she returns her attention back to the screen.

"While we're here," Gavin continues, "this is the photocopier, but Junior will show you how to use it, as well as the fax and the franking machine."

"What about the computer thing?"

"Do you know how to use a computer?" Tina asks over her shoulder.

"I played the occasional game on my kid brother's Sinclair Spectrum back in the day."

"Then, don't worry about it. It's a new system, and I'm only just getting to grips with it myself."

Gavin then leads me over to a filing cabinet, where he tugs open the top drawer.

"This is where all the property files are kept, in price order from lowest to highest."

He pulls out a random folder and opens it up on top of the cabinet.

"This is a PIF, or a property information form," he says, holding up a pre-printed sheet of paper. "All the vendor info is on the front and the viewing log is on the back. Every time you organise a viewing, you have to enter it into the log."

"As well as the viewing book?"

"Afraid so."

I'm wondering if I should be taking notes but I don't even have a pen, never mind anything to write notes on.

"It might be a good idea for you to go through the cabinet and familiarise yourself with our current instructions."

"I can do that. How many are there?"

"I'm not sure, to be honest — fifty or so. It changes day to day."

"And they're all in this cabinet?"

"The top three drawers, yes. The bottom one is for properties under offer, but you don't need to worry about that for the moment."

"Okay."

"Great," Gavin then says, clasping his hands together. "That should keep you busy until we head off to that repo. For now, I need a coffee."

He leaves me to get on with my task. I turn to the cabinet and pull out the first folder. Besides the PIF, the folder also contains about half a dozen copies of the sales particulars, and I presume that's what Gavin expects me to familiarise myself with. On the front, the particulars confirm that the property is a first-floor flat located in the town centre. Below the address there's a black and white photo of the building, plus a bullet list of features and the asking price: £38,950.

I've no idea if I'm supposed to remember every single property, but if nothing else, at least I'll get a feel for how much each kind of property is worth.

I return the folder to the cabinet and pull out the next. Ironically, it's for a flat in my development, Sefton Court, which is no great surprise as Lee brought two sets of particulars with him when he came to value my flat. There is, however, one significant change since I last saw a set of sales particulars for this property. The asking price is now £46,950 — three grand less than it was on Monday.

"Shitting hell," I hiss, thankfully not loud enough to catch Tina's attention.

I already know that we've no chance of selling the flat and covering the mortgage, but I had no idea how rapidly property values seem to be tumbling. Like it or not, I've no choice but to stick at this job and pay whatever I can towards the mortgage.

I glance at my watch. In forty minutes from now, I'm heading out with Gavin to see firsthand what happens if I don't.

Chapter 6

We leave the office at 9.45 am, by which point I can barely remember a thing about the properties I spent forty minutes researching.

"I'm parked just up the road," Gavin confirms.

"I meant to ask, where do you and Lee park if you're in and out all day?"

"Pot luck, mate. There's no parking at the office, so we just drive around until we find a space."

He then reaches into his pocket and pulls out a bunch of keys.

"This is mine," he confirms, coming to a halt beside a silver Ford Escort. "Got it last year."

"Nice."

"It came with my promotion to senior negotiator. Had a Fiesta before that — not the worst car in the world, but the Escort has independent suspension and ABS."

"Impressive," I reply, although I've no clue what he's talking about.

Gavin unlocks the car and places his briefcase on the back seat.

"Hop in then," he says. "Wait for an invite, and you'll be standing on the pavement all day."

I hurry around to the other side and get in.

"So, what do you drive, Danny?" Gavin asks as we fasten our seatbelts.

"Up until a few days ago, I had a Peugeot 205 GTi."

"Cool motor and bloody rapid, I hear. What made you get rid of it?"

"The same reason I'm now your new colleague: money, or lack of it."

"I did wonder. You're a fair bit older than the average junior negotiator. What did you do before?"

"I was assistant manager at Presto until they closed the branch."

"That's some come down. Still, I dropped out of uni and ended up working in Tesco, and I've done okay for myself."

"I thought Lee was joking when he made that dig about stacking shelves at Tesco."

"It was only ever a temporary job, and Lee knows that, but he never misses an opportunity to remind me that I worked for Tesco."

Gavin takes no more than a passing glance over his shoulder before pulling away from the kerb.

"What made you drop out of uni?" I ask.

"I only went because my parents pestered me to go. My A-level grades were crap, so I ended up doing sociology at Chichester. I did six months, and that was enough for me. I couldn't wait to get out of there and start earning."

"Did you know what you wanted to do?"

"Honestly, I didn't have a clue, so I ended up working at Tesco for a while, just to earn a few quid. Then, I bumped into an old schoolmate I hadn't seen for a few years. He'd bagged himself a job in estate agency and bought a flat off the back of his salary, whereas I was still living at home with my parents. Anyway, a few months later, I spotted an advert for a junior neg vacancy at Gibley Smith and applied. The rest is history, as they say."

"What about Lee? What's his story?"

"How did a Yorkshireman end up in Hampshire?"

"Yeah, that."

"He first met Dawn, now his wife, on a stag do in Blackpool back in the day, and she didn't fancy living up north, so Lee moved down here about twelve years ago. He worked in the car trade for a while before he got into estate agency."

"I see."

"He can come across as a bit of a blunt bastard sometimes, but he's alright, Lee. You'll get used to his ways."

I don't know if I'll ever get used to Lee's ways, or want to, but based on my initial impressions of Gavin, he seems like a nice enough guy. That said, I'm not a fan of his overly aggressive driving style. Based on the screams coming from beneath the bonnet, I don't think the Escort is a fan either.

"What do you think of Junior ... Tina?" Gavin then asks.

"She seems quite pleasant."

"There are two things you need to know about Junior. One, she's totally loved up, so don't get any ideas about making a move on her. Two, don't be fooled by the council-estate accent. Tina likes people to think she hasn't got much up top, but she's a smart girl. Ambitious, too, so underestimate her at your peril."

"Now you've got me worried."

"She's not a nutter," Gavin chuckles. "I'm just saying there's more to Junior than most people give her credit for, and it's better to stay in her good books ... particularly if you want an easy life."

Warning issued, Gavin throws the Escort into a left-hand corner and straight into a turning on the right.

"Welcome to Nutshell Close," he then says, easing off the accelerator. "Even numbers are your side, so keep an eye out for number 56."

As it transpires, Gavin spots the locksmith's van before I identify the house number. He pulls up behind it, kills the engine, and then turns to me.

"As this is your first repo, let's hope the former homeowners have already left. If they're still inside, I guarantee there will be either aggro or tears, and that usually means we have to wait around before we can do what we need to do."

"Are they usually gone when you turn up?"

"Ninety per cent are, but I had one a few weeks ago where the wife was hosting a Tupperware party in the lounge while the husband was upstairs, re-grouting the bathroom tiles."

"That's mad. I presume they all get fair warning about the bailiff turning up?"

"Yep, but some people just don't believe it'll happen. They get warning letter after warning letter, and I suppose the odd one decides to bury their head in the sand."

As Gavin gets out of the car, I pause a moment and consider whether I'm also guilty of burying my head in the sand. If I am, it's not just to avoid my mounting mortgage debt but also my former fiancée. I can't avoid either much longer but, for now, I'd rather focus on someone else's misfortune.

I join Gavin on the pavement and we approach the front path of number 56 — a tired-looking semi with an overgrown front lawn and window frames in dire need of a repaint. The front door is already open, and a silver-haired locksmith is in the process of changing the lock.

"Alright, Steve," Gavin says as we approach. "Is the bailiff around?"

"Morning, Gav," the locksmith replies. "Yeah, he's inside."

"Cheers."

I follow Gavin into the house and a hallway where it must be five or six degrees colder than outside. It's not just the ambient temperature that's jarring, but the sheer emptiness of the place. The previous owners clearly didn't want to leave anything behind, including the carpets, curtains, and even the light shades.

We step through a doorway on the left into what I presume is the lounge. Without any furniture, it's hard to say what purpose the room once served. The only noticeable feature is the male figure dressed in black, standing in the corner and scribbling on a clipboard.

"Hi," Gavin says. "We're from Gibley Smith estate agents."

"Morning, lads," the man says in a deep, gravelly tone. "John Fisher, bailiff."

"Are we okay to get on and measure up?"

"Help yourself. I'm just about done with my checks, so I'll grab a set of keys from the locksmith and be on my way."

"Great. Any problems with the house we should be aware of?"

"They've stripped every last fixture and fitting, but they ain't caused any damage."

"That's a relief."

"Sorry," I interject. "Why would they damage their own home?"

My question was aimed at Gavin, but the bald-headed bailiff answers with a snort. "Strangely, some people aren't happy about having their home repossessed, so they half destroy the place before we turn up."

"I don't suppose it matters if it's no longer their home," I reply.

"Oh, it matters because if the place is a bomb site, it affects the sale price. Can you guess who has to pay back any shortfall?"

"The previous owner?"

"You got it. The lender still wants their money back, and if the proceeds of the property sale don't cover the outstanding mortgage, they'll go after the former homeowner for whatever's outstanding."

The words insult and injury spring to mind, but I keep that view to myself.

After snapping his clipboard shut, John Fisher leaves us to it.

"It's bastard cold in here," Gavin remarks while opening his briefcase. "Let's get this over and done with."

He then hands me a plastic object slightly bigger than a cigarette packet.

"What is it?" I ask.

"It's an infrared tape measure. You're in charge of taking the room measurements."

Thankfully, Gavin offers a quick demonstration of the device before we tour the rest of the house.

We start downstairs, which consists of the lounge, an equally bare dining room, and a kitchen long overdue for a refit. It's no more homely upstairs. The first two bedrooms are just shells, and the avocado-coloured bathroom suite was probably fitted more than a decade ago and is showing its age.

Then we enter the third bedroom, which isn't much bigger than a cupboard.

"God, that's sad," Gavin remarks, nodding towards the right-hand wall.

I step forward to get a closer look. There are seven hand prints on the wall, spaced horizontally about ten inches apart and a varying mix of primary and secondary colours. The first is just a tiny blob of yellow paint and written beneath it in black marker pen are the words: *Milly at Six Months*. The next is bright red and slightly larger: *Milly at One Year*. In royal blue, the final print is of Milly's hand at three and a half.

"I wonder where Milly is now," I say wistfully. "It seems so cruel, kicking a family out of their home just because they're struggling a bit."

"Depressing as it is, mate, we've got a job to do. It's just bricks and mortar now."

It would be easy to accuse Gavin of being callous but I guess you just become hardened to the reality after a while.

In a way, it reminds me of my nan's funeral last year.

As we loitered at the graveside, waiting for Nan's nearest and dearest to toss a handful of damp soil into the grave and say their final goodbye, I noticed a couple of bored-looking council workmen sitting in a flatbed van a few hundred yards away. It took a moment to realise why they were waiting around a cemetery — they were there to fill the grave once the last of the grieving family had set off for the wake.

It's not quite the same, but now I'm the dispassionate bystander, trying to ignore the sadness of the situation and complete an awful but necessary job. Lee never mentioned that emotional resilience might be required for the role.

The final port of call is the rear garden. It's not quite as overgrown as the front but the patio is ridden with weeds, and the dilapidated wooden shed in the corner looks like it won't survive another winter, particularly if it's a windy one.

"What do you think the house is worth?" I ask as Gavin opens the briefcase and swaps the clipboard for a camera.

"You tell me."

"Um, eighty to eighty-five grand?"

"If it were in pristine condition inside and out, you wouldn't be far wrong. As it stands, though, I'd peg an asking price at £74,950, and the lender will probably accept an offer north of seventy grand."

If this house sells for a shade over seventy grand, that's not much more than we paid for our two-bedroom flat only last year.

"Don't shoot me down, Gavin, but that seems really cheap for a three-bedroom house."

"When it comes to repos, the lenders don't want empty properties sitting around for months on end, so they ask us to value accordingly. If you're in the market for a bargain, buy a repo."

"That doesn't seem fair on the former owners."

"It's not, which is why we tell anyone with mortgage troubles to sell up before the bailiffs come calling. Once a place is repossessed, the lender can sell it at any price they choose."

"Any price?"

"Within reason, yeah."

"Shit," I inadvertently blurt.

With Gavin's words reverberating around my head, I stare down the garden towards the rickety shed, wondering if it might serve as a temporary home should mine be repossessed.

"You okay, mate? You look a bit peaky."

"I've already told Lee, so I might as well confess my woes to you, too. Me and my ex bought a flat in Sefton Court last year, and I'm struggling with the mortgage repayments."

"Oh dear," Gavin replies, his expression pained. "Did you buy it new?"

"Yep, and we have a mortgage for just shy of sixty-six grand."

My colleague sucks air across his teeth and shakes his head.

"Want my advice?" he then asks.

"I've got a horrible feeling I don't, but go on."

"Get the fuck out of there as quickly as you can. The market is only going one way and the longer you leave it, the more debt you'll rack up."

Advice delivered, Gavin points the camera towards the garden and clicks off a couple of shots. If he turned the camera forty-five degrees, he'd capture the face of a man who knows he can't bury his head in the sand a day longer.

Like it or not, I *have* to see Zoe.

Chapter 7

If I needed any further motivation to confront my financial problems, and indeed my ex-fiancée, it came this afternoon. When I returned to the office with Gavin, he showed me the process once a property is repossessed. I say process, but Gavin implied it's merely a formality as he faxed the lender a one-page report with his recommendations and details of comparable properties.

That done, Lee said it would be a good idea if I spent a couple of hours touring the vacant properties for sale. Including the new instruction in Nutshell Close, which I'd already visited, there were twelve in total, and nine of those twelve were repossessions.

If touring a succession of cold, soulless, empty properties wasn't depressing enough, the final two happened to be in Sefton Court.

As Lee suggested when he came by to conduct his valuation, neither flat differed in terms of layout. The former owners of the ground-floor flat had redecorated, but the first-floor flat still had the original colour scheme, like ours, which is probably why I felt physically sick as I wandered around the empty rooms.

It made me think.

Prompted by the number of sci-fi films I've watched over the last decade, I've often wondered what I'd do if offered the opportunity to peer into the future, to catch a glimpse of Danny Monk's life twenty, thirty, or forty years from now. On the one hand, it'd be fascinating, but on the other, potentially terrifying.

Just twelve years on from leaving school, a few of the lads in my class are now almost unrecognisable. Tony Barron is so overweight that he has his own gravitational field, and Liam Ashby's once magnificent quiff finally lost its battle with male pattern baldness three years ago. As for Joe McDowell, he now resembles a mahogany mannequin due to his excessive and prolonged use of sunbeds. Then there's Gary Lucas who will forever remain twenty-six years of age because that's the age he swallowed his last ecstasy tablet at a rave in Southampton. Three days later, the doctors confirmed Gary was brain dead and promptly switched off his life support machine.

As I stood in the lounge of 19 Sefton Court, I got a glimpse of what lies ahead if I don't get my act together. I only spent five minutes in that flat but it was long enough to realise that the universe might be trying to tell me something: *Get your shit sorted, Danny, or very soon you could be turning up with a locksmith and a bailiff to repossess your own home.*

That's the reason why I'm now parked up on the corner of Windsor Drive as dusk descends.

I left the office at seven on the dot, intending to head home and grab a bite to eat but, by the time I unlocked the Volvo, my appetite had all but vanished. Instead of driving back to the flat, I bit the bullet and made my way in the opposite direction, to the Carter family home.

There's a light on in the lounge window so someone is in, but seeing as there's a space on the driveway where Zoe's dad would usually park his Jaguar, I presume he's out. That's no bad thing. I got on okay with Zoe's mum but her dad used to look down his nose at me. I never understood why, but I didn't much care as our paths rarely crossed.

I puff a deep breath and get out of the car.

The Carter residence is one of nine so-called executive homes built in the mid-eighties for those with aspirations of joining the middle-class set. Consequently, Zoe's parents would attend or host a dinner party almost every weekend, and I used to joke that it was likely a front for wife-swapping orgies. My fiancée never saw the funny side, probably because she didn't want to imagine her parents writhing around naked with the chartered accountant and his wife from across the cul-de-sac. Understandable, in hindsight.

I reach the front door and despite my stomach churning like a cement mixer, I manage to press the doorbell. The melancholy chimes of Big Ben echo from the hallway, followed within seconds by the sound of a lock disengaging. The door opens.

"Danny!" Zoe splutters.

I've not seen Zoe since the day she left, and I underestimated the impact of seeing her again. It's not as though she's made any effort but Zoe never had to. Even now, standing in the doorway with her hair tied back and dressed in a shapeless pair of jogging pants and a baggy sweatshirt, she'd still turn heads. That was something I once loved about her but now, I detest it. I don't want to look at her and feel the way I once felt.

"Zoe," I respond flatly. "We need to talk."

"Talk ... or argue?"

"I'm done arguing. It's about the flat."

"I guess you'd better come in."

"Are your parents at home?"

"They're out. Dinner with one of Dad's suppliers."

Zoe edges back into the hallway but keeps her hand on the door. Taking her gesture as an invite to enter, I step forward, passing uncomfortably close to the woman I've been intimately close to hundreds of times.

She closes the door.

"Why are you wearing a suit?" Zoe then asks.

"New job."

"I heard that the shop had closed down. I'm sorry."

"Not sorry enough to drop by the flat and see how I'm doing, though."

"If I recall, you said you never wanted to see me again. Ever."

I did, but that was only ever wishful thinking — an avoidance strategy to minimise the pain.

"That still stands, but as we're both still tethered to that bloody mortgage, we need to work out what we're going to do."

"Okay, come through to the kitchen, and I'll put the kettle on."

So far, so very civilised, but that in itself stings because I might have imagined Zoe breaking down in tears and confessing how she's struggled to live without me. Instead, she wants to sip tea and engage in polite conversation.

I follow her to the kitchen and make myself at home on one of the barstools at the breakfast bar while Zoe fills the kettle.

"What's your new job?" she calls out over her shoulder.

"Negotiator," I reply, dropping the junior part of my job title for purposes of pride. "In an estate agency — Gibley Smith."

"That's pretty cool."

"Yeah, it is."

I don't want to engage in idle chit-chat, but knowing Zoe's current career status might prove advantageous during what is likely to be a strained conversation.

"What's happening at the salon?" I ask. "Did you get that promotion?"

"Debbie decided not to open a second salon, so I'm stuck where I am for now."

"That's a shame."

It is, but not for me particularly.

The rumbling of the kettle helps to mask the long seconds of silence. There's no point trying to talk across the cavernous kitchen so I wait patiently for Zoe to bring the coffee mugs over. When she eventually does, she chooses to stand on the opposite side of the breakfast bar rather than sit on the stool next to mine.

"Thanks," I mumble as she places a mug before me.

"You're welcome."

I take a sip of coffee while Zoe taps her fingernails against the side of her mug — a long-standing nervous tic.

"How have you been?" she asks.

"Is that a serious question? How do you think I've been?"

"I meant, you know, in general."

"In general, life's been pretty shit."

"Alright," she replies defensively. "I was only asking."

"And the only reason I'm here is because one element of my now-shitty life needs sorting — the flat."

"I know."

"What you don't know is that we now have negative equity."

"Negative what?"

"It means the flat is worth significantly less than we owe on the mortgage."

"How much less?"

"My best estimate is about twenty grand."

"No way," she gasps.

"Yes, way."

"How is that even possible? I thought properties always went up in value, not down."

"Have you not read a newspaper or switched on the TV recently? The economy is shot."

"Of course I have, but ... twenty grand?"

"It gets worse. As of next week, we'll be three months behind on the mortgage repayments."

Zoe stops tapping her mug and stares back at me, her mouth agape, eyes unblinking.

"Pardon?"

"You heard me. We're three months behind on the mortgage repayments."

"We?"

"Yes, we."

"Why haven't you been paying the mortgage?"

"Because I'm skint, Zoe."

"I thought estate agents earned a fortune."

"I only just got the job. I've been unemployed for a couple of months."

"For crying out loud, Danny. Why didn't you tell me?"

It's a fair question. Fair, but not one I can answer without appearing weak.

"Because ... because I didn't want to see you, okay."

"I know things didn't end well between us, but I thought we could at least remain civil."

"Are you for real?" I snap. "Did you seriously think we could remain civil after what you did?"

"Yes, because as I've told you umpteen times, it was just a stupid one-off mistake."

"Forgetting to put the bins out is a mistake. Sleeping with one of your old schoolmates isn't."

"You know full well I didn't sleep with Wayne."

"You shared a bed."

"Yes, but we never ... I told you what happened."

"Ah, yes," I bark, flinging my arms in the air. "You did tell me, and those fucking words will remain forever etched in my memory."

On the night in question, Zoe had arranged to meet up with two of her old school friends, Claire and Vicky. They hadn't been out for a while and the plan was to meet at a new wine bar in town, gossip over a few bottles of Chardonnay, and then hop in a taxi and head home around eleven.

What actually happened is they bumped into some lads they went to school with, and when closing time at the wine bar arrived, they all went on to a nightclub together.

At some point in the early hours of the morning, Zoe left the nightclub with a twat named Wayne Pickford, and they ended up back at his flat.

Of course, I wasn't aware of any of this at the time. I fell asleep on the sofa at eleven on Saturday evening and only woke up when I heard Zoe creeping in at eight on the Sunday morning. She apologised and told me she'd stayed the night at Claire's because her friend was upset over some tiff with her boyfriend.

I trusted Zoe with my life, and I had no reason to doubt her story.

Unfortunately for my then fiancée, Wayne Pickford decided to brag about his conquest in the pub a few days later. A feature of living in a small town is that everyone knows everyone, and a guy I played five-a-side football with happened to be playing darts in the same pub that night. He called me the next day and recounted what he'd heard, but even then I didn't believe it. After work, I decided to drop by Claire and Ian's flat on the way home, and Ian admitted that Zoe hadn't stayed at their place and the couple hadn't had the tiff Zoe alleged.

Two lies could only lead to one conclusion — Zoe *had* spent the night with Wayne fucking Pickford.

The minute she walked in after finishing work, I confronted her with my allegation. At first, she denied it but when I threatened to find Pickford and beat the truth out of him, Zoe broke down and admitted her stupid one-off mistake.

Apparently, they kissed in the nightclub and then went back to his place, although Zoe had little recollection of how or why that happened. She did, however, manage to recall what subsequently occurred and, after hearing her confession, I'm unlikely to ever forget her exact words. She said, "Wayne just fingered me for a bit and then I wanked him off. He came and I fell asleep shortly afterwards."

It's one thing to hear your partner confess to cheating, but it's quite another for them to then downplay the magnitude of that betrayal. Zoe had the temerity to claim it wasn't so bad because she'd only committed a grade C infidelity. Grade A infidelity, she argued, was a full-blown affair and grade B was a one-night stand that included full penetrative sex. She seemed to think that her lack of enjoyment at the stubby fingers of Wayne Pickford somehow lessened the crime.

It didn't, and I told her we were finished. I also told her to pack her things and that I never wanted to see her again.

"You said you wanted to discuss the flat," Zoe says haughtily. "Not go over the same argument again."

I take a sip of coffee purely to keep my mouth occupied. I don't want to go over old ground any more than Zoe, but I just can't seem to help myself.

"We need to do something about the mortgage repayments," I say through gritted teeth. "And soon."

"Have you spoken to the building society?"

"No."

"Why not?"

"What exactly am I supposed to say to them?"

"The truth."

"Oh yeah," I huff. "I'm sure they'll be sympathetic if I tell them my fiancée moved out and then I lost my job. They don't give a shit, Zoe. The only reason to call them is to confirm how we're going to pay back the outstanding repayments."

"And how are we going to do that?"

"If I knew, I wouldn't be here. I sold the car a few days ago and paid a bit off, but there were other bills I had to pay."

"You sold your car?"

"Yes."

"But you loved that car."

"I did, but it seems I just can't keep hold of the things I love."

My off-the-cuff remark seems to throw Zoe momentarily. She swallows hard and then stares into her coffee mug.

"I am sorry," she says without looking up from the mug. "More sorry than you'll ever know."

"So am I, but what does it matter? We can't put the genie back in the bottle."

Seemingly transfixed by the plume of steam rising from her mug, my former fiancée appears lost in her own thoughts. I'm about to prompt her back towards the reason I'm here when she looks straight at me.

"We could," she says in a low voice.

"We could what?"

"Put the genie back in the bottle."

"You have access to a time machine, do you?"

"No, but we could put the last five months behind us and start again with a clean slate."

I remain silent, waiting for the punchline to her sick joke.

"Couldn't we?" she urges.

"Oh, you're actually serious?"

"Is it such a crazy idea?"

"It's batshit crazy."

"It's not, Danny — think about it. I could move back in and—"

"Whoa!" I interject. "As it stands, I'm a long way from accepting you back into my bed. A very long way indeed."

"Okay, I could move into the spare room."

I open my mouth but my brain trips over itself trying to compute a suitable response. Never in my entire life have I wished for something so badly while simultaneously loathing the object of that wish.

Zoe takes my silence as a positive sign and steps around the breakfast bar.

"Do you believe in fate?" she asks.

Still dumbstruck, I shake my head.

"I'm not sure I believed in it either, until this evening. It can't be a coincidence you turning up tonight."

"Eh?" is the best I can muster.

I then notice a look in Zoe's eyes, a sparkle I've only ever seen a handful of times, the last being on the day we moved into the flat.

She grabs hold of my hand. "Danny, I think this is fate, telling us that we need to try again."

Chapter 8

Standing at the patio doors, I stare out at the rainswept street. Maybe it's something to do with the hole in the ozone layer, but the autumn weather seems particularly schizophrenic this year. Yesterday, the sky was blue and the air still, but there's a howling wind this morning, and the rain is relentless.

My eyes drop towards the bistro table and chairs on the balcony. The wooden slats have not fared well in the year of exposure to the British weather and the metal parts no better. I wouldn't dare sit on either chair now. Like the flat itself, the cheap bistro set proved a poor investment.

It's not even eight o'clock yet, so too early to set off for work. I gave up trying to sleep an hour ago because my mind refuses to release its grip on the conversation with Zoe last night, and her shameless proposal. Thoughts alone are harmless, but when they're attached to emotions, the resulting flood of brain chemicals prompts all manner of physical side effects: increased heart rate, muscle tension, and low-key nausea. It's no wonder I had trouble sleeping.

I'm knackered, and yet, my mind won't stop tormenting me.

"Bloody woman," I mutter.

It's not the woman per se that's messed with my head, but the substance of her plan. God knows how she managed it, but Zoe found the sweet spot between ridiculous and unworkable. If it were simply ridiculous, I could have easily brushed it aside with a snort of derision. If it had been unworkable, I could have presented a robust fact-based defence. It was neither.

Worse still, it did indeed seem like fate had played a hand in its conception.

Unbeknown to me, Zoe's younger brother, Max, moved out of the family home three months ago. He's now living happily with his girlfriend in South London, having started a new job in the publishing industry. According to Zoe, this move had been on the cards for some time, and her parents had begun making plans of their own.

When those plans first came to fruition, Zoe and I were happily engaged and living in a shiny new apartment. And once Max moved out, the Carters would be left with an empty nest. So, with one eye on their retirement years, they made plans to sell the family home and downsize to a smaller property with a bigger garden. Wife-swapping convenience or not, Zoe's mum hated their postage-stamp-sized garden, and her dad hated the noise created by the younger children in the cul-de-sac. They wanted to move on, and that's exactly what they'd intended to do before their daughter turned up on the doorstep, complete with a suitcase and a sob story, back in the spring.

Five months later, Mr and Mrs Carter aren't willing to put their lives on hold while their daughter works out her living arrangements. Zoe's dad put the house on the market last week, but to ensure his daughter isn't left homeless, he offered her a cash lifeline of three thousand pounds. It would be enough for a deposit on a flat if Zoe were to buy again, but her dad assumed I'd buy Zoe's share of our current home, which obviously isn't going to happen.

Zoe planned to pay me a visit this week to discuss buying her share of the flat, but when I turned up at her door last night and gave her the damning news about our home, it planted a seed which quickly grew into her ridiculous plan. In her mind, she could move back to Sefton Court, use her dad's money to clear our outstanding mortgage debt, and then we could try rebuilding our relationship — the sweet spot between ridiculous and unworkable.

I was barely seconds into a scornful response when Zoe posed a question: am I still in love with her? I knew the answer, but I didn't want to give Zoe the satisfaction of saying it. However, the woman I once considered my soul mate had no trouble confessing how much she still loves me.

Even though I never admitted my feelings for Zoe, the fact I left Windsor Drive without dismissing her plan probably answered her question. I wish she'd never asked it, not least because I'm about to start only my second day in a new job. She asked me to think about it for a few days and then suggested we meet on Saturday evening. I don't think meeting up with her is a good idea, but my mind won't let me think about anything else.

I take one final glance at the bistro set and consider, only fleetingly, whether it's beyond repair. As metaphors go, I know it's lame, but that's where my head is this morning.

"Get it together, Danny."

I gulp the tepid remains of coffee and transfer the mug to the sink. The simple act of washing up helps switch my thought process. The distraction of work is *exactly* what I need. Being in the very flat that my cheating ex wants to return to isn't.

I grab my car keys and leave.

I'm not sure what the average age of a junior negotiator is, but I'd guess it's typically eight to nine years younger than I am. As he handed me a Yale key yesterday afternoon, Lee confirmed that my age was the only reason he was willing to trust me with a key to the office.

Victoria Road is almost deserted when I drive down it, so I decide to park near the office rather than the backstreet I used before. There's a one-hour parking limit, but I'd rather take my chances with a traffic warden than endure the guaranteed soaking I'll get if I park more than ten yards from the office.

I dash from the car to the front door, unlock it, and try to tug it open.

"Dickhead," I mumble once I remember to push.

Once inside, I brush the raindrops from my jacket and drape it on the back of my chair. I vaguely recall Tina saying that whoever is the first to arrive has to put the kettle on as a matter of priority, so I wander through to the back room and fulfil my duty. Seconds later, the front door rattles shut as Tina blusters into the office, shaking a semi-open umbrella.

"Morning," I call out. "Fancy a coffee?"

"I'd love one, thanks," she responds.

As I grab a couple of mugs from the cupboard, Tina enters the back room and hangs up her umbrella.

"How was your first day?" she asks.

"Interesting. And long."

"I don't know how you guys do it. I'm so glad I get to leave at half-five."

"Maybe I need to retrain; learn how to use a computer."

"If I can do it, anyone can."

Tina's modesty sparks a reminder of the conversation I had with Gavin yesterday and his warning not to underestimate our office administrator.

"I've always wanted to understand a bit more about computers. Maybe you could show me the basics if we ever get a quiet five minutes."

"I could, but it'll cost you."

"Name your price."

"A mini chocolate cheesecake from the bakery up the road."

"Alright, you've got yourself a deal, although you might have to wait until payday. I'm a bit strapped for cash at the moment."

"I could lend you some money if you're struggling. Not much, but some."

I'm slightly taken aback by the offer.

"Oh, um, that's really sweet of you, Tina, but I'm okay at the moment, thanks."

"Have I embarrassed you?"

"Not at all. I just wasn't expecting you to offer."

"I know what it's like when you're struggling with money, and it's not nice."

"No, it's not, but I'll survive. Who knows, maybe I'll sell a house on my second day, eh."

"I'll keep my fingers crossed for you. And if you change your mind about the money, just ask."

"Will do, and thanks again."

Tina then heads off to her desk, leaving me to make the coffee. Just as the kettle comes to the boil, Lee swaggers in and heads straight for the back room.

"Morning, Danny," he says, the pungent stench of cigarettes on his breath. "Kettle just boiled, has it?"

"It has. Would you like a coffee?"

"Tea with two sugars, ta."

"Coming up," I reply, reaching for another mug.

"What did you make of your first day as an estate agent?" Lee then asks.

"Yeah, it was good. A lot to learn, still."

"I'm glad you mentioned learning because we have a very effective training programme here at Gibley Smith."

"I'm definitely interested in advancing my career."

I'm more interested in advancing a pay increase, but I know the two tend to go hand in hand.

"Good, because the training programme starts today. It's called in at the fucking deep end."

"Um …"

"The diary is rammed with appointments, so you'll have to conduct a handful of viewings this morning. It's piss easy, so you've nowt to fret over."

"Well, if you think I'm up to it, I'm game."

"Good lad. Now, bring my tea through when it's ready, but make sure you let it brew for at least three minutes."

"Got it."

"See, you're a quick learner."

Lee flashes a grin and then leaves me to my tea-making duties. Once I've filled his mug with boiling water and jabbed the teabag with a spoon a few times, I pick up the two mugs of coffee and deliver one to Tina's desk.

"Thanks, Danny."

"You're welcome."

On cue, Gavin breezes in. Both he and Lee look straight to the clock on the back wall.

"A minute early," Gavin trills. "Get in!"

I have a feeling this is a game my two colleagues play most mornings.

"Aren't you a good boy," Lee responds mockingly. "I'll let Mummy and Daddy know that their little Gavin managed to get his fucking arse to work early for once."

"Yeah, very funny," Gavin snaps back before transferring his jacket to his chair.

Lee shakes his head and turns his attention to the office diary.

"Coffee?" I ask Gavin, merely to break the tense silence.

"I'd love one, mate."

"Make it quick," Lee says. "We need to get on."

I'm tempted to suggest that we could get on a lot quicker if I didn't have to brew his tea for three whole minutes, but it's already obvious that Lee can be a bit prickly in the morning. I hurry to the back room and complete my round of hot beverages.

The morning meeting begins.

Lee hurries through a round-up of yesterday's events and then moves on to today's diary.

"I've got a valuation in half an hour at 22 Loxwood Road for a Mr and Mrs Wigg. That address rings a bell for some reason."

"They bought the house through us two years ago," Gavin replies. "They're relocating."

"I remember. He was a Tory councillor, wasn't he?"

"Still is, for the time being."

"If I remember, he thought the sun shined out of Thatcher's arse."

"Probably best not to talk politics, assuming we want their business."

"I'll do my best."

Lee is yet to mention which way he leans politically but the look of disdain on his face suggests he's not a huge fan of our Prime Minister, or her party.

"Anyway," he continues. "Gav, you've got a valuation at half nine at 80 Coleman Road with Mr Stringer. Two-bed end terrace."

Gavin acknowledges the appointment with nothing more than a nod.

"And, Danny, your very first viewing is at ten. Luckily for you, it's at 19 Sefton Court with a Mr Patterson and a Miss Butler, first-time buyers."

"Okay."

"Soon as you're done there, get your arse over to 56 Nutshell Close. You've got a viewing there with Mr and Mrs Edgar."

I feel woefully ill-equipped to escort prospective buyers around properties, but I'd rather wing my way through a couple of viewings than sit and dwell on Zoe's plan.

"I'll run through a few pointers before I leave," Lee adds. "Just so you don't make a tit of yourself."

"Appreciated."

Just as Lee is about to move on to the next appointment in the diary, the phone rings. Tina is quick to answer it, announcing the company name. There's a brief pause before she speaks again.

"Yes, he does."

A strained frown then crosses Tina's face. Barely ten seconds after picking it up, she puts the phone down.

"What was that all about?" Gavin asks.

"I don't know. It was a woman, and she asked if Daniel Monk works here. I said yes, she thanked me, and then hung up."

All three of my colleagues turn in unison and look directly at me, as if waiting for an explanation. I don't have one and just shrug.

"Some woman wants to know where you work, eh, Danny," Lee says with a glint in his eye. "Have you got a stalker?"

"Eh? No."

"Remember that film from a few years back, *Fatal Attraction*?"

"The bunny boiler," Gavin says.

I actually went to see *Fatal Attraction* at the cinema with Zoe. It's true to say that the most shocking scene involved the protagonist's wife coming home to find their pet rabbit gently simmering in a large saucepan.

"That's the one," Lee says. "You haven't got yourself involved with a bunny boiler, have you, Danny?"

"No, and I don't have the faintest idea who just called."

"Let's just hope it's not another Mr Kipper," Gavin remarks.

"Who?"

"Don't you remember what happened to that estate agent, Suzy Lamplugh, back in 1986? It was all over the news for weeks."

"Vaguely. Didn't she go missing after showing someone around a flat?"

"Yep, she met with a bloke calling himself Mr Kipper, and that was the last anyone saw of her, the poor girl. Even now, it still makes my blood run cold."

"I've got a rape alarm if you want to take it with you on those viewings," Tina interjects.

"I'm sure I'll be fine, but thank you for the offer."

"Just don't get yourself abducted, okay," Lee says. "It's not easy finding a junior neg that knows how to make a half-decent cuppa."

"Thanks, I think, but it's probably just someone from the Job Centre checking up on me. I called them to say I wouldn't be signing on as I've found a job."

"Let's hope so, eh."

Frankly, being abducted would just about put the tin lid on what's been a dreadful year so far. Maybe I will borrow Tina's rape alarm.

Chapter 9

When Lee said his training programme involved being dropped in at the deep end, he wasn't joking. Well, he almost wasn't joking. Before leaving for his valuation, he gave me a few pointers and handed over the official Gibley Smith training manual. The dusty tome was so old that when I opened it up, I was mildly surprised to see it wasn't written in Latin.

Gavin also imparted a few words of wisdom before he left the office — never take a shit in a repossessed property, as the water supply is usually disconnected. He left before confirming if his advice was based on prior experience.

I close the training manual and put my jacket on.

"Are you off on your viewings?" Tina asks from her desk.

"In a minute."

"Are you nervous?"

"Not really. What's the worst that could happen ... actually, don't answer that."

"I won't," Tina sniggers. "But you'll be fine."

"Thanks. Can I ask you a question?"

"Sure."

"What happened this morning when Gavin arrived? He seemed quite annoyed by Lee's comments."

"Gavin moved back to his parents' house just after Christmas, and a few days later, his mum dropped off a Tupperware box with his lunch in it."

"Bit embarrassing, but hardly a stick to beat him with nine months on."

"It's because he's *still* living with his parents. He told us it was temporary after the divorce."

"Gavin's divorced?"

"He married his childhood sweetheart at twenty, and they divorced four years later. I think it was a mutual thing, but he doesn't really talk about it."

"Duly noted."

I grab the keys for the two properties I'm about to visit and Tina wishes me luck. Based on what little I've learned so far and the low-level risk of being abducted, I need all the luck I can get.

If there's any silver lining to my task, at least I know the way to the first property as it's literally a stone's throw from my own home. The rain has thankfully abated but the gloomy sky threatens more, so I hurry to the car and set off on the short journey back to Sefton Court.

Although both the parking bays belonging to flat number 19 are vacant, I park around the corner in my bay. Whilst I can feign confidence in front of the couple viewing the flat, the tatty Volvo screams loser.

I'm a little early, but I don't want to sit in the car and allow my thoughts to drift towards Zoe, so I make my way around the building and let myself into the communal hallway that leads to flat 19. I don't have to wait long for another car to pull up. I watch on as a youngish couple get out and then walk hand in hand towards the communal entrance. Assuming they're the couple I'm due to meet, I'm relieved they're young and, therefore, likely to know even less about property matters than I do.

I put on my best smile and open the door.

"Mr Patterson and Miss Butler?"

"That's us," the guy replies. "Gary and Lisa."

"Nice to meet you. I'm Danny from Gibley Smith."

We shake hands, and I invite them into the hallway. The training manual suggested I keep the conversation light at first and attempt to build a rapport.

"Have you come far this morning?"

"Not really," Lisa replies. "We live local."

"That's just as well, what with the rain and all."

The couple reply with strained smiles.

Having already exhausted my list of small talk topics, I lead the couple up the hallway and unlock the door to flat 19.

"Come on in," I say while holding the door open.

They follow me through to the lounge.

"This is the lounge," I announce as if it wasn't patently obvious to anyone but an idiot.

"It's a good size," Lisa says with a degree of enthusiasm.

"Plenty of room for furniture," I respond before quickly wishing I hadn't. What else would you put in a lounge apart from furniture? Livestock? A string quartet?

Gary makes for the patio doors and inspects the balcony beyond whilst Lisa drinks in the room. I need to ask a question that doesn't further imply that I'm a complete moron.

"How long have you been looking for a property?"

"Just a week or so."

"Okay, cool. What appeals about this place?"

"The price," Gary replies, turning away from the patio doors. "It's a repo, isn't it?"

"Yes, it's a repossession."

"My older brother bought a repo last month. He only paid sixty-one grand for a two-bed semi."

"Sounds like a bargain."

"It was, and that's what we're after."

"Definitely," Lisa affirms.

Lounge inspected, I guide the couple around the rest of the flat. Lisa's excitement seems to mount as we move from room to room but I suspect Gary is trying to keep a poker face. The tour ends back in the lounge.

"What do you think?" I ask. "Is it a contender?"

"Do you mind if we have another quick look on our own?" Gary asks.

"No problem," I reply, glancing at my watch. "But I do need to be away within the next ten minutes. I've got another viewing across town."

"We won't be long."

The couple then turn and head back towards the hallway. There isn't much I can do, so I lean up against the wall and stare at my watch. I can hear the couple talking in muffled tones but not what they're actually saying. For all I know, they could be plotting my abduction.

Five minutes later, they return.

"It's a nice pad," Gary announces. "And we'd like to put in an offer."

"Right ... um, great. How much would you be willing to offer?"

"Forty-four thousand."

"I beg your pardon."

"Forty-four thousand," Gary repeats.

It's not my flat, so there's no reason to feel so offended, but I do. Maybe it's because I happen to own an identical flat a hundred yards away, and I paid a hell of a lot more for it.

"You do realise these flats were selling for sixty thousand only last year, right?"

"So? That was last year, and prices were much higher across the board."

"I know, but ... forty-four thousand is a very low offer for a flat as lovely as this."

"It's as much as we can afford," Lisa says.

"Right."

"But, we're first-time buyers, and we've already sorted a mortgage with the Abbey National."

The mention of a mortgage triggers the vague memory of an instruction in the Gibley Smith training manual.

"It's great that you've already arranged a mortgage, but you will need to speak to our mortgage advisor. It's only a formality — we just need to double-check you're good for a loan."

"We are," Gary replies defiantly.

"I'm sure, but it's company policy, I'm afraid. We can't submit an offer until you've spoken to our mortgage advisor."

Even in my head, the policy sounds a bit iffy, but I don't want to get in trouble on my second day.

"I'll ask our mortgage advisor to call you later today, and then we can get that offer submitted for you. How's that sound?"

Based on Gary's frown, it doesn't sound good at all. However, he eventually nods his agreement.

"Excellent," I say, checking my watch. "I'll show you out."

I shake hands with the couple outside and assure them I'll get on to our mortgage advisor the minute I'm back in the office. With their offer way below the asking price, it seems a waste of everyone's time. Part of the job, I suppose.

First viewing done and dusted, I hurry back to the Volvo and then race across town to meet Mr and Mrs Edgar at 56 Nutshell Close. When I checked the freshly minted sales particulars before leaving the office, I was surprised to see the asking price set at precisely the figure Gavin recommended. I wrongly presumed that the lender might instruct a surveyor to ascertain a fair market price. I doubt the previous homeowners will be too chuffed when they spot their former home advertised in the paper for much less than it's likely worth.

I turn into Nutshell Close and pull up on the right-hand side of the road, some seventy yards short of number 56. There's a Mercedes saloon parked on the driveway of the house, and I presume it belongs to Mr and Mrs Edgar.

When I hurry up to the front door, I turn and smile at the couple. That smile isn't returned, but they both get out of the car.

"Mr and Mrs Edgar?" I confirm.

"That's right," Mr Edgar replies while locking his Mercedes. "And you're late."

I am late, but no more than a minute.

"Apologies. My last appointment overran."

The middle-aged couple don't say another word as I push open the door and invite them to enter first. Based on their stiff body language and stony faces, this is going to be hard work.

Once we're in the hallway, I close the front door and belatedly introduce myself.

"We tried selling our previous home through Gibley Smith back in 1981," Mr Edgar replies. "Atrocious service. Absolutely atrocious."

Mrs Edgar agrees with a nod and a huff.

"I'm sorry to hear that. I wasn't working for Gibley Smith in 1981."

Mr Edgar ignores my defence. He seems more interested in tapping his knuckle against the hallway wall.

"It smells peculiar in here," Mrs Edgar observes, breaking her vow of silence. "Most unpleasant."

"It's probably damp," Mr Edgar suggests. "Pound to a penny, the place is riddled with it."

"I think it's been empty for a little while," I say in defence of the house. "The lounge is to your left if you'd like to go on through."

Mr Edgar leads the way, tapping the wall as he goes. Quite what he's trying to ascertain is beyond me, but it's bloody annoying.

"Have you been looking for a new home long?" I ask once we enter the lounge.

"Four months," Mrs Edgar replies. "Although it's not for us. We'd never live in a house like this, would we, Jeremy?"

"Good God, no. It's for our son and his ... his wife."

Mr Edgar almost spits out the word wife.

"Oh, so they're the ones looking to buy, are they?"

"No, we'll buy the house, and they'll rent it from us."

"Ah, okay."

He returns to his wall tapping while Mrs Edgar frowns at the bare floorboards.

"These will need replacing," she remarks. "They squeak."

The couple continue adding to their complaints as we tour the ground floor. Apparently, the dining room is too dark, the kitchen is too small, and the garden is nothing short of a shambles. We return to the hallway.

"Would you like to skip upstairs?" I ask. "It doesn't seem like this is the house for you."

"We didn't come all this way to view half a house, young man."

"No, of course not. After you."

I wave the obnoxious couple up the stairs and follow behind, biting my tongue all the way.

"What happened to the people who lived here?" Mrs Edgar asks once we reach the landing.

"Sorry, I don't know."

"Were they ... foreign?"

"I couldn't tell you. I never met them."

She visibly shudders and then follows her husband into the main bedroom, where the complaints continue.

"The sockets look ancient," Mr Edgar says. "When were the electrics last checked?"

"I've no idea, I'm afraid."

"You're supposed to be selling a house, and you can't even answer a basic question about the electrics?"

"With respect, it's not our job to test the electrics, and as the house is being sold by a bank, it's unlikely they'll know."

"Unbelievable," he snorts before turning his attention to the last remaining untapped wall in the room.

Their feedback doesn't improve in the second bedroom, and Mrs Edgar refuses to even enter the bathroom. Finally, we reach the box room with the hand prints on the wall. I let them enter and then loiter in the doorway.

"I can't believe you have the cheek to call this a bedroom," Mr Edgar rants. "It's barely a cupboard."

"Look at that, Jeremy," Mrs Edgar gasps, pointing at the hand prints. "They actually kept a child in these conditions."

"It was likely feral," her husband snorts. "What kind of parent lets a child daub paint all over the walls?"

The training manual never mentioned tethers, but I've reached the end of mine.

"Clearly, this house doesn't meet your exacting standards, so let's not waste any more of your time."

I stand aside and wave the couple out of the room.

"We haven't finished yet," Mr Edgar barks. "We'd like to inspect the rooms for a second time."

Inwardly seething, I force a smile. "Help yourself, but I need to be away in five minutes. I'll wait on the driveway."

I stomp down the stairs before Mr Edgar can object.

Leaving the front door ajar, I lean up against the brickwork to the side of the garage and take a few deep breaths. I've dealt with plenty of arrogant arseholes in my years of working in retail, but the Edgars are on a different level. Maybe their attitude is no worse than I'm used to, but the difference is that I'm a junior member of staff, so I'm expected to suck it up. As a manager, I could deal with troublesome customers however I saw fit.

I let my mind drift off and reminisce about the career I lost. Those thoughts are then rudely interrupted when the Edgars appear.

"All done?" I ask, closing the front door to imply it was a statement rather than a question.

"Yes, and we'd like to submit an offer."

If Mr Edgar had asked me to join him and his wife for a threesome, I'd be slightly less shocked.

"You want to submit an offer?" I clarify. "For this house?"

"Do you have a hearing impediment? Yes, of course, this house."

"How much would you—"

"Fifty thousand," Mr Edgar snaps. "And we won't pay a penny more."

Whilst the lowball offer on the flat in Sefton Court might be considered naively ambitious, the Edgars' offer is downright laughable.

"You do know the asking price is £74,950, right?"

"Of course I do."

"And you want to offer £50,000?"

"Good grief. Yes."

"Okay, I'll ask my manager to put it forward. Have you arranged a mortgage?"

"We don't require a mortgage. It'll be a cash purchase."

"Right. Leave it with me."

"Call us the moment you have an answer. Understood?"

"Yep."

Not that I'd want to shake his hand, but Mr Edgar turns on his heels and walks towards the car where his wife is already waiting in the passenger seat.

"Prick," I mutter under my breath.

Mr Edgar suddenly spins around. "What was that?"

"I said, um ... quick. Your wife is waiting."

"Don't tell me to be quick, young man, just because you're incapable of managing your diary. I'll leave when I'm good and ready."

To make his point, he gets into the Mercedes and sits there with his arms folded. I double-check that the front door to number 56 is locked and then stride away. Their car is still on the driveway when I start up the Volvo. Either Mr Edgar is willing to waste his time as a matter of principle, or Mrs Edgar is giving him grief for not suggesting a threesome.

Whatever his reason, I'm not hanging around to find out.

Chapter 10

When I return to the office, Lee is back from his valuation but Gavin is still out.

"How'd it go?" my boss asks as I transfer both sets of keys to their respective numbered hooks in a filing cabinet.

"The good news is that I received offers on both properties. The bad news is how much they offered."

"Go on."

"The young couple offered forty-four thousand on 19 Sefton Court. That's as much as they can afford, apparently."

"Did you speak to them about a mortgage?"

"I did, and they've already arranged one with Abbey National, but they said our advisor could call them."

"I'll give you the number for Tracy in the mortgage admin department. Every time you get a lead, call it through to her and she'll pass it on to one of the advisors. What about the second offer?"

"Ah, yes," I grimace. "Mr and Mrs Edgar offered fifty grand on the semi in Nutshell Close. They're cash buyers, apparently."

"What?" Lee blasts. "I don't care if they're offering to buy the house with gold bullion and blowjobs; that's a fucking joke of an offer."

"I thought you might say something along those lines. Sorry."

"It's not your fault, lad. They made an offer on another house last month — twenty-five grand below the asking price. Pass me your viewing book, and I'll show you how to deal with the likes of the Edgars."

I step over to my desk, retrieve the viewing book, and pass it to Lee. He checks the Edgar's number and angrily jabs the buttons on his phone before lifting the handset. He then waits for the call to be answered.

"Mr Edgar? It's Lee Ross from Gibley Smith."

There's a brief pause before he speaks again.

"We spoke last month when you offered on that house in Laburnum Gardens, and I told you it's a waste of everyone's time unless your offer is within ten per cent of the asking price."

I can just about hear the elevated pitch of Mr Edgar's voice but I can only imagine his words.

"That house in Nutshell Close only came on the market today," Lee continues. "There's no way they'll entertain an offer of fifty thousand."

Mr Edgar's pitch increases by an octave or two.

"Yes, I know that a house is only worth what someone is willing to pay for it, but we've already received two other offers on that house this morning and both are within a few thousand of the asking price. Therefore, your offer is irrelevant."

Mr Edgar's voice increases in volume to the point I catch three words: *wasting our time.*

"And you're wasting mine, so I'm going to end this call. Goodbye, Mr Edgar."

Lee then slams the phone down.

"Twat," he spits.

"I take it Mr Edgar wasn't best pleased?" I venture.

"That's putting it mildly."

"Still, I don't suppose it matters if we've got two other offers."

"We don't have any other offers. I only said that to piss him off."

"Oh."

"Go grab the file for the Sefton Court flat, will you."

With Lee clearly agitated, I don't argue. It strikes me as just as much a waste of time as the Edgar's offer, but it's Lee's time to waste.

"Cheers," he says as I hand him the file. "Ring that mortgage lead through, and then you can start calling applicants about the house in Nutshell Close — see if we can't get some interest before the Edgars return with another shite offer."

"Will do."

After a five-minute conversation with Tracy in the mortgage admin department, I flip open the box of applicant cards and pull out the wad in the seventy to eighty thousand price bracket. At a guess, there must be thirty-odd cards, so I'm likely to be on the phone for a while.

Twenty minutes and a dozen calls later, I've managed to secure one viewing and seven people asked for a set of particulars to be sent in the post. I'm about to make another call when Lee yells across the office.

"Looks like you've made your first sale, Danny. Well done."

I stare back at him, perplexed.

"They accepted that offer on 19 Sefton Court."

This is likely a moment that every junior negotiator looks forward to and savours. Like the first girl you kiss or the first record you buy, the first property you sell must live long in the memory. It will for me, but for all the wrong reasons.

"You're supposed to look pleased," Lee remarks.

"I ... er, I am. It's great news."

It's anything but great news. Even with my limited knowledge of how the property market works, I know that my flat has just dropped another few thousand in value. If number 19 sold for £44,000, who would willingly pay more for an identical flat? No one.

I console myself with the knowledge that it doesn't make any real odds. If we'd sold the flat last week, we'd have lost a small fortune. If we sell it today, we'll still lose a small fortune, albeit not as small as last week. When you've got five figure negative equity, what difference does a few grand really make? If you're fucked, you're fucked.

I return to my calls, and by lunchtime, I've worked through all the cards, bar a few. I have three viewings for my efforts, plus a small stack of envelopes ready to post out once I've inserted a set of sales particulars.

With both Lee and Gavin out on appointments, I check with Tina if it's okay if I grab a bite to eat.

"You don't have to check with me," she replies. "Go for it."

"Do you want anything from Tesco?"

"Why are you walking all the way to the supermarket? There's a bakery just up the road, and they sell takeaway sandwiches in the cafe around the corner."

"Remember what I said about my finances? I've got to watch every penny, hence a DIY lunch from the supermarket."

With Tina confirming she doesn't need anything, I leave the office and saunter through the town towards Tesco. My journey isn't in a straight line as I want to avoid a certain hair salon at the far end of Victoria Road. That part of town has been a no-go zone for the last five months, as I couldn't bear the thought of bumping into Zoe. That hasn't changed, although my reasoning has. I told her I'd call the building society today, and I haven't had a chance, nor will I unless Lee and Gavin leave the office again.

I reach the supermarket and distract myself from thoughts of my ex-fiancée by browsing the chilled foods aisle in search of cheap sandwich filler. My budget will only stretch to either corned beef or luncheon meat, which is akin to choosing between bovine or porcine roadkill. Fortunately, my budget will stretch to a small jar of own-brand sandwich pickle, which should at least disguise the taste, if not the texture of the meat.

After grabbing the cheapest loaf of bread and a tub of margarine, I hurry through the checkout and make my way back to the office. When I step through the door, neither Lee nor Gavin are at their desks. This is good news. If I hurry, I can make a sandwich and then call the building society.

I get halfway across the office when Tina looks up from her computer monitor and beckons me over.

"Before you have your lunch, Danny," she says. "Can I have a quick word?"

Something about her tone of voice suggests her word will be serious.

"Um, sure. Have I done something wrong?"

"No, not at all. It's … it's that woman. She called again."

"What woman?"

"The one who called during the morning meeting and asked if you work here."

"How do you know it was the same woman?"

"Her tone of voice is quite distinctive, and she asked after you again."

"She asked if I work here?"

"No, she wanted to know … I wrote it down so I wouldn't forget."

Tina leans over her desk and consults a notepad.

"She said: Will Daniel Monk be in the office tomorrow morning?"

"What did you say?"

"I said, yes. She thanked me and then hung up."

"You said her tone of voice was distinctive. How so?"

"She sounded ... it's hard to describe but kind of tired, maybe even a bit sad. I'd also say she's an older lady."

"Great," I groan. "I have a geriatric stalker."

"I didn't say she was geriatric. Just mature, like, not young."

"I'm not sure her age is really the issue here, but thanks for the clarification."

"You've no idea who it might be?"

"Not a clue. I thought the earlier call might have been someone at the Job Centre but I can't imagine why they'd want to know if I'm in the office tomorrow."

Tina replies with a shrug of her shoulders and a semi-sympathetic smile. Her reaction is one I should adopt because a random woman enquiring about my work situation is the least of my problems. And maybe now is the right time to deal with the most significant of my problems. Hungry as I am, I can't put off calling the building society any longer.

"Putting my stalker aside for the minute, are Lee and Gavin due back soon?"

"Lee will be another half hour, I'd guess. Gavin popped home, so he'll be a while. Why do you ask?"

"I know we're not supposed to make personal calls, but I need to ring my mortgage company — it's kind of important."

"No one takes any notice of that rule. Besides, if you're stuck in the office all day every day, when are you supposed to make personal calls?"

"That is true."

"I've got a stack of dictation to get through, so you don't have to worry about me eavesdropping."

Tina then extracts a micro-cassette from a Dictaphone and puts on a pair of headphones.

"Go on," she then prompts. "And good luck."

"Thanks. I need it."

I hurry back to my desk and retrieve a letter from my jacket pocket. The bold font and red ink emphasise the seriousness of the content, not to mention a direct order that I call the building society's debt recovery department as a matter of urgency.

There's no putting it off any longer. I dial the number.

It's a measure of how seriously the building society takes debt recovery that my call is answered within five rings. The woman on the other end of the line, Alison, asks for my name and account number. As soon as she confirms my details, I bite the bullet and explain my situation.

"So you're now in full-time employment?" she confirms.

"Yes, but the salary isn't great, and I won't be paid until the end of the month."

"Will you be able to make this month's mortgage payment?"

"Honestly, no."

"I see you made a payment earlier this week, albeit only partially."

"It's all the money I had."

"Fair enough, but we need to set up a payment plan to cover the outstanding debt. Plus, we need to determine how you'll meet your future payments."

A nugget of advice Dad offered comes to mind.

"I'm hoping to find a lodger. That'll help with future payments."

"Right, and what about the outstanding debt? How much can you afford to pay each month towards that?"

It's a straightforward question, but there are two answers, both complicated. I don't know how much commission I'll earn from one month to the next, so it's impossible to commit to a set figure. Then there's the solution involving my cheating ex-fiancée. If I accept her proposal, I can completely clear the debt within a few weeks. It would, however, involve Zoe and I living under the same roof again.

"At the moment, I'm not sure, but I'm confident that I can clear the arrears by Christmas."

"I'm afraid we do need a fixed repayment plan in place to avoid escalation to the next stage."

"The next stage?"

"An application to the court for a repossession order."

"How long have I got before it gets to that stage?"

"We've got a backlog at the moment, so it could be four or five weeks before the papers are submitted."

"In which case, I'll get back to you next week once I've worked out how I'll clear the outstanding debt."

Alison adds a note to my file and then offers her advice, although it sounds more like a warning: avoiding the problem will only make matters worse. Much worse.

After ending the call, I sit back in my seat and puff a long sigh.

I managed to kick the can down the road a bit, but I'm getting worryingly close to the end of that road.

Chapter 11

After finishing work yesterday, I popped in to see my parents. Admittedly, I had an ulterior motive. I wanted to tell them how I was faring in my new job, but I also fancied a decent, home-cooked meal. However, the bangers and mash came at a price. Mum insisted I update her about the flat and my finances in general.

No man in his late twenties wants to receive a lecture from his mother, but in my case, a lecture is the lesser of two evils. To this day, neither of my parents knows the real reason why Zoe and I split up. As far as they're aware, we had a disagreement, reached an impasse, and decided to go our separate ways. It makes every conversation about the flat difficult because they don't understand my reluctance to sit down with Zoe and sort things out. My pride, however, remains a roadblock to the truth. I'd rather suffer my parents' frustration than admit my fiancée wanked off another man. Maybe one day, if the truth ever comes out, my parents will thank me for sparing them the sordid details.

When I arrive at the office, Tina is already in the back room.

"Morning," she says somewhat dolefully. "Coffee?"

"I'd love one, ta."

She opens the cupboard to retrieve a mug and then shuts the door with a touch too much force.

"Everything okay?" I venture. "You seem a little out of sorts this morning."

"It's nothing. Just a stupid row with Stuart."

"Stuart is your other half, right?"

"For now," she huffs.

I'm in no position to offer relationship advice, but I get the feeling Tina wants to get something off her chest. My prediction proves correct when she then turns to face me, hands on her hips.

"Can I ask you a question, Danny?"

"Of course."

"You've lived with a partner, right?"

"Um, yeah. My ex-fiancée."

"Did you find it hard when you first moved in together?"

"A bit. We all have our annoying little habits, and it takes a while to iron them out."

"Me and Stuart moved in together three months ago, but he won't stop with his annoying little habits. It's really starting to piss me off."

"Is he eating biscuits in bed?" I ask in an attempt to lighten Tina's stormy mood.

"No, it's far worse than that."

"Picking his nose?"

"Worse."

"Jesus. What exactly is his bad habit?"

"When we're both getting ready for work in the morning, Stuart thinks it's okay to take a dump while I'm in the shower."

"Ah, we had a similar problem in our first flat. When someone flushes the loo, the water in the shower is suddenly scalding hot."

"That's not the problem. We only have one toilet, and that's in the bathroom."

The real cause of Tina's angst suddenly becomes apparent.

"You mean …"

"Yes, Stuart thinks I'm being unreasonable because I don't like him taking a shit while I'm showering only a few feet away."

"Seems obvious, but have you tried locking the bathroom door?"

"Yes, but it's really easy to undo the lock from the outside."

"I see."

I don't, nor do I have any further advice.

"He said his ex never complained," Tina continues. "Do you think I'm being unreasonable, kicking off about it?"

"Not at all, although I don't know how he even manages to do his business when there's someone in the same room. I struggle to go when there's someone in the same postcode."

Tina chuckles, and it seems to take the edge off her frustration.

"I think I'll give him an ultimatum," she declares. "If he does it again, I'll wait until he's in the shower and then take a dump in the back seat of his car — tit for tat."

"Or shit for shat?"

"Yes!" she giggles. "Exactly that."

My purpose served, I leave Tina to watch the kettle boil and head to my desk. Glancing up at the clock, it's almost half-eight, and although it's no surprise Gavin is yet to arrive, Lee strikes me as the punctual type. With nothing else better to do, I open my viewing book, intent on double-checking I've copied all my viewings to the respective property files. Just as I'm about to transfer my jacket to the back of the chair, Tina arrives at my desk with a steaming mug of coffee.

"You're a star. Thanks."

"No problem."

"Lee is cutting it fine this morning," I say casually.

"He's not in today. There's a manager's meeting in Basingstoke."

I glance across at the diary on Gavin's desk, open at today's date.

"Just as well we're not that busy, eh?"

"And that's the way I like it," Tina smiles.

The front door then swings open, and Gavin breezes in.

"Morning," he says with a yawn. "Is there water in the kettle?"

Once he's sorted himself out with a mug of coffee and Tina has brought him up to speed on turd-gate, Gavin begins the morning meeting.

"Quiet day today," he begins. "I've got a repo at ten and then a valuation at half twelve. Danny, are you okay doing a viewing at 22 Linton Street at noon?"

The house in question is another repo and one that I viewed during Wednesday's tour of all the vacant properties.

"No problem."

The office phone rings, and, as seems to be the norm during morning meetings, Tina answers it at her desk.

"You up for a beer after work?" Gavin asks while we wait for Tina. "It's kind of a tradition on a Friday."

"I'd love to, but money is a bit tight at the moment."

"It's my shout. You can buy the beers on payday."

"Only if you're sure?"

"Yeah, no problem. We usually go to the Victoria Club above the Co-op. Do you know it?"

"Can't say I do."

"It's members-only, but I'll sign you in. And it's only a quid a pint if you're willing to suffer Fosters."

"What is it they say about beggars?" I respond with a grin.

Gavin is set to say something when Tina clears her throat to attract his attention.

"Gav, I've got this woman on hold, Mrs Weller. She owns a house on Echo Lane, and she's after a valuation."

"Christ, we don't get invited up there too often. When is she looking to book a valuation?"

"That's the thing. She insists it must be at ten this morning ... and she wants Danny to do it. I can't say for certain, but I think it's the same woman who called before."

I'm not sure which of us is more taken aback by Tina's revelation, but Gavin is the first to react.

"Put her through to my phone."

Our office administrator duly obliges, and Gavin picks up the phone on his desk.

"Mrs Weller, this is Gavin Flint, senior negotiator. I understand you'd like a valuation, correct?"

Silent seconds pass as Mrs Weller responds to Gavin's question.

"Okay, can I ask which number Echo Lane you live at and what type of property it is?"

As Mrs Weller relays the requested information, Gavin scrawls notes on a pad.

"And how many bedrooms?"

My colleague jots down the answer.

"I can be with you at eleven this morning if that works?"

Gavin's brow furrows as he listens intently for what seems an age.

"I do understand," Gavin then says. "Danny will be with you at ten."

He ends the call with a thank you and a goodbye. I fix him with a suitably confused glare.

"Why did you tell her I'd be there at ten?" I ask. "What do I know about valuing houses?"

"It was that or nothing, mate. She said if you can't do it, she'll call one of the other agents."

"At least she'd receive a visit from someone who knows what they're doing," I complain. "You'd be better off sending Tina."

"Not my job," she states.

"It's not really mine, either, yet. Gavin, it's pointless sending me."

"Who is she, anyway?" Tina asks.

"I don't know."

"You must do," Gavin suggests. "Why else would she specifically ask for you?"

I scratch my head, buying time while I consider the question.

"She might be one of my mum's friends," I venture. "That's all I've got."

"If that's the case," Gavin says. "You've already got a foot in the door."

"Whether she's a friend of my mum's or not, I can't go."

"Why not? If you go, at least we've got a chance of getting the instruction. She wasn't interested in anyone else doing the valuation, so you do it, or we lose out to another agent."

"It's just one house. Does it really matter if we're not in the running?"

"Ordinarily, no, but we're talking about a house on Echo Lane."

"I don't even know where Echo Lane is."

Gavin opens the top drawer of his desk and pulls out a map, which he unfolds on his desk.

"Come take a look at this," he says. "It's an Ordnance Survey map covering the western fringe of the town."

I reluctantly get up and stand beside Gavin as he runs his finger across the map.

"Echo Lane is one of the oldest roads in the town, and as you can see, there are only five properties along its entire length."

I stare down at the map, and it becomes apparent why I've never heard of Echo Lane. No more than a single-lane track leading nowhere, there's nothing around other than open fields and woodland.

"This is Mrs Weller's place," Gavin continues, tapping a section of the map at the furthest end of Echo Lane. "And look at the size of the plot."

The map outlines the boundary of each of the five properties, and even to my untrained eye, it's clear that the house in question sits within a sizeable slab of land.

"How big do you think the plot is?" I ask.

"Four or five acres, easily. Houses with plots that size rarely ever come to the market, and when they do, they go for serious money. And that means a serious commission if we get the instruction."

"Which is highly unlikely if you send me to value her house."

Gavin turns to me.

"Listen, mate, I know you're new to the game, but all you need to do is show up and turn on the charm. Wander around the house and say the right things, then tell her that the house is so unique that you'd like to conduct some further research before committing to a value. You can do that, right?"

"Well, um ... I suppose."

"Good man," Gavin says, slapping me on the upper arm. "And if you get her to instruct us, you can forget Fosters — I'll treat you to champagne later."

"I admire your optimism, but if I can avoid making a complete twat of myself, I'll consider that a win."

"As soon as we've finished the morning meeting, we'll grab a coffee, and I'll run through the basics. If you can run a shop, I'm pretty sure you can blag your way through a valuation."

I'm flattered by Gavin's confidence, but it'll take more than a fifteen-minute pep talk and a few pointers to allay my concerns. This seems like a terrible idea.

Chapter 12

I estimated that the three-mile drive to Echo Lane should take no more than fifteen minutes, but I left the office just after nine-thirty to be on the safe side. I'm nervous enough without the added stress of running late.

In fairness to Gavin, he did go to great lengths to ease my nerves. He suggested that I think of it as a date, and all I have to do is portray an air of confidence and charm even if I'm secretly bricking it. I've been on plenty of dates over the years, and, as now seems likely, there are more to come, so the comparison is useful. The worst that can happen on a date is you make a tit of yourself and you don't get a second date. The worst thing that could happen on this valuation is that Mrs Weller decides that I'm a tit and she'd rather use a different estate agent.

Besides, if this does go badly, I can blame Gavin for sending me. As for Mrs Weller insisting that she'd only accept the valuation if I do it, I can't think of any other reason than she must know one or both of my parents. Maybe Mrs Weller thinks she'll get a favourable commission rate by instructing a company that happens to employ a friend's son. I suspect she'll be less keen to strike a deal after I've wandered around her house like a lost child.

"Positive thoughts," I whisper as I leave the town centre behind.

Having studied Gavin's map in detail, the route to Echo Lane is now embedded in my memory. Once I've passed through the residential streets, I head towards the bypass. The part I'm unfamiliar with is the road that once formed the only route out of the town before they built the bypass in the sixties: Gallows Lane. Like so many old roads that once crisscrossed the county, it became obsolete once a quicker alternative route arrived.

As the houses on either side of the road thin out, I take the right-hand turn into Gallows Lane, passing a bright-red phone box on the corner. If my memory serves, there used to be a pub somewhere along Gallows Lane, but the name and the exact location escape me. There's no longer any evidence of its existence but then there's not much evidence of anything along Gallows Lane besides the odd cottage.

The final man-made structure on the lane is a post box. Beyond that, it's just grass verges and wild hedgerows until I pass a sign indicating the direction and distance to villages that wouldn't sound out of place in an Enid Blyton book.

I continue on, not entirely convinced that I haven't already passed Echo Lane. I know from the map that it's a right-hand turn and a narrow track, but that's all I've got to go on. Then, with my stress levels already on the rise, I suddenly pass a gap in the hedgerow. I slam on the brakes and come to a stop almost parallel to the track. There's no road sign to confirm if it is Echo Lane, but it is the first and only turning on the right I've passed. I reverse back a few yards and then point the Volvo in what I hope is the right direction.

A quick check of the dashboard clock confirms I'm still ten minutes from my appointment time, which is just as well. If this track ends up being a road to nowhere, at least I've got time to turn around and retrace my steps. Saying that, the track is so narrow it'd be difficult turning a motorbike around, never mind a hulking Volvo.

Moving at a snail's pace, I eventually reach the first sign of civilisation — literally a sign at the end of a driveway. I can't see the house, but the sign confirms that wherever it is, it's number 5. I press on and pass a similar sign for number 4. This must be Echo Lane, although the scale of it feels significantly larger than the paper inches of an Ordnance Survey map. I can see why Gavin got so excited — folk who want to live in a peaceful rural setting but remain within a ten-minute drive of the motorway network aren't spoilt for choice, and less choice means higher prices.

The lane continues to snake onwards and, to my concern, becomes even narrower. I eventually pass number 3, which is closer to the lane but protected by a tall hedge. Number 2 is similar to number 5 in that the only clue to its existence is a signpost at the end of a long driveway, although I can just about make out the silhouette of a building in the distance.

As I turn back towards the lane, the view straight ahead is a worrying one, and for a moment, I consider pulling over and walking the rest of the way. The tarmac road surface peters out and gives way to a rutted dirt trail, hemmed in on both sides by a thick wall of brambles. The lane is hardly vehicle-friendly, but this last stretch would challenge a tank. Fortunately, I'm driving one.

Gently lifting the clutch, I ease the Volvo forward.

A mate of mine once suggested off-roading as a possible event for a stag weekend, but he was quickly outvoted when someone else suggested Amsterdam. I wasn't keen on either option, but as I trundle cautiously along the final yards of Echo Lane, I can now say I've experienced both. Despite a few ominous knocks, the Volvo's suspension does a reasonable job of absorbing the worst of the ruts. Even so, it's an uncomfortable ride.

Although the road surface doesn't improve, the claustrophobic bramble bushes eventually thin out. I'm then presented with a view of open fields on my left and, as the lane gently sweeps to the right, a rusty five-bar gate straight ahead. Beyond that gate lays a meadow as vast as it is wild, and to my right, a crumbling drystone wall.

"Holy shit," I gasp when my eyes settle on the structure beyond the wall.

I've only been an estate agent for three days, but long enough to tell the difference between a desirable residence and a tumbledown wreck. Number 1 Echo Lane definitely sits in the latter category. A blanket of moss covers most of the roof, apart from the sections where the slate tiles have slipped into the guttering.

The view doesn't improve below the roof.

Most of the front elevation is covered by creeping ivy, and where the brickwork is exposed, there are dark patches of damp. Besides a weathered front door, each of the four windows to the front is hidden behind a closed wooden shutter. However, the shutters themselves are in such a state of neglect that they're more rot than wood.

It is, without question, the most sorry-looking house I've ever set eyes on.

With nowhere to park, I decide to abandon the Volvo where it sits. I then grab my clipboard from the passenger seat and mentally prepare myself. No wonder Mrs Weller was keen to book a valuation at such short notice — a strong gust of wind and her home is likely to collapse around her.

I get out of the car and make my way to what I imagine was once a front path. An army of weeds has colonised the paving, and if there was a front lawn, you'd be hard-pressed to tell where it once started and where it ended. It's so overgrown that it's past the point of requiring a gardener — what it really needs is a herd of ravenous goats or a few gallons of napalm.

Trying not to trip over the weed clumps, I zigzag cautiously up the path to the front door. There's no sign of a knocker or a doorbell, but there is a small brass plate fixed to the door at eye level. No more than four inches long and tarnished by the elements, I can just about make out the instruction etched into the brass: *Visitors — knock three times and then enter.*

Mrs Weller's security leaves a lot to be desired, but instructions are instructions. I rap my knuckle on the door three times and then turn the grimy doorknob.

The front door opens with an ominous creak.

I take a peek around the door, expecting to see a hallway stretching out in front of me. Instead, there's another door, in marginally better condition than the one I just opened. I step into the small entrance lobby and close the front door, but not before checking I can get out in a hurry should the need arise.

The space is so small that it doesn't seem to serve any function other than to add a barrier between the front door and the hallway. The walls are rough plaster, painted white, and the floor is covered in red quarry tiles. There is one striking feature, though, and that's the unnerving absence of sound. There's also a faint but peculiar smell that I can't quite pin down. It's a bit like that strange scent that hangs in the air before a thunderstorm.

Tentatively, I reach for the handle of the second door and push it open.

To my relief, there is a hallway beyond the door. The relief is coupled with surprise because the first impression is completely at odds with the exterior of the house. Perhaps fifteen feet in length and eight feet wide, the only word I can think of to describe it is immaculate.

Closing the door to the entrance lobby, I'm about to wipe my feet on the mat but, because the polished wooden floorboards are pristine to the point of untouched, I briefly consider removing my shoes altogether.

"Through here," a female voice then calls out.

"Okay," I reply, but it comes out as a croak, my mouth suddenly dry.

The voice came from beyond a partly open door at the end of the hallway, to the left of the staircase. After thoroughly wiping my feet, I cover the fifteen feet of polished oak planks whilst drinking in the rest of the hallway's features. There's nothing remarkable about it, other than the apparent newness. It kind of reminds me of our flat on the day we first viewed it. The walls, painted a warm stone colour, are so smoothly plastered that they reflect the soft glow of the recessed spotlights in the ceiling.

I reach the door where the voice emanated from and nudge it open.

"Daniel, I presume?"

I've barely had a chance to take in my surroundings, never mind question why Mrs Weller used the formal version of my name, when the woman herself strides towards me, her hand outstretched. At least I presume it's Mrs Weller.

"Good morning, Mrs Weller?"

"That's right," she replies as our hands interlock.

The handshake is enthusiastic but her hands are like ice. It's a relief when she finally releases her grip.

"Can I get you a tea, coffee ... a soft drink?"

"I'm okay, thank you."

She nods and then waves her hand towards a rustic-looking dining table with three matching chairs lined up on each of the two longer sides. "Please, take a seat."

I choose the nearest chair while Mrs Weller moves gingerly around the table to the opposite side. It's a good opportunity to weigh up the woman I need to charm. The shoulder-length silver-grey hair suggests she's a similar age to my mum, but her complexion is that of a woman maybe ten years younger. She moves with a certain degree of stiffness, suggesting her black trousers and blood-red turtle-neck sweater were chosen for comfort rather than fashion.

Mrs Weller pulls out the chair opposite mine and slowly lowers herself onto it. It's only then I notice another striking feature — her eyes. They're such a deep shade of brown that it's hard to distinguish between the pupils and the iris, giving them a sultry quality.

"You found the house okay, then?" she asks.

"No problem at all," I reply with a smile, conscious that I'm supposed to be a professional estate agent. "Although I didn't even know that Echo Lane existed before today."

Should I have said that? Fuck it — too late now.

"It's a bit off the beaten track, yes."

Mrs Weller returns my smile but doesn't follow up on her remark. I feel compelled to say something.

"So, you'd like the house valued, correct?"

"Yes, and I presume you'd like to have a look around the place?"

"That'd be a good place to start."

"Help yourself. You passed the stairs in the hallway and there's a lounge on the right, a dining room on the left."

"Er, you don't want to come with me?"

"The house is virtually empty so I don't think I've any reason to worry."

I don't know if this is normal, or Mrs Weller merely thinks I'm a closet kleptomaniac. Either way, I'm slightly relieved I won't have to walk around the house and provide a gushing commentary as we move from room to room.

"I'll be five minutes," I announce, getting to my feet.

"Take as long as you need. Are you sure you wouldn't like a drink?"

"Actually, I wouldn't say no to a glass of water."

"It'll be ready for you once you're done."

"Thank you."

I return the chair to its original position and open the clipboard. Gavin said I should make notes as I go, purely to give the impression I'm paying attention.

As I'm about to exit the kitchen, I catch sight of my own reflection in a window behind the sink. The reason I can see my own reflection is because of the shutters on the opposite side of the glass. The window frame itself, painted in gloss white, looks so fresh it could have been fitted yesterday.

Returning to the hallway, I reach the lounge door first and open it. It's an impressive size but that could be because there isn't a stick of furniture in the room. The emptiness is accentuated by my footsteps echoing off the floorboards, and the array of eight individual spotlights recessed in the smooth plasterboard ceiling. The walls are painted the same shade of stone as the hall and there are picture windows at both ends of the room. Like the kitchen, the frames appear new. I make a note to ask Mrs Weller if there's a reason why her perfectly appointed windows are hidden behind tatty old shutters.

I return to the hallway and open the door to the dining room. It's almost a carbon copy of the lounge, minus the stone fireplace.

Upstairs, a wide landing leads to three double bedrooms. They're just as pristine as the downstairs rooms and equally devoid of furniture, bar the main bedroom which houses a single bed, made up with crisp white linen. The bathroom is as good as I'd expect to find in a luxury hotel, with a free-standing bathtub, shower cubicle, plus a Victorian-style toilet and pedestal sink. It's so clean, so shiny, it's hard to believe anyone has ever used it.

As I return to the landing, I pass underneath a hatch which obviously provides access to the loft. I don't think I'm expected to check out the loft which, considering the state of the roof, is no bad thing. It does beg the question, though — the knackered roof must leak like a sieve, so why is there no evidence of water damage in any of the first floor ceilings?

I make a note on the clipboard and head back down the stairs.

Back in the kitchen, Mrs Weller is still sitting at the table.

"All done?" she asks.

"Yes, and you have a lovely home, Mrs Weller."

"Thank you. Come sit down."

There's a tall glass of water on the table directly opposite Mrs Weller; an indicator of where she expects me to sit. I oblige and take a quick sip, just to gather my thoughts. I've had an easy ride thus far but now the real test begins.

"How long have you lived here?" I ask — an ice-breaker Gavin suggested.

Mrs Weller sits forward and leans her elbows on the table. "That's not really relevant. Try again with a different question."

"Um, are you looking to sell the house, or are you just interested in ascertaining the value?"

"Neither."

It's not an answer Gavin covered in his pep talk. My mind struggles to formulate a suitable response.

"You're wondering why I specifically requested you to come here?" Mrs Weller rightly confirms.

"Um, yes."

"I'm not looking to sell the house, and the value is of no interest to me. I am, however, hoping I can strike a deal."

"A deal?"

"Correct, and not just any deal, Daniel. If you're up for a challenge, the reward will be the deeds to this very house."

Chapter 13

Before I fell into a retail career, I had three other jobs. My very first was on a youth training scheme, sanding chairs for a reproduction furniture company. The job proved tedious, and I resented working forty hours a week for twenty-five quid.

After three months, I was so desperate to leave that I applied for and accepted a job as a cashier at a petrol station. It proved just as tedious, but I earned three times as much. It was only a stopgap, and eventually, I landed a job with a CCTV security company, working in the office as a junior sales clerk.

The office manager was a forty-something bloke called Barry, and, as I would discover, Barry considered himself a bit of a joker. I was young and naive, not realising that anyone appointing themselves the office joker is, almost always, an utter bellend.

One week into my employment, Barry rushed over to my desk and handed me a scrap of paper. Stony faced, he said he was running twenty minutes late for an appointment, and I had to call the client he was due to meet and let him know. The scrap of paper contained the client's name and his office phone number.

Barry then bustled off to grab his car keys, and I, being a diligent young man, dialled the number. A woman promptly answered.

"Good morning. Frimpton Bird Sanctuary."

By that stage of my employment, I already knew we supplied CCTV to all manner of businesses and organisations, so I had no reason to suspect what was about to unfold.

"Good morning," I replied politely. "May I speak to Albert Ross."

"Who?" the woman replied.

"Mr Albert Ross. I believe he's due to meet my colleague Barry Dobson at eleven."

The woman sighed so loudly that I thought she might be hyperventilating.

"This is a bird sanctuary," she then said flatly.

"Right."

"You're calling a bird sanctuary to speak to Albert Ross."

"That's correct," I replied.

The woman then muttered what was likely an expletive.

"You haven't twigged, have you?"

"Um, sorry ... twigged what?"

"Albert Ross. Albatross."

The penny dropped at the exact same moment Barry reappeared, literally holding his sides in a fit of laughter. I apologised to the woman on the phone and hung up.

Initially, I accepted Barry's prank with good grace, but he then took great pleasure in telling everyone in the office. From that day forward, whenever our paths crossed in the staff room, Barry would ask if I'd spoken to Albert Ross recently.

I eventually left Mandell CCTV Services, but some months later, I bumped into one of my former colleagues. She told me that Barry had played one of his little jokes on the company's finance director, but it didn't go down well, and Barry was subsequently fired. That did make me laugh.

"Pardon my scepticism," I say, addressing Mrs Weller in a suitably suspicious tone. "But this has all the hallmarks of a prank. Did Lee or Gavin set this up?"

"It's no prank, Daniel."

"Maybe not," I reply, pushing my chair back. "But seeing as you don't need the house valued, I should probably get back to the office."

"No, wait. Please."

With that, Mrs Weller turns in her chair and opens a drawer behind her. She extracts a leather folder and places it on the table.

"If you can bear with me for a few seconds," she says, unzipping the folder, "I promise you'll want to hear my proposal."

Despite the absurdity, I can't deny that I'm mildly curious about where this is heading. It's the only reason I remain in my seat.

The folder contains two A4-size manilla envelopes, one significantly thicker than the other. Mrs Weller peels open the flap of the thicker envelope and pulls out a wad of paper, placing it on the table between us.

"The deeds to this house," she says matter-of-factly.

The typed information on the top page does indeed suggest I'm looking at a set of property deeds. However, I've never seen a set before, so for all I know, the rest of the pages could contain instructions for a Betamax VCR.

"These are the original deeds, but I do have a copy you can take away with you, if you'd like to get them checked by a solicitor."

"I'll take your word for it."

Mrs Weller then turns her attention to the second envelope, dipping her hand inside.

"And here," she says, pulling out a much thinner document. "Is a contract."

"A contract for what exactly?"

"For you, potentially, to become a very wealthy man, Daniel."

My host sits back in her chair and places the contract on top of the deeds.

"Do you have a rough idea of what this house is worth?" she asks.

"I, er ... not yet, no. I need to—"

"At this exact moment in time, it's worth approximately £200,000."

"Oh."

"Apologies for the subterfuge, but the value of the house today is academic. It's what it *will* be worth in years to come."

"Speaking from bitter experience, I can tell you there's no guarantee it'll go up in value."

"I know you're relatively new to the estate agency game, so I'll forgive your lack of knowledge. Over time, property values always go up. Always."

"I suppose it depends on what you mean by time."

"In this case, it's incidental, and for the sake of clarity, I'm not talking about the house on its own. It sits on a plot of approximately 5.4 acres, which, today, is wholly irrelevant. However, in years to come, the local council will need to build many hundreds of new homes for the town's growing population. They will then rezone this entire area, and do you know what that means?"

"We'll finally get a drive-through McDonalds?"

"Let's hope not," Mrs Weller huffs.

"I don't know, then."

"It means this house, or the land in which it sits to be precise, will multiply in value five, six, maybe even sevenfold once it falls within a zone earmarked for residential development. Whoever owns it will become an instant millionaire."

"Which does beg the question ... actually, it begs several questions. Firstly, how do you know what the council intend to do in the coming years? I can't even get them to confirm which day they're emptying the bins from one week to the next. Secondly, how do you know I've only just started at Gibley Smith, and why do you keep calling me Daniel?"

"It's your name, isn't it? Daniel Thomas Monk?"

"Yes, it's my name, but how do you know my middle name?"

"Because I couldn't recruit just anyone for this project. It had to be the right man."

More questions tumble through my mind. I need to prioritise the most pertinent.

"What makes me the right man, and what exactly is the project?"

"I'll come on to that, but first, let me just clarify your current ... situation."

I reply with a sceptical frown, but it doesn't invoke a reaction.

"You're twenty-eight years of age, correct?"

"Yes."

"Single."

"For now," I mumble, squirming in my seat.

"You're also in a bit of a pickle, financially."

"How do you—"

"How I know what I know is irrelevant," she interjects. "But I have conducted extensive research, and you are precisely the kind of man I need."

"If you really had done your research, you'd know that I'm almost certainly not the kind of man you need ... unless you're looking for a man with crippling negative equity, a failed engagement, and a job that pays almost half what I earned six months ago."

"Self-pity is such an unattractive trait, Daniel. It doesn't suit you."

"I'm just stating facts."

"What you failed to mention are your many positive attributes."

"Such as?"

Mrs Weller smiles and then fixes me with her big brown eyes.

"You're very handsome, for starters. Tall, broad-shouldered, and most men would kill for your jawline."

The smile remains, as does the intensity of her gaze.

"Thank you," I gulp, reaching for the glass of water.

"You're also intelligent, resourceful, and, most importantly, a decent man."

Considering we only met fifteen minutes ago, I decide to take Mrs Weller's compliments with a pinch of salt.

"In short, Daniel, you're the right man for this project."

"I'm flattered you think so, but what exactly do you think I'm so well qualified for?"

Mrs Weller dips her hand into the envelope again.

"Do you know what this is?" she asks, holding up a flat black object roughly five inches square.

"It looks like a computer disk."

"I believe the common term is floppy disk, and this particular disk contains all the information you need to undertake the task, should you choose to accept it."

I inadvertently respond with a snort of laughter. "Sorry, but this sounds a lot like the plot of a Cold War spy film."

"I understand you've every reason to be sceptical, but let me finish. The floppy disk contains a raft of personal information pertaining to a young woman, Kim Dolan. Everything from her O-Level results to her favourite sandwich."

"Who is Kim Dolan?"

"She's someone I need you to redirect. By that, I mean she's currently heading along a path that will, in time, result in a lifetime of sadness and regret. You can change that, Daniel."

"Can I? How?"

"By breaking up her current relationship. Kim is dating a man named Neil Harrison but he's not the man for her ... not by a long chalk. All you need to do is persuade Kim that there's no future with Harrison."

"No offence, but this sounds dodgy as hell. Even if I overlook the ethics of breaking up some random couple, how do I do it?"

"However you see fit. There's only one rule: you must not have sexual intercourse with Kim."

"Bit presumptuous."

"She's an attractive young woman. You will be tempted."

"Not if I get up and go back to the office. This is nuts."

"I can't deny it's an unorthodox task, but don't let that cloud your judgement. I'm offering you the opportunity to own this house, and if you grasp that opportunity, one day, you'll wake up as a millionaire. Think about that for a second, Daniel. Think about what your life will be like if you don't have to do a job you hate, live with constant money worries, or drive a second-hand Volvo, for that matter."

I have to give credit to Mrs Weller for her pitch. She's certainly identified where most of my current woes reside. I sit up and clear my throat.

"Let me get this straight. If I complete this ... project, you'll sign over the deeds of this house to me."

"Correct, which is why I prepared a legally binding contract — for your peace of mind."

"And you want me to trash this Kim's relationship?"

"I need to ensure she never wants to see Neil Harrison ever again."

"Why don't you talk to her? It doesn't make sense to ask some guy you've just met."

"She won't listen to me, and besides, I can't leave this house."

"Why not?"

"It's complicated. You wouldn't understand."

"Try me."

"For the purposes of comprehension, have you heard of the condition agoraphobia?"

"It's the fear of open spaces or something? The opposite of claustrophobia?"

"Loosely, yes. As I said, I cannot leave this house and I'd be grateful if we leave it at that."

Mrs Weller then leans forward and places the floppy disk on the table next to the deeds and the contract.

"I fully appreciate that this is a lot to process, so why don't you take away the disk and the contract, digest the content of both, and think about my proposal over the weekend? I've jotted my phone number on the back of the contract, so if you have any questions, please don't hesitate to call."

I momentarily stare at the document and the disk, unsure if I should even consider humouring this crazy woman.

"Go on," Mrs Weller then prompts. "There's no harm in taking them, is there?"

"I guess not," I reply, finally slipping both items into my clipboard.

"I do have one other incentive, which might help you make up your mind. I will pay you £200 a week to cover your expenses."

"Expenses?"

"I wouldn't expect you to be out of pocket while you're performing the task. The payment will cover your basic expenses: travel costs, food, and the like."

"And what if I fail? Would I have to repay any of it?"

"Firstly, I don't think you'll fail — I have every faith in you, Daniel. Secondly, they're expenses, so I wouldn't expect you to pay a penny back."

It's a measure of how desperate I am that even the prospect of owning a house and selling it in a few years for a million quid pales when compared to my immediate need for cash. Insane as this is, two hundred quid a week can't be sniffed at.

"When do you need an answer?" I ask.

"By 8.00 pm Monday. I would stress that you are the man I want for this project, but I do have alternative options. Time is not on my side, I'm afraid."

"Understood," I reply, glancing at my watch. "And I'd better be going."

"Of course. Do you have any questions before you leave?"

"No, I don't think so."

"Are you okay seeing yourself out?"

"Sure," I respond, getting to my feet. "It was nice meeting you, Mrs Weller."

Nice isn't the word I want to use, but I'm too polite to say what I really think.

"And you, Daniel."

I turn and take three steps towards the hallway, but then a question belatedly comes to mind. I turn around.

"Did you call my office on Wednesday morning, and yesterday, asking questions about me?"

"Guilty," Mrs Weller smiles back. "I was just double-checking."

"Double-checking what?"

"That you were where you're supposed to be."

Her answer makes no sense, but it's at least consistent with everything else she's said since I walked through the door.

"Right ... um, bye then."

"Goodbye."

I hurry down the hallway and then navigate the two doors to freedom. And sanity.

Chapter 14

I've wasted an inordinate amount of time wondering what would have happened if Zoe and I hadn't taken a wrong turn on our walk into town that fateful Saturday. We'd never have passed the Sefton Court development, and therefore, we'd likely have carried on, living our lives in our rented flat.

It wouldn't have affected the event that led to our breakup, but I'd have been in a better position to cope with the fallout.

As I drive back from Echo Lane, it also occurs to me that if we'd never bought the flat in Sefton Court, I'd never have called an estate agent to value it, and therefore, I wouldn't now be driving back from Echo Lane.

And there was I, thinking that fate had thrown its last curveball.

Before I left, Mrs Weller asked if I had any questions. However, in my eagerness to leave, I didn't probe how she knew so much about me and my life. How did she get that information and, more to the point, why pick me to derail a relationship involving two people I've never met?

It only takes the journey back to the office to make up my mind regarding Mrs Weller's proposal. The two hundred quid a week is a tempting carrot, but the whole deal is just so far-fetched I doubt I'd ever see a penny of it. I could just about get my head around her wanting to help out someone in a toxic relationship, but offering the house is just insane. There's no other word for it. Besides, I've got enough on my plate as it is.

Once I've parked up, I remove the contract and the floppy disk from the clipboard and shove both in the glove box. Now I just need to decide what I tell Gavin. It takes all of ten seconds to reach a decision — no one in their right mind would believe the truth, and I don't want my new colleagues to think I've got a screw loose. My mind made up, I waste another minute concocting a white lie.

I lock the car and hurry back to the office.

"How'd it go?" Gavin enquires the second I walk through the door.

"Um, fine, but she's definitely not selling."

"Why did she ask for a valuation, then?"

"Something to do with inheritance planning. Honestly, it went over my head, but she couldn't have made it any clearer that she's not selling up."

"Bloody time waster," Gavin huffs. "Did you mention the value?"

"No, but she did. She seems to think the house is worth about £200,000."

"What was it like?"

"Not much to look at from the outside but it's like a new house once you step through the front door."

"She's probably not far off with her estimate, which makes you wonder why she wasted our time. Anyway, get Junior to send out a standard valuation letter."

"Will do."

"Oh, and Danny."

"Yes?"

"Seeing as nothing came from it, let's not bother telling Lee. He'll get the hump with me if he finds out I sent you on a valuation."

"It's not as though Mrs Weller gave us much choice."

"I know, but Lee won't see it like that. It's just not worth the hassle."

"Understood. I'll keep it to myself."

"Nice one."

I wander over to the back of the office where Tina is on filing duty.

"Can you help me with a valuation letter?" I ask.

"Sure. Give me a sec."

Once she's finished with the last file, Tina beckons me over to her desk.

"Ordinarily," she begins. "You just fill out a property valuation form and drop it into my tray. I'll then type it up and send it out."

"Gotcha."

"But, seeing as it's your first one, I'll show you the process."

She places her hand on a clamshell-like device next to the keyboard.

"What's that?" I ask.

"It's a mouse. You use it to navigate around the screen."

"Cool."

I watch on as Tina clicks buttons on the mouse, and a blue box appears on the screen.

"Microsoft Windows?" I comment. "What's that?"

"It's the new operating system. Windows 3.0."

"Is it easy to use?"

"It is once you get your head around it. Mainly, I use the word processor called *Word*."

"Word?" I snort. "Is that the best name they could come up with?"

"You'll never guess what they call the spreadsheet program."

"Number?"

"No," she chuckles. "*Excel*."

Tina then moves the mouse around, and a little arrow on the screen tracks her actions.

"All of the standard letters are stored on the computer so I just need to open up the valuation letter and edit it. Then I just print it off — a piece of cake."

"Wow," I gush. "My mum's got a clunky old typewriter for whenever she has to write an important letter. Something like this would blow her mind."

"I used an electronic typewriter at college. It's like comparing a modern car to a horse and cart."

"I bet."

"Give me the details of your valuation, and I'll show you how easy it is to use."

I quote Mrs Weller's name and address, along with my completely pointless opinion of the value of number 1 Echo Lane. Tina edits the document on the screen and then clicks the mouse a few times.

"All done," she chirps. "Once the printer churns out your letter, sign it, stick it in the post tray, and I'll frank it later."

"Thanks, Tina."

My attention is then drawn to a semi-transparent plastic box next to the monitor.

"Are they floppy discs?" I ask.

"They are. I use them for backup copies of all our documents, and head office sends them out whenever there are changes to our standard letters."

"So, you just stick a disk in the computer and it opens up whatever info is stored on there?"

"It depends."

"On?"

"The type of file. The computer uses different programs for different files."

"Right."

"Why the interest?"

"I'm just curious. Someone gave me a floppy disk and … actually, just forget it."

As Tina returns to her duties, I wander back to my desk, chiding myself for even contemplating the contents of Mrs Weller's disk.

"All sorted?" Gavin asks.

"Yep."

"Do you fancy chasing up some of the outstanding viewings for feedback?"

"Sure."

"Just remember what I said. Vendors claim they want honest feedback but if you tell them the truth, they get the hump."

"Noted."

I call the first viewer on my list and as it happens, I couldn't have picked a better example to demonstrate why Gavin urged caution. Mr Stretten viewed a house in Pinehurst Road yesterday afternoon and he was all too keen on sharing his opinion of the place. In short, Mr Stretten said he'd rather move his family into a bomb-ravaged hut in central Beirut over the three-bed semi in Pinehurst Road. I didn't share that exact feedback with the homeowner, instead telling her that the Stretten family required a larger garden.

Over the ensuing hour, I realise why viewing feedback is a job for the junior negotiator. Logic suggests that if someone is genuinely interested in a property, they'll make an offer soon after viewing it. Therefore, I'm left to seek feedback from people who have no interest in the property they viewed. That's bad enough, but then I have to listen to the vendors moaning about our inability to find a suitable buyer. It's a horrible job.

Maybe that's why my mind drifts back to Mrs Weller's offer as I grab lunch in the back room. I promised myself I wouldn't dwell on it once I'd made up my mind but what if I'm about to tear up the equivalent of a Wonka golden ticket? On the face of it, the opportunity does appear every bit as absurd as a day trip to Willy Wonka's factory, albeit with fewer Oompa-Loompas.

But a tiny, tiny part of me can't let go of the fact it could be a genuine offer.

As I sit and chew on a corned beef sandwich, my mind swings back and forth. It can't be a genuine offer, surely. But what if it is? No one gives away a house for a favour. Then again, I read that almost a million people walked into a record shop and voluntarily purchased a copy of *Especially for You* by Jason and Kylie. The truth, no matter how baffling it sometimes seems, is the truth.

My thoughts are interrupted when Gavin wanders into the back room.

"Not disturbing you, am I?" he asks.

"No, it's fine. I'm about done."

"You alright? You look a bit perturbed."

"No, I was just thinking about this morning's valuation."

"What about it?"

"If the house is worth two hundred grand as it is, what would it be worth if you could build on the land?"

Gavin eyes me for a moment. "I thought you said the vendor wasn't interested in selling?"

"She definitely isn't. I'm just curious, that's all."

"As it stands, the size of the plot doesn't make a huge difference to the value. The access is shit, so it's no good for equestrian use, and no one wants that much garden. Imagine having to mow a lawn that size."

"But, if you could use the land for building houses, it'd be worth a lot more, presumably?"

"Yeah, a lot more, but if I were ten inches taller and not so pasty-faced, the girl behind the counter in Barclays might agree to go for a drink with me. As it is, I'm a short arse, and that land is designated greenbelt, so there's no chance of it being rezoned for housing."

"Never?"

"As Prince once said, never is a bloody long time ... or words to that effect. No one thought they'd ever get permission to build on Manor Farm, but now there are eight hundred houses standing on what used to be potato fields."

"Where's Manor Farm?"

"It's nowhere these days, but it used to be on the southern side of the town. It's now a housing development called Wellington Park."

"Oh, right. We've got a house for sale there, haven't we?"

"Yep, on Kestrel Drive. Well remembered."

"So, what you're saying is that Mrs Weller's plot of land isn't of any great value today, but it might be at some point in the future?"

"Yeah, but everything will be worth something if you hold on to it for long enough. A mate of mine owns a mint first-edition copy of Razzle from '83, and he reckons it'll be worth a small fortune in years to come."

"Er, Razzle is a wank mag, isn't it? You can hardly compare it to a plot of land."

"No, but it proves my point. Just think about all those antiques that sell for serious money — they were once just regular furniture."

"True."

"Anyway, I only came out here for a piss. I've got a valuation to get to."

Gavin disappears into the toilet and I amble to my desk. I've still got a handful of viewings to follow up, but now I've allowed the seed to germinate, I can't stop thinking about Mrs bloody Weller.

My thoughts are temporarily distracted when the office phone rings. Tina answers it before I get a chance. A few seconds pass and then she calls across to me.

"It's for you. A Miss Carter."

The only Miss Carter I know is a Miss Carter I'd rather not speak to. I lift the handset and tap the button to connect the call.

"Hello," I say gruffly.

"Hi, Danny," Zoe trills. "I hope you don't mind me calling you at work."

"I'm not supposed to take personal calls, so be quick."

"Sorry, are we meeting tomorrow evening or not?"

"Had a better offer have you?"

"No, I just want to get things sorted. I'm sure you do, too, right?"

"Yes, but I said I need time to think."

"I understand, but my parents received an offer on the house this morning, and they've accepted it."

"Good for them, but I don't see how that changes our situation."

"The couple who made the offer want to move in before the end of November at the latest, so I need to sort out my living arrangements, pronto."

"Oh."

"We need to decide what we're going to do, Danny."

This is it — decision time. On the face of it, I'm just meeting my ex for a drink but much like the wrong turn that led us to Sefton Court, this seemingly innocuous decision could trigger another series of calamities in the life of Danny Monk.

I am, however, running out of time myself. Procrastination is no longer an option.

"Alright," I sigh. "Tomorrow. Seven o'clock at The White Horse."

Chapter 15

After a ten-year retail career, I'm more than accustomed to working on Saturdays. The difference with Gibley Smith is that I at least get one Saturday off in three, although there's no midweek day off.

Lee wanders in just before nine.

"How'd it go yesterday?" he asks in lieu of a greeting. "The place didn't burn down without me, I see."

"Yeah, it was okay. Tea?"

"Aye. Please."

My boss conducts a quick cigarette inventory and then stands in the doorway to the back room.

"Did you go out for beers with Gav after work?"

"I did. Just a couple."

Much as Gavin wanted to make a night of it, I left The Victoria Club just after eight. It was an interesting place — a bit like the British Legion club my dad frequents, but with plusher carpet and flock wallpaper. Gavin introduced me to the owner, Nigel, and I left with an application form and a promise that membership would be a formality because I work in the property sector. I didn't have the stomach to tell Nigel that I can't currently afford the twenty-pound membership fee.

"Do we have a morning meeting if just two of us are in?" I ask, changing the subject.

"Not really. I'll have a nose in the diary, and if there's anything worth mentioning, we can discuss it."

Gavin was so keen to avoid Lee's wrath that he tippexed the valuation at Echo Lane from yesterday's diary page. In a way, I wish I could just as easily erase it from my thoughts, but I'm due to meet Zoe in ten hours, and I need to keep all options open just in case that chat goes as badly as I suspect it might.

It's a measure of how messed up my life is that I have two paths open to me. Either could potentially lead to sunnier uplands, but I've got grave reservations about both.

"Fuck sake," Lee mumbles while standing over the open diary on his desk. "I was hoping for a quiet day."

"I'm happy to get stuck in," I reply, although my offer is solely to keep myself occupied rather than to impress the boss.

"You can do the viewings this afternoon, but there are two valuations booked for this morning. No offence, lad, but I wouldn't trust you to value the change in my pocket just yet."

"No," I chuckle nervously. "You're probably right."

"Give it a few months, though, and we'll see."

Lee then turns his attention to a handful of letters in his in-tray. I return to the back room and start a job I am apparently qualified for.

Once I've made Lee's tea and I'm settled behind my desk, the office door swings open, and a couple enter. I glance across at my boss, but he's still preoccupied with yesterday's post.

"Morning," I say to the couple. "Can I help?"

"Yes, we'd like to go on your mailing list," the woman replies.

"No problem. Take a seat."

Judging by the husband's body language, I'd guess he's not thrilled to be house hunting at this hour on a Saturday morning. I don't have the heart to tell him it gets worse from here on in. Once you own a property, even a brand new one, every Saturday seems to involve a trip to either a DIY store or the nearest branch of Habitat. I once mentioned Zoe's obsession with titivating our flat to Mum, and she suggested it's a maternal nesting instinct. Dad suggested it's just an excuse to waste money on pointless tat. I lean towards my father's view.

Once I've copied all the couple's details to a card, and the woman has proudly informed me that they're newlyweds, I head to the filing cabinet and pull out the particulars of the properties in their price range: five flats and one tatty terraced house.

"Here's what we have available," I say, retaking my seat. "Would you like me to run through them?"

"Yes, please," Mrs Cosgrove replies enthusiastically.

Her enthusiasm wanes as she dismisses each of the flats for various reasons. The last resort is the scruffy mid-terrace house that currently belongs to the Midland Bank after they repossessed it.

"Ooh, a house," Mrs Cosgrove coos. "That's more like it, isn't it, Darren?"

"Uh? Um, yeah."

"Can we view it?"

"Any particular day or time? It's vacant, and we've got the keys."

"I don't suppose we could view it now?"

I glance over Mrs Cosgrove's shoulder towards my boss. "Lee, do I have time to show this couple the house in Brompton Road before your valuation?"

"As long as you're back by quarter past ten at the latest."

I turn my attention back to the couple. "I can meet you there in ten minutes."

"Brilliant," Mrs Cosgrove beams.

The couple depart, and I gulp down the rest of my coffee before snatching the keys from the filing cabinet.

True to my word, I turn into Brompton Road exactly ten minutes later. Being a Saturday morning, most of the residents are still at home, which is great for them but not so great for an estate agent in need of somewhere to park.

I pass the house I'm due to show to the young couple and eventually find a space eighty yards further on. By the time I reach number 22, the Cosgroves are already waiting outside. I wrestle with the new lock and invite them to follow me into the hallway.

Despite their lack of experience in the property market, the couple should have assumed that a two-bedroom house pegged at such a low price might not be in tip-top condition. The look on Mrs Cosgrove's face suggests her expectations stretched far beyond reality.

"It smells appalling in here," she remarks, wrinkling her nose.

"I think the previous owners had cats," I reply. "Possibly incontinent cats."

There's no way to sugarcoat it — this house does reek of cat piss.

"But, once you replace the carpets and redecorate," I add, trying to appear positive, "It'll make a lovely first home."

Sporting an admittedly insincere smile, I open the door to the lounge and wave the couple in.

"This is the lounge," I say in lieu of anything more interesting.

Mrs Cosgrove tentatively steps through the doorway, and her husband trudges behind. I'm about to follow when I hear a noise that could be described as a shriek, a retch, or possibly a combination of the two.

"I feel sick," Mrs Cosgrove announces as she hurries out of the lounge and makes for the front door.

The lounge is definitely ground zero for the offensive stench, and it is pretty pungent, but I don't know what they were expecting in a house listed at just £59,950.

I follow them to the pavement where Mrs Cosgrove is glaring back toward the front door, arms folded.

"How can you let people view a house that's so ... that's so ... inhospitable!"

I think she means uninhabitable, but I don't correct her.

"It's just a bad smell," I say.

"You should have warned us," she retorts before grabbing her husband's hand and dragging him back up the street.

"Bye, then," I mutter under my breath.

I lock the door and trudge back to my car. If there's a record for the shortest-ever viewing, surely my effort must be close to breaking it.

I start the Volvo, and just as I'm about to pull out and find somewhere to turn around, a delivery truck appears in my passenger-side window. It then slows to a standstill in the middle of the road, and two men get out. Based on their uniforms, I'd guess they're delivering something to one of the residents.

"Brilliant," I groan, realising I won't be going anywhere until the truck has moved.

It only takes sixty seconds for boredom to set in, and between impatient glances towards the wing mirror, my eyes fall on the glovebox.

"Leave it, Danny," I whisper.

My parents are never slow to remind me that I had two troublesome traits as a child: impatience and nosiness. Those traits manifested one Christmas when I was poking around their bedroom in search of my presents, and Dad caught me red-handed, shaking a wrapped box that could have contained an Evel Knievel Stunt Cycle. It might well have done, but Dad's punishment was one less gift on Christmas Day.

I can't help myself.

Reaching across the passenger seat, I open the glovebox. I then pull out Mrs Weller's contract document and the floppy disk.

Folding over the front page of the contract I attempt to read the first few paragraphs of text.

"Uh?"

I go over them again. Each sentence is written in complex legal speak, with a sprinkling of Latin terms thrown in for good measure. I understand most of the individual words, but collectively, the text is so incomprehensible it might as well be written in Welsh.

Frustrated, I stuff the contract back in the glovebox and slam it shut. My attention then turns to the floppy disk I left on the passenger seat. When I return to the office, Lee will be heading out, and I'll be left alone with a computer. Is there really any harm in seeing what's on the disk? It's not as though it commits me in any way.

The revving of a diesel engine snaps my attention back to the moment. I check the mirror and I'm relieved to see the truck slowly shrinking as it reverses back up Brompton Road.

Rather than returning the floppy disk to the glove box, it remains on the passenger seat for the short journey back to Victoria Road. When I eventually find a parking space, I tuck the disk inside my jacket before hurrying to the office. When I arrive, Lee is standing at his desk, checking the contents of a briefcase.

"How'd you get on?" he asks.

"Not great. We made it as far as the lounge, and then Mrs Cosgrove walked out. I don't think it's for them."

"It does smell a bit ripe in there."

"Can't the bank pay for someone to remove the carpets?"

"They don't give a shit, lad. They'll just keep reducing the price until someone snaps it up."

"Right."

"Anyway, I'm off. You'll be okay on your own for an hour or so?"

His tone implies a statement rather than a question.

"I'll be fine, I'm sure."

I celebrate Lee's departure with a mug of coffee and then make myself comfortable at Tina's desk.

"Here goes nothing," I mutter before pressing the power button on the front of the computer.

After a series of whirring noises, the Microsoft Windows logo eventually appears on the screen. With only my limited and probably irrelevant experience of a Sinclair Spectrum to go on, I lower my hand to the mouse and move it around the mat. The little arrow does what it's supposed to do, which is a good start.

After locating the correct slot on the front of the computer, I slide Mrs Weller's floppy disk in. A tiny green light flashes on the front of the machine, which I hope is a good sign. Then, suddenly, a box pops up on the screen. After staring at it for at least twenty seconds, it dawns on me that it's more of a window than a box. Logical, I suppose, considering it's called Microsoft Windows.

In the box, or window, there's a tiny cartoon-like illustration of a floppy disk. I move the pointy arrow to it and then press the left button on the mouse. Nothing happens. I think back to what Tina did yesterday, and I seem to recall she clicked the mouse button twice several times. I try again with an extra click, and the computer whirs into action again.

Another window appears, informing me that Microsoft Excel is loading. I can only hope that the computer knows what it's doing because I sure as hell don't. The screen suddenly changes again, and a page appears, broken into cells with horizontal and vertical lines. More importantly, though, is that in each of the cells along the two left-hand columns, there are rows of text. I sit forward and scan the information ...

Full name: *Kimberley Anne Dolan* **Age:** *26* **Date of Birth:** *17th August 1964* **Address:** *17 Marchwood Avenue, Frimpton, Hampshire SO21 2RG* **Telephone:** *0962 76030* **Height:** *5' 6"* **Weight:** *Approx. 8 st 6 lbs* **Bust:** *34DD* **Eye Colour:** *Brown* **Skin Colour:** *Medium to pale* **Hair:** *Shoulder-length light-brown* **Education:** *Frimpton Girls' School* **Job:** *Travel Agent* **Employer:** *Lunn Poly — Frimpton branch* **Favourite Meal:** *Duck chow mein* **Favourite Drink:** *Black tea, one sugar* **Favourite Alcohol:** *Malibu and Coke* **Favourite Film:** *Dirty Dancing*

The rows go on and on, listing every snippet of information about Kimberley Anne Dolan, from her childhood pet dog's name through to the traits she most admires and despises in a man. Whoever compiled the information went to great lengths to ensure it covers every facet of Kim's life and personality. If I happened to be in the market for a new girlfriend, which I'm absolutely not, the list of facts would make the process of chatting up Kim Dolan almost too easy.

Conscious that someone could walk in at any moment, tying me up until Lee returns, I replicate another of Tina's actions I remember from yesterday. I move the pointy arrow to the word 'File' and click it. A list of options appears, and I select 'Print'.

Behind me, a slight humming sound emanates from the boxy beige printer. Somehow, I've managed to access a computer file and print it off without any assistance or mishaps. If I can't get another job in retail, maybe I could retrain and get a job in the computer industry. Or not.

Once the printer has spewed out five entire pages of information pertaining to Kim Dolan, I extract the floppy disk and prod the power button on the front of the computer to turn it off. The screen fades to black and all the lights on the front of the machine dim to darkness.

With everything back as it was, I gather up the pages, fold them twice, and shove them in my jacket pocket. I don't know if I'll reference them again or if they'll end up in the bin, but if I do decide to take up Mrs Weller's offer, and I'm still erring against the idea, I can't keep accessing the info via the office computer.

Job done, I return to my desk and puff a long breath. I then happen to glance up at the clock, and it reminds me that I'm due to meet Zoe in only eight hours' time.

Thoughts of Mrs Weller and Kim Dolan will have to wait. For now, I need to determine a strategy for dealing with my former fiancée.

Chapter 16

With a towel wrapped around my waist, I stand in front of the open wardrobe, caught in two minds. On the one hand, I don't want Zoe to think I've made too much of an effort just in case it sends the wrong message. Saying that, I'm still not sure what the right message is. However, I'd quite like it if she experienced a moment akin to the losing contestants on the TV darts quiz, *Bullseye,* as they're shown the prize they didn't win. In my head, I can almost hear Jim Bowen's voice: *Sorry, Zoe, but look at what you could have won.*

Jim then continues. *I did warn you, Zoe — you get nothing in this game for two in a bed.*

Instantly, my thoughts drift away from the jovial TV host to Zoe and Wayne Pickford, lying in bed and groping wildly at each other's bits and pieces. My stomach instantly contracts as the flames of betrayal reignite.

I grab a pair of stonewashed jeans and a white linen shirt from the wardrobe. The very thought of Zoe's betrayal is enough to reset my forgiveness dial back to zero. I *do* want her to see the best of me; the best of what she sacrificed in return for a sordid one-night stand.

After getting dressed and styling my hair, I apply a few generous squirts of Zoe's favourite aftershave, Drakkar Noir. I'm not a huge fan, but she gifted me a bottle last Christmas after sniffing a sample in a department store. Barely fifteen minutes after I unwrapped the bottle and sprayed a little on my neck, Zoe unwrapped me. We went at it then and there on the sofa.

Happier times.

I slip on my black leather jacket, grab the door keys, and leave. I'm five minutes late, but I don't care. Within the first hundred yards, I regret putting on the jacket. If I'd bothered checking the weather on Ceefax, I'd have known that the forecast promised an unseasonably muggy September evening.

It's always hit and miss whether The White Horse is busy on a Saturday evening. Sometimes, they have a disco or a band, and recently, the landlord, Kevin, tried out a karaoke night. Based solely on the number of vehicles in the car park, it looks like there's nothing on this evening.

At five past seven, I push open the door to the main bar.

The second I step through the door, the walls close in on me. All I can see is the woman perched on a bar stool directly ahead. Dressed in a low-cut blouse and a denim skirt, it's patently obvious that Zoe had the same idea as I did. Much as it pains me to admit it, she looks hot as hell.

She flashes a broad smile my way and then hops off the stool. Before I can react, my ex hurries towards me like a military wife greeting her husband after a long tour of duty.

"It's so good to see you, Danny," she purrs in my ear as her arms snake around my waist.

"You too," I reply, although I immediately regret saying it.

Greeting over, I order a pint, and Zoe suggests we find a quiet corner to talk. It's obvious that she's got a game plan, and I need to keep my wits about me.

"How's the new job going?" she asks once we're settled on a sofa next to the inglenook fireplace.

"It's okay," I reply before taking a sip of lager. "Better than being on the dole."

"How are your parents ... and Robbie?"

"They're all fine."

"Have you seen your brother recently?"

"Yeah, he asked me to look after Hugo last month, so I stayed for the night while Robbie and Steve went to a friend's funeral."

"Sorry, who's Hugo?"

Zoe's ignorance regarding my brother and his boyfriend adopting a dog is a reminder that everyone else's life just carried on as normal after our relationship imploded.

"He's a rescue dog. Obviously, they'll never be able to have kids, so Hugo is the next best thing."

"What breed is he?"

"Pure-bred mongrel. Cute, though."

Zoe smiles and then reaches for her wine glass. "Remember when we talked about getting a dog?"

"I remember a lot of things we talked about and the plans we made. Didn't account for much in the end, though, did it?"

It wasn't intentional but my words are edged with bitterness.

"You're still angry with me?" Zoe pouts.

"Yes," I reply without hesitation.

"That's good."

"Is it?"

"If you weren't angry, it'd mean you don't care anymore."

Too late, I realise that I've walked straight into Zoe's trap. She *definitely* has a game plan.

"Whether I'm still angry with you or not is irrelevant. I can't ever forgive you."

"Don't you think the two are related? You can't forgive me because you're still harbouring so much anger, but if you were to let it go, you *could* forgive me."

Anyone who believes the stereotype that hairdressers are a bit dim would likely change their mind after meeting Zoe. She's anything but dim, as her counterargument proves.

"Which is why," she continues, "I still think we have a future together."

"What about trust?" I retaliate. "How can I live with someone I don't think I'll ever be able to trust again?"

"Did you trust me when we first met?"

"How could I? We didn't know each other."

"Exactly. I said the other night that I'd love us to start again with a clean slate so you can slowly build your trust in me just like you did the first time."

"Until you fancy hopping into bed with an old school buddy again."

"I've learned my lesson the hard way, Danny, and you have my word that I'll never cheat on you again. All I want is a chance to get back what we had."

Zoe leans forward and, deliberate or otherwise, provides an enhanced view of her cleavage. It's a killer tactic. I swallow hard and shift my gaze to the floor.

"I don't think we can," I reply in a low voice. "It's too late."

"As long as there's still love, it's never too late. You do still love me, don't you?"

"Yeah," I snort. "But you're missing the point — I don't *want* to love you."

"And that's because you're still angry. Everything you've said so far is understandable, but once the anger subsides, you'll be in a much better place. Don't give up on us just because you can't see past the anger."

She has an answer for everything, but she can't undo time.

"You've got no idea how I feel, Zoe," I say. "And I won't be able to shed the anger as long as I've got visions of you and that prick in my head. How do you propose getting rid of them, eh?"

"I never said it would be easy, but in time, we can do this ... together."

Now I've restoked the feeling I had back in the flat, it's time to blast a great big fucking hole in Zoe's masterplan.

"Do you remember Tania? The girl who worked in the shop for a few months last year?"

"Yes," Zoe replies flatly.

Of course, she remembers Tania, even though they only briefly crossed paths on one occasion. Once met, Tania was hard to forget: ash-blonde hair, crystal-blue eyes, and the kind of figure you'd usually only see on the cover of a lads' mag. Zoe hated Tania the moment she set eyes on her.

"You didn't like me working with Tania, did you?"

"Not especially," Zoe strops.

"Do you remember admitting that you felt threatened, even though I told you a thousand times you had nothing to worry about?"

"Why are we talking about Tania?"

"Because I want you to picture a scene. Imagine that I bumped into Tania in this very bar last month. We got chatting, had a few drinks, a few laughs, and at last orders, I invited her back to the flat."

"Danny, I don't want—"

"I haven't finished yet," I interject. "I listened to you; now you're going to listen to me."

I underline my point with a quick gulp of lager before continuing.

"We get back to the flat, open a bottle of wine, and then make ourselves comfortable on the sofa. One thing leads to another, and before I know it, we're ripping each other's clothes off."

"This isn't—"

"We take it through to the bedroom, and as I lie on my back, Tania straddles me. God, she's got such an amazing body and—"

"Stop it!" Zoe literally yells.

Two old blokes standing at the bar simultaneously throw a scowl in our direction.

"Tell me that didn't happen," Zoe then says, her voice low and strained.

"No, it didn't."

There's no disguising the sense of relief on my ex-fiancée's face.

"Did you feel awful just thinking about it?" I ask.

"Yes. Obviously."

"How awful?"

"Sick to my stomach awful."

"Now, imagine how bad it feels when you're forced to picture a scene that *actually* happened ... like you and lover boy rolling around in bed together."

"Don't, Danny. Please."

"Come on, Zoe, imagine it. That picture is the first one that floats into my mind when I wake up, and it's the very last I see before falling asleep at night ... assuming I manage to fall asleep. Day after day for the last five months."

"Okay, I get it."

"No, you don't. You seem to think I can just forget what happened, park my emotions, and move on. If it were that easy, don't you think I'd have done that by now? Do you think I enjoy my own mind tormenting me?"

I flop back on the sofa and squeeze my eyes shut for a moment. A hand comes to rest on my knee.

"I'm sorry," Zoe says feebly. "I hate myself for hurting you."

"Ironic," I sigh, opening my eyes. "Because I think I might hate you too."

"You don't mean that ... do you?"

I shake my head after a second's thought. "No. I just don't like you very much."

"Then why did you agree to meet up?"

"Because ... because we've got other issues to sort out. You might want to patch things up, but my priority is working out what the fuck we do about the flat."

"Did you speak to the building society?"

"Yes, and they're willing to cut us some slack, but they want the arrears cleared and assurances we won't fall behind with the repayments again."

"Are you sure selling it isn't an option?"

"Oh yeah," I scoff. "It's an option, alright, if you fancy taking on fifty per cent of a twenty-five grand debt?"

"Surely we won't owe that much if we sell it."

"Zoe, a young couple put in an offer for 19 Sefton Court the other day — a repossession. I didn't think for one second that the bank would accept their lowball offer, but they did."

"How lowball?"

"Forty-four grand."

"Oh."

"Is that all you can say? Oh?"

"What do you want me to say, Danny? I came up with a solution, and you've spent the last ten minutes telling me why it won't work."

"You moving back into the flat?"

"Yes. It makes sense."

"Financially, maybe, but not on any other level."

"So, what do you expect me to do? I need somewhere to live, and if it's not back at Sefton Court, I'll have to find somewhere to rent."

"You're just as liable for the arrears as I am, plus every bloody repayment for the next twenty-four years."

"Yes, I know."

"Then help me come up with a plan to deal with it."

"I did."

"That ain't happening. I don't want to live with you ... not now, anyway."

"But you're happy to saddle us with a mounting debt? That sounds a lot like pride over pragmatism to me."

Zoe sits back and folds her arms — a sure sign that she's nothing further to add to the conversation.

"I think the only fair option is that you pay half the arrears and a modest amount towards the monthly repayments until I sort out a long-term solution."

"I haven't got that kind of money," she snaps back. "And why should I pay anything towards the monthly repayments if I'm not living there? That's not fair."

"Remind me again how much your dad is giving you. Three grand, isn't it?"

"That money is for me to rent somewhere."

"You won't need that much."

"I might, and Dad will go apeshit if he discovers I bailed you out with his money."

"You're not bailing *me* out, Zoe — you're bailing *us* out."

My former fiancée leans forward and snatches her glass from the table. After tipping the last of the wine down her neck, she returns the glass to the table with almost enough force to break the stem.

"There's no need for a strop," I remark. "That won't get us anywhere."

"No? What will then because I'm out of ideas."

"I don't know."

Zoe tilts her head until it's resting on the back of the sofa. While she's staring up at the ceiling, I use the break in play to gulp another mouthful of lager. Silent seconds pass.

"Seeing as we've reached a stalemate," she then says, her tone softer. "Why don't we go back to the flat and continue talking there? It'll be more relaxed, and I'm sure we can come up with a compromise that works for both of us."

Even before I walked through the door, I had my suspicions that Zoe might try to fashion an opportunity to deploy her superpower if all else failed. Superman can fly faster than a speeding bullet. My ex can suck the skin from a banana.

"I'm fine here, thanks," I reply flatly.

"Suit yourself," she huffs.

Then, without warning, Zoe grabs her handbag and gets to her feet.

"What are you doing?" I ask.

"I'm leaving."

"But we've still got stuff to sort out."

"Here's the deal," she says defiantly. "I move back into the flat, settle the arrears and half the mortgage payments going forward, or I don't, and you find another way to keep the building society off our backs. You've got one week to make your mind up."

"That's—"

"Goodbye, Danny."

Ultimatum delivered, Zoe spins on her heels, strides towards the door, and leaves.

Chapter 17

The radio alarm clock beside the bed was a flat-warming gift from my parents. It's an upgrade on our previous alarm clock, bar one feature — the shrillness of the alarm itself. It's so loud, so jarring, it's the equivalent of being woken up by someone jamming a miniature cactus up your back passage while they simultaneously scream the lyrics to *Agadoo*. For that reason, I switched off the alarm so we'd wake up to the radio.

I'm wrestled from my slumber by the perky tones of Bruno Brookes on Radio 1.

"And no Sunday morning would be complete without this classic by The Commodores."

I don't know what world Lionel Richie inhabits, but I can't remember the last time I had an easy Sunday morning. This one is only seconds old, but it's already fucking awful.

I stayed in the pub after Zoe left yesterday evening, but only for twenty minutes. With just a fiver in my wallet, the only option to drown my sorrows involved a trip to the off-licence and three litres of Kestrel Lager. I'm not willing to test the theory, but Kestrel might be the only lager that tastes better after the human digestive system has converted it to piss.

I roll out of bed and stagger to the bathroom, my mouth dry and head pounding.

After emptying my bladder, the next priority is coffee and painkillers. There's barely any of the former, and when I search the drawer where we usually keep the latter, all it has to offer is half a packet of Rennie, a tub of Vicks VapoRub, and some corn plasters.

"Fuck sake," I groan, slamming the drawer shut.

The phone rings. I'm in two minds about answering it, but the ringing isn't helping my headache.

"Hello," I grunt.

"Good morning to you, too, son."

"Oh. Hi, Mum."

"Are you okay? You sound like you've just got out of bed."

"I have, as it happens."

"It's gone nine, you know."

"Yes, I do know, but I've been at work all week, remember. I fancied a lie-in."

"Of course. Sorry. How's it going?"

"Yeah, not bad."

"I'm glad to hear that. Do you have any plans this afternoon?"

"Nope."

"Robbie just called to say he's coming over later. I thought it'd be nice to have lunch together."

Even if I didn't fancy lunch with my parents, it'd be good to see my kid brother again. Besides, I can barely afford a Pot Noodle, so the offer of a free lunch is too good to decline.

"I'd like that. What time?"

"Robbie said he'll be here around one, so we'll eat at two."

"That works for me. Is he bringing Stephen?"

"No, and he was a bit cagey when I asked."

"They've probably had a row, and Robbie is sulking. You know what he's like."

"Indeed," Mum replies with a slight sigh. "Anyway, I'd better get on. I'll see you later."

I bid Mum goodbye and return to the kitchen. Once I've made myself a mug of coffee, I flop down on the sofa and close my eyes. I'd rather not, but I then replay last night's conversation with Zoe.

The Kestrel, dire as it was, helped blot out the worst of my indignation. This morning, however, I have to face the reality while stone-cold sober — my ex-fiancée has me over a barrel.

If the flat is repossessed and the building society chases us for the shortfall, Zoe can cry to Daddy, and he'll likely pay off his daughter's half of the debt. John Carter has built up a successful double-glazing company, so he's not short of a bob or two. My dad, on the other hand, wouldn't offer me a single penny on a point of principle, even if he had the money, which he probably doesn't.

For a moment, I consider whether I'm really just a chip off the old block and allowing principles to cloud my judgement. Allowing Zoe to move back in would solve my financial problems, for the foreseeable, anyway, but at what cost? Zoe has constantly claimed that her cheating was a mistake, but I've never seen it that way. She made a choice, or a series of choices, that she knew would hurt me. Even if I could find it within me to forgive her, how in God's name am I supposed to forget what she did? Sharing a flat with her would just prolong the agony.

I can't do it. I just can't. But what choice do I have?

Maybe it's the injection of coffee, but my brain suddenly finds another cylinder to fire on. I do have another choice, or at least there's an option to investigate one: Mrs Weller.

Gibley Smith employed me as a junior negotiator, so why am I ignoring an obvious opportunity to negotiate? If Mrs Weller's offer is genuine, and I'm her number one choice to aid in that ridiculous challenge, would she be willing to pay more than just my expenses? As it is, I very much doubt I'll spend anywhere near two hundred quid, so clearly money isn't an issue.

Trying not to let the headache win, I weigh up the pros and cons of getting involved in such a crazy proposal and what I might be able to squeeze out of Mrs Weller. I don't know how open she'll be to a renegotiated contract, but as the saying goes, if you don't ask, you don't get.

I need to do the asking first, though, and I guess there's no time like the present.

After slipping on a pair of joggers and a sweatshirt, I hurry down to the car park and retrieve Mrs Weller's contract from the glove box. I then return to the sofa and dial the phone number she penned on the back of the contract.

"Good morning, Daniel."

"That was ... wait. How did you know it's me calling?"

"You're the only person with my number besides the young lady I spoke to at your office."

My first thought is to ask why she has a phone if no one has her number, but it's hardly a priority.

"Right, um, anyway, I've been thinking about your proposal and, tempting as it is, my circumstances aren't ideal at the moment."

"I'd beg to differ. I'd say your circumstances are ideal — perfect, even."

"Maybe you could call my building society and discuss their interpretation of the word perfect. You might find they disagree."

"You're talking of matters financial?"

"Yes."

"Would you like to pop over, and we can see if there's a solution to that particular problem?"

"Er, yes. When?"

"As I said to you on Friday, time is of the essence. I'm available this morning."

"I need to grab a quick shower and a slice of toast, but I can be with you by half ten."

"Perfect. The front door is unlocked, so come straight in. I'll be waiting in the kitchen."

"Will do."

"See you shortly, Daniel."

She ends the call, and I return the phone to its base. This might still turn out to be a complete waste of my time, but that doesn't mean it's not worth a punt. Frankly, I'm willing to try anything if it offers an alternative to Zoe moving back in.

I get up and retrieve the last two slices of bread from the cupboard. The crusts would usually end up in the bin, but I'm so skint that I can't afford to throw away perfectly edible food.

Half an hour later, I'm back behind the wheel of the Volvo, heading west. The headache has now eased to a low throb, courtesy of two glasses of tap water, but I still feel less than chipper.

After navigating the tarmac section of Echo Lane, I slow the car to a walking pace as I cover the narrow, rutted track that leads to number 1. Twenty seconds of shaking, rattling, and rolling later, I turn off the engine and clamber out of the Volvo. I then take a moment to reappraise the house's exterior.

After standing by the front wall for a while, I conclude that my initial opinion hasn't changed. From the outside, the house still appears neglected to the point of abandonment. Why would anyone spend a fortune refurbishing the interior of a house but leave the exterior in such a state? I'm no builder, but it defies common sense.

"Common sense," I mumble under my breath.

Nothing is common about any of this, and it stopped making sense the moment I sat down at Mrs Weller's kitchen table on Friday.

I make my way carefully up the path and open the front door. After stepping into the pokey entrance lobby, the front door closes behind me, presumably due to its own weight or because it's fitted with self-closing hinges. I'm then met with the same sense of absolute silence, and the peculiar odour hasn't dissipated since my last visit.

Undeterred, I open the door to the hallway, wipe my feet, and take a couple of cautious steps across the polished wooden floorboards. There's no justifiable reason for it, but something about this house gives me the willies.

"Hello? Mrs Weller?" I announce. "It's only me. Danny."

"Come on through," she hails from the kitchen.

I find Mrs Weller sitting in the same chair she occupied on Friday, wearing exactly the same turtle-neck sweater.

"How are you, Daniel?" she asks.

"I'm okay, thanks. You?"

"That depends on how this conversation pans out. Please, take a seat."

I return to the same chair I parked my arse on during the last visit.

"So, you have a financial issue?" Mrs Weller begins. "Is that all that's preventing you from accepting my proposal?"

"Yes, and pretty much yes."

"Would you care to elaborate?"

Fortunately, I used the journey to Echo Lane to prepare a solid foundation for these negotiations.

"In a nutshell, I'm behind on my mortgage payments, and I barely earn enough to cover the current repayments, let alone the arrears."

"I see."

"I'm not sure you do. My former fiancée wants to move back in, and if I agree, she'll pay off the arrears and cover half the monthly outgoings. I'd rather she didn't move back in, but I don't currently have any other option."

"Why does that have any bearing on my proposal?"

"If my ex moves back in, it would be on the basis of us trying to repair our relationship. I can hardly swan off whenever I fancy to deal with your ... with Kim Dolan, can I?"

"Please, just cut to the chase. What is it you're asking for?"

"Bottom line, I need two grand to pay off my mortgage arrears. Unless you're willing to help me out, I can't help you."

Without replying, Mrs Weller slowly gets to her feet and moves stiffly towards the far side of the kitchen. She then opens one of the cupboard doors. It's hinged at such an angle that I can't see what's inside, but a slow succession of beeping sounds provide a hint. After several seconds, Mrs Weller raises her left hand, and there's another series of beeps.

She then turns to face me. "Two thousand pounds, you said?"

"That's right."

After nudging the cupboard door shut, Mrs Weller returns to the table. As she lowers herself back onto her chair she tries, and fails, to mask the obvious discomfort. Her movements remind me of the time Dad pulled a muscle in his back while at work — Mum said it was like living with the Tin Man from *The Wizard of Oz*.

Undaunted by her discomfort, Mrs Weller then places two rolls of banknotes on the table midway between us.

"Money is of no concern to me," she says. "So, there's your two thousand pounds, Daniel."

I'm so flabbergasted that she's agreed to my demand, finding the right reaction takes a moment.

"Wow ... great. Thank you."

"For your information, there's a safe in that cupboard," she then adds, pointing to the wall unit she just returned from. "Once the project is complete, the code is yours. You can have everything in there."

"That's very generous. What exactly is in there?"

"A significant amount of cash, plus an item that you'll only understand the value of once the project is complete. If I were to show it to you now, it would be meaningless."

"Right, um, dare I ask how much cash?"

"As I said, a significant amount."

"But how—"

"Do we have a deal or not, Daniel?"

She thrusts out her right arm, inviting me to shake her hand. There's two grand in cash only fifteen inches below her outstretched hand, and all I have to do is shake that hand and the cash is mine. Only a fool would turn their nose up at such a deal.

"I'm in," I smile, shaking her hand.

The handshake lasts an uncomfortably long time as Mrs Weller seems reluctant to let go. Eventually, she does, and then she slowly turns in her chair and opens a drawer.

"I have the contract ready for you to sign," she says over her shoulder. "Plus, the two hundred pounds for expenses and a document you might find useful."

She turns around and places a large envelope on the table.

"Did you access the information on the disk I gave you?"

"Yes, I did."

"That information will prove invaluable in your task, but alone, it's not enough. You need this."

Mrs Weller dips a hand into the envelope and withdraws a sheet of paper.

"This confirms a handful of locations and times where Kim Dolan will definitely be over the next two weeks. Each is an opportunity for you to talk to her without her boyfriend, Neil Harrison, interfering."

She sets the document aside and then returns her hand to the envelope. This time, she withdraws what looks like a copy of the contract, plus a pen.

"Ready to sign?" she asks, placing both on the table in front of me.

"To be clear, I don't have to pay a penny back if I fail?"

"Correct."

"And the deeds to this place will be signed over to me once I complete this task."

"The project, yes."

She calls it a project, and I call it a task. It's just semantics, so I pick up the pen.

"Where do I sign?"

"Flip through to the final page. Sign it, print your name, and add today's date."

I complete her first two requests but then hesitate.

"The 9th of September," Mrs Weller confirms.

"Right. Thanks."

"1990," she adds as if I didn't already know what year it is.

"That much I do know," I chuckle awkwardly before scribbling the date on the contract.

Once I've done what she asked, I slide the contract back across the table. Mrs Weller takes no more than a fleeting glance at the last page before returning the contract to the drawer. She then turns to face me, her expression unreadable.

"Can you come back this time next Sunday to provide a report on your progress?"

"No problem."

"If you have any questions or require guidance, don't hesitate to contact me, day or night."

"Understood."

"And one final thing before I let you get on with your day, Daniel — the timeline is non-negotiable. On Sunday, 23rd of September, Neil Harrison intends to propose to Kim, and if that happens, it'll be too late. Do you understand?"

"The 23rd?" I bluster. "That's two weeks today."

"Exactly. You cannot afford to waste any time, so please don't."

"I'll formulate a plan this afternoon. You have my word."

"Good. Now, don't let me keep you."

She slides the final document across the table. "And keep that safe."

"I will," I reply, plucking the rolls of notes and the document from the table and transferring them to my pocket.

"Goodbye, Daniel. I look forward to seeing you again next Sunday morning."

Not quite believing my luck, I hurry out of the kitchen and don't dare stop until I'm back in the Volvo. Even then, I start the engine and reverse straight back down the track without so much as a second glance at the house.

Only when I've put at least a mile of distance between myself and Echo Lane do I pull over and check the spoils of my negotiation, although calling it a negotiation is a stretch. I asked, and Mrs Weller obliged without complaint. Maybe I should have asked for more.

Each roll of notes is held together with a rubber band. I release the first band and count out the purple twenty-pound notes. There are fifty in total, and all appear to be genuine — a picture of Queen Elizabeth II on the front and William Shakespeare on the back, plus the dashed metallic thread running vertically down the middle.

I refasten the roll and check the second. It, too, contains exactly fifty used twenty-pound notes. After refixing the rubber band, I return both rolls to my jacket pocket and zip them up. The final check is the envelope containing the money for my expenses. I peel it open and count the twenty-pound notes — ten in total. I shove the envelope in my other jacket pocket and sit back in my seat.

Not only do I have enough money to clear the mortgage arrears, but I've also got enough to restock the kitchen cupboards. With another two hundred due next Sunday, I should also have enough to cover the next mortgage payment. What happens next month is still a problem, but at least I've bought myself some breathing space.

"Get in there!" I shout, slapping my hand against the steering wheel.

No matter how many houses I sell while I'm employed by Gibley Smith, I don't think I'll ever negotiate a better deal.

My jubilation is only tempered by the fact that the cash comes with a condition. Yes, I need to keep my end of the deal, but how hard can it be to break up some random couple?

Money for old rope, I reckon.

Chapter 18

"That was fantastic, Mum," I remark, patting my stomach. "Just what the doctor ordered."

"Thank you, and I'm pleased to see you're in better spirits than when I called this morning," she replies before shooting a glare at Robbie. "Unlike your brother."

"I'm fine," Robbie huffs from across the dining room table. "I'm just tired, that's all."

Having just polished off a large helping of Mum's trademark sticky toffee pudding, I'm amazed Robbie's fatigue hasn't been cured by a monstrous sugar rush.

"Has everyone had enough?" Mum then asks as she begins stacking the empty bowls.

"Leave that, Linda," Dad orders. "I'm sure our sons will be only too willing to wash up, being it's their job."

"Dad, we're not teenagers anymore," I object. "I think we're a bit old for chores."

"Not in this house, you're not," he replies with the driest of smiles. "And you're not too old for a clip round the ear, either, so less of the back chat."

Robbie, always keen to stay in Dad's good books, gets to his feet and gathers up the bowls.

"Come on," he says. "I'll wash, you dry."

Consigned to my fate, I reluctantly get to my feet and follow my kid brother out to the kitchen.

"It's about time they invested in a dishwasher," I remark as Robbie fills the sink with hot water.

"Knowing Dad, he'll probably buy one as a gift for their thirtieth wedding anniversary. He did mention he's got something special in mind."

"It'll be that or a new hoover. Do you remember Mum unwrapping the last one on Christmas Day?"

"Yeah," Robbie snorts. "In fairness, she did seem genuinely chuffed."

"There you go, then. That's Stephen's Christmas present sorted."

My brother responds with a strained smile.

"Where is he, anyway?" I ask. "Is he not a fan of sticky toffee pudding?"

"He's spending the day with his Mum."

"Why didn't you go with him? You haven't had a lover's tiff, have you?"

"Nothing like that, no. He just ... his head isn't in a good place at the moment, so I suggested he spend the day at his mum's."

"That doesn't sound like Stephen — he's the most happy-go-lucky guy I've ever met."

"He's going to a funeral tomorrow," Robbie responds in a suitably solemn tone.

"Oh, I'm so sorry. Two funerals in a month must be enough to mess with anyone's head."

"Five so far this year."

I almost drop the tea towel. "Five?"

"Yep."

Despite the two-year age gap, Robbie and I have always been close, right up until he moved to Brighton. As kids, we shared an almost telepathic understanding, which is why I always had my suspicions about his sexuality and why I was the first person he came out to.

Now, though, I'm struggling to decode my brother's body language, never mind his revelation.

"That's bloody tragic."

"It is, and the funeral tomorrow will the hardest yet. Poor Jason didn't even make his twenty-fifth birthday."

"What happened? Was it an accident, or …"

Robbie turns to face me, his eyes moist and his bottom lip protruding slightly. "Have a guess," he says quietly.

I don't have to guess, and I certainly don't need to say the four-letter word that I know strikes terror into my brother's heart every time he hears it.

"Oh God. I don't know what to say, Rob."

"Nothing you can say," he replies, turning off the tap. "It's just so fucking awful."

"I can't even imagine."

"You'd think that seeing our friends die so young would be the worst part, but it's not."

"No?"

"The worst part is thinking that if I hadn't met Stephen, I'd be lying in a cemetery by now."

"Don't say that."

"It's true. You weren't a great influence, Danny, and if I hadn't met Stephen, chances are that I'd have followed in my big brother's footsteps."

"What do you mean?"

"You used to let one girl out the back door while another was knocking on the front."

"I was never that bad."

"Weren't you?" Robbie coughs, giving me the side eye. "I think your memory must be on the blink."

"Okay, maybe there were a few girls, but you're not me."

"No, I'm not, but you don't know what the gay scene is like. Before this fucking disease was a thing, you could go out every night of the week and get laid if you fancied it. A lot of the guys I knew back in the day were like kids in a sweet shop. Those same guys are now either lying sick in a hospital bed or six feet under."

"I get that it must be hard, but you and Stephen ... you're sound, right?"

"Yes, we're sound, and never a day goes by that I don't thank my lucky stars that we met. How many people, gay or otherwise, ever find their soul mate? And if we hadn't met one another when we did ... that doesn't bear thinking about."

"Yep, I hear you. I also kind of envy you."

Robbie stops scrubbing a bowl and turns to me. "Really? Why?"

It wasn't just my parents I kept the truth about Zoe from.

"Don't you dare tell Mum and Dad this, but I wasn't entirely honest about the reason me and Zoe split up."

I then relay the true version of events, minus some of the less savoury details.

"I'm genuinely shocked," Robbie says once I've confessed all. "I didn't think Zoe was like that."

"Neither did I, which is why it felt like such a kick in the teeth. I honestly thought she was the one, and we'd get married, have kids, grow old together ... all that stuff."

"And now?"

"Now I can't imagine a scenario where I'd ever trust her again."

"So, it's over? Like, properly over?"

"I think so."

"Maybe it's for the best. She obviously wasn't the woman you're destined to spend the rest of your life with. Everything happens for a reason, Danny."

"I wish I could be so pragmatic about it, but I still feel like shit."

"Next time you're feeling sorry for yourself, you'd do well to remember how many times your kid brother has pulled his funeral suit out of the wardrobe this year. If that doesn't put things into perspective, you're a lost cause."

Robbie isn't one for instigating conflict, nor dolling out advice for that matter, which is why his words land like jabs to the stomach. I'm about to launch a half-hearted counter when Dad appears in the doorway.

"We were thinking of heading out for a stroll. Are you two coming along?"

"Is that a question or a demand?" Robbie replies while handing me a bowl to dry.

"I'd say a question, but you know your mother."

"Give us five minutes, and we'll be with you."

"Righto," Dad says, backing out of the kitchen.

"Christ," I groan. "The last thing I need is a stroll over the common. I've got stuff to do this afternoon."

"Maybe it'll do you good," Robbie replies. "Help you clear your head a bit. Help us both clear our heads."

"Yeah. Maybe."

We finish our chores and join our parents in the hallway.

It must be an age thing because I used to hate my parents dragging us out for a walk after lunch on a Sunday. However, an hour after we left the house, I return in a reflective but positive frame of mind. I could put it down to the warm sunshine and small talk, but really, I have my brother to thank.

After saying our goodbyes to Mum and Dad, we wander up the street to our respective cars. Mine happens to be the closest, although I hesitate when I get within ten feet.

"How far up the road did you park?" Robbie asks.

"Um, this is mine," I reply, nodding at the Scandinavian shitbox to my left.

"No way," Robbie gasps. "You're driving a Volvo these days?"

"It's a long story."

"Please tell me you've got a tin of Mint Imperials in the glove box and a tartan travel blanket in the boot?"

"Fuck off," I retort, trying to hold back a grin.

My new car proves the source of much amusement to my kid brother. After laughing raucously for what feels like an age, he finally wipes a tear from his cheek.

"Thanks, Danny," he splutters while trying to regain his composure. "I didn't think anything could cheer me up this weekend, but ... a fucking Volvo!"

His laughter is so infectious that, despite the lip-biting, I can't help but laugh along with him.

"Enough of this," I finally splutter. "I've got to get going."

"Why? Does the vicar need his car back before teatime?"

"You're a bellend."

"Yeah, it runs in the family."

Still grinning like we're back in junior school, we hug and say goodbye with a promise on my part that I'll head down to Brighton in a few weeks' time.

My smile lasts almost all the way back to Sefton Court, but it's long gone by the time I return to the flat and remove my jacket. It was great to see Robbie again, and despite his piss-taking, his advice did sink in. Now I've got some financial breathing space, I need to start putting the pieces of my life back together.

One not-insignificant hurdle stands in my way, though, and to overcome it, I need to sit down and ponder what I can do to undermine Kim Dolan's relationship. I can't very well turn up at Mrs Weller's house next Sunday with nothing but good intentions — she'll want to see some measure of progress. If not, I can probably kiss goodbye to the second expenses payment.

I grab a pad and pen from the kitchen drawer and perch on the sofa. Before I write a single word, I refer to the list of times and locations supplied by my sponsor. It's a fairly short list, primarily highlighting Kim's regular trips on her lunch break plus a few evenings out. I never thought to ask, but how does she know Kim Dolan's movements over the coming weeks? I can only assume she's a creature of habit or Mrs Weller keeps a crystal ball in that safe of hers.

The memory of the safe prompts another unanswered question. How much cash does she keep in there, and what's the mystery prize she mentioned? Something I need but won't understand until the time is right? It made sod all sense at the time and even less now.

Without the mental capacity to focus on anything but the immediate problem, I return to Kim Dolan's itinerary. The first item on the schedule relates to her job at the travel agency, Lunn Poly. She has lunch at one o'clock and almost always visits Wilson's Bakery for a sandwich.

With so little time to play with, that's got to be my first interaction with Kim Dolan. What I say to her and where I go from there is anyone's guess.

I've got a lot of thinking and planning to do.

Chapter 19

"3-1 to bloody Bury," Lee rants while puffing on a cigarette in the back room. "Useless bastards, the lot of them."

Lee's excuse for being in a bad mood this Monday morning is down to his football team, Rotherham United, losing on Saturday. I couldn't be less interested, but Tina is already at her desk, and Gavin hasn't arrived yet, so Lee has decided to vent in my direction. I just want a coffee.

"If you're a gambling man, Danny, stick a tenner on Rotherham going down this season. Easy bloody money, mark my words."

"I'm not, but I will."

I only have a passing interest in football and know precisely nothing about Rotherham United, apart from what Lee has relayed this morning. For a team he allegedly supports, his choice of language could be considered slightly negative. I make an attempt to lighten his mood.

"Still, England had a good run at the World Cup, eh?"

"You reckon?" Lee spits. "It's a measure of how shite we are that everyone thinks losing on penalties to the Krauts in the semis is some sort of achievement. And don't get me started on bloody Gazza. My fucking nana could have tucked that late effort away, and she wouldn't have booed like a baby in the middle of a game. Bloody pansy."

Having exhausted my knowledge of contemporary football, I flash my boss a pained smile and hurry to my desk. Just as I'm about to sit down, Gavin wanders in.

"Morning troops," he beams. "Everyone have a good weekend?"

"No, I did not," Lee blasts from the back room doorway.

Gavin's need for caffeine is obviously so great he's willing to listen to Lee's woes, and the two men disappear into the back room. I get up and step over to Tina's desk.

"Can I ask you a question?" I say in a low voice. "About our lunch breaks."

"Sure."

"You always take the full hour, right?"

She looks at me as if I've just enquired about her bra size. "It's what I'm entitled to. It says so in my contract."

"No, you misunderstand. I'm not criticising you for taking what you're entitled to — I just want to know what Lee's view is. I'll need to take a full hour several times over the next two weeks, you see."

"Ah, gotcha. Sorry. If you need to take a full hour, take it."

Tina then spins her chair ninety degrees and beckons me to lean in.

"Keep this to yourself," she says in a voice not much louder than a whisper. "If you check the diary, you'll find that Lee regularly has appointments booked for early afternoon. I know for a fact that some of those appointments are fake, and he goes home for a couple of hours."

"Really?" I whisper back.

"Gavin once drove up Lee's road and spotted his car parked on the driveway at the exact same time he was supposed to be at a valuation on the other side of town. The lying git then wandered back into the office just after two in the afternoon, complaining about what a waste of time his valuation turned out to be."

"That's a bit naughty," I snigger.

"Benefits of being boss, I suppose."

I thank Tina and return to my desk just as Lee and Gavin emerge from the back room, the former having turned his ire toward the match officials.

He finally shuts up, but only because we're already behind schedule with the morning meeting.

As Lee goes through the diary, I can't help but notice Tina's wry smile when our boss says he'll do a viewing at a vacant house at 1.30 pm, and he'll go straight after his lunch break because it's just around the corner from his home.

My morning will involve a viewing at 56 Nutshell Close, plus the tedium of following up on all the weekend's viewings. Fortunately, the scheduling means I'm free to leave the office just before one so I can enact the first part of Project Kim, as I've now labelled it. I also need to pop into the bank to deposit the cash payment I secured for said project. Sadly, it'll only remain in my bank account for a few hours before the building society claim their outstanding debt.

The meeting ends and I begin the first of my morning tasks. With twenty-six viewings to follow up, I'll be fully occupied until I head to Nutshell Close at half-eleven. I start working my way through the list, although when I reach the couple who viewed Brompton Road on Saturday morning, I complete the follow-up notes without ringing them for feedback. Call it a sixth sense, but I got the impression they weren't interested.

The two painstaking hours drag, and by the end of it, I've had a gutful of phone calls and forms. I'm about to complain to Gavin when a thought stops me in my tracks. He never specified the time, but at some point today — maybe even at this very minute — my kid brother will be standing over a freshly excavated grave, saying a final goodbye to a friend who passed way before his time.

Given the choice, I'll settle for disinterested viewers and disgruntled vendors every day of the week.

I head off to Nutshell Close, where I endure twenty minutes with Mrs Philpot and her unruly toddler. Probably three or four years old, the little shit spent the entire viewing in tantrum mode. No amount of juice or crisps seemed to satisfy his demands, so his mother spent most of her time dealing with him rather than deciding if 56 Nutshell Close might be a suitable family home. On the upside, he did trip over a clump of weeds on the patio, grazing his knee slightly. Karma.

After a slow drive back to the town centre, I waste another ten minutes driving around in search of a parking space. When I return to the office, only Gavin is at his desk. We go through the motions of him asking how the viewing went and me confirming it was a waste of time.

"You should have hung around a little longer on Friday evening," he then says, referring to our hour at The Victoria Club. "A couple of cute girls pitched up about ten minutes after you left."

"To be honest, mate, the Minogue sisters could have pitched up, and I probably wouldn't have shown an interest. I'm still working my way through the wreckage of my last relationship."

"That bad, eh?"

"Afraid so."

"Isn't that a good reason to get out there and enjoy yourself? Make the most of being young, free, and single?"

"Hmm, I'm not so sure. Are you enjoying being single?"

Gavin takes a second to consider my question and then puffs a long sigh. "Yes and no."

"What does that mean?"

"Did Tina tell you that I was married?"

"Um, she might have mentioned something."

"It's not exactly an office secret. I married stupidly young, and while all my mates were out clubbing at weekends and going on lads holidays, I was at home playing the dutiful husband role. Fast forward four years to when my marriage ended, and those same mates are all married with kids or in long-term relationships."

"Ah, I see. You want to make up for lost time, but your mates now spend their weekends playing happy families or wandering around DIY stores?"

"That pretty much sums it up, yeah. I need a wingman."

"A what?"

"You know, someone who'll come out on the pull with me."

Rather than expand on his statement, Gavin looks at me like a kid might look up at a department store Santa — a distinct level of expectation plastered across his face.

"What ... you mean me?" I splutter, slapping a hand to my chest.

"Alright," he frowns. "It was only a suggestion."

Too late, I realise my reaction might have been a bit over the top. I suddenly feel bad for him.

"No, no, don't get me wrong, mate," I say, perhaps over-correcting on the enthusiasm. "I'm just surprised you think I'd make a fitting wingman, that's all."

"You'd be better than Lee, that's for sure."

"Lee's married, isn't he?"

"Yes, but he also thinks he's a bit of a lady's man."

"Christ," I hiss, allied to a suitable grimace.

"Exactly. We went out for beers after work a few weeks back, and I got to hear some of his best chat up lines. And by best, I mean worst."

"You didn't get anywhere, then?"

"We got barred from The Red Lion. Lee tried his lines on the landlord's wife."

"It sounds ... traumatic."

"That's exactly what it was like. So, would you be up for a night out sometime?"

"Yeah. Why not."

His face lights up. "Cool."

Mission accomplished, Gavin doesn't push his luck by trying to tie me down to a specific date. Instead, he nips out for a sandwich. The last thing I need at the moment is to rekindle my misspent youth but I do have some sympathy for Gavin. It can't be easy searching for the second Miss Right on his own, and it must be nigh-on impossible with Lee in tow.

As soon as my colleague returns with his sandwich, I confirm I'm heading out, and I'll likely be a while. My first port of call is NatWest Bank. Mercifully, the queue isn't too long. The prune-faced woman behind the counter takes her time counting the cash, but not long enough to hinder my plans.

A few minutes before one o'clock, I hurry up Victoria Road towards Wilson's Bakery. I know for certain that Kim's place of work, Lunn Poly, is in the shopping centre, so I need to find a suitable spot where I can wait for her to approach the bakery. Fortunately, a bus shelter on the opposite side of the street offers the perfect vantage point. Barely sixty seconds after securing my spot, I realise there's an obvious flaw with my vantage point as a bus pulls up, blocking my view of the bakery.

I move slightly further up the street until I can see past the bus and then check the time — two minutes after one.

Any concerns I had about spotting Kim amongst the lunchtime shoppers prove unfounded when a young woman dressed in a scarlet red skirt and jacket crosses the street some fifty yards beyond the bus stop. No self-respecting woman would voluntarily wear such an unflattering outfit, so I can safely assume the woman now approaching the bakery is wearing the Lunn Poly staff uniform.

With my pulse quickening, I dash across the street and enter Wilson's bakery, only a few seconds behind the woman I hope is Kim Dolan. Inside, there's a short queue with a woman in red at the back. As I step up behind her, it dawns on me that Lunn Poly must have more than one employee at the local branch. I need clarification that this is Kim Dolan.

The queue moves quickly, and before long, just the two of us are waiting to be served. Willing the woman in front of me to turn around doesn't have the desired effect, but her hair length and colour correspond with the information on the floppy disk. One other nugget of information on the disk happened to be Kim's favourite perfume, and I'm just about close enough to pick out two distinct notes in this woman's perfume: jasmine and rose. It's a pleasant floral scent, but without knowing what Kim Dolan's favourite perfume actually smells like, it's a wholly irrelevant observation.

The assistant behind the counter asks what the woman in red would like. The reply is a brown-bread, ham salad sandwich and a packet of ready-salted crisps. The items are duly placed on the countertop, and the woman in red pays with a handful of coins. She then gathers up her order and turns around.

Our eyes lock for a fraction of a second before I shift my gaze to the Lunn Poly badge fastened to the woman's lapel.

Even without the information on the floppy disk and the badge confirming her identity, I'd bet my life that the woman in front of me is Kim Dolan. In that same moment, Mrs Weller's motive for interfering in this woman's love life becomes apparent — the physical similarities are so obvious, I'm pretty certain they must be mother and daughter.

Then, as quickly as our paths crossed, Kim Dolan strides past me and out the door.

"Can I help, love?" the woman behind the counter asks.

With my mind still trying to unravel the connotations of Kim Dolan's possible identity, I can only stare back at the woman, my jaw bobbing up and down.

"Um ... I'll have two beef and tomato rolls, please. With mustard."

I hadn't planned on buying lunch in Wilson's Bakery, but after a week of sandwiches a dog would turn his nose up at, I think I deserve a treat. Besides, I've still got the two hundred quid in my wallet and lunch surely counts as an expense.

I then spot a tray of cakes on a shelf. "And a cinnamon swirl, please."

Lunch acquired, I head back down Victoria Road, my thoughts dominated by the briefest of meetings with Kim Dolan.

When I arrive back at the office, another thought chases me in the door. If, as I suspect, Mrs Weller is Kim Dolan's mother, what's the deal with their relationship? Are they estranged? Is Kim's romance with Neil Harrison the reason?

As Gavin is on the phone and Tina is hammering away at her keyboard, I disappear into the back room and shut the door. Peckish as I am, I need a moment to dissect what I've just learned. Up until now, I had reservations about Mrs Weller's motives, but the more I think about it, it does make sense that she'd be willing to hire someone to sabotage a relationship if that relationship involved her own daughter. Is it worth a house, though? Parents say they'll do anything to protect their kids, but surely there are limits. Come to think of it, Mrs Weller said she couldn't leave the house, so why offer it as an incentive?

My rumbling stomach draws my attention back to lunch. There's only one way I'll get answers to my questions, and that's by asking the woman herself. For now, I've got more pressing matters to attend to — two beef and tomato rolls, not to mention a cinnamon swirl.

Chapter 20

There's a song I distinctly remember from my childhood because it featured on an album that Dad played in the car far too often. I think it was a band called The Eagles, but I can't recall the title of the song. What I do remember is the lead singer harping on about the number of women on his mind — seven, if memory serves.

I currently have three on my mind, and that's enough for any man, particularly at seven thirty in the morning.

The first of those women is Zoe. She called last night to see if I'd given any further thought to our conversation on Saturday evening. Not that I told her, but I've had many thoughts about rekindling our relationship, most of them negative. She reiterated her plea that we could start again with a clean slate if only I dealt with my anger. If her aim was to piss me off, she succeeded. That's the thing about cheating — once the act is over, it's done with. It's the partner that gets to suffer the long term consequences. I'm sure Zoe felt guilty for a while, but she's managed to block that out more successfully than I've blocked out the mental images of her indiscretion.

I ended the conversation by promising to call her with a decision by the end of the week — I didn't specify which week. While I had the phone in my hand, I dialled the number of the second woman on my mind to discuss the third.

When I asked Mrs Weller if Kim Dolan is her daughter, she provided the kind of answer I'd expect from a politician: a flat-out refusal to admit or deny the allegation. However, she confirmed that she is closely related to Kim, but I shouldn't dwell on that fact as it's not relevant to my task.

After firmly closing the door on that subject, Mrs Weller, much like Zoe, reminded me that time is of the essence. She then put me on the spot and demanded to know what I had planned. I blagged a reply, which is why I now have to visit Lunn Poly on my lunch break today. To add an extra layer of pressure, Mrs Weller suggested an ice-breaking tactic when I sit at Kim Dolan's desk and enquire about holidays.

I'm not comfortable with it, but having sold my soul for a substantial chunk of cash, I've no choice but to follow through. Whether it bears fruit or not remains to be seen.

"Tell him to fuck right off," Lee barks across the office.

"Do you actually want me to say that?" Tina replies, her eyebrows arched.

Our office administrator is on the phone with Mr Edgar because he wants to view the repossession in Brompton Road this morning. Judging by Lee's response to that request, I think he's had enough of the Edgars' time wasting.

"Put him through to me," our manager then demands.

Tina does as she's told without question.

"Mr Edgar, it's Lee Ross, branch manager. We spoke before when you offered on the house in Nutshell Close. I understand you want to view another of our properties."

I'm not sure we're supposed to be spectating Lee's phone call, but Tina and I listen intently.

"You can view the house, but if you're considering putting in another ridiculous offer, you'll be wasting our time and yours. Is that clear?"

I can just about hear Mr Edgar's voice but not well enough to understand what he's saying.

"Yes, the house needs work," Lee continues. "But that's already reflected in the asking price."

After another pause, he then glances at the diary on his desk.

"Fine," he eventually sighs. "My colleague Danny will meet you there at eleven o'clock."

Gobsmacked, I glare across at Lee as he ends the call.

"I thought you intended to tell Mr Edgar to ... what was the term?"

"Fuck right off," Tina helpfully interjects.

"Aye, I was," Lee replies. "But Mr Edgar said he'll complain to head office if we don't let him view the house, and that'll involve more bloody paperwork than I can be arsed with."

"So, I'm stuck with showing the world's fussiest house hunters a run-down property that stinks of cat piss?"

"Afraid so, lad, but you never know — maybe the Edgars are cat people."

There's no sense in arguing, so I don't. If there's any consolation, at least Lee didn't book the viewing for twelve o'clock. I've already told him I need to take my lunch break at noon as I've got a family matter to attend to. I just hope he doesn't wander past Lunn Poly while I'm hopefully discussing my fictitious holiday requirements with Kim Dolan.

Precisely one hour later, I'm back in Brompton Road. The Edgars are as charming as they were the first time we met and just as positive about the property they've come to view. Once they've wasted five full minutes complaining about the smell, Mr Edgar sets off on his wall-tapping expedition while his wife highlights everything she hates, from the wallpaper to the light switches. I like a moan as much as the next man, but it's not my entire personality. How the Edgars have reached their advanced years without spontaneously combusting remains a mystery.

They did eventually leave, but only after insisting I submit an offer of forty grand.

Thankfully, I don't have to hear Lee's reaction when I return to the office as he's out on a valuation. Or skiving. I jot down the details of the Edgar's derisory offer and leave the note on his desk.

"Right, I'm off out for a while," I tell Tina. "I'll be back by one."

"Got a hot lunch date, have we?" she replies with a cheeky smile.

"Not exactly, no. More of a mercy mission."

"Good luck."

I leave the office and make my way up Victoria Road to the shopping centre's main entrance. Although the centre itself only opened a decade ago, I now struggle to recall what was here before. I remember there were some voices of protest when the local council first suggested our town would benefit from a shiny new shopping centre, but those complaints patently fell on deaf ears. Why anyone would prefer the alternative is beyond me. I'm not exactly an avid shopper, but I like having all my retail needs under one roof. I can try on suits in Foster's Menswear, browse the range of unaffordable Hi-Fi units in Dixons, and pick up almost any type of gift from the Index catalogue shop. I can also book a holiday, should I ever find anyone to go with me.

I reach Lunn Poly and sneakily peer inside through the array of posters in the window. There are two desks near the front, and a woman in a red uniform is talking to a pension-age couple. To my relief, she's not the woman in red I first caught sight of yesterday. That woman in red is sitting at the adjacent desk.

Time to make my move.

I push open the door and enter. Kim Dolan immediately looks up and smiles, and for the briefest of moments, I fear she might recognise me from Wilson's Bakery. If she does remember stepping past a flustered estate agent yesterday, there's no obvious reaction to that same man entering her place of work.

"Good afternoon," she says crisply. "How can I help?"

"Hi there," I reply, doing my utmost to appear cool and confident. "I'm on the hunt for a suitable holiday."

"You've definitely come to the right place. Please, take a seat."

The seat in question is one of two in the same vivid shade of red as Kim's uniform. The staff must be sick of the colour by the end of the working week. I sit down and cross my legs.

"What kind of holiday are you looking for?" Kim asks.

"It's a bit of an odd one, and I don't know if such holidays even exist, but I'm specifically looking at holidays for solo travellers."

"Oh, they definitely exist," Kim replies positively. "We work with two tour operators specialising in solo travel."

"Great. Tell me more."

Kim gets to her feet. "Let me grab the relevant brochures, and we can talk about your specific requirements."

She turns around and steps over to a wall display stocked with a vast array of brochures. It's just as well she's got her back to me, otherwise she'd likely notice my admiring glance. Even in such a god-awful uniform, there's no hiding her shapely figure as she reaches up to grab a brochure from one of the upper shelves.

I avert my gaze just in the nick of time. With the brochures secured, Kim turns around and steps back to her desk.

"Right, then," she says, retaking her seat. "Did you have a particular country or destination in mind?"

"Hmm, I quite like the idea of America."

"Good choice. One of the tour operators has just released some great deals for holidays in Florida."

"That's not really my thing. It's all theme parks and Mickey Mouse, isn't it?"

"A bit, but at least we can cross one destination off your list. Is there another part of America you fancy?"

"There is, but I'm not sure it'll be a common holiday destination. Nashville."

"Nashville?" Kim parrots with a hint of surprise in her voice. "As in Nashville, Tennessee?"

"That's the one. The home of country music."

Just the mention of country music prompts a distinct shift in Kim's body language. It also prompts a clenching of my buttocks as I'm about to spin an uncomfortable lie. If this falls flat, at least I can blame Mrs Weller, seeing as this is her idea.

"Are you a fan of country music?" Kim asks, her arms now resting on the desk.

"Massive fan," I respond with a nonchalant wave of my hand. "And it's always been a dream to visit Nashville."

"Oh my God. I'm a huge fan of country music too, and I'd give my right arm for the chance to visit The Grand Ole Opry and The Country Music Hall of Fame."

"I can sneak you in my suitcase if you like?" I suggest with a grin.

"Gosh, I'd love that ... although I don't think my boyfriend would be too keen on me going on holiday with another man."

"That's a shame. Maybe he can take you."

"Sadly, country music isn't his cup of tea. He's more of a classical music fan."

"I guess you need to work on him for a while; try to change his mind."

"It'll be a long while," she sniggers. "Thankfully, I manage to see a few country artists a bit closer to home."

"Oh, right. I didn't realise there was much of a scene in Hampshire."

"There's not, really, but there is a country music night once a month at The Malthouse. Have you ever been?"

"No, can't say that I have."

The Malthouse is the local arts centre and a place I've spent many years avoiding. I can appreciate certain kinds of artistic events, just not poetry recitals and sculpture exhibitions.

"Some of the acts are a bit ropey," Kim continues. "But I've also seen some really good ones. You should definitely give it a go."

"I will. When's it on next?"

"Actually, this Thursday."

"Cool. I might just drop in. Will you be there?"

"I go every month with my best pal, Donna."

"I might see you there, then."

Kim flashes a half smile and then adjusts her position in the chair, almost as if she's switched back to travel agent mode.

"Anyway, if you're set on visiting Nashville, I don't think you'll find a package deal. I can still help you with flights and a hotel if you're interested?"

"Definitely."

"When were you thinking of travelling?"

"I'm flexible, but probably spring next year."

"And how long would you like to stay?"

"Let's say a fortnight."

Turning her attention to a notepad and pen, Kim then requests my name and contact number.

"Give me a day or two to find the best options, and I'll call you."

"That would be great. Thank you, Kim."

For a brief moment, the look of concern on Kim's face must mirror my own because she never told me her name. I then endure a few seconds of deep discomfort before realising the obvious. I point towards the badge on Kim's lapel.

"I presume Kim is your name?"

"Yes, of course," she replies with a less-than-subtle sigh of relief. "The company only introduced the name badges last month, and I'm still getting used to displaying my name to the world."

"No respect for your privacy, eh?"

"Nope, and what's worse is that I keep forgetting to take it off whenever I leave work. I don't mind customers knowing my name, but I'd rather not advertise it to every crank in town."

"I take your point on the badge, although the uniform on its own is quite ... distinctive."

"I can think of other words to describe it. Gopping being one of them."

"Maybe," I chuckle. "You carry it off, though."

Kim's cheeks adopt a pinkish hue as she avoids eye contact by looking at her notepad. My throwaway compliment seems to have pierced her defences.

"I'll, um, be in touch," she says coyly. "Unless you have any other questions."

"Not at the moment, thanks," I reply, getting to my feet. "I look forward to hearing from you."

She looks up at me with eyes so big and brown, they reinforce my theory that Kim must be Mrs Weller's daughter. As the woman herself refused to confirm as much, I could ask Kim, but that would completely blow my cover, and any chance of completing the task.

"Goodbye, Kim," I purr.

I then turn around and stride purposefully towards the door, happy in the knowledge that I've made progress. Not much, but some.

Chapter 21

When I wandered back to the office yesterday lunchtime, my bubble of positivity popped within seconds of opening the door. Lee had returned to find the offer from the Edgars. One minute, I was looking across a desk at a woman with come-to-bed eyes and the cutest of dimples, the next, I was facing an enraged Yorkshireman, his face scoured with more creases than a Bulldog's ball-bag.

Somehow, it was my fault that Mr and Mrs Edgar offered on the house in Brompton Road. I reminded Lee that he had warned them against making another low-ball offer, and they'd chosen not to heed that advice, so why would they listen to a lowly junior negotiator?

I'd like to say he calmed down a bit once he'd finished with me, but he then turned his attention to the cause of his ire, and a heated phone conversation with Mr Edgar ensued. As of today, the Edgars are now unofficially banned from viewing any of our properties. Their offer on Brompton Road was then submitted to the bin beneath Lee's desk.

This morning, he's back to his usual self, although it's not much of an improvement. The morning meeting is about to descend into an argument, but it has nothing to do with properties or time-wasting viewers.

"You're talking shite," Lee snorts. "Simply Red, I ask you."

I don't know how we got onto the subject, but Gavin is staunchly insisting that Simply Red's *A New Flame* was the best album of the eighties.

"It sold over a million copies," he argues. "That's how good it was."

"Jason Donovan sold over a million copies of his wanky album. Don't make it a classic, though, does it?"

"No, but we're talking about the best album — not the best-selling. I only mentioned the numbers to bolster my argument."

"You don't have an argument, lad. Everyone knows Def Leppard's *Hysteria* was the best bloody album of the eighties."

"And it's just a coincidence that they're from Yorkshire, is it?"

"I'm not biased. It just so happens that Yorkshire produces the best of everything: football clubs, cricketers, textiles, food and ale, musicians ..."

"Serial killers," Tina adds.

"Aye, them too," Lee responds with a disconcerting degree of pride.

"What do you reckon, Danny?" Gavin asks, turning to me.

"God, I don't know. Simple Minds, *Street Fighting Years*, maybe."

"What about you, Junior?" he then asks, looking across at Tina.

"I'd say Erasure," she replies. "I've got their album *Wild* on cassette in the car. It's brilliant."

"Erasure?" Lee scoffs. "Couple of tuneless poofs if you ask me."

I stare across the office at my boss, open-mouthed. It would be easy to say nothing, but too many people are too willing to take the easy option when it comes to this subject. I won't be one of them.

"Don't use that word, Lee," I say sternly.

"What word? Poofs?"

"Yes."

"Why the hell not?"

"Because it's offensive to gay people."

Puzzled rather than affronted, he turns to Tina. "You're not gay, are you?"

She shakes her head, and Lee asks Gavin the same question. He replies with a straightforward no.

"That just leaves you then, Danny," Lee continues. "And I know you're not gay, so who the fuck am I offending?"

"No, I'm not gay, but my kid brother is."

Silence.

"It's just a word," Lee eventually grunts when the silence becomes too uncomfortable. "I've got nothing against gay folk."

"I never said you did, but it's not just a word, is it? It's a slur."

"Okay. Point taken."

It's not exactly an apology, but at least he didn't double down. Lee then looks at the diary for a long moment before asking Gavin about a valuation booked for half nine, almost as if the previous conversation never occurred. To reinforce how little he wants to return to it, he addresses me.

"Danny, remember Mr Patterson and Miss Butler? The couple who offered on the flat in Sefton Court?"

"Er, yes."

"They're coming in at eleven to sign up with our mortgage advisor, so you've made yourself a bit of extra commission there."

I reply with a nod and a smile that barely registers as such.

"That's the good news," he continues. "The bad news is that she'll need to use your desk."

"Okay, so what do I do while my desk is occupied?"

"You go leaflet dropping."

"Eh? What's that?"

"Do you really need me to explain? You grab a pile of leaflets from the back room, drive out to some of the nicer roads, and then shove a leaflet through every letterbox. It's how we keep our name in the minds of potential vendors."

I knew that the junior part of my job title would condemn me to some of the less glamorous office jobs, but I didn't realise it would involve reliving my teenage years as a paper boy.

"Which roads?" I mumble.

"I'll give you a list. Just make sure you're ready to go by eleven."

As Lee moves on to the next item in the diary, my mind stays on the last two topics of conversation and whether they're related. Is he punishing me for calling out his use of the word poof? Is he so petty he'd punish one of his team just because they stood up to him? He's a bit of an opinionated loudmouth, but he doesn't strike me as the vindictive type.

Whether Lee's motives are benign or not, it looks like I'll be pounding the pavements later this morning. Thankfully, it's a pleasant enough day and if I want to stretch the silver lining, I can at least use the time to develop the Project Kim plan.

We finish the morning meeting and I pull out my box of applicant cards. There are two new instructions to tell them about, and I'd much rather call disinterested house hunters than acrimonious vendors who are already sick of being told that no one wants to buy their shitty home.

Jobs allocated, responsibilities delegated, everyone gets on with their morning, including me.

An hour of telephone calls results in three viewings booked and a dozen or so envelopes ready to be stuffed with sales particulars. Like any new job, it takes a while to get a handle on the best way to do it, and I think I'm slowly getting to grips with the process of matching properties with potential buyers. I now know, for example, that it's more efficient to confirm where the property is before I waste my time highlighting its features. Location is everything for many house hunters, it seems.

Half ten comes around and I decide to snatch a quick coffee before I head out with my stack of leaflets. With Lee out on an appointment, the atmosphere in the office feels less stressed. I check if Tina wants a cuppa and then wander through to the back room. While I'm waiting for the kettle to boil, I scan one of the leaflets I'm expected to deliver. It's written in marketing-speak and wholly uninspiring. There's a good chance that this leaflet, along with the rest I deliver, will make a short trip from the doormat to the kitchen bin, unread.

As I load a mug with coffee granules, I hear the front door open and the sound of a female voice in conversation with Gavin. A few seconds later, he pops his head around the door.

"The mortgage advisor is here, mate," he says. "Is she okay jumping into your chair?"

"She's early, but I guess so."

"Nice one. Do you want to come and introduce yourself?"

I don't really, but I follow Gavin out to my desk. I come to an abrupt standstill halfway across the office.

"You!" I gasp at the woman now sitting in my chair.

She stands up and holds out a hand.

"Yes, it's me," she says with a wide smile. "Cass O'Connor — nice to meet you."

My mind drags me back to July last year — specifically, the time Zoe and I spent completing mortgage application forms with Cass O'Connor. Even if she hadn't just introduced herself, there are two reasons why Ms O'Connor has stuck in my memory. Firstly, her distinctive hairstyle. I don't know what you'd call it, but her neck-length black hair is so sharply cut that the stylist must have used a razor rather than scissors. And when you factor in the level of shine, not to mention the paleness of her blue eyes, it gives Cass O'Connor an almost android-like aura.

However, the second and most relevant reason I remember her is because she's the mortgage advisor who told us that interest rates would tumble by the time our fixed-rate deal ended.

"You don't remember me, do you?" I say, leaving her hand hanging.

"Have we met before?"

"Yes, last year. You stitched us up with a mortgage on a new-build flat in Sefton Court."

"I do remember Sefton Court. It was the last development I worked on before moving to Gibley Smith, but I'm afraid I don't remember you ... sorry, what's your name?"

"Danny. Danny Monk."

"Nope," she says breezily. "Doesn't ring any bells."

"One mug punter much the same as the next, eh?"

"I beg your pardon."

"You told me and my fiancée that interest rates would come down, and there was no need to worry about our fixed-rate deal only lasting a year."

"Did I? Guess I got that wrong. Oops!"

"Oops?" I snap back. "Is that all you've got to say for yourself?"

Her smiley demeanour dissolves in an instant. "What do you want from me, Danny? I'm a mortgage advisor, not Mystic fucking Meg."

Her defence is followed by a glare so cold that it makes the hairs on the back of my neck stand to attention.

"You lied to us," I reply somewhat meekly.

"A lie implies intent. I made an educated guess."

"Educated?" I scoff. "That's a fucking—"

"Ahem," Gavin coughs. "Can we call a truce, guys? I need to make a call, and I don't want you two yelling at each other while I'm on the phone."

"Fine," I huff. "I'm going out, anyway."

I throw a final, defiant glare back at Cass O'Connor, and she replies with one of her own. Mercifully, she doesn't shoot laser beams from her eyes, cutting my legs at the knees. She's probably saving that for the next time we meet.

Now, with three good reasons for leaving the office, I grab a wad of leaflets from the back room and stomp my way to the door. If I was hoping for a dramatic exit, I failed — Gavin is immersed in a phone call, Tina is busily typing away, and the cyborg mortgage advisor is rifling through her briefcase.

The drive across town proves long enough for my indignation to simmer down. Whatever Cass O'Connor did or didn't say, I can hardly lay blame at her door for the way my life has turned out since she sold us that bloody mortgage. She didn't screw my relationship with Zoe, nor is she responsible for our negative equity or my position as skivvy in an estate agency. That doesn't mean I have to like her, but I can't blame her for the majority of my woes. It's not as though I'll have to see her very often, either.

I pull into a random road, parking both the Volvo and any further thoughts of Cass O'Connor. I've got more pressing women to contend with, and one of them will be at The Malthouse Arts Centre tomorrow evening. I need to work out how I take advantage of that fact.

With the sun high in a cloudless blue sky, I set about my task.

An hour into it, I'm almost out of leaflets and, to my surprise, a little disappointed. There's much to be said about wandering the suburban streets on a pleasant September day, mindlessly shoving leaflets through letterboxes. Not only has the spell out of the office soothed my soul a touch, but it's also provided time to nurture a plan for tomorrow evening. All I need is a willing co-pilot, and I think I know just the man.

I return to the Volvo and drive slowly back towards the town centre. If the gods are kind to me, Gavin will be in the office, Cass O'Connor will be done with the young couple, and Lee will be on another of his fictitious lunchtime valuations.

After stopping at Wilson's Bakery for a sandwich and a can of Lilt, I park the car and scoot back up Victoria Road. When I open the office door, it's immediately apparent that the gods don't actually hate me after all. Every desk is vacant, bar one.

"All done?" Gavin asks.

"Yep. Is Cass still around?"

"You just missed her."

Two out of three.

"Never mind. I was going to apologise, but I daresay I'll get another chance soon enough."

"You will. She's usually in here at least once a week."

"Good."

"What's the beef with you two? I got the gist of it, but you seemed properly pissed with her."

"It's nothing really. When me and my ex bought the flat in Sefton Court, we were spectacularly naive. Maybe Cass could have been a bit more honest about what we were letting ourselves in for."

"In her defence, we all have targets to hit, and sometimes you've got to be economical with the truth to ensure you hit those targets. That includes you, now."

"I suppose," I sigh. "Is Lee out on a valuation?"

"Allegedly."

Hat trick.

"Good, because I need to ask you something. Are you doing anything tomorrow evening?"

"Nothing exciting. I'll probably watch *Top of The Pops*, then have a bath followed by a resentful wank, and then cry myself to sleep."

The smile and the glint in his eye suggest Gavin is only joking, at least partly.

"Wow. That's ... tragic."

"Not as tragic as a Wednesday evening. No *Top of The Pops.*"

"There's *Bergerac* on BBC One."

"I don't know what that is."

"Something to do with a detective named Bergerac, set in the Channel Islands — Jersey, I think."

"Sounds riveting."

"I can't stand it, but my parents are fans. Anyway, if you're at a loose end, do you fancy coming with me to The Malthouse?"

"When I suggested a night out, I didn't have a Chekov play in mind."

"It's not a play. It's a country music night."

"Bloody hell," Gavin grimaces. "I'd rather watch a Chekov play ... or *Bergerac*, come to think of it."

"What if I told you that there will be two really attractive women there, and I vaguely know one of them?"

"Now you're talking," he replies, rubbing his hands together. "Are they both single?"

"Kind of."

"What does that mean?"

"It's complicated, but I like a challenge. Are you up for it?"

"Yeah, why not. Could be a laugh."

"Top man."

I don't think it'll be a laugh, but now I have my co-pilot, wingman, or whatever, my odds of success have just doubled, although double negligible is still negligible. At least I've now got a shot at Kim Dolan, and maybe Gavin will strike lucky with her friend. We could even leave The Malthouse with a new-found love of country music.

Stranger things have happened.

Chapter 22

Eleven o'clock on a damp Thursday morning, and I'm sitting in the Volvo at the end of Heron Close. When Lee suggested I attend a repossession this morning, it bolstered my theory that perhaps he still had the hump with me for calling out his homophobic language. However, Lee then confirmed that he has a meeting with our area manager set for half eleven, and Gavin has back-to-back valuations booked. I'm only here because no one else is available.

A locksmith's van is parked to my left, and we're both waiting for the bailiff. He's running late, but that'll be the least of his problems when he gets here. I check a copy of the repossession document for the third time, although I'm already certain that I'm outside the correct house: 9 Heron Close.

My confusion lies in the fact that, unlike the last repossession I attended, it appears that the outgoing owners of number 9 are still in situ and unprepared for the fate that's about to befall them. Besides a scruffy Ford Fiesta on the driveway, there are still curtains hanging from the windows at the front of the modest 1970s semi. Tellingly, though, there's a light on in one of the ground floor rooms and vapour clouds drifting from the boiler vent at the side of the house, indicating that the central heating is on.

A car appears in my rearview mirror, heading directly towards us. It stops short of the locksmith's van, and a dour-looking, middle-aged man gets out. Dressed in a black bomber jacket over a white shirt and carrying a clipboard, it would be a shock if he wasn't the bailiff. I get out of the Volvo and approach him.

"Morning. I'm Danny from Gibley Smith, estate agents."

"John Deacon, bailiff," he replies without taking his eyes off the clipboard.

"I think someone's still home," I remark.

"Not for much longer," the bailiff replies defiantly before setting off towards the front door.

I follow behind, as does the locksmith, and we loiter a few steps behind Mr Deacon as he rings the doorbell. I feel some degree of pity for whoever answers the door to find us three on their front path.

Seconds later, the door opens and, as I suspected, a confused-looking woman in her late-twenties stares back at us from the hallway.

"Mrs Ambrose?" Mr Deacon asks.

"Yes."

"My name is John Deacon, and I'm a court-appointed bailiff acting on behalf of the Bristol & West Building Society. I'm here to take possession of this property."

He holds out an envelope for the visibly stunned homeowner. "All the details are in there."

Mrs Ambrose, dressed in what might be either jogging pants and a sweatshirt, or pyjamas, eyes the envelope but doesn't take it.

"I think you're mistaken," she eventually says. "My husband dealt with the arrears last month."

"I'm not mistaken, Mrs Ambrose. If your account wasn't in arrears, the court wouldn't have issued a repossession order."

"There must be a mix-up somewhere. You'll have to come back later and speak to my husband."

"Mrs Ambrose—"

She goes to slam the door shut, but the bailiff manages to jam his foot in the way just before it closes. He then orders Mrs Ambrose to stand back as he forcibly barges his way into the hallway. I can't bear to watch what I fear is about to unfold, so I turn around and walk back up the front path towards my car. I'm in two minds about getting into the Volvo when a gruff voice calls my name. I reluctantly turn around.

"In here, now," Mr Deacon demands from the open doorway.

I trudge back down the path and follow the bailiff into the house. Standing in the hallway, he confirms the situation.

"Mrs Ambrose is currently on the phone to her husband but there's a kiddie asleep upstairs. Once she's accepted that she *will* be leaving this morning, I want you to watch over her while she packs a bag."

"Me?" I snort. "Isn't that your job?"

"I need to check the property over and ensure it's secure."

"Can't you do that afterwards?"

"I could, but then I'll be late for my next appointment, and my boss won't be happy. He'll probably call your boss, and before you know it, you'll be looking for a new job. Get it?"

Before I can protest, Mrs Ambrose returns to the hallway, her cheeks tear-stained.

"He didn't pay the arrears," she sobs. "He lied to me."

Mr Deacon steps towards the distraught housewife.

"I know this must be a shock," he says calmly. "But I'd like to make this as easy as possible for you."

"Really?" Mrs Ambrose whimpers.

"Of course. I'll give you twenty minutes to pack a bag with essential items, and then you can arrange with the estate agent a time to come back and collect everything else ... as long as it's within the next seven days."

If that's Mr Deacon's idea of easy, I dread to think what the hard option is. Being forced to pack naked as the bailiff whips her with a cat o' nine tails?

"Twenty minutes?" she blurts. "That's nowhere—"

"Nineteen," Mr Deacon interjects while staring at his watch. "Chop, chop."

He then turns to me. "Why don't you make yourself useful and help Mrs Ambrose? I'm sure she'll be grateful for the assistance."

Demands made, he strides towards the front door and begins issuing instructions to the locksmith. I have two options: tell the jumped-up prick where to stick his demands and then head back to the office, or try to assist the tearful woman standing across the hallway. As much as I'd love to give John Deacon the finger, I feel awful for Mrs Ambrose.

"What do you think you'll need?" I ask her.

"I ... I don't know."

"You've got a little one upstairs, haven't you?"

"Yes, our two-year-old, Harry. He's asleep at the minute."

"Shall we go wake him up, and I'll help you pack a few things?"

For the next fifteen minutes, I assist Mrs Ambrose — Jenny, as she insists I call her — as she stuffs clothes into carrier bags while trying to settle her confused toddler. We then transfer the bags and the child to her car.

"Um, where will you go?" I ask.

"Temporarily, to my mum's place. It's only a flat, so we won't be able to stay there for long."

"I wish there was something I could say or do to help, but ... I'm so sorry."

"Not as sorry as my husband will be when he shows his face," she replies, her tone understandably bitter. "But thank you, anyway."

"Right. Well, um, good luck."

She responds with a sad semi-smile and then reverses the car off the driveway. I stand and watch until the Fiesta disappears from view.

"All yours, mate," a voice booms from behind me. I turn around to find the locksmith holding up a set of shiny silver keys.

"Thanks."

"Don't get any easier, does it?" he says after a moment's hesitation. "Watching some poor bugger lose their home."

"This is only my second repossession, and that's two too many."

"Thatcher has got a lot to answer for, screwing us with double-digit interest rates and the bleedin' poll tax. Hopefully, the old bat is on the way out."

I've no strong interest in politics, but I can certainly relate to the locksmith's gripe about interest rates. I, however, still have a home, unlike Jenny Ambrose and her son.

After bidding the locksmith goodbye, I double-check the place is locked up, but not before reading the notice John Deacon taped to the front door, warning of criminal charges for anyone trying to force entry to the property. I don't know how these things work, now that everything the Ambrose family owns is locked in a house they no longer own, but I'm grateful it's not my problem.

I set off on the short journey back to the office.

My arrival coincides with Gavin's as he returns from the second of his valuations.

"How'd the repo go?" he asks as we both head to the back room in need of caffeine.

"It was bloody awful. The woman, Mrs Ambrose, was still in her pyjamas and she had no clue about the repossession order. Then, the twat of a bailiff only gave her twenty minutes to pack a few things and deal with her young son — he was fast asleep in bed when we pitched up."

"That's grim. I presume the house is still full of their stuff, then?"

"Minus a few bags of clothes, yes."

"That means one of us has to go back and hang around when they're ready to clear the place."

"Why?"

"Company policy. I guess they're concerned that if we just give the former homeowner the keys, they'll move back in and claim squatters rights."

"Pound to a penny, Lee gives me that job."

"I'll keep my penny, mate."

"Great," I huff. "That's something to look forward to."

"Take a book with you. It's better than sitting in the office listening to Lee moan about Rotherham United."

"True."

"Putting that to one side, we're still up for this evening, right?"

"Definitely."

"Where are we meeting, and what time?"

"Meeting? I presumed we'd go straight from work — it starts at seven."

"We'll look like a right couple of twats if we turn up in suits, don't you think?"

"Good point, but by the time I get home, change, and then get over to The Malthouse, it'll be nigh-on eight o'clock."

"Not if you've got a viewing at six, it won't."

"But I don't have a viewing at six."

"Not yet, but if you call that couple who are buying the flat in Sefton Court and ask them if they'd like to view their new home again at six, I guarantee they'll bite your arm off — ask if they want to measure up for curtains or show their parents.

You'll be done by half past, and it'll be pointless coming back to the office by that point."

"Oh, okay," I reply hesitantly. "Won't Lee get the hump if he finds out that I orchestrated the viewing?"

"He won't find out, and besides, if we didn't have to work such stupid hours every week, there wouldn't be any need to create dodgy appointments. Everyone does it."

"Do they?"

"God, yeah. There was this guy, Geoff, who used to manage the Woking branch, and he booked himself out of the diary for an entire Saturday a few years back: three valuations and nine viewings. No one gave it much thought until the area manager spotted Geoff on TV."

"On TV?"

"Yeah, Geoff was a massive Wimbledon fan, and they were at Wembley that day for the FA Cup final. He couldn't get the day off so he booked himself out on appointments all day. Would have got away with it if the BBC cameras hadn't caught him jumping around like a nutter after Wimbledon scored."

"That's shitty luck. I presume he was fired?"

"Nah, he just got a formal warning, but I don't think he cared. Imagine how gutting it must be, missing your team win the FA Cup because you can't get the day off work. I guess he thought a formal warning was a small price to pay."

Having heard Geoff's tale, and with Gavin's endorsement, I don't feel quite so guilty about setting up a viewing in the block of flats where I happen to live.

"What about you?" I ask. "Will you have time to get home and change?"

"Don't worry about me," Gavin replies with a wink. "I've got a valuation booked for six, and I guarantee I'll be out of there by quarter past."

"How can you be so sure?"

"It's my sister's house."

"Seriously?"

"Yeah. It's the ninth time she's had it valued in the last two years. One day she might put it on the market."

Chapter 23

As Gavin predicted, the young couple were only too pleased to view the flat again. When I arrived, they were joined by both sets of parents, and I loitered in the lounge while they wandered around. In a way, it was a bittersweet experience. It wasn't that long ago that Zoe and I toured an empty flat, excitedly discussing how we'd turn it into the perfect home. For their sake, I hope the prospective owners of flat 19 fare better on the relationship front than we did.

Fortuitously, the couple and their parents left after fifteen minutes, giving me enough time to nip back to my flat, bolt down a sandwich, and grab a quick shower. All that remains is a decision about what to wear.

What do you wear to a country music event? I don't even own a plaid shirt, never mind a Stetson.

I settle on a pair of stonewashed jeans, a black polo shirt, and my go-to leather jacket. A few squirts of Kouros cologne complete my preparations. There is no time to waste worrying about what kind of style might appeal to Kim Dolan.

The Malthouse Arts Centre is only just over a mile from the flat so, knowing I'll likely require a few glasses of Dutch courage, I decide to walk. Besides, after a hectic and frankly awful day at work, the walk is a welcome opportunity to decompress.

I arrive at The Malthouse and make my way to the bar, where I've arranged to meet Gavin at seven. It's pretty busy, and, to my relief, everyone is dressed for an evening at the pub rather than a hoedown. I don't know what I expected, but I'm glad I can blend into the crowd.

As I wait to be served, I scan the room for Kim and her friend. However, as the doors to the main hall are already open and the first of two acts is due to start any minute, there's a chance she's already taken her place near the stage.

With the crowd quickly dispersing, it's my turn at the bar. I order a pint, and a surly barmaid duly pours my drink.

"£2.10, please," she says, placing the glass on the bar and slopping ten per cent of it on the mat.

"£2.10?" I question. "Bit pricey."

"Take it up with the management committee."

I slap the right change on the bar and take a gulp from the glass, purely to occupy my mouth in case I say something I might regret.

"Your round, is it?" a familiar voice asks.

I turn around and almost spit a mouthful of lager in Gavin's face.

"What the ..."

"You like the outfit?" he asks, flashing a wide smile.

"It's ... bloody hell, Gav," I splutter. "Have you got a horse parked up outside?"

Gavin clearly does own a plaid shirt — a striking red and yellow plaid shirt with decorative metal collar tips. If only the crimes against fashion stopped there.

"They're a bit big," he says, noticing my saucer-like eyes trained on his fancy cowboy boots. "I had to wear two pairs of socks."

I don't know where to begin.

"Mate, I'm ... first question: why do you even own a pair of cowboy boots?"

"I don't. They're my dad's."

"That kind of explains the size issue, so I suppose I should ask why your dad owns a pair of cowboy boots. He doesn't work on a ranch, I'm guessing."

"He's a plumber, but he and Mum were into line dancing for a while until he hurt his back."

"Oh, I see. I presume the shirt is his, too?"

"He said I could have it."

"I bet he did."

With Gavin slightly crestfallen, I backtrack to save his feelings.

"It's cool," I say. "I'm just a bit concerned that ... people might assume that you're a hardcore country music fan, and you're not, are you?"

"Not really, no, but you're forgetting something."

"Am I?"

"I bullshit for a living, Danny. I'm sure I can talk my way out of any country music-related situations."

"Fair enough. Pint?"

"Love one."

I summon the surly barmaid again, and she duly serves Gavin with ninety per cent of a pint.

"So, where are these girls you mentioned?" he asks before taking his first sip of lager.

"I assume they're in the hall, waiting for the first act."

"Who's playing?"

I nod towards a poster beside the bar. "Nikki Amato — soloist."

"She any good?"

"Your guess is as good as mine. The same applies to the main act, The Gerry Armstrong Band."

"Didn't Gerry Armstrong play for Watford in the early eighties?"

"Possibly, but I'm willing to go out on a limb and say it's not the same fella."

"It could be."

"Seems unlikely."

"Why?"

"Er ... I don't know."

"I guess we'll find out later."

"I'm sure we will, but for now, we should probably go and see what the support act is like."

"Lead on."

With the Sundance Kid trailing behind, I stride over to the double doors leading into the main hall. A disinterested kid checks our tickets and waves us through to a small anteroom, which, I presume, helps stop the sound from leaking into the bar area.

We pass through another set of double doors into the main hall.

"Christ, I didn't think it'd be this popular," Gavin remarks.

Neither did I. I also presumed there would be rows of seats lined up in front of the stage, but the audience is standing — unsurprising, really, as it's a music gig. The stage is lit with a single bluish spotlight, highlighting a woman on a stool as she makes the final tuning adjustments to her guitar.

"Good evening, everyone," she then says into the microphone, her voice low and husky.

"Was that an Irish accent?" Gavin asks.

"I think so."

"That's not very wild west."

"Ireland is west of here, so it kind of is."

As Nikki Amato begins her set, I scan the audience in search of Kim Dolan but it proves a futile challenge. It's too dark, and I can't see beyond the taller members of the audience.

"Should we move to the front?" Gavin asks.

"I'm okay here unless you want to move?"

"Not really, but I thought you wanted to find the girls."

"Even if we spot them, we can't exactly wander over and spark up a conversation in the middle of a set, can we?"

"Good point. We'll strike during the interval, yeah?"

Strike is not the word I'd have chosen, but I nod in agreement with my diminutive colleague.

As I've paid a fiver for a ticket and I've nothing better to do, I lean against the back wall and take in Nikki Amato's set.

My country music experience is limited to the acts that have crossed over into the mainstream, like Dolly Parton, Kenny Rogers, and Willie Nelson. Even then, I'd be hard-pressed to list many of their hit singles. I seem to recall Kenny Rogers telling the tale of *The Coward of The County* and Dolly Parton lamenting her career choices in *9 to 5*.

As for Willie Nelson, he only came to my attention after the Pet Shop Boys secured the Christmas number one a few years ago. I had no idea that their chart-topper, *Always on My Mind*, was written by Willie Nelson, and he'd had a hit with it. I have Dad to thank for sharing that titbit of musical trivia after he picked me up from the train station last year and *Always on My Mind* was playing on the radio. He spent most of our journey complaining that Messrs Tennant and Lowe had butchered one of his favourite songs, and he wouldn't let me out of the car until he'd found the Willie Nelson version on one of his many cassettes and forced me to listen to it.

Nikki Amato's take on country music, however, is distinctly different from anything I've heard before. It could be the absence of banjos and harmonicas, or it could be the husky lilt of her Irish accent, but the first three songs are surprisingly stirring.

"She's good," Gavin comments as the audience enthusiastically claps at the end of Nikki Amato's fourth song.

"Yeah, she is," I reply, my eyes still glued to the stage. "I might even buy her CD."

Two songs later, Ms Amato brings her set to an end. Being this is a small town arts centre and not Wembley, there's no call for an encore or any grand exit, just polite applause and a few whoops as the singer hops off her stool and wanders towards a door at the side of the stage.

The main lights come on, and a voice announces that there will be a twenty-minute interval before the next act.

"Let's get to the bar before the masses," I tell Gavin.

I desperately want another pint, but I'm also conscious that there are only a handful of tables in the main bar, and grabbing one will make it much easier to lure Kim over.

My urgency is rewarded once I secure a tall table at the far side of the bar, complete with four empty stools.

"Your round, Gav," I say, keeping my eyes trained on the stream of people exiting the hall. "Better be quick if you don't want to wait all evening to be served."

"Righto."

As Gavin scoots off to the bar, I focus my attention on the doors to the hall. Assuming Kim and her friend were near the front, logically, they should be amongst the last to exit. That, of course, would depend on them being here at all, which I've yet to confirm.

A few more stragglers pass through the doors. Then, long seconds tick by without anyone else exiting the hall. I'm about to glance across and check on Gavin's progress when a tall, gangly woman emerges from the hall. She stops and turns around as if she's waiting for someone, and then, to my relief, Kim Dolan steps through the doorway.

She's here, thank God. Now, I just need to *accidentally* cross paths with her.

"One pint of overpriced lager," Gavin says, placing a plastic glass on the table.

"Cheers."

"There's some bloody weird people in here," he then remarks.

"Weird, how?"

"Standing at the bar, I kept getting funny looks."

"It's probably because you're an unfamiliar face," I lie. "I'm sure most of this crowd come every month, and you're like the new kid in school."

"Yeah, you're probably right."

I'm about to take a sip from my pint when I catch sight of two figures approaching our table — one significantly taller than the other.

"Hello again," Kim Dolan says playfully. "Fancy seeing you here."

"Oh, hi," I reply.

"You decided to check out the gig, then?"

"Yeah. Thanks for the tip-off ... Kim, right?"

"You've got a good memory. This is my best friend, Donna — remember I mentioned her when we were discussing your holiday requirements?"

The tall woman I hope to palm off on Gavin throws an awkward wave my way.

"Hi, I'm Danny," I respond. "This is my—"

"Good evening, ladies," Gavin boldly announces before I've finished introducing him. He then thrusts out his hand towards Kim. "Gavin Flint. A pleasure to meet you."

Both women shake Gavin's hand in turn, although neither appears comfortable with it.

"Can I get either of you a drink?" he then asks.

"I'll just have a Coke, please," Donna replies. "I'm driving."

"I'm not sure what I want," Kim says. "I'll come to the bar with you, Gavin."

My colleague's eyes light up. We've only been at the table a minute, and already, my plan is in danger of running off the rails. It should be Donna heading to the bar with Gavin, although my initial hopes that they'd experience a spark might have been optimistic. I don't know a lot about Gavin, and I know nothing about Donna, so it could be that they have a lot in common. However, that's not to say they'd make a good couple, at least not physically.

In the time it takes to kick myself, Gavin and Kim are gone, leaving me alone with Donna.

"Do you like country music, Danny?" she asks.

Ah, shit.

Chapter 24

I wonder if there is such a thing as Idiots Anonymous. I can imagine sitting in a circle with other idiots, confessing that I, Daniel Thomas Monk, have plummeted the depths of idiocy.

How, in God's holy name, did I not see what Kim had in store?

"So, what do you do for a living?" Donna asks after my fumbled answer to her last question.

Notwithstanding the fact that I'm not in the least bit attracted to Donna, even our names don't blend well. Donna and Danny smacks of a lame Eurovision act from the seventies.

"I'm an estate agent," I reply, hoping my profession alone might put her off.

"That's cool."

"It's not. The pay is awful, and this morning I helped evict a young mother and her child from the family home."

"Oh."

Too late, I realise my strategy of keeping Donna at arm's length might come back to bite me on the arse if she relays any of this conversation to Kim.

"I'm only kidding," I say with a half-hearted chuckle. "The pay isn't that bad."

Donna responds with a lopsided smile.

"So, um, what do you do, you know, for work?"

"Me, I'm a model," she replies.

"Wow, that's ... that must be amazing. What do you model?"

She leans forward and holds her right hand out.

"My hands," she confirms.

"Right. They are nice hands, not that I'm an expert or anything."

"I did a shoot for Elizabeth Duke this morning. Engagement rings."

"Sorry, I don't know who she is."

"She's not a person," Donna sniggers. "Elizabeth Duke is the Argos jewellery brand."

"Oh, gotcha."

"I did Ratner's last month. Did you know they're the biggest jewellery chain in the UK?"

"I did not," I reply. Nor could I give less of a shit.

I need to excuse myself before this goes any further, and Donna wrongly assumes I'm interested in her.

"Sorry, I just need to nip to the loo."

With no clue where the toilets are, I embark on a haphazard tour of The Malthouse before finding the gents off a random corridor. I take a precautionary pee, wash my hands, and then count to sixty just to allow enough time for Gavin and Kim to return from the bar.

It's a relief to see them at the table when I amble back.

"Did I miss anything?" I ask, stepping back into the fold.

"We were just talking about Nikki Amato," Kim replies. "What an amazing set."

"I said the same to Gavin, didn't I, mate?"

"Yes, you did. And I concurred."

"I take it you're a big fan of country music, Gavin," Kim then enquires.

"What gave it away?"

"The shirt, maybe."

"Do you like it?"

"It's ... bold."

"Thanks."

"What artists are you into?" Donna asks.

"Um, all of them," Gavin replies in the least convincing of lies. "I've got loads of country albums. Hundreds."

"You must have a favourite."

"Ah, there are so many, it's impossible to pick one."

"Go on," Donna urges. "You can tell a lot about a guy by the music he likes."

"Well, er ... " Gavin splutters. "I'm quite keen on The Wurzels."

Donna looks at Kim. Kim looks at Donna. I look up to the ceiling and silently ask God what he's playing at.

"The Wurzels aren't a proper country music act," Kim responds.

"They are," Gavin rebuffs. "They're from the West Country, and they wear dungarees."

Kim and Donna share another look before announcing they're off to the loo. I watch them all the way to the far side of the bar, Kim's shoulders shuddering with laughter as they walk.

"The fucking Wurzels?" I spit as soon as the girls are out of sight.

"Sorry. My mind went blank."

"They're not even a proper pop act, never mind a country act."

"Didn't they sing a song about a combine harvester?"

"Yes, but ... they're a parody band. They take the piss out of other artist's songs."

"Oh, I didn't realise," Gavin says somewhat sheepishly. "Have I blown my chance with Kim?"

Not for the first time this evening, I find myself struggling for a suitable reaction.

"Kim?" I finally snort. "Are you ... "

"She insisted on helping me at the bar, so I reckon I'm in there."

Much as I'd like to blame Gavin for jumping to such a wrong-headed conclusion, I need to take the lion's share of the blame. I should have briefed him properly before we met Kim and Donna.

"Kim is the one I'm trying to ... to pull."

"You never said."

"Well, I am now. I asked you along so you could get to know Donna."

"Mate, she's not really my type."

"Why? What's wrong with her? I think she's quite attractive."

"She is, but ... I'm not sure I fancy her."

"You're kidding, right? She's a model, you know."

Gavin looks up at me, bemused. "What does she model? Guttering?"

"Alright, she's a bit taller than you," I reply, trying to stifle a laugh. "But that's not a deal breaker, surely?"

"A bit taller? She's almost the same height as you, which suggests—"

"Not gonna happen," I interject. "I'm mad about Kim."

"You barely know her. She told me at the bar that you only met two days ago when you were asking about holidays in Lunn Poly."

"True, but ... but I saw her first."

"What are you? Eight?"

"Alright, forget who saw her first. I'm telling you now that Kim isn't an option, okay?"

"She likes my shirt. What's that if it's not a come-on?"

I could bash my head against the table but that would only waste the valuable seconds before Kim and Donna return to the table. I've no option but to tell Gavin the truth, or at least a version of it.

"Kim isn't interested in you, mate. She's already in a relationship."

"Eh?"

"Cards on the table. A family friend is concerned about Kim's relationship, and she asked me to ... that family friend wants Kim to ditch her current boyfriend, and she asked me to help."

"Help?"

"Yeah."

"In what way?"

"She didn't say exactly, but reading between the lines, I guess she wants me to lure Kim away from her current boyfriend. And she was also adamant that it has to be me."

Gavin rubs his chin while processing my confession.

"Are you winding me up?" he then asks.

"No, I swear it's the truth."

"So Kim is definitely off limits?"

"I'm afraid so, but if you're interested in Donna, go for it."

"Hmm, I don't know."

"Think of the kudos, telling your mates you're dating a model."

"Is she really a model?"

"Hands, apparently. She did a shoot for engagement rings this morning."

"I see," Gavin muses. "She does have nice hands."

"Yeah, and I bet she's got nice ... I'm sure you'll find she's got many redeeming qualities once you get to know her."

My colleague takes a slow sip of lager and then gives me a thumbs up. "Okay, I'm in."

"Cheers," I puff. "Now, I need to ask a favour."

"Go on."

"You cannot mention any of this to Donna, or Kim, obviously. Come to think of it, I'd rather you didn't tell anyone."

"Mum's the word."

"I mean it, Gav. I told you the truth because I trust you — don't let me down."

Ever since Zoe cheated, I've struggled to trust anyone, and Gavin is the least likely of exceptions considering he's a self-confessed bullshitter. However, as long as he thinks I've taken him into my confidence, he's less likely to blab about Project Kim.

"I really appreciate that, mate," he replies almost earnestly. "It means a lot, and I won't let you down."

Gavin couldn't have cut his agreement any tighter as I spot Kim and Donna making their way back to the table.

"They're on their way over," I say in a low voice. "Just play it cool, okay, and for the love of all things holy, please don't mention The Wurzels again."

"Gotcha."

I turn and smile at the two women as they approach. My aim is to appear friendly, but it's a fight not to let the relief reach my face. In their shoes, I'm not so sure I'd have returned to join us.

"We were just talking about your modelling career," I say to Donna as she reaches for her Coke.

"Were you?"

"Yeah, Gavin happened to mention that you've got really nice hands, didn't you, Gav?"

"I did," he blurts.

"That's very sweet of you to say," Donna coos, although her gratitude is aimed more in my direction than Gavin's.

I feign a smile and then turn to Kim. "What would you say your best feature is?"

Fortuitously, I already know the answer, courtesy of Mrs Weller's exhaustive list of Kim Dolan's loves, likes, and dislikes.

"I'm not really sure."

"You do have incredible eyes if you don't mind me saying."

"Oh, um ... really?" she stammers, blushing slightly. "Thank you."

"Mine would be my buttocks," Gavin announces, ruining the moment. "They're very firm and particularly pert ... so I've been told."

No one seeks to confirm Gavin's claim one way or another.

"What about you, Danny?" Donna asks. "What's your best feature?"

I was hoping that Kim would ask that very question, but now I'm faced with a dilemma. If I say anything vaguely positive or interesting, Donna might take it as encouragement. If I say something lame or trite, Kim will think I'm a dickhead.

A voice suddenly booms from the PA system, encouraging patrons to return to the main hall as the second act is about to take to the stage. Perfect timing, and I use the distraction to finish my pint rather than answer Donna's question.

There is, however, still enough time to throw a question at Kim. "What do you know about the band that are up next?"

"They're brilliant," she replies. "A complete contrast to the first act."

"In what way?"

"They're far more upbeat. If you're lucky, you might even see me dance."

"Is that an invite to join you and Donna for the second act, then?"

"By join, you mean loiter around the edge of the stage with us?"

"Yeah, that."

"It's a free country," she replies with a grin.

It's all the encouragement I need. I beckon Gavin to follow as we trail Kim and Donna into the hall. From there, we move around the edge of the floor towards the stage, where a five-piece band are conducting sound checks. Not one of them is wearing a plaid shirt or cowboy boots, but a cracked series of letters printed on the bass drum confirms they're the Gerry Armstrong Band.

If anyone was still in doubt, the lead singer introduces himself and his bandmates. I wouldn't swear on it, but I'm sure I detect a slight Geordie accent.

They begin their set with an up-tempo tune that sounds much more like the country music I'm familiar with, probably because it involves a fiddle and a banjo.

"This is one of my mum's favourites," Gavin shouts in my ear. "She learned all the steps at line dancing."

"There are steps?"

"Yeah. Want me to show you?"

"Absolutely not. You can clap your hands or shuffle on the spot, but that's the limit."

Having put Gavin back in his box I glance across towards Kim and Donna. The subject of my task is closest to me, but her attention is fixed on the stage rather than the curious estate agent next to her. Both women are clapping their hands and jiggling their hips in time to the music, and I must admit, Kim's jeans and a snug-fitting sweater are a vast improvement on the Lunn Poly uniform.

Then, Kim suddenly turns her head and catches me staring. I open my mouth to say something purely to alleviate my awkwardness, but to my surprise, she responds with a smile. She then says something to Donna, and the two women giggle before returning their attention to the band.

Over the course of the ensuing set, I happen to glance across twice more. I get away with it the first time, but Kim catches me on the second. Again, she doesn't seem troubled that another man is patently attracted to her, although that same man is conscious of Mrs Weller's strict instructions. However, if there's any chance of undermining Kim's relationship within the requested timeline, I can't afford to be anything less than bold, and that will require more than an admiring glance or two.

The lead singer announces the final song of the night, *Queen of Hearts*, and although I've never heard of it, the crowd responds with a cheer. By the time the chorus begins, I realise I have heard the song before, albeit a pop-inspired version. I'm sure it was in the charts when I was a teenager, and I remember it well enough to sing along. Credit to Gavin for joining in even though he improvises most of the lyrics. Badly.

The song comes to an end, as does the night's work for the Gerry Armstrong Band. My work, however, is far from over. I can't let the evening just fizzle out.

As soon as the lights come on and the crowd mills back to the bar, I throw a question out.

"It's not even ten yet. Anyone fancy going on to Jaxx?"

The prospect of a few hours at the only nightclub in town, and a dive of a nightclub at that, is hardly enticing, but it's all I've got.

"Count me in," Gavin announces. "But give me a minute. I'm busting for a piss."

He hurries off to the loo. No one checks out his buttocks.

"What about you two?" I ask Kim and Donna. "Fancy a few drinks? I might even show you my best moves on the dancefloor."

"I'm game," Donna replies.

"I'd love to," Kim says in a tone of voice that implies she really wouldn't love to. "But I've got work in the morning."

"Come on," I urge. "We'll have you home by midnight, Cinders."

She ponders my proposal momentarily before taking a step closer to me.

"I really can't," she says. "But if you're free on Saturday evening, how do you fancy joining us in a foursome?"

"Yeah, I'd love to."

"Shall we say seven o'clock at Martinelli's?"

"The bar on Station Road?"

"That's the one."

"Great. I look forward to it."

Kim then checks her watch and turns to Donna. "We'd better get back to the car park before your ticket expires."

The two women then say goodbye and ask me to apologise to Gavin for not hanging around. They hurry away, leaving me standing in a near-empty hall while the band pack away their gear.

A minute passes, and just as I'm about to retreat to the bar, my colleague returns.

"Where are the girls?" he asks.

"Good news and bad news, mate."

"Let's have the bad news first."

"Kim wasn't up for Jaxx because she's got work tomorrow."

"That's a bummer. What's the good news?"

"She suggested we go out as a foursome on Saturday evening. You up for that?"

"Definitely," he beams.

"Good man. They did stipulate one condition, mind."

"What's that?"

"Absolutely no cowboy boots."

Chapter 25

When Zoe moved out, I suspect my libido left with her. Understandably, considering the reason behind her departure, I couldn't bear thinking about sex for weeks. Those weeks turned into a month, and then two, and then three.

In a way, it was similar to the time, as a teenager, I spent the evening at Gary Dougherty's house when his parents were out. For entertainment, we decided to sample the contents of the drinks cabinet, settling on a bottle of Harveys Bristol Cream, which we duly polished off. I ended the evening draped over the toilet, dry retching and, to this day, even the slightest whiff of sherry makes me gag.

For similar reasons, my brain cannot detach the broader subject of sex from Zoe's indiscretion, so every time a sexual thought floats into my mind, I feel slightly nauseous. Once the nausea passes, anger rocks up, and that's not in the least bit sexy.

However, last night, I had a dream. A psychologist might suggest it had something to do with spending part of yesterday evening with an attractive woman, but the dream was very much centred on a different woman — the last one I wanted in my dreams. In the dream, Zoe and I were enjoying a bout of wild sex on the balcony just after daybreak. On the street below, the milkman passed by in his float, seemingly oblivious to Zoe's cries of passion.

I don't know the meaning of the dream but, when I woke up, I felt properly revved up, to the point I had to deal with the resulting erection whilst taking a shower. Besides leaving a sexual footprint, the dream also left an emotional one, and for the first time since she suggested it, I gave Zoe's plan some proper thought.

And so, as I stand in the back room at Gibley Smith, waiting for the kettle to boil, I'm torn between the love and hate I still harbour for my ex-fiancée. Up until I called by her house last week, I was willing to settle on hate, but ever since Zoe suggested we try again, I've been unable to ignore the dull ache in my heart. I wish I could just flick a switch and cast her from my memory altogether, although that might prove confusing whenever a letter arrives with her name on it or when I eventually sell the flat.

I push thoughts of Zoe to the back of my mind when Tina wanders in.

"Morning," she says with a yawn.

"It certainly is. Cuppa?"

"Yes, please."

"How are things with Captain Crapper?" I ask, grabbing a mug from the cupboard.

"Who?"

"Your other half."

"Oh, him," she sniggers. "No further incidents to report, thankfully."

"Has he finally seen the error of his ways?"

"Only after I made a threat. I told him that every time he took a dump while I was in the bathroom, I'd enforce a seven-day sex ban. So far, it seems to be doing the trick."

So much for putting the subject of sex to bed.

"Nice one, although if my ex had curled one out while I was in the shower, that would have put me off sex for a year, never mind a week."

"I have longer punishments for other behavioural issues."

"Such as?"

"Two weeks after we moved in together, he went out drinking with his brother. He came home at midnight, drunk as a skunk, and pissed in my wardrobe. That resulted in a month-long ban. Then there was the time I caught him flirting with one of the girls in his office. That was a three-month ban, although I did give in after seven weeks."

"Sounds a lot like puppy training."

"He *is* a puppy, really. He's only twenty, and most young lads are dopey twats ... no offence."

"I'm flattered you think I still qualify as a young lad. I certainly don't feel young these days."

"What is it they say? You're only as young as the woman you feel?"

"What do they say if you don't have a woman to feel?"

"Dunno," she shrugs. "Find one, I guess."

"I thought I had, but ..."

Tina has inadvertently reactivated the dull ache.

"But?" she probes.

"Forget it," I reply, returning my attention to the kettle.

Tina takes the hint and, after hanging up her coat, retreats to her desk.

Lee and Gavin eventually arrive and after swapping small talk for five minutes, we settle down for the morning meeting. The first order of the day relates to the last.

"Listen up," Lee says. "If anyone books an appointment after five o'clock today, I'll have their bollocks for breakfast. Understood?"

"I'm okay, then," Tina chimes in. "Seeing as I don't possess a pair."

"Tits on toast, then," Lee retorts. "It's Friday, and, as it's my day off tomorrow, I'm planning on a long session at the Victoria Club later. I don't want to be sitting in some boring bastard's lounge at six o'clock while they relay a history of every bloody property they've ever bought and sold."

"Does that apply to me and Danny, too?" Gavin enquires. "No appointments after five?"

"Aye, it does. It's your round if memory serves."

I'm not in the mood for another night out but I like the idea of doing next to nothing from five o'clock onwards. If Lee pushes it, I suppose I might join my colleagues for a quick pint.

We get on with the meeting, and I receive my orders for the day. My tasks for the morning are tedious but then Lee drops a bombshell. Mr and Mrs Ambrose, formerly of Heron Close, want to gain access to clear the rest of their belongings at one o'clock.

"They'll be there for hours," I complain.

"Two, to be precise."

"How are they supposed to empty the house and load it into a truck in two hours?"

"They've got two hours to empty the house. Who said anything about waiting around while they load a bloody truck?"

"I don't understand."

"It's pretty straightforward, lad. They take everything out of the house and stick it on the driveway. Once the house is empty, you lock up and get your arse back to the office."

"But what if it rains?"

"If it rains, it rains," he shrugs. "The building society said they'll pay Gibley Smith for a member of staff to sit there for two hours, so that's their lot. If they don't like it, tough."

I think back to when I was a manager, and I gave instructions to my staff. I'm confident they never thought it, but I'm sure I wasn't such a bullish oaf.

Thankfully, Lee is out on appointments most of the morning, so I can complete my tasks without his dulcet Yorkshire tones reverberating around the office. By late morning, I confirm with Tina that I'll take lunch at noon as I'm due at Heron Close by one.

At five to twelve, I grab my jacket, leave the office, and hurry up Victoria Road to Wilson's Bakery. My strategy of leaving just before the lunchtime rush pays dividends — I secure my chicken and mayo baguette within a couple of minutes. I pay the woman behind the counter and dash back to the door. Just as I'm about to step through it, a figure appears from nowhere. Despite my best efforts to come to a halt, my momentum carries me through the doorway, and I bump into the figure. It all happens in a fraction of a second, which is why it takes a moment to realise it's not just any figure.

"Oh," I splutter. "Er, hi."

Zoe looks up at me. "More haste, less speed, eh?"

"Yeah. Sorry."

"It's okay. How are you?"

Up until five seconds ago, I was fine. Granted, I wasn't looking forward to sitting in my car for two hours while a resentful family empty their former home, but overall, I was okay. Now, I'm not.

"I'm ... not bad. You?"

"So-so," she replies with a strained smile.

"Something up?"

"Kind of."

Zoe places her hand on my upper arm and guides me away from the bakery door, so we're standing just to the side.

"I know you asked for time," she then says, quietly enough not to be heard by anyone heading into the bakery. "But ... I'm finding it hard. I miss you, Danny."

I wish Zoe had told me her parents' cat had just died — I never liked the sly little shit. If she had, an invisible hand wouldn't now be squeezing my heart.

"I know," is all I can say.

"You know?"

"Yes, I know it's hard. I know only too well."

"But it doesn't have to be, does it?"

I look over Zoe's head to the street beyond and puff a long sigh. "I'm not there yet."

"Will you ever be?"

I think back to last night's dream and how I felt when I woke up this morning.

"Maybe."

"That's not much for a girl to cling to."

I don't want to look at Zoe because I know my defences will crumble, but I can't help myself. In that moment, blinded by her perfectly formed features, it's too easy to forget what she did.

"Come over to the flat on Sunday afternoon, and we'll talk."

"Really? Like, a proper talk?"

"Yes. Two o'clock."

"I'll be there."

I may have just made a grave mistake, but here and now, I can't think that far ahead.

"I'd better get back to work," I say, checking my watch for effect. "Lots to do this afternoon."

Zoe then moves a fraction closer to me. "I don't suppose I could have a quick hug before you shoot off?"

How often is a hug request denied? One in every hundred? Thousand? It must be rare because declining the request feels like a dick move, whilst accepting it is oh so easy.

I don't want to feel like a dick, so I let Zoe wrap her arms around me. Visions of balconies and milk floats drift through my mind.

I break from the hug. "Um, gotta go. See you Sunday."

For every yard of pavement between the bakery and the office, I question what the hell just happened. One random meeting with my ex, followed by a concession and a hug that went on for far too long. More than that, though, I feel ... not angry.

Am I finally coming to terms with what Zoe did? Is this that mythical moment of acceptance I've heard about? Does this have anything to do with last night's dream and the feelings I had when I woke up this morning?

So many questions, so few answers.

I return to the office and head straight for the back room. I won't find answers in a chicken and mayo baguette, but it's a worthwhile distraction.

Chapter 26

Post Zoe, I spent a large chunk of my afternoon with three angry men: Mr Ambrose, his brother, and some random mate with a Luton van. They weren't so angry when I first arrived and let them into the house, but they definitely were after I told them they'd have to move everything outside before loading the van.

They wasted ten minutes arguing with me and another five hurling abuse. I've been called many things by many people over my twenty-eight years, but *capitalist wankstain* was a new one. I informed Mr Ambrose that he wasn't the only one with financial problems and, if the abuse continued, I'd lock up the house and leave.

The threat worked and they begrudgingly began shifting furniture.

They were still emptying the house when three o'clock arrived, and, by all rights, I should have locked the house up and made my way back to the office. However, they only had a dozen boxes and a couple of mattresses to move, and it seemed churlish not to grant them another fifteen minutes. Perhaps understandably, considering the circumstances, gratitude for my gesture was in short supply.

Three hours after leaving Heron Close, I'm standing with two men, and one of them is almost as angry as Mr Ambrose's van-driving mate.

"That was a foul shot," Lee blasts. "You nudged the bloody cue ball."

"No, I never," Gavin responds, holding back a smirk. "You're just a bad loser, mate."

"Danny! You saw it, didn't you?"

"Keep me out of this. I just came out for a quiet pint."

Gavin might have a point. Lee really doesn't seem willing to accept his defeat at the pool table with good grace.

"This is bollocks," he huffs. "The only fair way to sort it out is to play again."

"It's Danny's turn."

"He doesn't mind waiting," Lee says before turning to me. "Do you, Danny?"

"Anything for a quiet life."

"Good lad. You can get the next round in while you're waiting your turn."

Fortunately for Lee, the cost of three pints is a price I'm willing to pay to get away from my boss for five minutes. He's loud enough in the office, but out in the wild, with a pint of Stella in him, he's verging on obnoxious.

"Same again?" I enquire.

"Aye," Lee responds while feeding another coin into the pool table.

"I fancy something different," Gavin says after a quick ponder. "I'll have a vodka and Um Bongo."

"Um Bongo?" I reply quizzically. "The kids drink? With vodka?"

"Yeah, it's lush. Have you never tried it?"

"No, nor have I ever tried gin and Kia-Ora or a whisky Tizer, because I'm an adult."

"You're missing out, mate."

"I can live with that, and you can live with a pint of Fosters. I'm not embarrassing myself at the bar by asking for a vodka Um Bongo."

"Gav," Lee then barks. "It's your break."

Discussion over, I leave them to it and traipse through an archway back to the Victoria Club's main bar. It feels busier than last week; a mix of office types enjoying post-work drinks and early birds out for a Friday night session. The owner, Nigel, claims he's running an exclusive club, but based on this evening's clientèle, he might want to remind his door staff of that claim.

On the upside, the bar is well-staffed, and a cheery, middle-aged woman with wildly permed hair asks for my order the minute I step forward.

"Two pints of Fosters and a Stella, please."

"Coming up, love."

While I wait, my mind turns to a subject that's dominated my thoughts most of the afternoon. I probably should be thinking about tomorrow's foursome with Kim and Donna, but I can't shake my earlier meeting with Zoe. It's not that meeting, as such, but what might happen on Sunday afternoon.

My defences are on the wane, and I know deep down that there's a chance they'll crumble if Zoe tries hard enough.

"£3.45, please, love," the barmaid says.

I hand over a fiver, wait for my change, and then carefully transfer the three pints back across the bar area to where my colleagues are playing pool.

"Drinks up," I announce, carefully lowering the glasses to a table.

"Cheers," Gavin says before downing the dregs of his current pint.

Lee doesn't say anything as he's focussing hard on a shot, carefully lining up the cue and stroking it back and forth like a seasoned pro.

"Who's winning?" I ask although I don't really care.

"If he sinks this shot, he's got two balls left before the black. I've got three."

I gulp a mouthful of lager and then watch on as Lee continues to painstakingly line up his shot. If there's any justification for the time he's taking, it's the difficulty of the shot. The cue ball is at one end of the table, only two inches from the cushion, and the ball he's aiming for is at the far end, nestled just to the side of the black.

Finally, Lee thrusts his arm forward, and the cue ball shoots up the table. It strikes the desired ball but at the wrong angle, sending it towards the jaws of the pocket before rebounding to the centre of the table. The cue ball, however, catches the black ball perfectly. It bounces off the cushion towards the right-hand pocket.

"No, no, no!" Lee shouts as the black ball rolls slowly towards the pocket.

Inch by inch, it loses momentum, but inevitably, it plops into the pocket.

Game over.

"Fuck sake," Lee snaps, slapping his cue on the table.

"Unlucky, boss," Gavin says.

"Nothing unlucky about it. The bloody table isn't even."

Something tells me Lee is a sore loser, but I don't think either of us wants to risk his wrath by pointing it out. He consoles himself by lighting a post-defeat cigarette.

"You're on, Danny," Gavin says. "Rack 'em up."

I slide a twenty-pence piece into the slot, safe in the knowledge that I only need to hang around for the duration of this game and one pint of lager, and then I can make my excuses.

"Heads or tails?" Gavin asks as I place the balls in the triangle.

"Heads."

Unsurprisingly, considering how much bad luck I've attracted this year, it's tails. Gavin breaks.

It's fair to say that my colleague is a much better pool player than I am. He sinks four consecutive balls before missing a tricky shot into the middle pocket. However, he leaves the cue ball so close to the cushion that even the relatively straight shot before me is more difficult than I'd like.

I lean forward and line up the cue. As I crouch down, I notice two figures in my peripheral vision, entering the pool room and moving towards a table in the corner. I only catch a glimpse as one of them steps forward and places a coin on the edge of the table, indicating that he wants to play the winner. I then happen to glance up.

My stomach spins a full revolution when our eyes meet.

The last time I saw Wayne Pickford, he was getting out of his car across the road from the Blockbuster video store. It was exactly one week on from Zoe's confession, and that chance encounter felt like a gift from the gods — a chance to vent the white-hot rage that had built up in the days after that tosser had destroyed my relationship.

I confronted Pickford, half expecting a grovelling apology and some measure of remorse. He knew full well that Zoe was engaged to another man, but that didn't stop him from luring her back to his place. However, after I pointed out the error of his ways, Pickford was anything but remorseful. We had a brief exchange of words, and then I lamped him. He went down and stayed down. Satisfied with my work, I walked away.

Our paths haven't crossed since that day.

"You," he sneers. "The fucking coward who threw a lucky punch and then ran away."

I stand upright, my right hand gripping the cue so tightly that my knuckles are paper white.

"Run away?" I growl back. "You were lying on the floor and crying like a pussy. How would you know what I did?"

Pickford steps around the table. He's two or three inches shorter than me and stocky. What Zoe ever saw in him will remain a mystery that not even she can explain.

"Wanna try it again, big man?" Pickford spits. "See if you're so lucky a second time."

I'm not stupid enough to make the same move I made the last time we met, knowing that's exactly what he expects. Despite his goading, I respond with the driest of smiles.

"I'm in the middle of a game of pool. You'll have to wait."

"See," he spits. "Coward."

If I genuinely thought that punching Wayne Pickford would alleviate the pain of Zoe's betrayal, I'd have already thrown a right hook. I know from experience that it makes no difference. I felt a second or two of satisfaction when I decked Pickford back in the spring, but afterwards, I felt just as wretched as I did when I first spotted him across the street.

"Just sit down and wait your turn, dickhead," I retort.

To underline my point, I step back to the pool table and line up the shot I was about to take before Pickford wandered in. My eyes flick from the cue ball to Pickford and back again as I cock my right arm to take the shot. Just as it seems I've called his bluff, he suddenly lurches forward, swinging an arm wildly towards my now exposed flank. Too late, I try to move out of the way of his fist, but it glances my ribcage with enough force to undermine my balance. My legs don't move quickly enough and before I know it, I'm falling backwards. Inevitably, I land flat on my arse, the cue clattering against a chair next to me.

With my pride suffering more than my ribs, I scramble backwards as Pickford looms over me, seemingly keen to continue his assault. I'm in serious trouble if he chooses to lay the boot in.

"Oi!"

I look up just as Pickford glances towards whoever called out. We both spot my boss approaching the scene. Lee stops no less than two feet away from Wayne Pickford, so they're almost eyeball to eyeball.

"I'd fuck off if I were you, lad," Lee says in a level voice.

"Mind your own business, old man. This is between me and him."

"Old man? That's a bit ageist, don't you think?"

"I won't warn you again," Pickford snarls, taking a step forward in an attempt to intimidate Lee. "Back the fuck away."

Rather than comply, Lee tilts his head back and looks up at the ceiling. Instinctively, Pickford mirrors my boss's action, presumably to see what the older man is looking at. In less time than it takes for me to draw a breath, Lee bends his knees slightly, arches his back, and then violently thrusts his head forward.

The Yorkshireman's forehead strikes Pickford's nose with such force it bursts like a dropped haggis landing on a stone floor. Blood and mucus spray out in all directions before Wayne Pickford collapses to his knees, clamping both hands to his face.

It takes a moment for the shock to pass and for my brain to issue instructions. I scramble up, my eyes still fixed on Pickford as his muffled wails fills the room.

"Shit," I gasp, lost for any other meaningful reaction.

Pickford's mate then steps forward. "What the fuck, man?" he yells at Lee. "You've busted his nose."

"Aye. You want a go, too?"

Based on his body language alone, I suspect he doesn't.

"I'm bored of playing pool," Lee then casually remarks, addressing me and a clearly stunned Gavin. "Fancy a game of darts in The Fox & Hounds?"

Chapter 27

Gavin sits back in his chair and repeats the question. "Who was he?"

In the cold light of a Saturday morning, I'm not in the right head space to provide chapter and verse on the identity of Wayne Pickford.

"Just some bloke I had beef with."

"He said you punched him. Why?"

"Gav, it's too early, and I've only had one cup of coffee. Can we drop it?"

"You know Lee will ask the exact same question on Monday morning, don't you?"

"Why does Lee care?"

"Er, in case the guy grasses him up to the police."

"He won't," I say dismissively, turning my attention to the diary. "He doesn't even know who Lee is."

"But he knows who you are, and that's my point."

"He doesn't know my surname. And even if he did and told the police, I wouldn't give them Lee's name. Not least because I don't have a death wish."

"I should have warned you," Gavin chuckles. "Lee can be a bit of a nutter when he gets riled up."

"A nutter in every sense of the word. He's mental."

"True, but if Lee hadn't dealt with that bloke, he'd have kicked the shit out of you."

"No, he wouldn't," I respond defensively. "I was about to get up when Lee intervened."

"Yeah, right."

"I was."

Gavin replies with a wry smile before getting to his feet.

"Anyway," he sighs. "Suppose I'd better be off."

"I'll see you later."

"I'll probably stop off at McDonald's on the way back. Fancy a bacon and egg McMuffin?"

"Yeah, go on. Ta."

My colleague snatches up his car keys and leaves the office. Despite calling the homeowners earlier, he couldn't get them to shift the ten o'clock valuation to a later time. He also claims he's not suffering a hangover.

We promptly left The Victoria Club after the incident with Wayne Pickford. Seemingly untroubled by his assault, Lee wanted to continue the evening at The Fox and Hounds, but I made an excuse about a family party I had to attend. Lee then press-ganged Gavin into going with him, and by all accounts, Gavin managed to get away just after nine. He never clarified if he meant nine o'clock or nine pints.

On the drive back to the flat, I attempted to unravel how I felt about the previous hour's events. Much like the minutes after I punched Wayne Pickford outside Blockbuster, the satisfaction of seeing him suffer proved short-lived. I concluded that even if I watched him being slowly fed into an industrial mincer, it wouldn't make me feel any better. His suffering, warranted or otherwise, isn't the antidote to mine.

Seeing him again, though, did summon up the feelings I thought I might have finally buried. It's akin to the time I had toothache as a kid, and I refused to tell Mum because I knew she'd drag me to the dental surgery. After a week of suffering in silence, the agony finally eased, and I congratulated myself on avoiding a trip to see our sadistic dentist, Dr Pringle. Three or four days passed, as did any residue pain, and I'd all but forgotten about the toothache until I tucked into a Marathon on the way home from school. Halfway through it, I bit down on a peanut and could have cried; it hurt so much. Twenty-four hours later, I was in the waiting room at the dentist, having confessed to Mum that I'd been suffering for a while. Her sympathy was in short supply.

My current pain, much like that I suffered as a kid, will likely continue to ebb and flow, but there's no simple fix, no twenty-minute filling.

The phone rings, and I take a call about a property that Gavin sold three days ago. The caller isn't interested in being added to the mailing list and promptly hangs up. While I've got the phone receiver in my hand and the office to myself, I dial a number I should probably have called a few days ago.

Robbie picks up on the third ring.

"I wasn't sure you'd be up this early," I say as a greeting.

"Early?" my brother snorts. "If Hugo doesn't get his walk by eight, he sulks all day."

"You spoil that dog."

"No, Stephen spoils him. Anyway, what's up?"

"Nothing."

"So, why are you calling?"

"Does something have to be wrong for me to check in on my kid brother?"

"Usually, yes."

"Fair point," I snigger. "But genuinely, I'm just calling to see if things are okay after ... you know."

"After the funeral?"

"Yep, that. How's Stephen?"

"Still a bit subdued, but he's alright, considering what he's been through over the last year."

"And you?"

"I'm doing okay. We're heading into town a bit later to book a holiday. I thought we could both do with some time away."

"Does that mean you need a dog sitter?"

"A friend of Stephen's has offered to take Hugo for a week, but that doesn't mean you're not welcome to come down and stay for a while if you need a break from the norm."

"It's a bit tricky with the new job as I work most Saturdays, but I will come down soon."

Robbie is momentarily distracted as he shouts an order at — presumably Hugo — to stop chewing the rug.

"Bloody dog," he groans, returning to the conversation. "I love him to bits, but I could kill him sometimes."

"I wonder how many times Mum and Dad have said that about you or me."

"You, a lot. Me, not so much."

"I probably deserved it."

"You *definitely* deserved it," Robbie laughs. "And I'd bet there were a fair few girls who would have happily killed you back in the day, too."

"Harsh."

"You were a shit, Danny."

"I was young and stupid. And I'm sure those girls would be delighted to know how my antics have come back to bite me on the arse."

"Are you talking about karma or Zoe?"

"Both."

"Karma is indeed a bitch, but what's the score with Zoe? Any developments."

"Yes and no," I sigh. "She's coming over tomorrow afternoon."

"Seeking forgiveness?"

"Something like that. She wants to move back in, put her mistake behind us and move on."

"And I take it from your tone that you're ..."

"Honestly, Rob, I don't know what to do."

"Ah, so there is a motive for the call. You want your little brother's advice."

"No," I huff.

"Sure?"

I don't have anyone else to ask, and whether it was a subconscious motive for calling or not, there is a good reason to seek Robbie's advice.

"What would you do if Stephen cheated on you? Would you take him back?"

"Depends on what you mean by cheating. A one-night stand is very different from an affair."

"Is it? Both involve lies and deception."

"Yeah, but if we're talking about what Zoe did, she was drunk, and it was a one-off. An affair involves lying consistently over a prolonged period — it's cold, calculated and, in my book, unforgivable."

"So you're saying you'd never forgive Stephen if he had an affair, but you'd give him a second chance if he had a one-night stand?"

"More or less, although I'd cut his balls off either way."

"A strong incentive never to cheat."

"I can think of a stronger one," Robbie responds. "Love."

"Zoe claims she still loves me."

"I'm sure she does, and she probably loved you all the while she was fondling another man's tackle, but it didn't stop her, did it?"

"Eh? You're now contradicting yourself. You said you'd forgive Stephen for a one-night stand."

"We're not talking about Stephen, are we? I'd forgive Stephen because we've been through so much together, and I can't imagine my life without him, no matter what mistakes he might make."

"Right. I get you, I think."

"Do you?"

"Um …"

"Listen, Dan, I know you don't want to hear this because it's … well, we don't do this kind of chat, but just ask yourself a simple question. When Zoe cheated on you, did it take more than she ever gave you? If the answer is no, she's still in credit, and it's worth trying again. If the answer is yes, maybe it's time to move on."

I'm not sure when it happened, but somehow, my kid brother is now a half-sensible grown-up. I wouldn't go as far as saying wise because I've seen what he wears on a night out.

"Thanks, bruv. I hear you."

"You'll let me know what happens?"

"Sure."

"And you'll try and get down here soon? It'd be great to have a night out."

"Yeah, I will. Promise."

After a quick chat about Mum and Dad and a request to pass my regards on to Stephen, I end the call. I can't deny that listening to a voice that doesn't reside in my head made a change, as did hearing a different perspective, but I don't know if I have the answer to Robbie's question. Has Zoe taken more from me than she ever gave?

Before I get the chance to ponder that question, the door opens, and a thirty-something couple wander in.

"Can we go on your mailing list, please?" the guy asks.

"Sure. Grab a pew."

Twenty minutes later, I've booked Mr and Mrs Morgan a viewing at the freshly cleared former home of Mr and Mrs Ambrose. It's funny, but they didn't think they could afford a house in Heron Close, and they were visibly delighted when I showed them the draft sales particulars. One family's loss is another's gain.

As the Morgans depart, Gavin returns, clutching a brown McDonald's bag in his hand.

"Hungry?" he asks, shaking the bag.

"I was."

"I'll eat yours if you're not. I reckon I can manage three bacon and egg McMuffins."

"I didn't say I wouldn't eat it."

I trail Gavin to the back room, where he hands me a greasy bun-shaped package.

"Looking forward to tonight?" he asks while unwrapping the first of his McMuffins. "I am."

"You weren't that keen on Donna two days ago? What's changed?"

"Beggars and choosers," he chuckles. "Besides, I'm sick of sitting at home with my folks on a Saturday evening. You've no idea how depressing it is."

"I might have a vague idea."

"No, mate, you don't," he replies, holding his late breakfast inches from his mouth. "Saturday night TV starts with Noel Edmonds, then it's Paul Daniels followed by Russ Abbot. By nine o'clock, I'm ready to gouge my own eyes out."

"Okay, you win — that's a grim lineup."

"And that's a good night. I once sat through an entire episode of *All Creatures Great and Small* and, let me ask you, have you ever experienced boredom so extreme that it physically hurts?"

"I think so," I reply after a moment's thought. "I once endured a double period of geography where the teacher droned on about different types of lakes."

"God, I think I suffered the same lesson."

"Well, I guess if we struggle for conversation later, we can woo the girls with our knowledge of oxbow lakes."

"They'll be putty in our hands," Gavin laughs before biting into his McMuffin.

"I hope so, Gav, because I've only got until next Sunday to tempt Kim away from her other half."

"Why the deadline?"

"Her boyfriend is due to propose, apparently."

"Seriously?"

"Yep."

"How do you know?"

"The woman who asked me to intervene told me."

"Yeah, but how does she know this dude is going to propose to Kim?"

"Maybe he asked her permission," I reply with a slight shrug. "I didn't get around to asking."

"All sounds a bit dodgy to me, mate. What's in it for you, besides a possible bout of naked wrestling with Kim?"

"That's not an option. It was made clear that I can go so far, but under no circumstances am I allowed to sleep with Kim."

Gavin chews on his McMuffin for a long moment before responding.

"So, you're being asked to play a game with no prize if you win? Why the fuck would you even bother?"

It's a legitimate question, but I can't tell Gavin the truth. I have a signed contract confirming the deeds of 1 Echo Lane will be mine once I've completed Mrs Weller's project, but I'm still mildly cynical myself. I can only guess what my colleague's reaction might be. There is, however, a less outlandish explanation and one that's a lot closer to the truth.

"Between you and me, Gav, there's a few quid in it *if* I pull it off."

"You're being paid to split Kim and her bloke up?"

"When you say it like that, it sounds bad."

"I'm not judging, Danny. If it means an evening out on the town, I couldn't care less."

"Oh, okay. To be honest, I'm not confident I'll pull it off, anyway, so it's probably academic."

"I don't know. The way Kim looked at you on Thursday evening, I reckon you're in with a shot."

"You think?"

"Definitely. Believe it or not, a girl used to look at me like that once."

"What happened? Did you date?"

"Better than that — I married her."

"But now you're divorced."

"That is true, and towards the end, she couldn't bear looking at me at all. Still, she did look at me fondly once, and that's better than not at all, eh?"

"I guess so."

I take a bite of my McMuffin and then ask an obvious question.

"Your divorce — was it amicable?"

"For her, yeah. I didn't want to divorce at all, but it wasn't up for negotiation."

"No?"

"Paula just came out with it one day while we were on the way to the garden centre — she didn't love me any more. Simple as that, really."

"You didn't ask why?"

"Of course, but that's a question I wish I could undo because I wasn't ready for the answer."

"Why? What was the answer?"

"She said she no longer found me attractive to the point that the mere thought of us having sex again made her feel physically sick."

"Ouch. Sorry."

"It's not what I wanted, but it's what I've got, and I'm trying to make the most of it."

I can't say I know Gavin well, but if I had to use just one word to describe him, it would be positive. Standing here now, I wonder how much of his banter and bravado is a façade because his back story sounds anything but positive. Indeed, it sounds like he's still hurting after the collapse of his marriage. However, we're not best friends, and I don't know him nearly well enough to probe.

Maybe there's more at stake this evening than just Mrs Weller's request. Maybe it's also an opportunity to help Gavin rekindle his mojo and rebuild his self-esteem.

As if one challenge wasn't enough.

Chapter 28

Am I going on a date?

If I had a dictionary, I might be inclined to look up the meaning, but I reckon it says something along the lines of a date being a social or romantic meeting.

I'm meeting Kim in a bar, and that's social, but there are two factors that muddy the waters. Firstly, there will be four of us there tonight. Indeed, Kim used the word 'foursome'. I suppose it could be a double date, but that leads me to the second and most pertinent factor, although it's more a question I can't answer. Why did she invite us out at all?

As I make my way along the street towards The Frog & Anchor public house, where I'm due to meet Gavin, I turn the question of Kim's motive over for the umpteenth time since it first crossed my mind in the shower earlier.

It's Saturday evening, traditionally the one evening of the week a young couple might have plans together. Could it be that Kim's other half has plans of his own like a stag do or a poker night with his mates, and Kim was heading to Martinelli's this evening anyway? It makes sense. Kind of.

Overthinking is a curse and, in this instance, unhelpful. I need to be on my A-game, and if I'm to make headway with Kim, she'll need to spend the evening with the confident, witty, and charming version of Danny Monk. It's been a long time since he's been out, never mind on a date that might not even be a date, so I hope he's not too ring-rusty.

I push open the door to The Frog & Anchor's public bar and stride in.

After a quick scan of the room I spot Gavin at the bar. He's in the process of ordering a drink, which gives me just enough time to appraise his choice of attire. There's no cowboy boots or plaid shirt with metal-tipped collars, but his outfit is severely lacking in the style stakes: beige chinos with clumpy-soled loafers and a dark-blue Harrington jacket that looks at least one size too big.

He turns and notices me moving slowly in his direction.

"Were you waiting outside for me to order?" he says with a grin. "Pint?"

"Please."

Beneath his Harrington jacket, he's wearing a sweater with horizontal stripes in navy and off-white. Swap the jacket for a blazer and he'd have the full Rick Astley ensemble — if Rick Astley shopped at C&A.

"What do you think of my cologne?" Gavin then asks, presenting me with his neck.

I cautiously oblige with a quick sniff.

"Well?" he then prompts.

"It's nice," I reply, hoping my expression doesn't betray the truth. "What is it?"

"It's called *Obsessive*."

"That name sounds familiar. Calvin Klein?"

"Avon."

"Oh."

He pays for our beers while I check the time.

"We'll have to make do with just the one in here," I say as Gavin passes me a pint. "It's just gone half-past."

"I know. You were supposed to be here half an hour ago."

"Was I? I thought we said half six."

"Never mind, you're here now," he says. "But you had me worried."

"Worried how?"

"I thought you had changed your mind about taking me with you."

"That'd be a shitty thing to do, dropping you at the last minute. Why would I?"

"Um, forget it," he replies, avoiding eye contact. "Anyway, here's to a successful evening."

Gavin raises his glass, and I mirror his action. "Here's hoping. Cheers."

In the office, my colleague has always struck me as confident but here, he seems on edge.

"Everything alright, mate?" I ask. "You seem a bit nervy."

"I'll be fine once I've had a beer or two. I've never been much good when it comes to chatting to women."

"I know this sounds like a cliché, but just be yourself."

"That's what my dad said."

"It's good advice."

He smiles up at me, and for a minute, I'm transported back in time to my teenage bedroom. I remember Robbie asking my advice just before he set out on his first date. I think he was about fourteen, and, thinking back, perhaps he was nervous because he was about to go on a date with a girl. Suffice it to say the evening didn't go to plan, and although I've never asked him, it was probably an early step in Robbie accepting his sexuality.

Gavin's nervousness is born of a different concern, but it's just as evident.

"In the history of the phrase, no one has ever relaxed after being told to just relax, so I won't say it."

"Good. It doesn't work."

"But think of this another way. We're just two mates, going out for a few beers and to enjoy the evening — that's the top and bottom of it. The fact that we'll have female company for part of the evening is only a footnote. Okay?"

"Gotcha."

"And if that fails to calm your nerves," I say with a nod to my glass. "There's always alcohol."

"Amen to that."

Gavin then deftly moves the conversation to safer ground by asking what I think about my new career, and the whole estate agency game.

"Is it what you expected?" he adds as a supplementary question.

"Yes ... and no."

"But mainly no, right?"

"What makes you say that?"

"Because I remember what it was like when I first started. I absolutely loathed the first few months. And I thought about jacking it in on a daily basis."

"What stopped you?"

"My dad had a chat with me, and relayed a few tales from his time as an apprentice plumber. He said every job is the same — you start at the bottom and get given all the crap tasks because that's all you're capable of doing. But, if you keep your head down, work hard, and stick to it, soon enough you're giving the crap tasks to someone else because you've got something worthwhile to do."

"Your dad isn't wrong but at my age I wasn't anticipating starting again at the bottom."

"You won't be at the bottom long. I'll bet you a barrel of beer that you're promoted by the New Year."

"You think?"

"Yeah, I do."

"Shame it's up to Lee and not you, then."

"Lee likes you."

"Seriously?" I snort. "If you're right, I'd hate to think how he treats staff he doesn't like."

"Trust me, I've seen it first hand and he's an absolute arsehole, but that day when you pulled him up about ... about that word he used ..."

"Poof."

"Yeah, that. He didn't go off on one — he backed down. Believe it or not, that's his way of showing respect."

"Hmm, okay."

"And don't forget last night and what he did in The Vic. He could have walked away but he fronted up to that bloke."

"True, but he didn't have to headbutt him."

"And that bloke didn't have to stick you with a cheap shot while you were at the pool table. In my book, he got what he deserved. I know it doesn't seem like it, but Lee values loyalty, and he was just sticking up for one of his own."

It's an interesting take, and I can't deny I'm secretly pleased that Gavin thinks that Wayne Pickford got what he deserved. Lee's loyalty is another matter, though, and my views on loyalty have shifted in recent months.

"Maybe you're right," I say, purely to draw a line under the topic. "For now, let's just focus on having a drama-free evening."

"Yeah, cool."

We both take a moment to gulp back lager.

"Can I ask you a question?" Gavin then says. "About this arrangement of yours."

"What arrangement?"

"Kim."

"Oh, that. It's more of a task, but yeah. Fire away."

"Exactly what are you planning to do? I mean, you want to break up her relationship, but how?"

"That's a really good question but I don't have a good answer. To be frank, Gav, I'm making this up as I go along."

"You think she might get off with you and then ditch her boyfriend?"

"That's one possibility, I suppose. The woman who dragged me into this obviously thinks that'll work."

"What about you, though?"

"What about me?"

Gavin takes another quick gulp from his glass.

"Let's say you get off with Kim and she does ditch her boyfriend. Then what?"

"Then it's job done."

"That's it? You never see her again?"

"Um, I don't know. I genuinely haven't thought that far ahead."

"Would you want to date her? Actually, scrub that question — what man in his right mind wouldn't want to date a woman that hot?"

"Granted, she's attractive, but I'm not in the market for a new relationship."

"Because the last one ended badly, right?"

"Yeah."

"Maybe a new relationship is *exactly* what you need. It's what I need."

"Not enjoying single life, then?"

"Sometimes I do, but I miss having someone to do stuff with. You know, just silly things like going to the cinema or a bite to eat at the Wimpy."

"Maybe tonight is the night your luck changes and you find Miss Right."

"Frankly, mate, I'll take Miss Anyone. I'm not a fussy man."

"Fair enough," I snigger. "And on that note, let's finish these and get going, shall we?"

We empty our glasses, return them to the bar, and head for the door.

The main reason we chose to meet in The Frog & Anchor is the proximity to Martinelli's Bar, as it's only a minute's walk. The secondary reason is because I'm not a huge fan of Martinelli's Bar so the less time we spend there, the better.

"Do you remember the Railway Tavern?" Gavin asks, referring to the traditional pub that once occupied the building before it became Martinelli's Bar a few years back.

"Yep. I took my kid brother there for his first pint."

"I don't understand why they gutted the place and turned it into a bar. It was fine as a pub."

"It's the nineties, Gav. Wine bars and bistros are all the rage, so I understand."

"I've never been a fan of wine bars."

"Why not?"

"Don't like wine."

"As good a reason as any."

"And I don't much like the kind of people who drink in wine bars."

"Really? I always assumed that the average estate agent would feel right at home in a wine bar."

"I'm sure some do, like our area manager, Andy. Have you met him yet?"

"I've not had the pleasure."

"You know there's a lot of negative stereotypes about estate agents, right? Well, Andy Shaw is the living embodiment of all those negative stereotypes. I've never met a bloke so full of himself."

"Does he get on with Lee?"

"Lee has to keep in Andy's good books but he thinks he's a prick. I don't agree with Lee on a lot, but we're in total agreement when it comes to our area manager."

"Well, now you've painted him in such a positive light, I can't wait to meet the guy."

We reach Martinelli's and I enter first, holding the door open for my reluctant colleague. Within a second of entering, and despite it not being overly busy, it's easy to understand why Gavin isn't a regular. It's not so much the sterile décor, the multitude of mirrored pillars, or even the coldness of the blue neon sign that dominates the left-hand wall. It's the people — all under thirty, all decked out in the latest fashions, and all preened to perfection.

I make a beeline for the far right-hand corner of the room, away from the neon haze and close to the end of the U-shaped bar. Gavin draws up beside me as I wait to be served.

"At least the music isn't blaring," I remark, scraping the barrel of positives. "The last time I was here, it was deafening."

"Give it time."

A young barman steps over and asks what we're having.

"Two pints of lager, please."

"We don't serve pints. Bottles only."

"Since when?"

"Since management decided."

"Fine. Two bottles of lager."

"Castlemaine, Becks, or Grolsch?"

"Grolsch, I guess."

Within seconds, two dark green bottles appear on the bar in front of us. The barman removes the caps, which are fastened in place by some over-engineered metal clip.

"That'll be £5.80, please."

I stare back at the barman, open-mouthed. "£5.80 for two bottles of beer? Are you sure?"

"That's what the till says."

I extract a tenner from my wallet and begrudgingly hand it over. My change is returned just as begrudgingly.

"Here," I say to Gavin as I pass him one of the bottles. "Savour it, as I won't be revisiting the bar with any frequency this evening — not at £2.90 a bottle."

"Outrageous," he snorts. "And we don't even get a bloody glass."

We stand and sip our overpriced beer for a few minutes, mindlessly commenting on how much we both preferred the Railway Tavern, when Gavin announces he needs the loo.

"If I'm not back in ten minutes," he says. "It's because I'm stuck behind a queue of blokes admiring themselves in the mirror."

"It's not as though there aren't enough mirrors in here, but I take your point. Good luck."

Gavin hurries off to the loo, keeping his head down all the way. I then happen to glance at my watch while sipping from the bottle of Grolsch. It's now a few minutes after seven. Even in the ten short minutes we've been here, the number of patrons has probably increased by twenty per cent. It's not exactly packed, but there are no longer any free tables and at least half the floor space around the bar is now occupied.

Suddenly, just beyond the left shoulder of a guy waiting to be served, I see a face I recognise. She then turns her head to the right, and a smile breaks across her face as she changes direction and heads towards me.

"Hey," Kim says as she steps past the last human obstacle. "Sorry, we're a bit late."

"No worries."

Unsure how to greet a woman I don't know that well, I settle on a smile. Donna isn't so reserved and greets me with a peck on the cheek. As she steps back, Kim turns ninety degrees and places her hand on the arm of some dude standing next to her.

"Danny, this is Neil," she says. "My boyfriend."

Chapter 29

If the man standing opposite me had a miniature tit where his nose should be, I don't think I could look any more surprised. As it is, he doesn't have a tit in the centre of his face or any other unusual features. With slicked-back fair hair, Neil Harrison is of average build and a shade under six feet tall.

That is all academic, though. What isn't academic is his presence. Kim never mentioned bringing her bloody boyfriend when she suggested a foursome.

Oh shit!

The very second I finally shake Neil Harrison's hand, the foursome becomes a fivesome as Gavin returns from the toilet. He immediately fixes Harrison with a confused frown, and that's the exact same expression Kim adopts as she glares at Gavin.

Foursome.
Foursome.
FOURSOME.
Fuck!

Much, much too late, I realise what Kim had in mind when she suggested the four of us meet tonight. The invite only extended to me to join her, Donna, and Neil fucking Harrison.

"I'll get the drinks in," Harrison says. "You boys alright for beers?"

His question quickly proves an irrelevance as he makes his way towards the bar without waiting for us to answer.

"What an unexpected surprise," Kim says through gritted teeth. "Nice to see you again, Gary."

"Gavin," he corrects.

"Sorry. Gavin."

"Um, I think there's been a slight breakdown in communication," I interject. "When you suggested a foursome, Kim, I thought ..."

"You thought what?"

"Well, um ... me, you, Donna, and Gavin."

"Why would I suggest that? You know I have a boyfriend."

"But I don't," Donna adds, fluttering her false eyelashes in my direction.

I feel like Wile E Coyote from the kids' cartoon at the exact moment he steps into his own trap rather than the Road Runner. Laid out, bare, it all seems so obvious now. What is less than obvious is how I deal with the ramifications.

"My apologies," I say with the feeblest of laughs. "Seems we've got our wires crossed."

"It's okay," Kim replies in a slightly less confrontational tone. "I'm sure Gary understands the situation, don't you, Gary?"

"Gavin."

"Whatever."

"Yeah, I understand," Gavin says flatly. "Four's company, five's a crowd."

"Perhaps we'll catch up with you another evening."

My colleague nods solemnly before putting the bottle of Grolsch to his lips, presumably to empty it before departing.

This isn't right.

"Gavin is here with me," I say. "He's not going anywhere."

"But Gavin wasn't invited," Kim protests.

"I don't care. If he's not welcome, we'll leave you to it and find a pub where we are."

Out of the corner of my eye, I catch Donna making a face at Kim. She could be pleading with her friend, or she could be suffering a stroke. Bearing in mind her age, a stroke seems unlikely.

"Fine," Kim then says with a sigh. "He can stay."

"Gee! Thanks, Miss," Gavin responds sarcastically. "I'm humbled, but I'm not staying where I'm not wanted."

He then thumps his empty beer bottle on the bar, turns, and strides away.

The word disaster barely covers how badly this evening is panning out. I look across at Kim, but she just drops her gaze to the floor, possibly in shame. With a shake of my head, I place my bottle on the bar next to Gavin's and then follow in his footsteps.

Out on the pavement, I catch sight of my colleague some fifty yards away, just outside the kebab shop.

"Gav, wait up," I call out.

He stops, turns around, and waits while I jog up to him.

"Are you alright?" I ask.

"I'm fine," he says flatly.

"Screw them," I huff, nodding back towards Martinelli's. "Fancy another pint in The Frog & Anchor?"

"I'm not in the mood," he replies after a moment's thought.

"I'm sorry. Kim was bang out of order."

"You don't have to apologise, but yeah, she was."

"I don't know why she was so rude. She wasn't like that on Thursday."

"Honestly, Danny, it doesn't matter. It's not the first time a woman has talked to me like I'm nothing, and I daresay it won't be the last."

"That doesn't make it right."

"Nope, but it doesn't change anything either."

I take a step closer and gesture in the direction of the pub. "Come on, let's go get a pint."

"I appreciate the offer, but I'd rather just go home."

"Mate, don't let Kim get under your skin."

Gavin digs his hands into his jacket pockets and finds a tepid smile. "It's nothing to do with Kim. I just fancy watching *All Creatures Great and Small*."

"Yeah, right," I snort.

"I do, and besides, you still have a task to complete, don't you?"

"Forget that. I can hardly make a play for Kim with her bloody boyfriend there, can I?"

"Are you likely to get another chance?"

"I don't know, but after witnessing her shitty attitude, I'm not sure I care."

"You cared enough to try on Thursday and again tonight, so it must be worth the effort."

"Kind of, I guess, but—"

"Then get back in there and do what you can. I don't want you abandoning your evening on my account."

Caught between abandoning my colleague or the mission, I don't know what to do other than to look to the sky and puff a deep breath.

"I'll do a deal with you," Gavin then says. "I'm more than happy to abort this evening and head home on the proviso you come along with me to an event at the end of the month."

"Er, okay. What event?"

"A singles night at Jaxx Nightclub. I saw it advertised in the local paper, but the thought of going alone doesn't much appeal."

It doesn't hold much appeal for me either, alone or otherwise, but if it adds a positive sheen to an otherwise crappy evening for Gavin, it's a small price to pay.

"Alright," I say, holding out my hand. "Deal."

We shake hands, and Gavin then orders me to get my arse back to the bar.

"You sure you're alright with this?" I double-check.

"One hundred per cent," he replies with a grin. "Now, piss off."

He turns and continues on his way without so much as a glance back. I, however, remain planted on the pavement. Gavin has made a decision, and now it's my turn. The prospect of rejoining Kim is even less appealing than a singles night at Jaxx, and my gut is screaming at me to follow my colleague's lead and abort the evening.

My head then reminds me why, despite sound reasons not to, it has to overrule my gut: my financial situation. Having paid off the mortgage arrears, I've managed to release the immediate pressure. However, the challenge of meeting next month's mortgage payment and every payment thereafter remains. Notwithstanding the improbable lure of a free house, I need Mrs Weller's next expenses payment. And for that, I need to demonstrate that I made some effort to complete her task. I'm due to visit Echo Lane tomorrow with an update, and as I stand here now, I don't have anything positive to report.

Reluctantly, I turn and trudge back to Martinelli's Bar. It's difficult to imagine what I might achieve, but I need to achieve something — any crumb of positivity to keep Mrs Weller onside and the cash flowing.

As I zigzag back across the bar to where I left Kim and Donna, I belatedly consider how best to play the hand fate has dealt. Making any kind of move on Kim is no longer an option, presuming Neil Harrison is unlikely to approve, but perhaps it's an opportunity to pump Donna for information on the couple — see if there are any cracks in their relationship I might exploit between now and the looming deadline.

Judging by the look on both Kim and Donna's respective faces, they're surprised by my return. Neil Harrison appears wholly disinterested.

"Oh, you're back," Kim says.

"I am ... if the original offer still stands."

"It stands," Donna blurts.

"Great."

I quickly check that they all have full glasses. "I need a drink. Anyone want anything while I'm at the bar?"

As I predicted, both girls politely decline the offer but Harrison empties his wine glass and holds it towards me.

"I'll have another if you're buying," he says with a shit-eating grin. "Chardonnay — make it a large one, chap."

"Sure," I reply before taking the glass. "Once you say please."

"Please," he sneers before rolling his eyes.

I somehow manage to maintain my cool and step over to the bar. I've barely said a dozen words to Neil Harrison, but it's enough to forge an opinion — he's an arrogant twat.

Once the barman finally decides to serve me, I order another bottle of Grolsch and a regular glass of Chardonnay. I then return to the huddle and hand Harrison his drink.

"One Chardonnay," I say with a wide smile.

"That's not a large glass."

"My apologies. I could have sworn I asked the barman for a large one."

I didn't, and I'm not inclined to return to the bar.

"Cheers, everyone," I say, ignoring Harrison's complaint and raising my bottle.

Back in the game, I participate in a ten-minute small-talk session, primarily driven by Kim and Donna. The conversation then turns to careers as Donna asks a question about the property market. Gavin had warned me that if I ever tell anyone I'm an estate agent, they'll automatically seek my opinion on the state of the property market. It seems he wasn't wrong.

"It's great if you're a first-time buyer, but prices are tumbling, so it's hard for sellers."

"Sounds like you sold up at the right time, Neil," Kim says, looking up at her boyfriend.

"I sold up at the right time because I knew it was the right time," he replies smugly. "And I made a killing in the process."

"Local was it?" I ask, although I couldn't care less. "Your property?"

"No, in the City. I worked up there for eight years and bought an apartment in '84. Sold it in late '89 and damn near doubled my money."

I feel obliged to ask, although I've already got an inkling of his answer.

"What did you do in the City?"

"Stockbroker."

Of course, he was.

"And now?"

I'd love nothing more than to hear he's unemployed, but something tells me he isn't.

"I set up a telecoms business last year."

"Telecoms? Like phones?"

"Cellular phones," he replies, reaching for his hip. "Like this."

Harrison pulls a dark-grey block from a belt clip and holds it about twenty inches from my face. I've seen similar phones on the news and the odd TV show, but they're typically larger, bulkier.

"State of the art, this one," Harrison continues. "The Nokia Cityman 100."

The overall shape and the rubber aerial remind me of a walkie-talkie set Robbie unwrapped on his twelfth birthday. They looked the part, but their range was so poor that you couldn't use them anywhere further than the next room.

"How much would one of those set me back?" I ask.

"If you wanted to buy it outright, without a contract, I could get you one for close to a grand."

A grand? For a glorified walkie-talkie? Some people have more money than sense.

"Tempting, but I think I'll stick to the BT phone in my lounge."

"Trust me, Danny, you'll have one before long — everyone will."

"Yeah," I scoff. "Sure they will."

Kim, perhaps noticing that Harrison and I aren't exactly getting on like a house on fire, moves the conversation on.

"Anyone like a top-up?" she asks, holding up her empty glass.

"I'll have a Grolsch, please."

"Same again for me," Donna chirps.

Kim then grabs her boyfriend's hand and almost drags him towards the bar, leaving me with her friend. I suspect that was the reason she offered to buy the next round.

"So, Danny," Donna begins. "Have you been here before?"

"Once. Not my cup of tea, if I'm honest. You?"

"I've been here a few times but not for months. The last time was with my ex, back in February. We broke up shortly after, and I've been single since then."

"Oh, right."

"What about you? How long have you been single?"

The moment I realised what Kim had in mind for her proposed foursome, this conversation was inevitable. I need to keep Donna on side, but I don't want to give her the impression I'm offering anything more than friendship.

"Not long," I sigh. "Split up from my fiancée a few months back."

"Oh dear," Donna responds dolefully. "I'm so sorry to hear that. Was it amicable?"

"It wasn't amicable at the time, and it still isn't. We own a flat together, so that makes our situation ... messy."

Donna replies with a sympathetic pout but doesn't comment further. It's my cue to start probing her for information on the couple at the bar.

"How long have Kim and Neil been together?"

"About ten months."

"Next step, engagement and wedding bells, eh?"

"Probably," Donna replies, but not with any degree of enthusiasm.

"You don't fancy the idea of being Kim's chief bridesmaid?"

"Of course I do — she's my best friend."

"But?"

"Who said there's a but?"

"No one, but ... let me put it another way. Do you reckon Kim has found her Mr Right?"

"Why are you so interested? Do you fancy her?"

I've clearly pushed too hard too soon. I need to backtrack a little.

"I'm just making conversation, Donna. Don't get me wrong, Kim is an attractive woman, but she isn't my type."

"So, if Kim isn't your type, what kind of woman is?"

"I'm open-minded," I reply with a semi-smile, hoping it'll lower Donna's barriers. "And, for the record, I was only asking about Kim and Neil because Gavin fancies her."

It's not an ideal tactic, but as Gavin is unlikely to meet Kim and Donna again, I'm sure he won't mind being my sacrificial lamb.

"Does he?" Donna responds, her left eyebrow arched.

"He's nothing if not ambitious, Gavin," I chuckle.

"I hate to be the bearer of bad news, but I don't think he's in with a chance. Kim is smitten with Neil."

It's only slight, but Donna's tone definitely had an intonation. Disappointment, maybe? It's time to take a chance.

"I don't know the guy, obviously, but I wouldn't have pegged him as Kim's type. He doesn't strike me as a country music fan, for starters."

"He definitely isn't, but they say that opposites attract."

"True, so would you say that Neil is your type?"

"Absolutely not," she spits. "I'd never date a man like him."

"Like him?"

There's a slight moment of hesitancy before Donna responds to my question.

"I can trust you, right? You won't repeat any of this to Kim."

"Mum's the word. Promise."

She glances across at the bar and then steps closer to me.

"Did you ever see the film *9½ Weeks* with Kim Basinger and Mickey Rourke?"

"Yeah, I watched it on video a couple of years back. Not my thing."

"Nor mine, but you know how Mickey Rourke's character was like ... controlling and manipulative? That's what Neil is like."

"Didn't they do all kinds of mad sex shit?"

"I'm not talking about Kim and Neil's sex life as such. It's more the way she is when he's around. She's like a different person."

Now Donna has mentioned it, Kim's demeanour has definitely switched this evening, and the way she spoke to Gavin seemed at odds with the woman we spent part of Thursday evening with. It'd certainly explain why Mrs Weller is so keen to undermine Kim's relationship with Harrison.

Before I can press Donna for more intel, Kim and Harrison return. As little as I want to be here, I'm now intrigued enough to hang around a while longer.

The drinks continue to flow for the next ninety minutes, but not necessarily the conversation. The foursome increasingly becomes two twosomes as Donna drags me to the bar when it's her round and sticks to me like a limpet when it's mine. The same could be said for Kim and Harrison, although there is a moment when I notice him chatting to some guy he bumped into on the way to the toilet. It wasn't the conversation that caught my attention; more the way Harrison continually glanced past the other guy's shoulder towards a gaggle of girls who barely looked old enough to buy a drink. Kim happened to mention it's her boyfriend's thirty-second birthday next month, which made his leering close to noncey.

My opinion of Harrison was already low, but seeing him eye-up those girls pushed it to the floor.

As nine o'clock comes and goes, I begin drawing up my excuses to leave. I've seen enough of Kim's relationship with Harrison to forge a solid opinion, and with Donna sinking her seventh glass of wine, she's now less of a reliable source of information and more of a drunken nuisance.

She catches me checking the time.

"The night is still young," she slurs.

"Shame I'm not."

"Don't be stu … stupid. You're only … what … how old are you?"

"Too old for this shit," I mutter under my breath.

"Pardon?"

"I said, twenty-eight."

"Exactly!" Donna booms theatrically before almost losing her balance.

Another reason I'm keen to leave is because the music is now so loud, conversation is almost impossible. As one track ends, it strikes me as the perfect opportunity to tell Donna I'm leaving. Alas, the lull is too short, and before I've had a chance to say a word, the opening beats to *Groove is in The Heart* by Deee-Lite fill the room.

"I bloody love this song," Donna screams in my ear.

Whilst Donna is patently pissed, I'm more than a bit tipsy myself, which is probably why I'm so slow to react when she grabs my hand and tugs me towards a group of revellers dancing in the packed floorspace midway between the bar and the exit. However, my legs don't quite coordinate, and I stumble along behind, slightly off balance. Then, when Donna suddenly stops, I almost crash into her.

Our bodies press together momentarily, and before I can apologise for almost knocking her over, Donna clamps my face in her hands. Paralysed by confusion, not to mention seven bottles of Grolsch, I barely move a muscle as a pair of Chardonnay-flavoured lips make contact with mine.

I've kissed a few women in my time, but in every instance, it was because I wanted to. Here, now, I don't want Donna's lips on mine, and I definitely don't want her eel-like tongue making further progress.

The second the shock subsides, I pull back. I then have to blink twice because there are now two female faces in close proximity, both looking directly at me. The first and nearest is Donna's, and she seems confused. The second, and the one I'm even less pleased to see, is staring daggers at me, eyes wide and mouth agape.

"Shit," I gulp. "It's ... this is not what it looks like."

Zoe's best friend, Claire, doesn't flinch, but her expression morphs into one of utter disdain. She then slowly shakes her head.

"You're an arsehole, Danny!"

The perfect end to the perfect evening.

Chapter 30

I'm never drinking Grolsch again. The ratio of unit consumption to next-day headache is completely out of kilter, and two hours after getting up, I'm still suffering.

The dull headache is not the only cause.

Five or six years ago, a Government minister by the name of Michael something-or-other found himself in a bit of a pickle. He was having an affair with his secretary, and on one quiet afternoon in his office, the honourable member was on his knees, head buried between his secretary's thighs, slurping away like a bear at a honey pot. That was the moment when the office door swung open, and a member of the shadow cabinet barged into Michael's office, furious about some last-minute amendment to a bill.

According to the national newspaper that scooped the exclusive story, the shocked minister turned away from his secretary's crotch and spluttered the immortal words, "This is not what it looks like."

The only reason I remember the story is because after I read it, I spent the rest of the day trying to come up with an alternative explanation to what Michael denied he was doing. An excessively thorough search for a lost contact lens? A spot of amateur gynaecology?

Nothing I came up with seemed plausible, and the newspaper article didn't state what excuse the Government minister offered — probably because the scene was *exactly* what it looked like.

I, on the other hand, uttered that line because it happened to be true — Donna's spontaneous attempt to snog my face off was exactly that, and it most certainly wasn't consensual. I did try explaining that to Claire, quite vociferously, but she wasn't having it. In the end, her meat-head boyfriend strongly suggested I leave the bar, or he'd rearrange my facial features.

Up until quarter past nine this morning, I thought that maybe Claire had listened when I pleaded with her not to report what she'd seen to Zoe. That was before I answered the phone.

I was annoyed by my ex-fiancée's lack of belief when I told her exactly what happened, but that annoyance quickly turned to apoplectic rage as Zoe accused me of stringing her along. The tipping point arrived with her sheer hypocrisy — like I was the one who destroyed our relationship by being unfaithful. I pointed out that nothing happened with Donna, but even if I was complicit in the alleged kiss, I'm a single man. Unlike her, I didn't cheat on anyone.

We spent five long minutes yelling at one another before Zoe stated that, in no uncertain terms, she would not be coming over this afternoon. She also said that as far as the mortgage is concerned, I'm on my own.

Before I could remind my ex of her responsibilities, she called me a two-faced bastard and then hung up.

Not the best start to my Sunday, and there's a good chance it's about to get worse.

The Volvo's shock absorbers groan in complaint as I ease the old car along the final section of Echo Lane. Once I reach the end, I switch off the engine and pause for a moment. What exactly do I tell Mrs Weller?

Having already had one financial door slam shut in my face this morning, I can't afford a second.

"Be positive," I murmur as I get out of the Volvo.

For the third, and possibly last time if I can't convince Mrs Weller there's grounds to continue her task, I push open the front door to 1 Echo Lane. I then loiter in the small entrance lobby for a moment, purely to check I wasn't imagining the complete lack of sound and the odd odour. I stand completely still and focus, but all I can hear is my own heartbeat. As for the odour, it's exactly how I remembered it, which is to say that I remember it being almost indescribably unique.

No wiser, I push open the main door and step into the hallway, calling out my name.

"Come on through, Daniel," comes the reply.

I enter the kitchen to find Mrs Weller sitting in the same chair, wearing the exact same clothes.

"Good morning," she says, looking up at me.

I haven't seen Mrs Weller since I first clapped eyes on Kim in the bakery, and although I recall being taken aback by their physical similarities, those similarities seem all the more stark, having seen both women within a fifteen-hour time window. If it transpires that they're not mother and daughter, I'll eat my dad's hat.

"Good morning," I reply, doing my best to appear upbeat.

"Take a seat."

Not wanting to break our routine, I plonk my backside on the chair directly opposite.

"Pleasantries out of the way," Mrs Weller begins. "How are you getting on?"

"No small talk today?" I remark jovially.

"I don't have time, Daniel," she replies wearily. "*We* don't have time."

"Right, well ... um, there's good news and there's bad news."

"Explain."

"The good news is that I went along to that gig at The Malthouse on Thursday and it went well. I spent the latter half of the evening with Kim, and we really clicked, so I thought. At the end of the gig, she asked if I'd like to go out with her on Saturday — last night — as part of a foursome."

"A foursome? With whom?"

"Me and her, obviously, plus Kim's mate Donna and my colleague, Gavin."

"The four of you went out last night?" Mrs Weller confirms.

"Yeah, but that's where the good news ends. Turns out that I got the wrong end of the stick — Kim turned up with Donna *and* her boyfriend."

"Oh no," Mrs Weller groans.

"That's more or less how I reacted. When Kim suggested a foursome, it was purely to set me up with Donna."

"Stupid, stupid, girl," Mrs Weller says under her breath.

"Anyway, my colleague buggered off after Kim told him in no uncertain terms he wasn't welcome, and I hung around for a couple of hours. I left after Donna tried it on with me."

Mrs Weller closes her eyes and puffs the longest of sighs. I don't know what to say, so saying nothing is probably for the best.

"So, there is no good news," she eventually says. "Just bad news with a prologue."

"I'm sorry," I shrug. "According to Donna, Kim is smitten with this Harrison bloke."

"I know that much, Daniel, but I really thought she'd take a shine to you. You're everything that Harrison isn't."

"Skint, you mean?"

"Kim doesn't realise it, but Harrison's wealth will prove to be her undoing. She might initially enjoy the trappings of his success, but a cage is a cage, no matter how gilded it might be."

"Donna did say he was ... controlling."

"That's a polite way of putting it, and it's a shame that Donna isn't willing to share her concerns with Kim."

"I got the impression Kim wouldn't listen. She seems a different person when Harrison is around."

"That's the first part of the game, Daniel. Alienate friends and family, then there's no one to undermine his authority. He's a devious and deceitful man, Neil Harrison."

"He's also got ... sorry, forget it."

"Go on."

"It's not important."

"Whatever it is, I want to hear it. Please."

"It's just that I noticed Harrison chatting to some other guy when Kim was dancing with Donna. He kept looking across and smiling at a group of teenage girls."

"I wish I could say I'm surprised, but knowing what I know about Neil Harrison, it's no less than I expected from him."

"But, his roving eye is a good thing, right? If he's eyeing up other women, it suggests he's not happy with Kim, and if you're not happy with someone, you're not likely to propose to them, surely?"

"If only that were true," Mrs Weller replies dolefully. "Harrison wants Kim as a wife, not for love, but as a trophy ... a pretty woman to stand by his side as he plays the part of a decent, honourable man. The reality is that he'll cheat on Kim before and after they marry, but by the time she discovers his infidelity, it'll be too late."

"I get that you have a low opinion of Harrison, and I understand why, but you don't know for sure he'll cheat on Kim."

"Yes, I do," she replies so vociferously I'm not inclined to argue.

Her mild outburst seems to heighten Mrs Weller's despair. The last time I saw a face so etched with worry was last November when Mum received a call from Stephen telling her that Robbie had a severe bout of flu. Perhaps with good reason, she feared that Robbie's self-diagnosis was a smokescreen for the illness he couldn't bring himself to consider. Mum sobbed when Robbie called a week later to say his test result had come back negative.

"Isn't there something else you can do?" I ask. "If Harrison is that much of a tosser … pardon my French."

"What do you suggest?" Mrs Weller replies curtly. "I genuinely thought she just needed to meet a better man; someone who had all the qualities she once deemed essential in her idealised view of the world. It seems I misjudged how far she's fallen under Harrison's spell."

"Um, I don't know."

Mrs Weller rests her arms on the table and bows her head forward slightly. It could be the gesture of a woman deep in thought, but it could just as easily be a sign of a woman on the verge of giving up.

After what feels like an age, she lifts her chin.

"I think it's too late, Daniel," she says. "I appreciate you did what you could, but it was always going to be a long shot. Maybe if we had more time or you'd met Kim earlier, you'd have achieved our objective. But, alas, we all run out of time in the end."

As much as I sympathise with Mrs Weller's obvious disappointment, my greater concern is the end of this meal ticket.

"Does this mean our deal is off?"

"Not off, just unfulfilled."

"What's the difference?"

"Our contract stipulates that you have until next Sunday to terminate the relationship between Kim and Harrison but, as you've learned, Kim appears impervious to your charms. A few more days will not change that."

"No, but, er ... what if I can find another way to split them up?"

"Such as?"

"I know a couple of blokes who'd give Harrison a good kicking for a few hundred quid. That, alongside a warning to stay away from Kim, might work."

"A marvellous idea," Mrs Weller says with a snort of laughter. "If only it were that easy."

"Surely it *is* that easy."

"You didn't read the contract, did you, Daniel?"

"Well, not every page, no."

"Did you read any of it?"

"Honestly, I couldn't make head nor tail of the legal language."

"That would explain why you never read the clause about inflicting harm on any third party in order to achieve the task. It's strictly forbidden."

"Call me naive but why not change the contract, and remove the clause?"

"Because I never created it, and I have no power to change it."

"Who did then? Can't you ask them?"

"I can't tell you, and no. The contract is the contract, and that's non-negotiable."

Frustrated as I might be, the woman sitting opposite is patently in a much worse place if her expression and body language are any barometer.

"There must be something I can do," I say in lieu of any constructive suggestions. "We have seven days, right?"

"It's six, actually, but that's academic. Six days. Six weeks. Six months. What does it matter if Kim has already sold her soul to Harrison?"

"It matters if there's another way, and I'm willing to try anything if it's that important to you."

"Tell me what that other way is, Daniel?" Mrs Weller says, almost pleading. "I'd love to know."

"You've put me on the spot and … and I don't have an answer, but let me at least give it some thought, eh?"

"There's no time."

"All I'm asking is that you give me a day or so. If I can't come up with something within forty-eight hours, I'll admit defeat and walk away, no hard feelings."

Mrs Weller sits back in her chair and, once again, closes her eyes. To my surprise, a smile eventually creeps across her face.

"What's so amusing?" I ask.

"Not amusing," she replies, opening her eyes again. "Ironic."

"What is?"

"Ever heard the saying: God loves a trier?"

"Maybe, yes."

"Kim loves a trier, too. She always valued a positive attitude, which is why I had such faith in you."

It's been a while since anyone has tagged me as positive, but there was a time before my relationship with Zoe imploded when I considered myself an optimist.

"If you're not ready to give up, Mrs Weller, neither am I. All I want is a chance to see what I can come up with."

"I guess there's nothing left to lose, so why not."

"Great," I say, feigning a smile to hide my relief. "You won't regret it."

Inadvertently, it seems I've already adopted estate agent levels of subconscious bullshit because, deep down, I'm far from certain that regret won't pitch up before the week is out.

"I'd better get going," I then say, getting to my feet. "Lots to think about."

"You'll let me know as soon as you've come up with something?"

"You have my word."

"Thank you, Daniel, and good luck."

I flash Mrs Weller a smile and say goodbye. Not that I'm bothered, but she doesn't offer to see me to the front door.

I wander back across the kitchen and out to the hallway but, after only half a dozen steps, I'm suddenly struck by a wave of nausea, likely due to last night's Grolsch consumption. Pausing for a moment, I take a few deep breaths and then continue towards the front door.

I don't make it.

A searing pain suddenly burns behind my eyes, akin to a migraine, accompanied by a tinnitus-like ringing in my ears. I close my eyes and press my fingertips to my forehead, praying it's just a sign of dehydration rather than something more sinister. The agony eases a fraction, and after a few seconds, I dare to open my eyes again.

One blink, maybe two, but in that millisecond, my eyes and my brain seem to disconnect. Rather than reporting the same polished wooden floorboards and smooth plastered walls, my eyes paint a very different picture: roughly hewn planks of timber beneath my feet and bare brick walls. For just that millisecond, my imagination conjured up a vision of what the hallway might look like if its condition mirrored the exterior of the house.

I squeeze my eyes shut.

When I open them, the pain behind my eyes is all but gone, and the scene is exactly as it was when I first entered the hallway.

What. The. Fuck.

By the time I reach the front door, it's as if nothing had happened. The low-key headache is still in situ but it's been there since I woke up.

I hurry out through the lobby to the front path where I stop to gulp back some fresh air.

Whatever just happened can only be due to tiredness, stress, or my brain reacting to the emotional pressure I've endured of late. Maybe it was just a warning sign — I need to lighten my load somehow. It can't be a coincidence that the illusion occurred only seconds after I promised Mrs Weller I'd find a solution to her problem.

"What are you doing, Danny?" I whisper to myself.

A new job with long hours, constant financial worries, an ongoing battle with my ex-fiancée, and I've just committed myself to fixing a problem I've no clue how to fix.

I plod over to the Volvo and fall into the driver's seat. A few more deep breaths and I feel a little better, at least physically. I then look across at the house and the open fields beyond. It's all I need to answer my own question — I'm doing this because the house before me is the prize if I succeed.

One problem. Six days.

If the old version of Danny Monk had any say, he wouldn't shirk from the challenge. He certainly wouldn't complain about tiredness or stress — he'd get the hell on with it.

I need to find him again.

Chapter 31

On the drive back from Echo Lane yesterday, it dawned on me that solving Mrs Weller's problem would, in turn, solve most of my problems.

Whether I'm mentally up to the challenge or not, I conceded that I have no choice but to try. It's an all-or-nothing gamble. Win, and my life will become immeasurably easier. Lose, and there's a good chance that my woes will rapidly escalate, not least because the incident in Mrs Weller's hallway might indicate I'm on the brink of a nervous breakdown.

Nevertheless, with more determination than I've mustered in a long while, I spent the entirety of the rest of my Sunday trying to think of ways to split up Kim Dolan and Neil Harrison. I scribbled down pages of notes. I war-gamed several different scenarios. I even resorted to watching *Songs of Praise* in the hope of divine intervention.

All those hours of solo brainstorming failed to produce a solution, however, they did set my mind on a path towards a new approach. That approach was born of my own circumstances and what happened with Zoe.

It dawned on me that Mrs Weller's initial idea of using me as bait to lure Kim away from Harrison wasn't entirely flawed, just back to front. Mrs Weller thought that I might be able to turn Kim's head so she might cheat on Harrison, but that tactic didn't even get off the ground. What she hasn't considered is putting temptation in Harrison's path and seeing if *he* bites.

It's the longest of long shots, but if I can create a situation where Harrison is unfaithful to Kim, and I can secure evidence of his cheating, that would surely destroy their relationship. I've only got my own experience to go on, but it certainly did the trick when Zoe finally fessed up.

All good in theory, but there's one major hurdle I need to overcome — how in Christ's name do I orchestrate a situation where Harrison cheats on Kim? There's also the smaller but still not insignificant hurdle of obtaining proof of any subsequent indiscretion.

It's a problem that dominates my thoughts to such a degree that, when I pull into a parking space outside the office, I've barely any recollection of the journey from the flat.

I hurry inside, keen to put the kettle on and consume a mug of coffee so strong it can't fail to fire up my flagging imagination. To my surprise, Gavin is already loitering in the back room.

"Bloody hell, Gav," I gasp. "Did someone set your bed on fire this morning?"

"Eh?"

"You're first in."

"Oh right, yeah. I'm still half asleep."

"Why are you here early? It's not like you."

"I stupidly agreed to give a mate and his missus a lift to the airport this morning. I've been up since five."

"I see. Where are they off to?"

"Torremolinos. Two weeks of soaking up the sun to celebrate their first wedding anniversary."

"Alright for some."

"Don't I know it," he grumbles. "There's no better reminder of how crappy your life is than sitting in a car with a happy couple about to jet off on holiday together. I thought I was going to puke at one point."

"Your time will come, mate. We're still on for that singles night at the end of the month, aren't we?"

"You remembered."

"Of course. We made a deal, and I never welch on a deal."

Gavin finds a smile and then grabs another mug from the cupboard.

"Coffee, I presume?"

"Thought you'd never ask."

As we wait for the kettle to boil, my colleague casually enquires about Saturday's events and how the evening panned out.

"It was a fucking disaster," I snort before explaining just how much of a disaster it was.

"Is that the final nail in the coffin with your ex?" he asks once I've unloaded.

It's too early to explain the full details of why my relationship ended, and even if it wasn't, I don't think I'm ready to reveal the truth to a colleague.

"Yeah, I think we've reached the end of the road," I reply.

"That's shit. Sorry, mate."

"Thanks, but dealing with the fallout of my messed-up relationship is the least of my troubles. Kim isn't likely to ditch that bellend she's dating any time soon, and that means I'm less than a week away from breaking a promise."

"To split them up?"

"Yep."

"What's the plan now?"

"Good question. I spent all day yesterday trying to come up with ideas, and I reckon the only surefire way to make it happen is to tempt Harrison into cheating on Kim."

"And how are you going to do that?"

"Absolutely no idea. The first problem is finding a young, attractive woman willing to act as bait. That in itself seems an insurmountable challenge considering how little time I've got to do this."

Gavin responds to my dilemma by turning his back on me and silently spooning coffee granules into the two mugs.

"Hire an escort," he then says in a low voice.

"Pardon?"

"You could hire an escort," he repeats casually, turning to face me. "Just an idea."

I consider his suggestion for a moment.

"That's not a bad idea, but I wouldn't know where to hire one. I mean, it's not like hiring a suit, I presume — you can't just browse the escort services in the Yellow Pages, can you?"

"No, but ..."

"But?"

"Speak to Tina."

Stunned by Gavin's suggestion, my mouth bobs open.

"Not like that," he responds, rolling his eyes. "I don't mean Tina is moonlighting as a call girl."

"What do you mean, then?"

My colleague shuffles uncomfortably on the spot while studying the cracked lino beneath our feet.

"Well?" I prompt.

"She'll probably cut my bollocks off for telling you, but Tina knows an escort."

"Really? Dare I ask how that came up in conversation?"

"Earlier this year, I was due to go on a date and I asked Tina for a few tips, hoping to up my dating game. I didn't even get to try those tips as the woman I met made an excuse and left after ten minutes. Anyway, the next morning, Tina asked how it went, and I told her the sorry story. I then asked, tongue in cheek, if she had any single friends who'd be willing to have sex with a desperate estate agent."

"Right."

"Tina said she did, but it'd cost me a ton."

"A hundred quid?"

"Yeah. I thought she was only joking but I pushed her, and she admitted that one of her old school friends is on the game."

"Oh. Did you, um …"

"No, I did not," Gavin protests. "I might be desperate, but paying for sex isn't my thing."

"Hey, I'm not judging, mate. Give it a few more months of celibacy, and I might consider it."

"You wouldn't, would you?"

"Never say never, but with my financial woes, I doubt I could afford more than three minutes with an escort even if I fancied hiring one."

"It's been so long for me three minutes would be ample time," Gavin sniggers. "And that would include getting undressed."

"Mate, I'm sympathetic, but it's way too early to be thinking about you getting undressed … or getting jiggy."

The kettle boils, and Gavin turns his attention to the mugs again.

"Do you think Tina might put me in touch with her friend?" I ask.

"No harm in asking, but she'll want to know how you found out, and that means admitting that I told you."

"Yeah, I get that, but it was your idea in the first place."

"I was trying to help."

"And you definitely did, mate," I respond enthusiastically. "I hadn't even considered using an escort, so I owe you a pint for coming up with the idea."

I deploy my best smile and hope that Gavin accepts being a sacrificial lamb. It's the second time in the last few days, but he doesn't know about the first. Hopefully, he never does.

"Alright," he eventually sighs. "But let me talk to Tina first."

"Good man," I beam, slapping him on the back. "Just keep one hand on your plums when you tell her."

"Don't worry, I will!"

It's not exactly a solution to my problem but if I can rope Tina's friend into my plot, at least the bait element is in hand. That said, the rest of the plot is still far from developed. I might need to pay Kim another visit at lunchtime and hope she'll unwittingly help fill in a few gaps.

"Oh, I need to warn you," Gavin says, passing me a coffee mug. "Rotherham won 5-1 at the weekend."

Maybe it's the lack of sleep or because my thoughts are so distracted, but I can't fathom why Gavin feels the need to warn me about a random football result. I respond with a quizzical frown, and then the penny drops.

"That means Lee will be in a good mood, surely."

"No, it means he'll bang on about it all day. Trust me, he's worse when they win, and Saturday's result was the best they've had in months."

Right on cue, the office door swings open and Lee strolls in.

"5-1 to the Rotherham!" comes the chant as he steps into the back room. "5-1 to the Rotherham!"

"Morning," I say, purely to stop him chanting.

"And a bloody good one it is, too, lad ... unless you're a Wigan fan, that is. Fucking drubbed, they were."

"Weren't Rotherham drubbed last week?" Gavin remarks.

"That was a blip."

"What was the term you used to describe the players? A bunch of wage-stealing, talentless shitehouses, wasn't it?"

"Happen I might have been a tad harsh. Has the kettle just boiled?"

"It has."

"Knock us up a brew, will you, lad," he then says to me. "I need to prep for the morning meeting."

He turns and heads to his desk, and Gavin follows behind. I wonder if I should bring up what happened in the Victoria Club on Friday, but as Lee hasn't mentioned it, maybe it's better to keep quiet on the subject.

I get on with making Lee's tea and, as I'm delivering it to his desk, our fourth and final member of staff hurries into the office, looking somewhat flustered.

"Sorry," Tina pants. "I've had one of those mornings."

"Don't sweat it," Lee replies, eyeing a letter in his right hand. "Get yourself sorted and Danny will make you a brew."

I'm about to object to being treated like a tea boy when it occurs to me that I need to stay in Tina's good books this morning.

"Tea or coffee?" I say brightly, flashing her my best smile.

"Coffee would be lovely, thanks."

Still wearing my plastic smile, I turn and trudge back to the kettle.

The morning meeting seems to go on forever as we cover both Friday's and Saturday's events. It turns out that I surpassed my target for viewings, and two of those viewings resulted in sales. Apart from making a few phone calls, I had zero input on either deal, but I'm willing to take the credit.

"Keep this up," Lee says. "And it won't be long before we can drop the junior part of your job title."

"Thanks. Does that mean I get a pay rise?"

"Aye. Your salary will go from bloody crap to just plain crap, and you'll still be expected to make the tea."

"Gosh, that's some incentive," I mumble.

The meeting ends, and Lee begins preparing for his first appointment of the day — a repossession booked for ten o'clock. When he first mentioned it, I was mildly surprised to hear the house is on the same development of executive homes as Zoe's parents' place. It never occurred to me that high interest rates and a failing economy would hit the well-heeled, too, but clearly, no one is exempt. Whoever they are, the current homeowners are about to have the shittiest of shitty Monday mornings, that's for sure.

I start the arduous task of following up the weekend's viewings and manage to get through half of them before Lee departs. The moment he leaves, I draw Gavin's attention.

"Are you going to talk to Tina now?" I whisper.

"I suppose," he sighs. "But if she gets violent, you'll back me up, right?"

"One hundred per cent."

"Okay, here goes."

Rather than get up from his desk, he sits upright and clears his throat.

"Junior," he calls over. "Can you come here a sec?"

Tina, presuming Gavin's request is work-related, grabs her notepad and steps over to his desk.

"Be quick," she says, plonking herself down on one of the client chairs. "I've got a ton of work to get through this morning."

"Don't worry, I'm not about to add to your workload," Gavin replies. "It's um ... I have a confession to make."

"What have you done?"

"I might have let it slip to Danny that your friend works in the, er ... adult trade. He was asking about escorts, you see."

"Not for me," I blurt. "For the record, I'm not looking to use an escort. Well, not personally."

Tina shoots a look my way before turning her sights on Gavin. I don't know her well enough to unscramble her expression, but it strikes me as puzzled more than angry.

"Let's just row back a bit here," she then says. "Firstly, Gavin, you're a twat. I told you that in confidence."

"Sorry," he murmurs.

"It was my fault," I interject. "I desperately need an escort, and Gavin was just trying to help me out."

Our office administrator stares back at me, unblinking. "Why do you need an escort?"

"To cut the longest of long stories short, there's a woman I know who's involved with a guy, and he's an absolute piece of work ... you know, the toxic type no parent would ever want their daughter to bring home."

"And?"

"I've cobbled together a plan to split them up, but to do that, I need an attractive young woman to lure this bloke into cheating on his girlfriend, Kim. I haven't worked out the details, but the goal is to capture a photo, which I'll then show to Kim. That should be enough for her to end the relationship."

"I see," Tina says impassively, crossing her legs.

Having said more than I intended, I await the verdict as Tina sits silently, digesting my plea.

"This isn't a wind-up?" she asks.

"No, it's a genuine plan."

"It's a crazy plan."

"Admittedly, it's not without potential pitfalls, but I'm running out of time."

"What's the hurry?"

"The arsehole intends to propose to Kim this weekend. Once that happens, it's game over."

Tina pauses for a moment and then gets to her feet. Without saying a word, she trots over to her desk, rummages around in her handbag, and then scribbles something on her notepad while Gavin and I watch on.

She returns, holding out a slip of paper.

"This is Candy's number."

"Candy?"

"Not her real name, obviously. It's her work name."

"Oh, okay," I reply, taking the slip of paper. "I really appreciate it, Tina."

"Fair warning, though. Candy doesn't come cheap, and she doesn't put up with any bullshit."

"A bit like you then, Junior," Gavin chuckles. "I mean, the not putting up with bullshit part."

Ignoring our colleague's misplaced wisecrack, Tina leans over my desk.

"Have you ever had any dealings with an escort before?"

"Can't say that I have."

"I haven't spoken to Candy in a few weeks, but the last time we met up, she told me she'd just hiked her rates. Be prepared to pay at least £100 an hour."

"That seems a lot of money."

"You can definitely find girls who'll work for less, but your job requires a girl with a certain set of skills if you don't want this bloke sussing out he's being played. Candy studied drama at college, so she knows how to put on an act."

"She studied drama? At college? How on earth did she end up becoming an escort?"

"Money, pure and simple. She's just turned twenty-one, lives in a swanky flat, drives a brand new Golf Cabriolet, and goes on holiday four times a year."

"Wow."

"Yeah, but she has to shag fat ugly men," Gavin points out.

"Yep," Tina says, turning to face Gavin. "That's exactly the point I made when she first told me about her line of work. But then she asked me a question."

"What question?"

"Tell you what, I'll put it to both of you," Tina says, stepping back from my desk. "Imagine an old woman, massively overweight, with bad breath and really poor personal hygiene. Would either of you have sex with her for £50?"

"I sure as hell wouldn't," I reply.

"Christ, no," Gavin says.

"What about £100?"

We both reply immediately with the same answer: no chance.

"How about £1,000?"

"Still a hard pass from me," I say.

"Same," Gavin says after a suspiciously long pause.

"£10,000," Tina then says. "Would that be enough?"

"Um, no," I say after giving it a moment's thought.

"Will she expect oral?" Gavin enquires. "If not, sure, I'd have a go for ten grand."

"You've gotta go down on her if she asks."

"Eww. No, then."

"Think hard about this next number," Tina then says, folding her arms. "Fifty. Thousand. Pounds."

It's only a hypothetical question, but I find myself pondering what difference fifty grand would make to my life. I could pay off half of our negative equity, sell the flat, and buy a new car, and I'd still have enough money to start afresh.

"That'd do it for me," I say. "I'd be up for it."

"Me too," admits Gavin. "But I'd politely ask that she washes her minge first."

"Nice," Tina grimaces. "And that's not really the point."

"What is, then?"

"The point Candy made to me is that almost everyone would sleep with a random stranger *if* the price were right. You've both said you'd sleep with a woman you don't find attractive for fifty grand, and that's how much Candy makes in a year by working just two hours a day."

"I've never thought of it like that," I admit.

"Me neither," Gavin adds. "Maybe I'm in the wrong game."

"Or you're the wrong sex," Tina sniggers. "It's only the blokes who are desperate enough to pay for sex. No offence, but no woman would pay either of you a hundred quid for a shag."

"Yeah, but I'd only charge you a tenner," Gavin retorts. "Mates' rates."

"Thanks, but no thanks," Tina laughs as she makes her way back to her desk.

I glance at the slip of paper. "Cheers for this, Tina," I call across to her. "I really appreciate it."

"No worries, and mention my name when you speak to Candy — say we're friends. She won't cut her rates, but she'll be more likely to help."

"Will do."

It's only just gone ten o'clock, and I've already made progress with my plan. Admittedly, it's been one of the more surreal Monday mornings I've experienced, but at least I now have a vague chance of completing Mrs Weller's task.

By lunchtime, I should know just how vague.

Chapter 32

For the next ten minutes, I need to put aside all thoughts of escorts and the hypothetical sex with a woman whose description matches one of the dinner ladies from junior school.

Standing a dozen yards beyond the bus shelter, I watch and wait for Kim to make her daily pilgrimage to Wilson's Bakery. My plan, if you can call it that, is to maintain my position until Kim has bought her lunch and then accidentally bump into her on the pavement. That part of the plan is sound, but what happens thereafter is in the lap of the gods. After Donna attempted to stick her tongue down my throat on Saturday evening, I spent ten minutes negotiating with Zoe's best friend before departing Martinelli's Bar. I never said goodbye to Donna, or Kim for that matter, so there's no telling what the latter's reaction will be when I approach her.

Just after one o'clock, a figure in a bright-red jacket and skirt crosses the road. My heart begins beating faster as I watch Kim enter the bakery. A minute passes, and then another.

"C'mon, Kim," I whisper.

Almost on cue, she exits the bakery, checks the road for traffic, and crosses. I, in turn, stride back down the road to the point where our paths will intersect.

I'm twenty feet away when Kim notices my approach. It begins with the first flicker of recognition, followed by a lukewarm smile as I slow my pace to a standstill.

"Hi," I say.

Kim stops a few feet away, and the smile dissolves.

"Oh, it's Harry Houdini," she says, her voice dripping with sarcasm. "The great escape artist."

"Sorry?"

"Saturday evening ring any bells? One minute you were there, the next you disappeared."

"Did, um, Donna tell you what happened?"

"She said you shared a kiss, and then you chased some woman across the bar. Donna then popped to the loo, but when she came back, you were nowhere to be seen. She was really upset, you know."

"I'm sorry I didn't say goodbye, but that woman who witnessed Donna's move on me happened to be my ex-fiancée's best friend."

"So?"

"Did Donna mention that I only broke up with my ex a few months ago, and because we own a flat together, the break up is ... let's just say it's complicated. What Zoe's friend witnessed hasn't exactly calmed the waters."

"Why did you split up?"

I'd rather not admit the real reason, but garnering Kim's sympathy can't do any harm.

"She cheated on me," I reply in a suitably crestfallen tone.

"Oh. I'm sorry."

"It's okay," I shrug. "Life goes on, but I hope you can understand that I'd rather avoid making my situation any more complicated than it needs to be."

"Does that mean you're not interested in Donna?"

"It means I'm not interested in a relationship with anyone at the moment. Donna is lovely, but it wouldn't be right getting involved with her while I'm still unpacking the emotional baggage of my last relationship."

Kim's lukewarm smile returns. "That's obviously disappointing for Donna, but I think your reasoning is admirable. Most men would jump into bed with the first available girl and hope that fixes the problem."

"Yeah, well, I'm not most men."

"So I'm discovering, Danny."

The look she then adopts is hard to decipher, but if I didn't know her relationship status, it would be easy to assume a flirtatious undercurrent. Perhaps more telling is the change in her demeanour when Neil Harrison isn't around.

"Did you and Neil have a good evening on Saturday?" I ask, moving the subject to the very reason I orchestrated this encounter.

"It was alright, but Donna was a bit wasted, so we had to leave early and get her home."

"That's a shame. I was actually hoping to speak to Neil again at some point."

"Why?"

Time to put on my estate agent's hat and let the bullshit flow.

"I had a viewing booked this morning, but the guy who booked it failed to show up. When I returned to the office, my colleague said the guy called a minute after I left, cancelling the viewing."

"Ah, right. A mobile telephone would have been handy."

"Exactly. Neil mentioned buying one on Saturday evening, and I'd like to pop by his office and have a chat about my options. Unfortunately, I didn't get the chance to ask the name of his company or where his office is."

"That's because you buggered off without saying goodbye."

"Guilty as charged," I reply, holding my hands up. "Sorry."

"Apology accepted, and I'll explain to Donna what happened."

"Thank you."

"And Neil's company is called Harrison Telecoms: Unit 2, Silverlake Business Park. Do you know it?"

"I don't, but I'm sure one of the guys in the office will know where it is. Is, um, Neil there most of the time?"

"He doesn't really talk much about his work, so I honestly don't know. It might be best to give him a call before dropping by."

"I'll do that."

Kim then glances across the road at nothing in particular.

"I'd better let you get back to work," I say. "Enjoy your lunch."

"I will. Oh, and before I forget, I've got those details you enquired about."

"Details?"

"Hotels and flights to Nashville. Remember?"

"Ah, yes."

I'd all but forgotten about my initial ruse to interact with Kim.

"Would you like me to fax them over to you?"

"That'd be great. Thanks."

"I'll do it later this afternoon."

"Righto."

My mission accomplished and the conversation exhausted, I should be on my way. However, the paper bag in Kim's hand is an opportunity to test an obscure fact Mrs Weller provided on her floppy disk. For no other reason than my own curiosity, I want to test how good her intel is.

"What are you having for lunch?" I say, nodding to the paper bag. "I'm looking for inspiration."

"Nothing exciting. Just a chicken salad sandwich."

"Here's a top tip for you, next time, ask for a bacon and marmalade toastie. It sounds like a weird combo, but trust me, it'll blow your mind."

"Oh, my God!" Kim gasps. "That's my all-time favourite sandwich, and I thought I was the only weirdo who ever ordered one."

"You've obviously got good taste."

Just not in men.

"Anyway, good to see you again, Kim."

I turn and set off back down Victoria Road, resisting the urge to glance back to where I left Kim standing. Not that it matters now, but I can't help but wonder how we might have got on if we'd met before Harrison got his claws into her.

In a different life, who knows?

After checking that Kim has continued her walk back to work, I cross over the road and backtrack to the bakery. Once I've acquired a cheese and ham sandwich, I take a slow walk back to the office, using the time to work through the next stage of my plan.

When I step through the door, I'm greeted by a statement I instantly wish I could unhear.

"I lost my virginity to an old clunker," Lee says from behind his desk. "Did her up against the back wall of the bingo hall. I was sixteen, and she was fifty-one."

Across from Lee, Gavin is perched on the edge of his desk, his face etched with disgust.

"Shall I come back in ten minutes?" I venture.

"I asked Lee that question we discussed earlier," Gavin confirms. "He said he'd shag a fat old woman just for the hell of it."

"Too bloody right I would," Lee says. "There's many a good tune played on an old fiddle."

"Even if that fiddle smells like a fishmonger's apron?"

"Thanks for that, Gav," I groan. "I'm about to eat my lunch."

I leave them to it and head to the back room, closing the door behind me.

As I sit and chew on my sandwich, I attempt to put the various pieces of my plan in order. I'll only get one shot at this, so it's crucial I get my proverbial ducks in a row. There's also the small matter of convincing Mrs Weller that it'll work, and I'm less than fifty-fifty on that myself. However, I need money to pay Candy, which requires another visit to Echo Lane and a one-time opportunity to pitch the maddest of plans.

My thoughts are temporarily put on ice when Lee suddenly bursts into the back room.

"Sorry, lad. I'm busting for a piss, and I've got a valuation in ten minutes."

He continues on to the toilet but leaves the door wide open.

"We might need to hijack your desk again tomorrow morning," he calls out. "Cass is coming in at eleven-ish for another mortgage appointment."

"Right."

"Ooh, I need this," he then groans.

What follows sounds a lot like someone slowly emptying a bucket of soup into a garden pond. I drop the last piece of my sandwich in the bag and toss it in the bin.

Having relieved himself, and me of my appetite, Lee heads off to his valuation. Gavin leaves ten minutes later to conduct a viewing. With Tina sporting her dictation headphones, it's the ideal opportunity to set up my meeting with Neil Harrison.

After a quick call to Directory Enquiries to get the number, I ring Harrison Telecoms. A perky young woman answers almost immediately.

"Can I speak to Neil Harrison, please?"

"May I ask who's calling?"

"It's Danny Monk."

"Will Mr Harrison know what it's regarding?"

I bloody well hope not.

"Tell him I'm following up on the conversation we had on Saturday evening."

"Hold the line."

While I wait for my call to be transferred, I run through what I'm about to say to Neil Harrison. I feel woefully underprepared but I'm pretty sure of one thing — Harrison is a man driven by money. He might see that as a strength, but I'm hoping it'll also be his blind spot. That, and his penchant for attractive young women.

"Neil Harrison."

"Hi, Neil. It's Danny Monk — we met at Martinelli's on Saturday evening."

"You're the estate agent?"

"That's me."

"What can I do for you?"

The words might imply friendliness but his tone is cold to the point of complete disinterest.

"Mobile telephones."

"What about them?"

"The phone you showed me on Saturday evening costs a grand, right?"

"Correct."

"Would I be right in assuming you'd do a deal at a lower price if the order was for more than one phone?"

"How many units?"

"Potentially, hundreds."

This is the make or break moment. The prospect of selling hundreds of phones in one deal could be chicken feed to his company.

"Yes, we can certainly entertain a discount for an order of that size. Who's the customer?"

"My company. We've got over a thousand staff, and most of them are in and out of the office all day, so a mobile phone would be a godsend."

"I'm sure that's true but, with respect, why are *you* calling me rather than someone from your senior management team?"

"Because our regional manager happened to be in the office this morning when I returned from an aborted appointment. I told him that, as a company, we must lose hundreds of hours every week because once a staff member leaves the office, there's no way to contact them. I then mentioned that I know someone who runs a mobile telecoms company."

"And?"

"And our regional manager, Andy, asked me to call you to see if you'd be interested in sitting down with him and exploring a deal he can then take to the board."

"I see."

I don't like the hesitancy in his voice or the subsequent silence. Is he just playing hard to get or have I underplayed the offer?

"We're both busy men, Neil, so if you're not interested, be honest. I'll call Andy and let him know."

"No, no, I'm interested. Definitely."

There's a hint of emotion in Harrison's response. Not exactly excitement, but measured enthusiasm.

"Okay, great," I respond. "Are there any days or times this week that would be better for you?"

"I can't do Wednesday morning or Friday afternoon, but my diary is fairly open this week."

"I'll report back to Andy, and if you can bear with me until tomorrow morning, I'll confirm a day and time for him to drop by your office."

"I'll look forward to it."

Having achieved exactly what I hoped to achieve, I make an excuse about another call and say goodbye to Neil Harrison. The trap is set — all I need to do now is convince a woman I don't know to act as bait and then sell the whole mad idea to another woman and ask her to fund it.

It might say junior negotiator on my business cards, but I'll need the negotiating skills of the United Nations to pull this off.

Chapter 33

As I sit and sip an obscenely expensive glass of orange juice, I try to remember what normal felt like. The last notable day of normality must have been early spring. It probably involved Zoe and me wandering around the shops on a Saturday afternoon, followed by a trip to Blockbuster to hire a film before picking up a takeaway on the way home. After the film, we might have had sex — I can't remember, but we had sex a lot, so it's highly likely.

If someone had told me that, come September, we would no longer be a couple, and I would be sitting in a hotel bar waiting to meet an escort, I'd have laughed in their face.

And yet, here I am.

I managed to call Candy halfway through the afternoon, and after using Tina's name as a starting point, I fumbled my way through a vague explanation of why I needed an escort. To my surprise, and relief, Candy didn't baulk at the idea. In fact, she explained that my particular requirement actually had a name: a honey trap. She then suggested we meet at the Aston Grange Hotel at precisely 7.15 pm.

Perched on a stool at the bar, I check my watch for the fifth time in the last five minutes. It's not quite a quarter past yet. I know next to nothing about the hotel trade, but I presume Mondays are one of the quieter days if the lack of customers in the bar is any gauge. The plinky-plonky jazz music playing in the background could also be a factor in keeping people away — it's certainly beginning to get on my tits.

The door from the reception area swings open, and a woman strides in. It takes no more than a glance to discount her as Candy, being she's probably mid to late twenties and dressed in business attire. At a guess, I'd say she's more likely a high-flying company exec.

I take another sip of orange juice.

"Danny?"

I turn and reply to the woman's assumption with a look of confusion. It's the businesswoman.

"Um, yeah."

She thrusts out her hand. "Candy. Nice to meet you."

"Oh, sorry … hi," I splutter before hopping off the stool and belatedly shaking her hand. "Can I get you a drink?"

Like the shopkeeper in the kids' cartoon, Mr Benn, the barman seems to magically appear from nowhere.

"Evening, Graham," Candy purrs.

"Good evening, Miss Dubois. Usual?"

"No, I'll just have a Diet Coke, please. I'm driving."

It now makes sense why Candy suggested this venue. She's obviously a regular. As for her surname, I have an inkling that Dubois is no more her real surname than Candy is her real first name.

I get my wallet out to pay for Candy's drink, but she orders me to put it away.

"On my tab, please, Graham."

"Of course."

Once Graham serves her drink, Candy suggests we take a seat. I let her lead, and she guides me towards two leather armchairs positioned in a bay window.

We sit down, and I try to tally the woman in front of me with the woman I work with every day. Tina is cute in a girl-next-door kind of way, but Candy is in a different league altogether. It could be her perfectly tailored suit that skirts the finest of lines between sexy and sophisticated, or it could be her rich auburn hair or the designer spectacles, but it's hard to imagine the two women in the same year group at secondary school.

"So, you went to school with Tina, huh?"

"I did, yes. And we grew up on the same estate, although our lives went in different directions from the time we left school, it's fair to say."

"That's quite the understatement," I chuckle nervously. "I hope you don't mind me saying, but you look more, um, mature than Tina."

"You're saying I look old?" Candy gasps, slapping a hand to her chest.

"God, no ... I mean—"

"I'm joshing with you, Danny. Yes, I know I look older than Tina, but that's because I thought I'd wear my honey trap outfit tonight: mature, respectable, but a little bit sexy."

"Oh, I see."

"What were you expecting me to wear, out of curiosity? A boob tube, mini skirt, and six-inch stilettos?"

That's not quite what I had in mind, but it's not far off.

"To be honest, Candy, I had no preconceived ideas."

"Of course, you didn't," she replies with a wry smile. "But I hope what I'm wearing is acceptable for your purposes."

"Very much so."

"Good, now maybe you can fill in some of the gaps from our conversation earlier. Tell me who you hope to catch out, how, and most importantly, why."

"Sure, but is the why part relevant?"

"I do have some morals, Danny, and I'm not willing to destroy some random guy's life unless he deserves it, no matter how much money is on offer. So, explain."

I've only known Candy Dubois for five minutes, but she's already smashed several of my preconceptions about the kind of woman who works in the sex trade. She clearly has scruples.

"The man in question is manipulative, controlling, and frankly, an arrogant arsehole. The longer he stays in a relationship with his partner, the greater the risk he'll completely brainwash her."

"Why doesn't she just leave him, then?"

"Some people don't realise they're in the wrong relationship until it's too late. I don't know the ins and outs, but a close family member is deeply concerned."

"So concerned they're willing to try a honey trap?"

"If that's what it takes, yes. This prick was also a stockbroker, a yuppie type, and that's reason enough in my book."

"Does he wear red braces and carry a Filofax?" Candy asks playfully.

"Almost certainly," I reply, smiling back. "I haven't checked, but I'd also bet he drives a Porsche."

"Okay. I'm in," Candy grins. "Some men deserve to be taken down a peg or two."

"Great. I guess the next question is ... cost."

"I can't tell you that until I know what you want me to do."

I sit forward and start relaying my somewhat sketchy plan to Candy.

"This guy, Harrison, owns a mobile telecoms business, and I've dangled a carrot in the form of a lucrative contract to supply my company with hundreds of mobile telephones. I've told him I'd arrange a meeting with my regional manager this week, but obviously, that's just to lure him in."

"Very good. Continue."

"Once I've set a day and time for the meeting, he'll be waiting in his office for my boss to turn up, but this is where you come in ... hopefully. I need you to turn up instead, full of apologies, and tell Harrison that the regional manager is stuck in a meeting elsewhere. You then say he asked you to discuss the basic details of what Harrison's company can offer."

"So, what's my role? The regional manager's secretary?"

"I thought personal assistant. Any lesser role and Harrison might not take the interview — I can imagine him referencing monkeys and organ grinders."

"PA it is, then."

"Now, this is the part of the plan where I'm solely reliant on you. I need you to flirt like mad with him and then, once the meeting is finished, devise a way of luring him out to your car, where I'll be waiting with a camera."

"And what exactly are you expecting me to do once I get him to my car?"

"A full-on snog should be enough, but any kind of physical interaction that can't be misconstrued as innocent."

Candy nods slowly and then takes a sip of Coke.

"I like the plan," she then says. "Bar one element."

"What's that?"

"If I meet him at his office, he might not bite. It needs to be somewhere he doesn't feel like anyone he knows might be watching."

"That's a good point. Where would you suggest?"

"Here is as good a place as any. Plus, he's more likely to respond to my flirting after a glass or two of wine."

"Perfect. I haven't confirmed any details yet, so I can suggest my regional manager wants to buy him lunch — no one ever turns down a free lunch."

"It sounds like we have the makings of a plan, and we can cover the finer details on the day."

"That brings me nicely to my next question. When are you available?"

"Wednesday or Thursday this week. I'm away for most of next week, I'm afraid."

"I don't want to push my luck, but I don't suppose you could do tomorrow? It just so happens that I have an excuse to be away from the office for an hour or two."

"Let me check my diary."

Candy dips a hand into her designer handbag and pulls out a small, leather-bound notebook. She flips it open and runs a manicured finger down the page.

"I can do tomorrow, but I've got an appointment at two o'clock, so I'd need to be away by half one."

"That should work if I tell Harrison to be here at noon. Will that give you enough time to … to do your thing?"

"I'm a fast worker, Danny," she replies before returning her diary to the handbag. "And I don't like to brag, but I've yet to meet a man impervious to my charms."

Candy follows up her statement by subtly glancing down at her own breasts. Point made.

"Um, that's … great," I respond, my cheeks burning slightly.

"Now, I guess there's just one loose end to tie up. My rate."

I brace myself, although I'm not really sure what to expect beyond the guide price of £100 an hour that Tina suggested.

"The total price for my service is £500. Payment to be made upfront and in cash."

"Oh."

"More than you expected?"

"I'm not sure, but it sounds okay … I guess."

"Not to put too fine a point on it, but what you're asking me to do goes way beyond what a typical client wants. I'm not just lying on my back and thinking of England for twenty minutes."

"No, I hear you, and I'm sure it'll be fine. I just need to run it by the family member I mentioned."

"Do you think they'll object?"

"Based upon the last conversation we had, I doubt it. The woman, Mrs Weller, appeared desperate."

"For what it's worth, I take my job seriously, and I wouldn't charge so much for my time if I didn't think I could deliver."

"No sense me trying to haggle, then?"

"You can try, but it won't get you anywhere."

Not that it's relevant, but my curiosity regarding Candy's career gets the better of me.

"Do many of your clients haggle?"

"If any man tries to argue with what I charge, he automatically discounts himself as a potential client. I'm running a business, and my time has a value."

"Is that how you see it? A business?"

"I'm no different from a hairdresser, really. People are paying for my time and expertise."

"It's not quite the same, though, is it? Don't take this the wrong way, but I doubt many girls at secondary school sit down with their careers advisor and ask how they become an escort."

"True, and no offence taken, but those same girls will happily spend decades doing a job they don't much like for not a lot of money. I love Tina to bits but I couldn't do what she does."

"I'd imagine quite a lot of people say they couldn't do your job."

"Having sex is easy. Anyone can do it."

"Alright. Wouldn't, not couldn't."

"And they're fools."

Candy pauses for a moment and then looks at me above the frame of her glasses.

"How old are you, Danny?" she asks.

"Twenty-eight."

"And when did you leave school?"

"Twelve years ago."

"So, you've been working for twelve years, and you *still* have thirty-seven years to go before you reach retirement age."

"Unless I win The Pools, I guess so."

"I've just turned twenty-one, and I've been in this game for two and a bit years. I'll be retired by the time I'm your age."

"Really?"

"I invest half of my income, and if those investments pay off, I can look forward to spending the rest of my life doing exactly what I want to do rather than working my arse off to make someone else rich."

"Wow."

"So, maybe those career advisers should think again. I'm certain most girls would rather spend just ten years being wined, dined, and treated like a princess over cutting hair for forty years with nothing to show for it at the end."

Candy makes a good argument, but she's glossed over the less savoury aspect of her job, which, if all goes to plan, will include snogging that smarmy turd, Neil Harrison. For that alone, I reckon five hundred quid is too small a price.

"Anything else you want to know?" she asks before checking her watch.

"Not that I can think of."

"If you want to go ahead tomorrow, I need to know by 10.00 am. Any later, and you'll have to pick another day."

"I'm heading off to see Mrs Weller now, so I can call you later this evening if that's okay?"

"I'm seeing a client, so leave a message on my answerphone. If it's a go, we can meet here at half eleven tomorrow just to prep before the main event."

"That sounds great."

Candy empties her glass and gets to her feet. "It's been nice meeting you, Danny."

"You too," I respond, holding out my hand.

"And if you ever get tired of working long hours in an office, there's a growing market for male escorts, you know. I'd happily show you the ropes ... so to speak."

My cheeks glow again, although I'm not entirely sure if Candy's suggestion is serious or not.

"I'll, um, bear that in mind."

"You do that," she replies with a broad smile. "And let me know either way about tomorrow."

"Of course."

She throws a wave my way before turning on her heels and sashaying back across the bar.

Whether Candy was serious or not, if I can't convince Mrs Weller that my plan is viable, selling sex might well become my last resort. Who'd be willing to pay for it, though, is an entirely different matter.

Chapter 34

As I drive up Echo Lane, the vista is noticeably different from my previous visits. Dusk is fast approaching and as the sun drops towards the horizon, the long shadows create an almost eerie feel to the lane as the Volvo bumps over the final yards.

Keen to get away before darkness really sets in, I hurry up the path and open the front door. I'm too tired and too hungry to loiter around in the entrance lobby and march straight through to the hallway.

"It's me, Mrs Weller," I call out. "Danny."

"Come on through."

Although she never specified if there's too late a time to drop by, I did call Mrs Weller this afternoon and check if it was okay. She reminded me that time is of the essence, and not to worry whatever the hour.

Despite the intensity and obscurity of our relationship, I don't yet know Mrs Weller well enough to comment on the fact that she's still wearing the same outfit and sitting in the same chair. I briefly consider a lame joke about her being there since yesterday morning, but the concern on her face suggests my humour wouldn't be well received.

"Sit down," she says flatly.

I silently oblige.

"You said you had a plan," Mrs Weller begins before I've even made myself comfortable.

"I do, but it's ... well, it's a little unorthodox, and I can't guarantee it'll come off."

"At this point, any plan is better than the alternative."

If it wasn't for the obvious anxiety in her eyes, I'd be tempted to press her on what that alternative might be.

"All I ask is you keep an open mind," I say.

"My mind is as open as it's ever likely to be, Daniel — that much I can promise you."

Promise made, I begin relaying the details of what I have in mind for Neil Harrison. To her credit, Mrs Weller sits and listens without comment. By the time I reach the final details, I have to admit it doesn't sound quite as batshit insane as it did this morning, but then I'm not the one being asked to fund it.

"What do you think?" I ask, trying to prompt some kind of reaction.

Mrs Weller doesn't say a word as she gets to her feet and steps across the kitchen. She then opens one of the cupboard doors and within a second, I realise what she's doing. The digital beeps suggest she's opening the safe, which could be a positive sign. Either Mrs Weller is about to hand over five hundred quid, or she keeps a pistol in the safe, and she's about to shoot me in the face for concocting such a ridiculous plan.

I watch on as Mrs Weller closes the safe, followed by the cupboard door. She then turns and almost hobbles back to the table.

"There you are, Daniel. Five hundred pounds in cash, as requested."

She places the pile of notes in the centre of the table and retakes her seat.

"Oh. Great. Thanks."

"You appear surprised."

"Um, not surprised as such. I thought you might take a bit more convincing, that's all."

"I have faith in you. If you think there's a chance this plan will work, I'm willing to help you in any way I can."

I'm slightly taken aback by her words. This woman who claims to know so much about me really doesn't know me at all. I could be lying through my back teeth purely to get my hands on more of her cash.

"That's very kind of you to say."

"It's not kindness, Daniel. This project won't succeed unless I have faith in you."

Assuming Mrs Weller is Kim's mother or at least a very close relative, there's something unsettling about the way she uses technical language to describe a family member's plight. Not that Kim is ever likely to find out about these meetings, but I wonder how she'd feel about being the subject of a project.

"Seeing as we're being frank, are you going to tell me what your relationship is to Kim?"

"I've said all I'm willing to say on that for the moment. However, if you are successful, I hope everything will become clear."

"Everything?"

"I'm sure you still have lots of questions. You certainly will once we know if your plan is a success … or not."

"I certainly have questions, like why you're willing to give away a house. Contract or no contract, you can't deny it does seem too good to be true."

"There are many things in life that might be considered too good to be true, as you'll discover. That doesn't mean they're not."

"So, the house will definitely be mine, will it?"

"I understand your scepticism, but the house will be yours once the project is complete, as will the contents of the safe."

"Are you going to tell me what's in the safe?"

"There's some cash which, as we've established, you may require to complete the project, but that's by no means the most valuable item in the safe."

"What is, then?"

"All in good time, Daniel. I've put my faith in you so I'd like to ask you to do the same, please. Can you do that for me?"

My eyes fall to the pile of notes on the table. A not insignificant sum of money, tendered with no scrutiny or questions, much like the rest of the cash that Mrs Weller has donated. I've no reason to trust this woman but neither do I have any reason not to.

"Yes, I can do that."

"Good," Mrs Weller says, finding a smile for the first time since I walked through the door.

"Um, unless there's anything else you need to know, do you mind if I scoot off? I've not eaten yet and could do with an early night. Big day tomorrow."

"Of course. You go."

I gather up the pile of banknotes and tuck them into my jacket pocket.

"When will you know if the plan has succeeded or not?" Mrs Weller asks as I get to my feet.

"By lunchtime, but then I need to get the photos developed — assuming Harrison walks into the trap. I think Boots do a four-hour service, but that might be cutting it fine to get the photos back before they close."

"Wednesday, then?"

"I think so, yes. I'll drop them by as early as I can."

"Drop them by?"

"Yes. You'll want the photos, right?"

"Why bring them here? It's Kim who needs to see them."

I stare down at Mrs Weller, perplexed.

"Sorry, are you suggesting that I show the photos to Kim? Surely it should be someone close to her that breaks the bad news."

"It has to be you, Daniel. There is no one else."

"But ... she'll assume I've got an ulterior motive."

"You do, though, don't you? You want this house."

"Yes, but Kim doesn't know that ... does she?"

"What Kim does or doesn't know is irrelevant. Just give her the photos and let fate deal with the fallout. Is that clear?"

"Do I have a choice?"

"I'm afraid not."

"No, I didn't think so," I huff. "But, for the record, I'm not comfortable with it."

"I wouldn't expect you to be, but it's our only option."

I'm too knackered to argue, and something tells me that I could stand here all night and not get a straight answer out of Mrs Weller, anyway.

"I'll see you on Wednesday."

"Good luck, Daniel."

"Cheers."

I wearily traipse back towards the hallway. As I reach the front door, I pause for a moment and look around. Is it really plausible that this place could be mine within the next few days? Maybe, because I've endured so much bad luck this year, the gods have decided to even things out — the gift of a house would certainly tip the scales in the opposite direction.

As tantalising as it is to imagine owning this place, I can't get carried away. There's the small matter of pulling off my plan and then Mrs Weller making good on her promise. Neither are certainties, that's for sure.

I drive home on auto-pilot, stopping at the chippy to grab a late dinner. Some might call it supper, but Dad once said that no man of working-class roots should ever use that word.

Besides, I don't think the middle classes would ever consider saveloy and chips suitable supper fare.

It's getting on for nine o'clock by the time I flop down on the sofa with a plastic tray and a fork. I unwrap my dinner and eat straight from the greasy paper. The chips are heavenly and the saveloy delicious, although I avoid dwelling on the contents of the latter.

There was a rumour at secondary school that the canteen saveloys contained pig anus, and sawdust swept up from an abattoir floor. That rumour never stopped Kevin Porter from bolting down eight saveloys in one sitting, thus cementing his position as the wackiest lad in school. Kevin now works in local government.

Hunger addressed, I consider drinking the last can of lager in the fridge. It might be just enough to drown out the noise in my head.

I get up and, on the way across the lounge, notice the blinking green light on the answerphone. Chances are, it's a message from Mum or a company I owe money to. It's too late to respond to either, but I know it'll bug me unless I check who called.

I place my tray on the coffee table, step over to the answerphone, and press the play button. A near-robotic voice confirms I received a message at 7.22 pm. The message begins: *Danny, it's me. I've been doing a lot of thinking since our conversation yesterday and I think we need to sit down and work out what's best for us both going forward. Unless I hear otherwise, I'll come over tomorrow evening at half seven. See you then.*

As much as I want to crack open the can of lager, I play the message again. It's not that I didn't understand Zoe's message, more the tone of voice she deployed. It wasn't edged with anger or irritation nor laced with regret or apology. In fact, there was barely a hint of emotion at all.

I hover over the answerphone, unsure whether I should just pick up the phone and call Zoe or delete the message. She is right in one respect — we do need to sit down and work out what's best for us both. Then again, the timing sucks. I've got enough to deal with tomorrow, and the last thing I need is a serious chat with my former fiancée.

Reaching for the handset, I stop myself. Tomorrow isn't the ideal time to deal with Zoe, but neither was yesterday, the day before, or any day since she moved out. I can't put it off any longer, circling around my problems rather than facing them head-on.

I tap the delete button.

Tomorrow should prove to be a pivotal day in Kim Dolan's life. Perhaps mine and Zoe's, too.

We'll see.

Chapter 35

A random itch on my thigh requires attention. I give it a brief scratch and then await the warm embrace of sleep once more. Something isn't quite right, though. In that brief second when my eyes flickered open, I'm sure the wall opposite the bed was bathed in muted light. It can't be morning already, surely. I force my eyes open and focus on the red digits of the alarm clock. 8.05 am.

"Fuck!"

Panic-stricken, I scramble out of bed and dash to the bathroom. I've got twenty-five minutes to empty my bladder, shower, get dressed, and drive into town.

Not the ideal start to what is likely to be a stressful enough day.

Twenty-four minutes later, I bring the Volvo to a screeching halt some hundred yards past the office. Hungry, bleary-eyed, and desperate for caffeine, I then jog back up the road and barge through the office door at exactly half-eight.

"Made it," I pant.

"Made what?" Lee asks from his desk.

"I got here on time."

"What do you want? A gold star? A pat on the fucking head?"

"Neither — I just want a coffee. Have I got time to make one?"

"Aye, but be quick."

I notice Gavin isn't at his desk, nor is he loitering in the back room when I get there. For all my panic, my colleague seems fairly relaxed when it comes to his time keeping. After flicking the kettle on, I load a mug with three heaped teaspoons of coffee granules and two of sugar. For the first time since I glanced at the alarm clock, I can pause for a moment and breathe. Then it hits me — what lies ahead today.

Even before I head out to meet Candy later, I've got to get to grips with the office camera, and for that, I require Gavin's input. For now, I need a coffee more than I've ever needed one. I pour the boiling water into the mug, stir it, and transfer the black nectar to my desk. Just as I sit down, Gavin wanders in.

"Morning," he chimes.

"You're late," Lee blasts. "Again."

"Yes, and I was also late getting home last night — it was eight o'bloody clock when I finally left Juniper Drive. I've never known a couple ask so many dumb questions."

"Did you get the instruction?"

"Yep."

"I'll let you off, then," Lee mumbles.

"How gracious," Gavin snorts. "Anyone want a brew?"

Tina and I both decline the offer but Lee holds out his empty mug. Another five minutes pass before we're all at our desks and the morning meeting can begin.

I'm only half-listening as Lee rattles through yesterday's events, but when he relays what's in store for us today, my ears prick up.

"I'm attending a repo at Sefton Court at ten this morning," he says. "Number 43."

"Another one?" I gasp.

"Aye. Won't be the last, either, I reckon."

I was in such a rush to leave the flat this morning, I didn't notice any of my neighbours moving out. That assumes they aren't just going about their day as normal, pretending that their worst fear isn't about to materialise. It's bad news for them, because it will, and it's bad news for me because it means another flat identical to ours is about to hit the market at a rock-bottom price.

If there's any positive to grasp, it's that Lee will be out of the office in just over an hour's time.

"Gav, you can do the valuation at Windham Close at eleven. I think they're wasters, mind, so don't hang around too long."

"Wasters?" I enquire.

"Folk who just want to know how much their house is worth. They've no intention of selling up, so it's a waste of our bloody time."

Lee then refers to the diary again before addressing me.

"Cass is in at eleven, so you need to make yourself scarce for an hour or two. We booked two valuations from your last leaflet drop, so it was time well spent."

The first time Lee asked me to trudge door to door, sticking leaflets through letterboxes, I was incensed. Now, I couldn't be more relieved. I've structured my entire plan on Cass O'Connor coming in, and Lee demanding I drop leaflets again.

"No worries," I respond, trying not to appear too keen.

Lee continues listing the rest of the appointments and tasks for the day, but all I care about is what happens at the Aston Grange Hotel at lunchtime. Everything appears to be falling nicely into place, but there are still many ways my plan might implode.

Best not to think about how. Best not to think at all.

The meeting draws to an end and Lee wanders out to the back room for a smoke. Tina then beckons me over to her desk.

"How'd it go with Candy?" she asks in a low voice.

"She's on board, so I owe you one."

"I bet she's charging you a fortune."

"She's charging someone a fortune — I'm just glad it isn't me."

"What did you think of her?"

"She's ... she's quite a remarkable young woman, and not what I expected at all."

"Yep, she's quite something, for sure. I kind of envy what she's achieved."

A response drifts into my head and moves towards my mouth, unfiltered.

"It's never too late for a career change."

Tina stares up at me, wide-eyed. "You're suggesting I should give up my job and sell sex for a living? How dare you!"

"Um, God ... no, that's not what I meant. I was thinking, you know ... like I changed careers to work here."

She snorts something under her breath but then chuckles to herself. "You're so easy to wind up, Danny."

"I'm not ... usually," I say after puffing a sigh of relief. "I've got a million and one distractions today, so my head is all over the place."

"Sorry, I didn't mean to tease you."

"No, it's cool. I'm just a bit stressed."

"Anything I can help with?"

"I don't think so, but thanks."

I return to my desk.

With Lee puffing away in the back room and Gavin on a phone call, I decide it's as good a time as any to commit my plan to paper, just to ensure my scheduling is thoroughly nailed down. If I mess up at any point, it'll probably flush the whole plan down the pan.

I grab a sheet of paper from the drawer and write out a timeline of how I see events unfolding. It doesn't take long, and the exercise has the added benefit of bolstering my optimism. The only element I have no control over is Candy and her ability to reel Neil Harrison in, but he'd have to be blind or gay not to be enticed by her charms.

Once Lee has left to meet another bailiff at Sefton Court, I waste no time addressing the first item on my list. I turn to my colleague before he picks up the phone again.

"Gav, have you got a sec?"

"Sure. What's up?"

"I need to use the office camera at lunchtime. Can you show me how to use it?"

"Can do, but what do you need it for?"

I relay a brief overview of what I've got in store for Neil Harrison.

"Bloody hell, mate," he reacts. "Whoever this woman is, she *really* doesn't want Kim dating that twat, does she?"

"That's putting it mildly."

"And what about you?"

"What about me?"

"You're jumping through a lot of hoops to help this woman. I hope she's looking after you."

Gavin then raises his eyebrows, the implication clear.

"Yes, she's looking after me but not in that way."

"If you say so, mate," he sniggers.

I roll my eyes, and Gavin retrieves the office camera from a drawer. At first glance, it's a complicated-looking beast.

"I'm assuming you've used a camera before?" he says.

"I've used one of those Kodak point-and-click cameras, but that's as far as my photographic knowledge extends."

"This isn't much different," he replies, leaning forward so I can see what buttons he's about to press. "Unless you're a budding David Bailey, you can ignore most of the functions."

"Good to know."

"Basically, you've got the buttons for the zoom function, which might come in handy if you're a distance away, and then you just press this button to capture the shot."

"Seems simple enough."

"I presume you won't be taking photos inside."

"I hadn't planned to. Does it matter?"

"If you're taking photos inside, you'll need to add the flash unit."

"Yeah, Harrison is many things, but he's not blind. A sudden flash going off might give the game away."

"You raise a good point. Anyway, how many photos are you hoping to capture?"

"Not sure. Maybe five or six."

"Do you have to reel the film on with your Kodak camera?"

"Yes."

"This does it automatically, but it takes a second, so don't get too trigger-happy. There's a little light in the top-right corner of the viewfinder — when it's red, wait, and when it's green, you're good to go. Got it?"

"Got it."

Another concern then crosses my mind.

"Lee isn't likely to need the camera this afternoon is he?"

"I don't think so, but he might be in the office when you get back, so you'll need to explain why you took the camera out with you."

"Yeah, I hadn't thought about that. Any ideas?"

Gavin turns to his left, and the panel on the wall displaying all the available properties for sale.

"Hmm," he then muses. "The photo of 22 Brompton Road is pretty shit. As it's a nice day, I think you should take a better one while you're out dropping leaflets."

"Thanks, mate. I really appreciate it."

"Do you?"

"Of course."

"Good, because I've got just enough time for a quick coffee before my appointment."

He hands me the camera and then his empty mug.

"Me and my big mouth," I laugh. "But fair enough."

I head to the back room and pay my dues. Twenty minutes later, Gavin heads off for his valuation, but not before wishing me good luck. I snatch up the phone and dial the number for Harrison Telecoms. The receptionist puts me straight through to Neil Harrison.

"Morning, Neil," I say breezily.

"Good morning, Danny," he responds in a slightly more friendly tone than the last time I called.

"Listen, I need to be quick, but I have good news and bad news. The good news is that my regional manager, Andy, is really keen to meet you. In fact, he's so keen to discuss this deal that he wants to know if you're available for lunch today at noon at the Aston Grange Hotel."

"Today?"

"Yeah, sorry it's such short notice, but Andy is away on holiday next week, so his diary is a bit hectic."

"It's okay. I can be there at noon."

"Brilliant. I'll let him know, and I hope the meeting goes well — we're all desperate to get our hands on a mobile telephone."

"Sounds good. And thanks again for setting this up."

I have to stifle a snort of laughter at his terminology. I'm certainly setting him up, but I think his gratitude will be short-lived.

After confirming Andy will meet him in the bar, I end the call and puff a deep breath. The mouse is now heading straight towards the trap, unaware that the sexy cheese waiting for him will prove his downfall.

Alas, I'm only able to bask in my satisfaction for five minutes. Lee returns to the office, and he's not alone.

"Hello again, Danny," Cass O'Connor says as she steps towards my desk. "In a better mood today, are we?"

"I'm fine, thanks," I reply with a plastic smile. "I presume you'd like my desk?"

"If it's no bother."

She could use Gavin's until he returns, but I get the feeling that Ms O'Connor is the type who bears grudges. If she can inconvenience me, even just a little, it's a form of payback.

"No bother at all," I respond, maintaining my smile but never letting it reach my eyes. "Anything to help a colleague."

I get up and step away from the desk, allowing her to sit in my chair.

"If you're feeling particularly helpful," she then says, grinning up at me. "I wouldn't say no to a nice cup of tea."

I glance over my shoulder. Lee is in the back room, probably enjoying a post-repossession cigarette. I lean over my own desk and raise the brilliance of my smile to the maximum.

"I am feeling particularly helpful," I say in a low voice. "But *you* can piss right off to the back room and make your own tea."

"Tut, tut, potty mouth," she replies, seemingly undaunted by my retort. "A simple no would have sufficed."

We glare at one another for a moment before I grab the camera and turn away. As little as I like Cass O'Connor, I've got more pressing concerns than a mortgage advisor with an attitude problem.

I wander through to the back room, where Lee is sucking the life out of his cigarette.

"I'm about to head out leaflet dropping."

"Alright, lad."

He then notices the camera in my hand.

"What are you doing with that?"

"As it's a bright, sunny day, Gavin asked me to get a new photo of 22 Brompton Road — the current one isn't great. Would you like me to take any others while I'm out?"

"Actually, we need one for this flat in Sefton Court, from the rear. It looks like that'll be on the market by the end of the week."

"Dare I ask how much for?"

"You might want to sit down — £44,950."

"Shit," I groan. "Why so low?"

"We sold the last one for forty-four grand, and this one is a bit tattier. If anyone offers a number north of forty grand, I reckon the lender will take it."

If I was hoping for a dollop of positivity before embarking on my lunchtime mission, Lee has just ramped up the pressure. My negative equity is increasing by the day, and if I can't meet Mrs Weller's challenge, my last hope of escaping mortgage purgatory is as good as over.

Everything now rests on an escort who may or may not be called Candy Dubois and the roving eye of a random dickhead who runs a telecoms company.

One way or another, this is going to be some afternoon.

Chapter 36

I decide to drop by Brompton Road before heading to the hotel. I'd rather hurry straight back to the office once I've captured Harrison's deceit, hopefully in time to get the photos developed before the end of the day. It also gives me an opportunity to test out the camera so I'm familiar with the various buttons.

After spending five minutes on Brompton Road, testing the zoom function and firing off shots from three different angles, I feel suitably competent.

I give the Volvo a good workout on the two-mile journey to the Aston Grange Hotel and arrive on the stroke of half-eleven. As I pull into a parking bay and kill the engine, a white Golf Cabriolet pulls up directly opposite. There are two distinct and notable features about the car that snare my attention. Firstly, it's H-reg, so virtually brand new and a limited edition model in Alpine White. Secondly, the woman smiling at me from the driver's seat.

We simultaneously exit our vehicles, and one of us glances admiringly back towards theirs. It's not me.

"Good timing," Candy beams as she steps towards me. "I need a strong man."

"I'll go ask in the bar," I reply with a grin.

She giggles and then beckons me over to the boot of her Golf.

"Shall we get the admin out of the way?" Candy then asks after opening the boot.

"Um, admin?"

"Payment."

"Yes, of course."

I extract the wad of notes from my jacket pocket and hand them over. Candy quickly flicks through them and confirms the amount is as agreed.

"Would you grab that for me?" she then asks, nodding at an oversized black briefcase. "It's an essential prop."

I grab the handle and, keen to prove my masculinity, casually flex my arm to lift the briefcase out. It doesn't budge.

"What the hell have you got in here?"

"Four house bricks and a five-kilo kettlebell."

"Explains it," I grunt, pulling out the case. "Do you always carry building materials and gym equipment when meeting clients?"

"Not as a rule," Candy replies, closing the boot. "But what gentleman can resist aiding a poor woman with a hefty briefcase full of files and folders?"

"Ah, I get it. This is to lure Harrison back to your car."

"Exactly."

"You really are more than a pretty face. I hadn't even considered how you'd manage that."

"Are you flirting with me, Danny?"

"I can't even remember how to flirt, but if I am, my cheeks are usually a giveaway."

"They are a little on the rosy side."

"That'll be the exertion of carrying this bloody thing," I chuckle, nodding down to the briefcase. "Shall we head inside before my shoulder dislocates?"

"Lead on."

As we walk, Candy begins relaying her strategy.

"I'll approach him when he arrives and make the apologies for my boss being unavailable."

"I've already told Harrison that Andy Shaw is on holiday next week, so his diary is rammed."

"That's good, as it'll seem less fishy that I've turned up in his place. The plan is to just have a light lunch — I'll tell him I've got to be away by one-ish, and then when he's not boring me about mobile telephones, I'll flirt my arse off."

"You won't overdo it, though, will you? He might get suspicious if you're too overt."

"Are you questioning my experience and judgement, Danny?"

"Er, no, not at all."

"Good, because I've yet to meet a red-blooded man that I couldn't twist around my little finger if I so wish. You've nothing to worry about on that front."

"Yes, of course. I trust you."

"Pleased to hear it," she says firmly. "Now, once one o'clock comes and I wrap up the meeting, I'll ensure he notices how heavy my briefcase is, and he'll offer to carry it to the car."

"You're sure of that?"

"I know you said he's an arsehole, but even arseholes can't resist playing the knight in shining armour. It's an ego thing."

"True."

"And once I've lured him back to the car, I'll whisper a few sweet nothings and then go in for the kill."

"Great, but make sure you're standing where I can capture a clear photo. This will all be for nothing if I can't get evidence of Harrison cheating."

"Understood. Where will you be?"

"Sitting in my car, but I'll park it a few bays away so don't worry if you can't see me."

"Okay, cool."

We enter the hotel bar, and Candy guides me to her preferred table. I then give her a description of Neil Harrison and we cover the last few points. Considering her role, Candy should be the one wracked with nerves, but she couldn't be any cooler.

"This will be a walk in the park," she assures me. "Now, get out of here in case he pitches up early."

"Right, yes ... I'm going. Good luck."

"Don't need it," she replies with a wink.

I scoot back to the Volvo and decide to move it a few bays further along, tucked discreetly behind a Range Rover. The view of Candy's Golf isn't quite as good but I'm far less likely to be spotted by Harrison when taking the photos.

Now, there's nothing left to do but sit and wait. And fret.

With nothing else better to occupy my mind, I stare at the dashboard clock. The minutes tick by and my heart rate picks up a few extra beats with every one of them. Candy only has one hour to work on her mark, so he'd better not be late.

At two minutes to twelve, I hear the sound of a car approaching. The Range Rover partially obscures my view, but if I sit bolt upright and twist to the right, I can just about see through the side windows.

A silver Porsche slows to a near standstill right behind Candy's Golf, and the driver reverse parks into the space I recently vacated. It's exactly the car I imagined Harrison might drive, but until the driver gets out, I can't confirm if my assumption was correct.

I shrink back into my seat and wait to hear the sound of a car door slamming shut. Then, I'll wait ten seconds, by which point the driver should be walking towards the hotel entrance.

Holding my breath, I wait. Seconds pass, and, to my relief, I hear the sound of a car door closing.

Ten, nine, eight ...

I reach four and sit upright again, focussing on the narrow band of tarmac visible through the Range Rover's windows. There, some fifty yards away, is a tall figure in a suit swaggering towards the path that leads to the hotel entrance. As he gets further away, almost beyond my direct view, he happens to turn his head to the left to look at a sign.

"Yes!" I whoop.

Neil Harrison then hurries on, out of view.

I relax back into my seat, knowing that the stress respite will be brief. Any minute now, Neil Harrison will realise that he's not meeting Gibley Smith's regional manager but his PA. If Candy fails to convince him that she's worthy of his time, Harrison will walk away, dashing my plan in the process.

I return my attention to the dashboard clock.

Inevitably, I try to picture the scene in the hotel bar. How would I react if I turned up to what I presumed would be a constructive and potentially lucrative meeting, only to discover the person who holds the keys to the deal has sent a makeweight?

I'd be pissed, for sure, but Candy is one hell of a consolation prize.

I close my eyes and take a series of deep breaths. I've done all I can, and sitting here stressing won't change the outcome.

As my heart rate slowly returns to normal, I focus on the sound of birds in the hedgerow behind the Volvo. Besides their chirps and tweets, the scene is otherwise silent. For a short while, I manage to escape my own thoughts and drift towards a state of nothingness. It's almost meditative, but I doubt even the Dalai Lama could train his mind to evade the shitstorm of troubles I'm currently contending with.

One of those troubles then barges Neil Harrison out of the way and steps into the spotlight of my attention. Bloody Zoe.

Even if events go exactly as planned in the next hour or so, I still have a showdown with my ex-fiancée looming. I could go into that conversation knowing that my financial problems are behind me, but even if that is the case, there's still the emotional turbulence to weather.

I love Zoe, but I hate her.

No, that's not right. I don't hate her — I just don't like her very much. Even putting aside what she did to me, the last two weeks have revealed previously unseen dimensions to her personality, and some of those dimensions are deeply unappealing. They're certainly not traits you'd choose in a soul mate. Maybe, by definition, that means Zoe never was my soul mate. And yet, I was convinced she was. I'm still not convinced she isn't.

As a headache begins to form, I open my eyes and glance at the clock: 12.11 pm. A small but powerful wave of relief washes over me. If Harrison wasn't willing to sit down with Candy, he'd have returned to his car by now. Another tick against another part of the plan.

Unbelievably, this might actually work.

The relief soon turns to regret — I wish I'd grabbed something to eat before driving over here. I haven't eaten since last night's late chippy dinner, and now the stress and adrenalin have eased a touch, hunger is making its presence felt.

Do I dare drive to the nearest petrol station and grab a Cornish pasty? Is there sufficient time before Candy completes her challenge? I don't even know where the nearest petrol station is, let alone if they sell snacks. And what if the Volvo chooses to play up whilst I'm parked up on a petrol station forecourt?

Hungry as I am, it's too much of a risk.

I close my eyes and try to clear my mind again, which is nice until I just about catch myself nodding off. This is awful on so many levels. How police detectives manage to sit in their cars for hours on end, doing nothing, is beyond me. I've managed thirty minutes, and I'm already bored out of my tiny mind.

To alleviate the tedium, I switch the stereo on. When I first took ownership of the Volvo, I set the first pre-set station to Radio 1, and that's all I've listened to since. I've not had any need or motivation to check out the remaining pre-set stations but I guess now is as good a time as any.

If I needed any evidence that whoever owned the Volvo before me was of advanced years, it comes when I select the second pre-set station. One of BBC Radio 3's sombre presenters introduces their next offering: *Martinu Symphony No 1.*

If there's one genre of music guaranteed to induce sleep, it's Classical. I jab the next button. A play on BBC Radio 4 is just as likely to send me to sleep. Buttons four to six aren't even tuned to a station, so I return to my choice of Radio 1. Newsbeat has just started.

The presenter's remit on Newsbeat is to make complex issues digestible to a younger audience and less depressing than other news outlets. Even so, today's roll call of grim news covers the inquest into the 1988 Clapham Rail Disaster, where thirty-five people died, the mounting crisis in The Gulf, and the latest unemployment stats. The presenter then cuts to a clip from Labour's Shadow Minister for Employment, Tony Blair, who warns that the government's fiscal policies are the cause rather than the cure to the country's economic ills. I mentally tune out — I've no interest in the views of another here today, gone tomorrow politician.

To lighten the mood after Newsbeat, the DJ, Gary Davies, decides an up-tempo song is in order. *Tonight* by New Kids on The Block wouldn't have been my choice — not now, not ever.

As the clock continues to count down to one, I half-listen to the radio and semi-daydream about how my life might change for the better if I pull off this challenge. The radio proves a distraction, so I turn it off.

Barely sixty seconds later, the sound of laughter from the far side of the car park drags me back to the here and now. It's too early for Candy and Harrison but I double-check by inspecting the view through the Range Rover windows.

"Crap!"

I just catch sight of a grinning Neil Harrison carrying a briefcase whilst walking slowly towards a white Golf Cabriolet. Candy appears to be leading him into the final stage of the trap, but she's a good five minutes ahead of schedule.

Suddenly panicked into action, I snap out my hand to grab the camera from the passenger seat, but in my haste, it slips from my grip, bounces off the edge of the seat, and drops into the footwell. It takes a few seconds of frantic scrambling to retrieve it, and by the time I line up the viewfinder to my left eye, Candy and Harrison are already standing near the Golf's boot.

I could kick myself. Another few seconds and I might have blown the one and only chance to capture what I suspect is about to unfold.

Candy closes the boot and slowly steps backwards whilst continuing a conversation with Harrison. Step by step, she manages to manoeuvre him to the side of the car, just short of the driver's door. Standing so close together, face to face, it's now obvious that Candy is about to deliver on her side of the bargain — Harrison has the look of a young child staring into a toy shop window.

I click the button on the top of the camera to capture my first shot. On its own, it's not evidence of betrayal, but, as the first page of the story I want to tell Kim Dolan, it's compelling.

Harrison then dips a hand into his jacket pocket and passes his new acquaintance what looks like a business card. Candy slips it into her pocket and then places a hand on Harrison's upper arm. Words are exchanged, and the expression on my target's face alters.

My hired help steps so close that their bodies must be almost touching, and she then beckons Harrison to lean in close. I realise she's about to whisper something in his ear. Whatever her words, they're brief and obviously enticing, as Harrison doesn't straighten up afterwards. I take another shot as Candy reaches up and places her hand on Harrison's left cheek. Another shot.

Time seems to stand still as the couple remain entirely motionless. Whatever Harrison has done thus far, however much he has flirted with or ogled Candy, it's all meaningless unless he takes this final step.

Inch by painstaking inch, Harrison bows his head forward as Candy moves her hand from his cheek to the back of his head. I take two photos in quick succession and then a third as their lips meet. My one fear was that the kiss might not appear damning enough, but that fear is quickly dispelled as the couple engage in a long, passionate snog. My cause is aided when Harrison's right hand moves south and begins pawing at Candy's buttock. I capture four more photos before the couple break for air. They talk for a moment and then Candy opens the driver's door and gets in her Golf. Harrison says goodbye with a lecherous smile before turning around and striding in the direction of his Porsche.

No longer concerned with what's happening in the car park, I double check the small LCD display on the back of the camera. It confirms the next shot will be the fourteenth on a roll of twenty-four — three shots at Brompton Road and the ten I've just snapped.

I carefully place the camera on the passenger seat and puff a huge sigh of relief. The sense of elation is intense, and I have to release it by pummelling the lower half of the steering wheel with my clenched fists. It takes every ounce of resolve not to get out of the Volvo and perform a victory dance in the car park.

I've done it.

I've actually done it.

The most insane of plans, plotted and executed without so much as a glitch. Granted, there's still the unpleasant task of showing the photos to Kim, but I'm doing her a massive favour — that much is now evident.

I glance at the dashboard clock again. This time tomorrow, I should be the proud new owner of a house on Echo Lane. That thought prompts a smile. I thought that 1990 was set to be the shittiest year of my twenty-eight, but it could well prove to be the most incredible. Incredible and pivotal.

No looking back now. Time to move forward.

Chapter 37

If I needed any further proof that my luck is on the turn, it comes as I drive down Victoria Road in search of a parking space. Twenty yards ahead, a black Ford XR3i indicates to pull out of a spot. I flash my headlights to let him out and then quickly manoeuvre the Volvo into the vacant space.

With the camera in my hand, I get out of the car and hurry down the road to Boots. The last time I visited the photo processing counter was back in the spring after Zoe and I spent a long weekend in London as a treat. We travelled up on the Friday, and in the afternoon, we climbed Primrose Hill. Standing at the top, we asked a fellow tourist if he'd take a photo of the two of us, with the entirety of London sprawled out behind us as the backdrop. We looked so happy in that photo, so much in love.

Unfortunately, we booked our trip in mid-December, possibly weeks before some bright spark decided to organise a mass protest against the poll tax on the Saturday of our break. That same bright spark underestimated how much angst had built up over Thatcher's new tax, which is probably why over two hundred thousand people turned up, and, unsurprisingly, the protest turned into a riot.

We avoided the worst of the trouble, but only by staying clear of several places we'd hoped to visit, including Trafalgar Square and Whitehall. When we finally got to walk along

Whitehall on Sunday, it was like wandering through the set of a post-apocalyptic movie, such was the devastation.

I glance at my watch as I approach the middle-aged guy behind the photo processing counter. It only then occurs to me that I might have a small problem.

"You'll think I'm an idiot," I say sheepishly. "But this is a friend's camera, and they never told me how to get the film out."

"It's your lucky day," the guy replies with a smile. "I dabble in amateur photography, so I might be able to work it out for you."

I hand the camera over, and the cheery Boots' employee prods a couple of buttons on the back. The camera then makes a whirring sound for a few seconds.

"All done."

"Brilliant. Thank you."

"You're welcome. I presume you'd like to process the film?"

"Yes, please. The four-hour service."

The guy then glances up at a clock on the wall and grimaces. It's exactly 1.31 pm.

"I think this is where your luck runs out. We shut at half five, so you won't get the photos today."

"It's only a minute late."

"Ordinarily, that might not be a problem, but we've got a backlog of orders today. I'm sorry, but tomorrow morning is the best I can offer."

"I guess I'll go with that, then."

He helpfully transfers the film to an envelope, requests my name and phone number, and then hands over a receipt.

"Do I pay now?" I ask.

"On collection."

I thank him again and hurry to the other side of the store to grab a sandwich and a bag of crisps. I'm so hungry I end up buying two BLT sandwiches and a bag of Monster Munch — a worthy reward for a plan well executed. While I'm queueing to pay, there happens to be a display opposite, full of boxes of Cadbury's Roses. The selection of chocolates is now considered the standard when it comes to saying thank you, and it crosses my mind that I do have someone I need to thank. I step over to the display and grab a box.

Once I've paid for and bagged up my items, including the camera, I dash back down Victoria Road, hoping to God that Lee doesn't ask too many questions about my supposed leaflet drop.

As it turns out, I needn't have worried. Neither Lee nor Gavin are at their desks, and it's also a blessing that Cass O'Connor has gone. I notice she's left her tea-stained mug on my desk, though — a petty act of retribution, I suspect.

"How'd it go?" Tina asks from behind her keyboard.

As hungry as I am, I owe her an answer.

"Brilliantly," I reply, stepping over to her desk. "And you deserve a massive thank you."

I dip my hand into the carrier bag and pull out the box of Roses.

"Unfortunately," I say, placing the chocolates on Tina's desk. "They didn't have massive boxes, so I had to settle on medium."

"For me?" she gushes. "You didn't have to."

"It's the least I can do. If you hadn't introduced me to Candy, I'd never have pulled off Project Kim."

"I'm just glad it went as planned."

"It did, and although she'll never know your involvement, Kim also owes you and Candy a debt of gratitude. She's really dodged a bullet."

"Happy to help for the sisterhood," Tina chuckles whilst opening the Roses. "And the chocolates, obviously."

My stomach then rumbles so loudly Tina tips the box in my direction.

"Sounds like you need feeding."

"Thanks, but I've got a late lunch planned," I reply, holding up the carrier bag.

"You're sure? I can't promise there will be any left by the time you've eaten your lunch."

"You go for it," I smile before heading to the back room.

After bolting down the sandwiches and demolishing the Monster Munch, I put the kettle on. Lee must have some kind of kettle detection sense as he wanders in just as it clicks to the boil.

"Don't say it," I remark as he opens his mouth. "I know my place — milk and two sugars."

"I was only going to ask how the leaflet drop went but, seeing as you're offering, go on then."

I perform my tea-making duties and then return to my desk. The sense of elation I felt in the hotel car park has all but gone, leaving my mind to dwell on this evening's conversation with Zoe. I don't want to think about it or what her motives might be.

It's not the distraction I'd have chosen, but Lee asks what I'm doing.

"I was about to follow up on a couple of outstanding viewings."

"Leave that for now. I'm heading out on a valuation in five minutes, and you can come with me."

"Er, okay."

He doesn't explain why he wants me to accompany him, and that immediately sets off an alarm bell. Have I done something wrong? Does he know that I lied about the leaflet dropping earlier? Will my boss headbutt me on the way to his car?

My mind scrambles for an answer, but after five minutes of nervous paper shuffling, I still can't think of a reason Lee wants me to join him.

"Ready, lad?" he asks, getting to his feet.

"Yep."

We leave the office and walk down Victoria Road to where Lee has parked his car: a powder-blue Ford Sierra.

"I fucking hate this thing," he complains while unlocking the doors. "I had a 1600 Orion Ghia before this, but the bastards at head office made me hand it over when it hit three years."

We climb into the object of Lee's disgust.

"Now everyone thinks I'm a bloody sales rep," he continues while putting on his seatbelt. "And it's a shite drive, to boot."

"If it's any consolation, it's better than my Volvo."

"At least you can sell your car. I'm stuck with this bastard thing for two more bloody years."

He starts the Sierra and pulls away. We're on the opposite side of the town centre before he speaks again.

"There's a reason I wanted to drag you out on this valuation," he says. "Two, as it happens."

"Oh?" is all I can muster in response, my mouth dry.

"How are you finding things?"

"Things?"

"You know, the job."

"It's early days, but yeah, I'm enjoying it."

"It's work, lad — you're not supposed to enjoy it. What I mean is, do you reckon you'll stick at it?"

I ponder Lee's question for a moment.

"And don't tell me what you think I want to hear," he adds. "Tell me what you really think."

"Truthfully, it's hard starting at the bottom again, and the long hours are a bind, but it's a better job than I thought it was going to be."

"It'll get easier."

"So Gavin said."

"Which brings me back to my original question: do you think you'll stick at it?"

"I think so, yes."

"Good, because I reckon you've got what it takes to make a career out of it. You're a bit of a fucking poser, mind, but beyond that, I like the way you've settled in."

"Um, thanks, boss ... I think."

We reach a roundabout and Lee gives way to a car exiting the junction on our right. Without indicating, that car turns left. My boss opens his window and leans out.

"Indicate, you daft twat!" he yells, to no obvious avail.

"Some folk shouldn't be allowed to drive," he mutters, returning his attention to the roundabout. "Mainly, those with tits."

I remain silent as we proceed on to the next exit, heading towards the southern edge of the town.

"What was I saying?" he then asks.

"You were saying I've settled in well, and you'd like to double my pay."

"Nice try, sunshine," he snorts. "Unfortunately, I don't get to decide how much anyone in the office is paid. Saying that, though, I do get to decide on who's hired and fired and who gets promoted."

"Right."

"So, if you can keep doing what you're doing, I can justify dropping the junior part of your job title next month."

"Oh, wow. That'd be great."

"There's an extra couple of grand on your basic, and you get a company car. It'll only be a Fiesta but at least you won't have to pay for insurance and tax or owt like that."

"Honestly, I'm ... I don't know what to say. Thank you."

"Don't thank me, lad. Gav and Junior both think the sun shines out of your arse for some reason, and they'd rather you stay. I couldn't give less of a fuck, myself."

Lee's statement is followed up by a wry smile, perhaps suggesting that he might, at least, give a tiny fuck.

"You said there was a second reason for bringing me along to your valuation."

"Aye, there is. It's called training."

"Training?"

"Am I speaking in tongues?" he huffs. "Yes, training."

"Training to value houses?"

"No, elephants, you dozy git. Yes, houses."

"Right."

"Don't sound too excited."

"No, I'm chuffed that you think I'm ready."

"You're a long way from ready, and the only way you'll get there is by watching and learning from a master like me. From now on, I want you to attend at least two valuations a week."

"I'm up for that."

Anything is preferable to being stuck in the office.

"There's another good reason for fast-tracking your training," Lee continues. "Woolwich Property Services have just employed a smarmy arsewipe by the name of Jamie Brice. He was one of the top negotiators at our Winchester office before Woolwich poached him, and do you know the secret to his success?"

"No idea."

"He's a poser, like you. The housewives love him and once he turns on the charm, they're like putty in his hands. I want you to be our version of Jamie bastard Brice."

"Well, er, I don't know if that's really me."

"Course it is, lad," Lee replies with a dismissive flick of his hand. "Obviously, you'll never be as charming or good-looking as me, but we need to fight fire with fire. Woolwich now have their smarmy, twenty-something salesman, and you're going to be ours, only better."

"Okay, I'm game if you think I'm right for the role."

"I wouldn't be wasting my time if I didn't think you were."

I've only known Lee for a few weeks, but I get the feeling he's not one for gushing praise. However, that doesn't mean I'm not flattered by his offer of a modest promotion and even his misplaced faith in my ability to charm the housewives of Frimpton.

As we reach the edge of a small housing estate, it occurs to me that maybe, just maybe, I might be able to make a go of my newfound career. It's not a career I'm mad about, but, as Lee himself implied, no one goes to work for the love of it.

"Oh, there's just one other thing," my boss then says. "Cass."

"What about her?"

"I don't know what the deal is with you two, but you need to sort it out. I can't have you bickering like kids in the office."

"Have you said the same to her?"

"Not yet, no, but I will."

"Alright, I'll try to build bridges."

Lee pulls over in front of a tired-looking semi and kills the engine.

"That's what I wanted to hear. And, for the record, Cass is alright when you get to know her."

"I'm sure she is," I reply with a half-hearted smile.

"See — you're learning," Lee says, grinning like an idiot. "That was bullshit, but almost believable bullshit."

Chapter 38

My eyes flick left and right. I can't decide, and I've only got a minute to make up my mind. On the one hand, I quite fancy a pizza but on the other, I've eaten nothing but crap for days, and I really should eat something vaguely healthy.

Reluctantly, I return the pizza to the chiller and plod over to the till to pay for a beef casserole.

It's a quarter past seven by the time I walk through the front door of the flat. Although I'm only minutes away from a showdown with my ex-fiancée, that wasn't my first thought when I pulled into the car park. Lee asked me to get a photo of the building for our latest repossession, and I clean forgot.

I hope his bullshit detection meter isn't functioning tomorrow.

Standing in the kitchen, I read the instructions on the microwave meal I just purchased. However, my appetite seems to have left all of a sudden, which is no real surprise. I put it in the fridge, hoping my appetite will return once Zoe has been and gone. With ten minutes to spare before she arrives, I've got just enough time to make a phone call I haven't had the opportunity to make all afternoon. I dial Mrs Weller's number.

"Hi, it's only me, Danny."

"I've been waiting for you to call, Daniel. What news?"

"I'll have to be quick as I'm expecting a guest any minute, but it's good news — Harrison took the bait, and tomorrow morning, I'm due to collect photos of him kissing our escort friend."

"Are they convincing photos?"

"Um, I'd say so, for sure. Not only are they kissing, but he took the opportunity to have a proper grope of her backside."

"I'd like to say I'm relieved, but I know how much it'll hurt Kim when she sees those photos."

"Yeah, about that. I was thinking I could just pop into Lunn Poly when Kim is at lunch and drop them on her desk."

"Absolutely not," Mrs Weller says assertively. "You must give them to her in person and ensure she looks at them."

"Really?" I groan. "Do I have to?"

"Yes, I'm afraid you do. It's the only way we can guarantee the task is complete."

"Alright, I'll do it."

"Good, and when do you anticipate you'll speak to Kim?"

"I'll intercept her on the way to the bakery tomorrow."

"That sounds ideal, and I know it won't be easy, Daniel, but I promise you it's for her own good."

"I hope you're right because—"

"I am right, and the next time we meet, I'll explain why."

"On that note, I could pop in on my way home from work tomorrow evening so we can sort out the ... you know ... the details of our deal."

"Of course. What time might I expect you?"

"That depends on my boss, but no later than eight."

"Perfect."

"Right, I'd better go."

"Thank you for calling, and I wish you luck tomorrow. And however Kim reacts, know that you're doing the right thing."

I end the call, still not one hundred per cent sure about anything, but I'm in too deep to backtrack. As little as I want to break the bad news to Kim, I suppose it's fitting that the messenger has also experienced cheating.

The sound of the front door opening immediately snuffs any further thoughts of Kim. I can't believe Zoe let herself in, but I suppose this is still her flat as much as it is mine.

She steps into the lounge and, for a moment, it would be easy to imagine things are today as they once were. My fiancée has just returned home from work. There's no welcome home hug or kiss on this occasion, although it does appear Zoe hasn't bothered to change out of her work clothes.

"Hey," I say, purely to break the silence.

"You okay?" she replies, just as flatly.

"Fine, thanks. Do you want something to drink?"

"No, I'm good. I just want to talk."

She takes a moment to look around the room before flopping down on the sofa. I choose the armchair.

"I've missed this place," Zoe then says, brushing her hand across the arm of the sofa.

"You were the one who walked out."

"I didn't walk out — you told me to leave."

"Like I had a choice."

"Let's not go there again, eh? I'm tired of apologising for what happened and ... and if you don't believe me now, you never will."

"Believe that you're sorry?"

"Yes."

"I think you are sorry, Zoe. You're sorry, I'm sorry ... doesn't make me feel any better, though."

"Will anything make you feel better?"

"I don't know," I reply with a shrug.

"And what about my feelings?"

"Your feelings?"

"After what you did on Saturday."

"I didn't do anything."

"Fuck sake, Danny — you were snogging another woman's face off."

"If that's what Claire thinks she saw, she must have been pissed because — as I told you on Sunday — that's not what happened. A woman kissed me, but I played no part in it."

"Even if you didn't instigate the kiss, you were out in a bar with her, weren't you?"

"I was at a bar with a group of people. Don't make it sound like I was on a date because I wasn't."

"Will you see her again?"

"Probably not, but if I do, it won't be romantically."

Zoe looks up at the ceiling for a moment, maybe to inspect the shade she spent so long choosing in Habitat.

"I'm willing to forgive you," she then says. "If you promise it didn't mean anything."

I've had a long day. I'm tired and hungry, and my brain is frazzled, which is why I have to double-check what I think I just heard.

"I'm sorry. *You're* willing to forgive *me*?"

"If you're telling the truth, yes."

Rather than respond with indignation or anger, I take a beat and let Zoe's temerity sink in. It's almost impossible to believe anyone could possess so little self-awareness, never mind someone I know intimately.

"You're acting like the wronged party here, Zoe. You do realise that, don't you?"

"You were seen kissing another woman. Of course, I'm the wronged party."

"There are two flaws to your argument. Firstly, and I don't know how many times I have to say this, but I didn't kiss anyone — someone kissed me. Secondly, it might have escaped your attention, but we're no longer together. Who I kiss is no concern of yours."

It wasn't my intention to sound quite so cold, but Zoe's pained expression implies I failed.

"We were talking about trying again," she responds with a slight sniff. "That's what you led me to believe."

"Yes, we were talking about it but … but the fact remains that we're not a couple."

"Now you've had a taste of single life, you're backtracking. Is that it?"

"No."

"I don't believe you."

"Believe what you like, but nothing has changed since last week."

"What does that mean? I need to know where I stand."

"It means … I still don't feel I can trust you, and I'm a long way from being able to forget what you did."

Zoe stares back at me, open-mouthed. "And what about what you did and how that made me feel?"

"For the umpteenth—"

"No, Danny, you can't have it both ways. I hurt you, yes, and I wish I could turn back time and undo that, but you hurt me too. Surely that's quits now."

"Quits? Are you serious?"

"Yes."

"This isn't a game of tit-for-tat, but even if it was, you can't compare what happened on Saturday to what you did."

"So my feelings aren't important? The hurt you caused me doesn't matter?"

Like so many times in recent months, an all-too-familiar sense of anger bubbles to the surface.

"Zoe, you went back to another man's flat, got undressed, presumably, and climbed into bed with him. I've only got your word that you never had full sex, but you went as near as dammit. How the fuck does that even compare to some pissed-up woman planting a kiss on me?"

"I'm not saying the acts are comparable, but the feelings are. I hurt you, and you hurt me — can't we just draw a line under it and move on?"

"Wait, are you suggesting that what Claire witnessed on Saturday somehow cancels out what you did?"

"No."

"It bloody well sounds like you are."

Zoe snorts an exasperated sigh and flings her hands in the air.

"You're not listening to me," she barks. "All I'm saying is that if we're both feeling hurt, it must mean that we still love one another. And if we both still love one another, surely that's reason to try again."

Frustrated as she might be, Zoe's argument has some logic. However, when have love and logic ever worked seamlessly together?

"It's not that simple," I mutter.

"Yes, it is. All I need is a straightforward yes or no. Do you want to try again, Danny?"

"I don't know."

"Let me make this simple for you. I've seen a flat I really like, but the agents reckon if I don't put down a holding deposit tomorrow, it'll be snapped up by someone else."

"That's not fair, Zoe. Don't pressurise me."

"But it's okay for me to feel pressure? I need a place to live, and if you don't want me back here, I need to find somewhere else."

"This isn't fair. I—"

"Just say yes," Zoe pleads. "I know it won't be easy at first, but we'll make it work. What we had was perfect, and it can be perfect again if we're willing to give it a try."

What we had *was* perfect, but it can never be that again. If you break a vase, you can glue it back together, mask the cracks, but it will forever be flawed. Perfect is, by its very definition, free from flaws. Even if we never mention him again, Wayne bloody Pickford will forever remain a significant crack in our relationship.

"I can't," I say quietly. "I'm sorry."

"That's it, then? We're officially done?"

"We were officially done the moment you hopped into bed with another man."

"It was one mistake," Zoe yells back at me. "One. Fucking. Mistake."

"You just don't get it, do you? It's not about … actually, just forget it. I'm tired of being angry, tired of going over the same ground … I'm just tired of it all."

"Fine," Zoe huffs, getting to her feet. "I get the message."

She steps over to the coffee table and smacks her keys down. "Guess I won't be needing these ever again."

She then turns to me, hands on hips. "Have a nice life, Danny, and I hope for your sake that one day, you don't look back and kick yourself for this."

I look up at my ex-fiancée and then at the keys on the coffee table.

"I know you're angry, Zoe, but we still have stuff to sort out."

"No, we don't. You've made your position quite clear."

"On our relationship, yes, but we need to discuss what we do about the mortgage."

Zoe tilts her head back and expels a near-maniacal snort of laughter.

"You don't want me," she then growls. "So you're on your own."

"What?"

"You heard me. If you think I'm willing to pay a penny towards the mortgage while you're living here, you're off your rocker."

"It doesn't matter what I think. We both signed those mortgage forms, so we're both liable."

"The difference is, you're living here, and I'm not. As far as I'm concerned, this is your flat and your problem."

"Zoe, I can't afford the repayments."

"Tough," she shrugs. "I offered you a solution, and you turned it down."

"Maybe you could offer that same solution to the building society when they're about to repossess the flat — see how that pans out."

"Again, not my problem."

"It will be because if I can't meet the mortgage repayments and this place ends up being repossessed, we're both legally liable for any shortfall."

"So you say, but my dad thinks otherwise. He reckons they'll just write off the debt."

"Wow," I cough. "Your dad is fucking deluded."

"I don't care what you think. As I see it, I've got nothing to lose if I just wait and see what the building society does. I'm certainly not going to pay any part of the mortgage on this place while you relive your youth, shagging anything that moves."

"That's not fair, Zoe."

"Nope, but fairness cuts both ways. You're not willing to give me a second chance, so that's that — mortgage or no mortgage, the second I walk out the door, I'm out of your life for good."

It is the ultimatum of ultimatums. Let her walk out, and there's no going back.

I slowly get to my feet and face Zoe.

"This might sound strange, but earlier today, I sat in my car and watched a guy cheat on his girlfriend. It was only a kiss, so not as bad as what you did, but she'll suffer as much as I did."

"What's some random couple got to do with us?"

"Nothing, I thought, but it just hit me. I know for sure that they'll break up, like I know for sure that it's always the wronged party that suffers the most in a breakup — it's not fair, but life isn't. That woman will feel angry and humiliated, and she'll shed plenty of tears, but it'll probably turn out to be the best thing that could have happened."

"I don't get it. Why?"

"Because once she's past the pain, she'll get on with the rest of her life, and she'll be happy again. It might not be next week or next month, but at some point, she'll look back and realise that what she had just wasn't meant to be."

"What are you saying?"

I consider her question carefully because, for the first time in a long while, I think I might have the answer.

"It pains me to say it, but if I want to be happy again, I *have* to let you go ... for good."

Chapter 39

Cathartic is too strong a word, but when Zoe left the flat last night, it certainly felt like a number of negative demons left with her. I still spent a good hour sitting on the sofa in silence, wondering if I'd made a huge mistake. At one point, I reached for the telephone, intent on calling her, but I never got as far as dialling the number. It kind of reminded me of giving up smoking — for the first week, it was hellish, but I kept reminding myself that the craving would eventually fade, and one day I'd wake up feeling fitter and healthier. The fact that a pack of ciggies hit an eye-watering £1.50 was of no consequence, or so I told myself.

This morning, having enjoyed something resembling a decent night's sleep, I can feel the slightest glow of an emotion I haven't experienced in ages — excitement. Yes, it's mixed with trepidation after Zoe's refusal to accept any responsibility for our mortgage debt but, this evening, I'll head to Echo Lane to sit before Mrs Weller and confirm I've fulfilled my end of our deal. If she's true to her word, and I have a contract that should ensure as much, that house will be mine.

I've also allowed myself to consider what I might do with the house. If there is any chance that the council change their planning rules in the coming years, the land will be ripe for development, so selling it now might not be a good idea. I could rent it out, I suppose, although I've no idea if the monthly income will cover most of my mortgage payment. If it does, I'll have to do some work to the outside as it currently looks like a wreck, but a few weekends of hard graft and Dad's assistance should have it looking half-decent in no time.

There is the small matter of breaking Kim Dolan's heart to overcome, but, like me, she'll recover, and her life will be immeasurably better without a cheating partner in it.

I enter the office with a slight spring in my step and head straight for the back room, whistling as I go.

"Someone's in a good mood," Tina remarks as she flicks the switch on the kettle.

"Good might be a stretch but I'm definitely in a better mood than I've managed in a while."

"What's brought that on?"

"I think I've finally settled the situation with my ex."

"Amicably?"

"Not really, no, but it's time to move on."

"Good for you," Tina smiles. "And talking of break ups, how did your friend react when you showed her those photos? I bet she went ballistic."

"I haven't picked the photos up from Boots yet, but I plan on seeing Kim at lunchtime. Can't say I'm looking forward to it."

"I do feel sorry for her, but if I were in her shoes, I'd rather know than not. You're doing the right thing, Danny, although I'm glad I'm not the one who has to tell her."

"Yeah, it's shit, but one day she'll thank me. Probably."

Tina holds her hand up, fingers crossed, before turning her attention back to her morning brew.

Lee and Gavin then arrive in quick succession and after five minutes of small talk, we settle down to the morning meeting.

Now that Tina has put the thought in my head, and the task is only a few hours away, my mind wants to dwell on the impending conversation with Kim rather than what Lee has to say. I just about catch his confirmation of two valuations today — one at eleven and one at half-eleven — before my name is mentioned.

"Um ... sorry?" I splutter.

"I said, cloth ears, you're doing a viewing at 22a Union Street at half ten."

"Yes, right. No problem."

The flat in question is situated at the top end of town and only a five-minute walk from the office. As it's located above a fried chicken takeaway, I'm surprised anyone wants to view it, but it does present an opportunity. I have to pass Boots on the way back so I can collect the photos then rather than waste ten minutes of my lunch break.

Lee rattles through the rest of the day's business and then asks if anyone has any questions. I do, although it's not related to my plans for the day. Not directly, anyway.

"Quick question. A mate's parents are thinking about renting out their house and they were wondering how much a tenant might pay each month. Any ideas?"

"They'd need to speak to Vicky in the lettings department," Lee confirms with minimal interest.

"Yeah, I did say that was probably the case, but they're only after a ballpark figure at the moment."

"Where is it?" Gavin asks. "Their house?"

"I, um, can't remember the name of the road, but it's near Echo Lane. Three bedrooms, detached."

"What do you reckon, boss?" Gavin asks, turning to Lee. "About six to seven hundred a month?"

"Aye, about that. Could be slightly more if it's in good nick."

"Thanks," I say. "I'll pass that on."

Everyone gets on with their respective work while I scribble down a few sums on a scrap of paper. It then becomes clear that the sums are more than just a series of numbers — they're potentially a permanent solution to my property woes.

Even if I take Gavin's lower estimate of the rental income of a detached house, six hundred quid would cover three-quarters of my monthly mortgage payment. Add in the modest pay rise I discussed with Lee yesterday, not to mention the benefit of a company car, and my finances should look an awful lot rosier in the coming months.

Thinking longer term, there's still the issue of the negative equity, but if I've learned anything in my brief estate agency career, it's that when property prices hit rock bottom, there's only one way they can go. If I can hold on for a couple of years, maybe the flat will eventually be worth more than the outstanding mortgage.

I pause for a moment and consider the significance of this day. Will I look back at it as the day I closed one chapter of my life for good and started a new one?

Maybe.

There was a time, not so long ago, when I couldn't imagine life without Zoe. Actually, I could imagine it, but I just didn't want to because all I could envisage was a miserable, pointless existence. That could be the reason why I've wallowed in my own misery for so long, but no more. Sitting here now, pretending that I'm checking through my viewing follow-ups, I can see a life worth living post-Zoe.

Whoever said that money doesn't buy happiness has clearly never had to cope with negative equity and a cheating partner.

Much as I'd love to dwell on the possibilities of my future, I probably need to get on with my job, otherwise Lee might see fit to revoke the promised promotion.

For the next hour, I make phone calls, fill out forms, and generally listen to folk whine. Viewers are frustrated that they've wasted their time looking at a property that doesn't meet their expectations, and homeowners are frustrated that another viewing has failed to produce an offer. Both seem to think it's my fault.

Mercifully, the time arrives for me to head out. I grab the keys to 22a Union Street, double-check I've got the receipt for my photographs, and leave the office.

The walk up Victoria Road takes me past Boots, and perhaps if I had more time, I'd be tempted to pick up the photos. However, I don't want to risk being late for the viewing if there's a queue at the photo processing counter.

I reach the end of Victoria Road and turn right, then left into Union Street. Despite being within the northern part of the town centre, most residents would consider Union Street the very arse end. It's populated by tattoo shops, takeaways, and second-hand record stores, not to mention a number of empty units previously occupied by businesses that failed to weather the recent economic storms. For that reason, 22a Union Street is the cheapest property on our books. That, and the stench of cooking oil that lingers around the ground floor entrance.

There's a chubby bloke with curly hair standing near the door; a set of our sales particulars in his hand.

"Mr Harper?" I enquire. "I'm Danny from Gibley Smith."

"That's me," he replies wearily.

I unlock the door and lead Mr Harper up the stairs. I don't know anything about his circumstances, but age-wise, he appears too old to be a first-time buyer.

"Are you looking for investment properties?" I ask, guiding him into the lounge.

"Chance would be a fine thing," he snorts. "I'm scraping the bottom of the property barrel because it's all I can afford."

"Right."

The bare floorboards and peeling wallpaper in the lounge do little to raise Mr Harper's spirits, nor does the wailing siren of a police car as it navigates the traffic beyond the only window in the room. He's equally unimpressed by the dingy double bedroom, tired kitchen, and mould-ridden bathroom.

"What do you think?" I ask as we return to the small landing.

"It's a shit hole," Mr Harper replies.

"Ah, but it's a very cheap shit hole," I counter with faux positivity. "The vendor is desperate to sell, so he'll probably take an offer of around £37,000."

Mr Harper scratches his chin for a moment. "Would you mind if my wife came and viewed it, maybe tomorrow?"

"No problem. Are you considering an offer, then?"

"Am I hell," he spits. "But she's being such an unreasonable bitch in our divorce settlement, I want her to see firsthand what I can afford once her lawyer has finished shafting me."

I don't recall this situation being referenced in the staff training manual, so I'm unsure how to respond.

"Um, sorry to hear that," I say meekly. "Give the office a call when you've spoken to your wife, and we'll sort something out."

I escort the deflated husband back down the stairs and leave him to sample the joys of Union Street. Maybe his opinion of the flat will improve after he's bought himself a two-piece chicken meal or a second-hand copy of Dire Straits *Brothers in Arms* on cassette. Unlikely, but you never know.

My time with Mr Harper, brief as it was, at least served as a life lesson. As I hurry back along Union Street, I remind myself that no matter how crap life seems, there's always some poor bastard in a worse situation. Up until yesterday, I was that poor bastard.

A minute later, I reach Boots and make my way to the photo processing counter. There's a queue and only one person serving. Fortunately, it's not my time being wasted, vindicating the decision to pop in now rather than on my lunch break.

Almost ten minutes later, I reach the counter and hand over the slip for my photos.

"I won't be a tick," the flustered young shop assistant says before she turns and searches a row of shelves behind her.

Long seconds pass, and a few more customers join the queue behind me.

"Sorry," the assistant calls out over her shoulder. "I'm having difficulty finding your photos."

My heart sinks to my stomach as the implication of Boots losing my photos sinks in. Everything I went through and everything I've planned, all for nothing because someone didn't do their job properly.

The young assistant then turns around. She has an envelope in her hand, but her expression doesn't fill me with confidence.

"This doesn't have a name on it," she says sheepishly. "But it's the only order unaccounted for."

She flips open the envelope and holds it up so I can see the top photo.

"Thank God," I pant once I see the photo of a house on Brompton Road I captured. "Yes, those are my photos."

"Thirteen prints in total?" she confirms.

"That's right."

"That'll be £9.99, please."

I feel like asking for a discount due to the unnecessary stress, but I don't think the customers in the queue behind me would appreciate the additional wait. Instead, I slap a tenner on the counter, snatch up the envelope, and tell the assistant she can keep the change.

As much as I want to loiter outside Boots and check the photos, I'm aware that I'm already pushing my luck time-wise. I left the office almost forty-five minutes ago for what should have been a thirty-minute appointment. Still, having almost soiled myself in Boots at the thought of losing the evidence of

Harrison's betrayal, waiting an extra few minutes to view the photos is no big deal.

I stow the envelope safely inside my jacket pocket and stride back down Victoria Road.

As I approach the office, I quickly concoct a reason why it took so long to view a pokey one-bedroom flat. It seems unlikely Lee will notice or care, but I don't want to get in his bad books.

My excuse becomes a moot point when I wander in.

"Did you get lost or stop off for a tattoo?" Gavin asks.

"Er, neither? Where's Lee?"

"Weren't you listening in the morning meeting? He's at the eleven o'clock valuation, and I've got one in fifteen minutes."

"Ah, right."

I sit down at my desk and pull out the envelope.

"I had to pop into Boots to collect these," I say.

"Is that what I think it is?" Gavin responds. "The evidence of dirty deeds?"

"Yep."

I pull open the flap and extract the photos.

"What do you reckon?" I ask Gavin, showing him the photo of 22 Brompton Road.

"That's a pretty decent shot, actually."

"Cheers."

"Anyway," he says, getting to his feet. "As much as I'd love to stay and check out your photography skills, I've got a valuation to get to."

"Yeah, okay," I reply, my attention fixed on the first photo that doesn't feature a terraced house. "See you later."

Gavin departs while I slowly flick through the damning evidence of Neil Harrison's betrayal. I'm so focused on the photos that I barely take any notice when Tina steps up to my desk.

"Are those the photos of Candy and that bloke?" she asks, perching herself on one of the chairs opposite.

"Yep," I reply, unable to take my eyes off the photo of Harrison groping Candy's arse.

"Can I see?" Tina asks.

"Sure."

I hand her the photos and sit back in my chair as Tina flicks through the culmination of my hard work. This should be a moment of immense satisfaction — I should be elated at beating the odds and completing what seemed like an impossible task. I should be frothing with excitement at the prospect of collecting my reward later.

So why do I feel so awful?

Tina finishes looking at the photos and places them in a pile in the centre of my desk. She looks up, and our eyes meet. I know in that instant that her thoughts likely mirror mine.

"Your poor friend," she says. "She'll be devastated when she sees those photos."

"I know."

"The guy is obviously a piece of shit, and she'll be better off without him, but ..."

I cast my mind back to the day Zoe admitted what happened with Wayne Pickford. Every word of her confession felt like a punch to the guts. Blow after blow, I literally felt punch drunk at the end, but that wasn't the end — it was only the beginning. I would suffer for days, weeks, months. Unable to eat, unable to sleep, unable to function.

My circumstances differed from Kim's, but she'll feel the same pain, the same sense of humiliation, and then she'll have to live with the anger.

No one deserves that.

"Can you do me a favour, Tina?" I ask, gathering up the photos and returning them to the envelope.

"Sure. What's up?"

"I need to go somewhere for an hour, and if Lee asks where I am, can you tell him I'm on a viewing?"

"Take the keys for Brompton Road, and I'll tell him you've got back-to-back viewings."

"Thanks."

"Can I ask where you're going?"

I get to my feet. "On a damage limitation exercise."

Chapter 40

I take two wrong turns, adding an additional five minutes to my journey. If the circumstances were different, I'd be annoyed at the delay, but the extra minutes offer valuable thinking time.

The sign for Silverlake Business Park comes into view. I flick the indicator stalk and slow down before taking the final right-hand turn. My ultimate destination, unit 2, is on the right — a white, flat-roof building with two windows and a door on the left side of the front elevation, plus a roller shutter on the right.

I pull into one of the parking bays signposted for visitors and silence the Volvo. There's a silver Porsche parked a few bays along, so it seems the man I'm here to see is inside the building. I probably should have checked before driving over here, but then there's a lot about this plan that I haven't thought through. Maybe that's no bad thing because I'm far from sure it's a good idea. All I've got to go on is that look in Tina's eyes and the residue pain of my own memories.

I reach into my jacket pocket and pull out the envelope. All ten photos are present and correct, as is the strip of negatives, but they'll be staying in the car — an insurance policy in case events spiral out of control.

I open the glovebox and tuck the strip of negatives inside.

It's tempting to remain in the Volvo and spend the next twenty minutes formulating a strategy or simply determining if I'm doing the right thing. I don't have twenty minutes and even if I did, I'd rather go on my gut instincts. This is one of those scenarios where too much thinking might prove my undoing.

I get out of the Volvo and stride purposefully across the car park. The door has a sign next to it, confirming the name of the business: Harrison Telecoms.

Without breaking stride, I push open the door and step into what is clearly a reception area, complete with a young receptionist behind a desk. She greets me with a polite smile.

"Can I help you?"

"Is Neil around? I need to see him as a matter of urgency."

"He's in his office, but I'm not sure if he's busy. Let me check for you."

The receptionist gets up and disappears through a door behind her desk. You'd think a telecoms company might have a more efficient method of staff communication.

I kill time by pacing up and down the carpet until the door opens and the receptionist reappears, closely followed by Neil Harrison.

"Hello, Danny," he says, offering me his hand. "To what do I owe this pleasure?"

"Any chance I could have a quick word? Somewhere private."

"Will it take long? I've got a meeting across town at one."

"Ten minutes. Tops."

"Come through to my office."

I follow Harrison back through the door to a corridor with four doors leading off it. We stop at the first on the left, which is the only one currently ajar.

Harrison enters first, and I ensure the door is shut once I'm in his office. It's not an impressive space — a desk with a chair on both sides, a couple of filing cabinets, and a bookshelf containing half a dozen trophies and not a lot of books. Telling.

"Grab a seat," he says, lowering himself into a leather swivel chair behind the desk.

I make myself comfortable, although it's only in the physical sense. On every other level, I'm a long way out of my comfort zone.

"I presume this is about yesterday's meeting?" Harrison begins.

"It is ... in a way."

"Did your boss tell you he couldn't make it? He sent his PA instead."

"Candy?"

"That's her. Bit of a slapper but great tits."

"Nice arse, too, so I'm led to believe. Very gropeable."

I'm not convinced gropeable is a word, but it serves a purpose as Harrison squirms a little.

"Quite," he replies with a thin smile. "Have you heard anything more about this deal?"

"No, but I do have another proposal I'd like you to consider."

"I'm listening."

My heart is going ten to the dozen, but I need to appear calm and confident. Accordingly, I sit back in my seat and cross my legs.

"What you're going to do for me, Neil, is meet Kim for lunch and gently tell her that your relationship is over because you don't really love her."

It's a strong opening gambit, and accordingly, Harrison stares back at me, unblinking.

"What?" he snorts. "Are you on drugs?"

"No."

"Drunk then, because no one of sound mind would sit in my office and say what you just said."

"I'm of perfectly sound mind, thanks, and you *will* do as I ask."

"Will I now?" he says with a dry smile, folding his arms. "I won't, but I'll humour you. Why would I ditch my girlfriend on your say so?"

I maintain my poker face and slowly reach a hand into my pocket, withdrawing the envelope.

"You're going to do it because, if you don't, Kim will get to see these photos."

I open the envelope and slide the first photo across the desk. Harrison, seemingly more puzzled than concerned, leans forward and glances at it. His reaction isn't quite what I hoped.

"It's an innocent photo of me and a business acquaintance," he says nonchalantly. "But you know that."

"I wouldn't say it's entirely innocent, but I take your point."

I flick to the back of the pack and extract the most damning of the photos.

"This one, however, might take a bit more explaining."

Harrison doesn't immediately look at the photo I slide across the desk. Instead, he fixes me with a cold stare.

"What's your game here?" he asks, the photo still unchecked. "Because whatever it is, you're messing with the wrong man."

"No game, and if you bothered to look at the photo, you'd see that you're in no position to make threats."

Finally, his eyes flick towards the desk, and they immediately widen.

"There's no explaining that photo, is there, Neil? It's exactly as it looks — you, snogging an attractive young woman while groping her backside."

He continues to stare at the photo but doesn't touch it. I'd love to know what's going through his mind, but whatever he's thinking, he must realise he's screwed.

"Do we have a deal?" I ask.

"My God," he scoffs. "Are you really so desperate to get into Kim's knickers that you followed me around with a camera?"

"Nope. I've no interest in Kim besides ensuring that she doesn't end up tethered to a prick like you."

"How noble, but you've overlooked one minor detail — I can twist Kim around my little finger, so even if you show her your grubby photos, I'll talk my way out of it."

I had a feeling that he might try to call my bluff, but thanks to two wrong turns, I have another card up my sleeve.

"I'm sure you could, Neil, but Candy isn't a PA. In fact, she doesn't even work for Gibley Smith."

Harrison looks perplexed but not concerned.

"Candy is what you might describe as a call girl."

The penny doesn't so much as drop but based on Harrison's jaw bobbing up and down, it clangs to the floor like a metal dustbin lid.

"Are you fucking sick?" he eventually blasts. "You hired a prostitute to set me up?"

"I wouldn't put it quite like that, but yeah, that's the gist of it."

His face reddening, Harrison leans forward and points a finger in my direction. "I'm going to—"

"Shut it," I snap. "You need to hear me out."

Even if he wanted to continue his protestations, his jaw is set rigid, teeth gnashing.

"I know what a manipulative, controlling arsehole you are," I continue. "However, you might be able to convince Kim that you're sorry and it was just a one-off mistake, but how about your parents or your business contacts? Maybe the Freemasons or the Rotary Club? I can get dozens of copies of that photo printed and I can send them to all manner of people, together with a letter outlining your relationship with Candy Dubois. That letter might imply that you regularly pay Candy for kinky sexual services. Maybe a bit of light bondage or role play. I could say how much you love being tied up while Candy shoves Lego bricks up your arse or how you love dressing up as a schoolgirl and being caned. As you've discovered, Candy is a convincing actress, and she'll go along with whatever tales I decide to tell."

Silent seconds pass. Harrison just sits there, glaring at me.

"Why are you doing this?" he eventually hisses.

"I told you. Kim is better off without you."

"You just want to have a crack at her yourself. That's what this is about, isn't it?"

"As I said, I'm not interested in Kim but even if I were, it doesn't change your situation. Go and see Kim, gently end the relationship, and you'll never see or hear from me again. Ignore my warning, though, and you'll leave me no choice but to show the photos to Kim ... and then I'll start writing those letters."

Neil Harrison might be many things, but I doubt he's a fool. I can almost hear the cogs whirring as he looks at the photo on his desk. In his shoes, I'd be weighing up my options too.

"Get out of my office," he says.

"Do we have a deal?"

"Fuck off."

"I appreciate you're angry, but you need to think rationally here, Neil. You don't love Kim, so it's not as though you're losing anything you care about. Or is it just because you don't like being told what to do?"

"I said, get out!"

To emphasise his order, he stands up. Slowly, I get to my feet, but I don't take my eyes off the man opposite, not even when he edges around the desk.

"I won't tell you again," Harrison warns.

"Do. We. Have. A. Deal."

Before I even uttered the first word of my question, I had an inkling what reaction it might provoke. In the time it takes to adjust my feet and take one step back, Harrison's right arm is already arcing towards my head. I'm no boxer, but I experienced enough scraps in my younger days to instinctively appreciate the difference between a genuine threat and some chancer taking a swing. Based solely on his technique, Neil Harrison falls firmly into the latter camp.

Fights are always won and lost in fractions of a second. Swing wildly, and you give your opponent time to duck but, duck too soon, and you give your opponent time to adjust their attack. Harrison's timing is woeful, as is his reaction when his fist cuts through the empty air previously occupied by my head.

His body twisted, balance compromised, it's almost criminally simple to counter Harrison's punch with one of my own. I thrust a jab towards his exposed flank — hard enough to hurt but not so potent it might crack ribs.

My punch happens to coincide with Harrison finally losing balance. It's possible he might have fallen over of his own accord, but my jab certainly helped. He crashes against the edge of the desk and then lands hard on the floor. His survival instincts then kick in as he scrambles to get back to his feet, but a sudden jolt of pain undermines his progress. Then, I see it — the look of realisation in his eyes. I've been on the end of a few hidings myself, and I know what fuels that look. It's a mix of pain and humiliation, fear and loathing. It's the look of a man who knows he's beaten.

By my reckoning, the threat to share the photos with Kim and then expose Harrison as a sexual deviant should have been enough to seal the deal. There was no need for physical threats, never mind actual bodily harm, but it wasn't my play. Now the door is open, I'd be stupid not to walk through it.

I grab the back of the chair I vacated a minute ago and reposition it. Then, I perch my backside on the edge and lean forward, my elbows resting on my thighs.

"That wasn't very clever, was it, Neil?"

There's little to no reaction to my question.

"You know what?" I continue. "I've had a rough couple of months but, looking back, I've also learned a valuable lesson — anger is a toxic emotion. It rots your brain, clouds your judgement. At times, I was so angry I couldn't think straight ... hell, I tried everything to overcome it, but the one thing I didn't try was to let go of what I couldn't control."

I sit back and cross my legs. Harrison shuffles a few inches back.

"I get it, Neil, I really do. You're angry because I'm forcing your hand, but you need to look at the bigger picture. I lost focus because I was so angry, but now I know what I want, nothing will stand in my way ... nothing and no one, especially you."

To emphasise my warning, I shoot Harrison what I hope is a threatening enough glare.

"Anyway," I say, adopting a chirpier tone. "I should let you get on. You've got a chat with Kim to prepare for."

I stand up and return the chair to where I found it.

"Remember what I said, Neil. One ten-minute conversation with Kim and your life carries on as normal. But, if you let the anger get the better of you, you'll regret it — that's a promise."

Mission accomplished, I turn and stride towards the door. When I reach it, I turn and pose one final question to the man on the floor.

"Oh, I forgot to ask. Any chance we can still do a deal on a mobile telephone?"

He doesn't say it, but the look of contempt implies a no.

"Never mind," I smile back. "I've heard they make you impotent, anyway."

Chapter 41

I sit for a moment, listening to the tick-tick of the engine as it cools down after the journey across town. In a way, I'll miss the Volvo when I finally get a company car. Maybe it's a sign I'm getting old but there's a lot to be said for dependability and comfort.

I pat the old girl's steering wheel and clamber out.

There seems little sense in locking the car because there's no one around. Besides the handful of folk who live in the houses further down Echo Lane I doubt there's anyone within a mile or two. It's just me, serenaded by the gentle rush of the wind and the evening song of Mrs Weller's avian neighbours.

I reach the head of the front path and stop as a cold shiver runs down my spine. I spin around, half-expecting to see someone standing close by, but the scene is unchanged from seconds earlier. Looking out across the fields, with the sun skirting the treetops in the distance, I could almost thank the primaeval part of my brain that forced me to turn around. The view is as tranquil as it is beguiling — the English countryside at its finest.

I've had no reason to consider it until now, but should the town planners ever grant permission for this swathe of land to be built upon, would that really be a good thing? Financially, yes, but in every other way, once these fields are littered with boxy houses and strips of grey tarmac, that's it — they're gone forever.

I'm getting ahead of myself.

After drinking in the view for a few seconds more, I turn and continue up the path.

I don't linger in the entrance lobby because I'm too anxious — I just want to sit down in front of Mrs Weller and confess that I didn't do exactly as she asked. In no way do I regret my decision but, seven hours after my visit to Silverlake Business Park, I've no idea if Neil Harrison did as he was told.

Pushing open the door, I call out. "It's only ..."

The rest of the sentence dies in my throat as the front door closes behind me, and I'm suddenly cast into darkness. For some reason, the hallway lights are switched off.

"Hello? Mrs Weller?"

Silence. I wait for a moment and call out again. No one replies.

The lack of light might be explained by a power cut, but where is Mrs Weller?

Slowly, my eyes adjust to the darkness but only enough to highlight the outline of the staircase and the doorway to the kitchen. However, my sense of smell soon fills in for the lack of visual information. The air is heavy with the scent of decaying wood and damp brickwork.

This isn't right, and I feel compelled to investigate, but the prospect of walking blindly into the darkness doesn't hold much appeal.

I turn around, step back through the entrance lobby, and open the front door. The contrast between the stale, musty air inside the house and the gentle breeze outside is profound.

An obvious solution to the light issue would be to prop the front door open, and the drystone wall offers up plenty of temporary doorstops. I retrieve a suitable stone from the top of the wall and carefully transport it back along the weed-ridden path.

With the front door wide open, I enter the entrance lobby again and open the door to the hallway.

"What the ..."

Now bathed in light I can clearly see the hallway, but it bears absolutely no resemblance to the pristine space I admired on my first visit. The scene does at least explain the smell of decay. The once smooth, plastered walls are now bare brick and the floorboards are rough, uneven, and in some places, missing altogether. As for the staircase, half of the spindles are missing, and every tread is sagging and splintered.

In a way, what I'm seeing makes perfect sense because the hallway now mirrors the outside of the house. It is what I'd expect to see in an abandoned house left to rot for years, decades even. What makes zero sense is how this has happened in the forty-eight hours since my last visit.

Scarcely able to believe my own eyes, I take a couple of tentative steps into the hallway. Each footstep is greeted by a groan from the spongy floorboards.

"Hello?" I call out again, more in hope than expectation. "Anyone home?"

The silence is disconcerting, but then I'm suddenly struck by a sense of déjà vu. What day was it? Sunday? I put the sudden migraine-like symptoms down to a hangover, but no amount of dehydration would explain the fleeting visions I experienced — visions of bare brick walls and rough floorboards, similar to what I'm seeing now.

Coincidence, surely, or just a trick of the mind. Shaking off the unease, I continue forward.

After half-a-dozen cautious steps I reach the doorway to the lounge but the door itself isn't there. Shards of light leaking through the gaps in the window shutters offer a clue to the general condition of the room, and I quickly conclude that it's in no better state than the hallway.

I continue on towards the kitchen.

The daylight weakens as I approach the doorway but, much like the lounge, there's just enough light leaking through the rotten window shutters to keep the darkness at bay.

I step into the kitchen and pause while my eyes adjust to the gloom. Considering the state of the hallway and the lounge, I don't know why I'm shocked to find there's no table and chairs, or polished stainless-steel appliances, or expensive-looking wall units. The only way of determining that this is indeed a kitchen is a stained and chipped Belfast sink beneath one of the windows and a cast-iron stove mottled with rust and soot spots.

I look up to the ceiling, or what's left of it. Most of the plaster has crumbled away, revealing a lattice of narrow wooden struts. A lot of it looks rotten, but the damp hasn't deterred the spider community if the thick expanse of cobwebs is any barometer.

As I stand and try to make sense of what I'm seeing, a belated thought strikes. Is this now my house? I did what I was asked, and I have a contract to confirm the deeds are now mine, but what use is it? It's a wreck, and it'll take more than a few weekends to make it habitable, not to mention tens of thousands of pounds I don't have. It's a problem that requires unpicking but in the big scheme of unanswerable questions, it's hardly a priority. Yes, the house needs a fortune spending on it but how the fuck did it end up like this in just a couple of days?

I step further into the kitchen, brushing an errant strand of spider's silk from my cheek.

Then I spot it — the safe that was previously hidden in a cupboard.

Roughly the size of a small suitcase and fixed to a wall in the corner of the room, it's the first time I've actually seen it. I hurry over and take a closer look. Clad in grey steel, there's a numeric keypad with a calculator-like display above it, although the display is currently dark. There's also a hefty-looking lever handle to the left of the keypad.

An obvious question floats into my mind. Why is the safe still here when every other fixture and fitting has gone? I don't know, but it's a relief to see it because it's a single shred of physical evidence that I didn't imagine what this room looked like two days ago. It's enough to protect my sanity ... for now.

I reach up and grasp the handle. If the safe is locked, the fact it's still here will be of little relevance.

"Please don't be locked," I murmur before levering the handle ninety degrees.

I'm rewarded with a metallic clunking sound and a single beep. It then occurs to me that I've not seen a single light switch or wall socket since I entered the house. I turn around and slowly survey the walls, and then look up to what's left of the ceiling. There's no evidence of wiring or even a power supply connected to the house.

Does the safe have an internal power source? A battery?

It's another question I can't answer but it's wholly irrelevant. What is relevant is what's actually in the safe. I tug the handle, and, to my relief, the thick metal door eases open.

Although I still don't know where the power is coming from, I'm pleased to see the designers incorporated two small lights into the safe's design: one above each of the two shelves. That millisecond of being pleased then blossoms into full-blown delight when my eyes fall on the stack of bank notes tucked away on the bottom shelf. At a glance, there must be seven or eight individual bundles, but my attention is then drawn to a white envelope lying next to the cash — my full name printed on the front.

I tear it open and extract two sheets of A4 paper, stapled together. Without reading a single word it's obvious the letter was produced with the aid of a word processor, similar to Tina's, rather than a typewriter.

With barely any light in the kitchen, I place the letter near the bottom shelf of the safe and begin to read.

Dear Daniel,

Firstly, I can only apologise for the state of the house, and I know you must have many questions. I'll try my best to answer them in this letter. I'm sorry I couldn't be there in person to explain but as I told you on several occasions, I could only spend a finite amount of time here.

Let me begin by explaining the reality of Kim's life if Neil Harrison had proposed this Sunday, and she'd accepted. This might sound like a work of fiction but sadly, it is a description of the future Kim had waiting for her.

On Saturday 11th of May 1991, Kim Dolan and Neil Harrison married at a registry office in Chiswick, London. Besides two of Neil's colleagues who served as witnesses, no one else attended. By that point, Harrison had turned Kim against all of her friends and family, thus denying her father the opportunity to walk his youngest daughter down the aisle.

Shortly after they married, Harrison insisted that Kim quit her job so she could perform her duties as a housewife and, eventually, a mother. They moved into a house in Winchester, and from that moment onwards, Harrison controlled every facet of Kim's life.

Then, on the 14th of February 1993, Harrison loses his temper after Kim finally finds the strength to say she wants to end their marriage. They argue and, after a brief struggle, Kim manages to flee the bedroom. She got as far as the landing but then Harrison punched his wife in the back of the head as she reached the stairs. Kim's last memory of that scene centred on the indescribable pain as she crashed from the top stair to the very bottom.

I won't bore you with the full version of Kim's life from that moment on, but you should know that she broke her back in that fall. That fragile, shattered woman would spend six months in hospital and another two years learning how to walk again. By that point, Harrison will have divorced her, although Kim will never see a penny of his money. He will, however, leave her with something — a lifetime of near-constant pain from her injury and deep psychological scars that will never heal.

That is the future you prevented.

Just before one o'clock this afternoon, Neil Harrison walked into Lunn Poly and asked Kim if he could have a quiet word. They went into the staffroom and then Harrison stated that their relationship was over as he wanted to focus on his business.

I can only guess, but I assume you decided not to show Kim the photos because you knew, from your own experience, how much the betrayal would hurt her.

I'm sorry to say, Daniel, that was a mistake.

Kim needed to understand what kind of man Neil Harrison is, and by sparing her feelings, you left the door open for that bastard to rekindle their relationship at a later date. Fate, unfortunately, isn't easily deterred and although Kim's future won't involve a fall down a flight of stairs, it will still involve years of misery at Harrison's hand.

This could have been avoided if you'd shown Kim those photos.

Now, I cannot say you failed in your task because you did undermine Kim and Harrison's relationship, albeit temporarily, but it is now impossible for me to give you the deeds to this house. I appreciate that this will seem unfair, but I need to enact clause four of our contract, which states:

In the event that the task, herein referred to as "the Assignment," fails to be completed, whether due to culpa lata, vis maior, casus fortuitus, or any cause attributable to the Obligor or any third party, the Obligor shall ipso facto forfeit, relinquish, and irrevocably surrender any and all rights, titles, claims, or interests in the property, nullifying any prior or future assertions of ownership.

As frustrated as you must be feeling right now, I hope the cash in the safe eases your frustration slightly. Take it — you deserve it. You also deserve an explanation of how we've arrived at this point.

You asked if Kim and I are related, and I apologise if I seemed cagey in my response. If the truth didn't defy belief, I suspect you would have guessed in a heartbeat. You see, Daniel, Weller is my mother's maiden name, and for reasons that should now be obvious, I couldn't use the name on my birth certificate: Kimberley Anne Dolan.

I can almost imagine you now; standing in that kitchen, a look of disbelief on your face, and wondering if this is all an elaborate prank. I wouldn't blame you. However, take a look around. The house as you see it has not been occupied since 1958, which is why it is in such a terrible state of repair. The inside of the house — as it was on your previous visits — is how it will look in the future.

I appreciate that this is a lot to take in, and you probably think I'm insane — sometimes I wonder it myself, but it is the truth.

There is nothing more I can do but offer you a choice. You can simply walk away, and if you never return to this house or think about Kim Dolan again, I wouldn't blame you. But

I know you must have questions and I hope you're willing to take a leap of faith.

There's an item on the top shelf of the safe. If you want to know the relevance of that item as well as the answers to your questions, return this letter to the safe, close the door, and enter the code 2-0-2-4 into the keypad. Then, turn the handle back to the horizontal position. Within a few minutes, you'll know the truth.

The choice is yours, Daniel.
With warmest regards
Kim/Mrs Weller

Chapter 42

"Yeah, right," I snort after reading the letter for a second time.

I shouldn't be surprised that Mrs Weller has wheedled her way out of our deal, or that she's not here to explain why — her offer always seemed too good to be true. If it wasn't for the sizeable chunk of cash sitting in the safe, I'd be mightily miffed.

As for the letter itself, it's a work of fiction, obviously, composed by a woman with serious psychological issues. However, I can't deny that some of her outlandish claims might answer a few of my questions.

That doesn't make them the truth, though.

It reminds me of a conversation I had with my nan in the weeks before she passed away. She'd been ill for a while and knew her time was running out, and I asked if she was scared.

"Not in the slightest," she replied. "God will see me right."

Nan was a dedicated Christian and we'd spoken about her faith a few times over the years. During my rebellious teenage years, I pushed back against her beliefs and asked questions that have likely been asked a million times by most atheists and agnostics.

Why does God let people suffer?

How can God let children die?

Why is there no evidence of God's existence?

Nan answered all of my questions with unshakeable conviction, using verses from The Bible to back up her position. I have to admit that her words softened my stance because she patently believed in what she was saying but, deep down, I didn't truly believe her answers.

Bible stories make sense, but so too do fairy tales.

I fold up the letter and return it to the safe. Whilst my hand is in close proximity, I then grab the stack of notes. There are seven bound up in batches of roughly £1,000, plus a thinner wad of loose notes. All told, I'd estimate there's just over seven grand in cold, hard cash.

It's not a house, unfortunately, but it's enough cash to keep my financial troubles at bay for a year or so. Small mercies.

I distribute the notes between three of my jacket pockets and then return my attention to the safe. Easily overlooked, there's a small box on the top shelf, barely two inches wide and covered in a black, suede-like material. After a quick inspection, I flip the lid open to reveal a pair of silver cufflinks inlaid with pearl.

I don't understand how they're relevant to me, or why I would consider them of greater value than the stack of cash, as Mrs Weller previously claimed. Even if they came from a high-end jewellery shop, they can't be worth more than a few hundred quid.

Another question I can add to the list of those I'll never answer. But, of all of them, there is one that I fear might niggle for a very long time: why me?

Whatever this is, and whatever the truth behind it, I don't understand why Mrs Weller roped me in. Of all the men she could have selected, there's no obvious reason why she chose me.

I pocket the cufflinks and shove the safe door shut with more force than necessary. Frustration, no doubt. I don't like being lied to, or tricked, but deep down, I'm still that kid who couldn't wait until Christmas Day to discover what presents his parents had bought.

There's a lot I don't like about all of this, but not knowing is by far the worst part.

Now that the safe door is shut, the keypad is directly in front of me at eye-level. What did the letter say? Enter the code 2-0-2-4, turn the handle, and I'll get the truth within a few minutes.

"The truth," I huff.

Jesus never walked on water. Mrs Weller cannot possibly be Kim Dolan.

Can she?

No.

Obviously.

So, who is she?

My calf muscles tense as I prepare to turn around and leave. Moving is so hard-baked into our brains that we never think about it — we just do it. Instructions are issued and the corresponding muscles carry out those instructions. We all do it from the second we wake up until the moment we fall asleep at night.

On this occasion, my limbs choose to ignore the instruction.

Instead, I raise my right hand and jab the #2 button on the keypad. The safe makes the same beep sound I heard before, and the display above the keypad shines a bright red number two. I press #0, then #2 again, and finally #4.

I check the display: 2-0-2-4.

Unsure what to expect, I grab the handle and yank it upwards until it's back at the horizontal position. Nothing happens.

Now what?

My answer comes with a dull pounding across the top of my skull, no doubt a result of tiredness. I've wasted enough time and I feel like shit.

I release my grip on the handle and my legs belatedly accept the instruction my brain sent twenty seconds ago. I turn around.

The pain is sudden and excruciating, like white hot needles jabbing at the back of my eyeballs. At the same time, a high-pitched ringing threatens to shred my eardrums.

Then, as quickly as it arrived, the pain begins to dissipate but, whatever fuck-awful event my body is enduring, it's not over. My vision begins to swim as I'm struck by a wave of nausea. It's so intense I squeeze my eyes shut and bend over, ready to spill the contents of my stomach.

The expected vomit-storm fails to materialise, but my legs then buckle and, without even feeling it, I collapse to the floor. The smell of damp wood is then replaced by another scent — familiar, but I can't pin down where I last smelt it.

Then, I sense what can only be death. Even if I wanted to struggle, I have no energy, and I'm not even entirely sure I have a body anymore. I feel nothing.

And then I do.

Much like waking from a bad dream, I open my eyes in a state of panic.

I'm not dead, I think. Dead men don't feel cold tiles pressing against their cheek, or see table legs inches from their face, surely?

I dare to turn my head a fraction and then let the scene sink in. It takes a good few seconds to recognise my surroundings — Mrs Weller's kitchen.

Still groggy, I clamber to my feet and lean against the pine table for a moment, just to be sure I don't pass out again. Whatever just happened to me must have messed with my head because for a good twenty minutes, I could have sworn the kitchen looked like a room in a Dickensian hovel.

It is now exactly as it was the first time I stepped foot through the doorway, bar one less-than-obvious difference. Perplexed, I step over to the window and look out to a beautifully landscaped garden. Someone has opened the rotten shutters and I can now see what I couldn't before.

A manicured lawn stretches some two hundred yards towards a boundary of mature trees. Just beyond the glass there's a circular table with six chairs sitting beneath a huge parasol. There's also a low L-shaped sofa with bright mustard-coloured cushions, and a matching coffee table. It all looks expensive, and too good to be left outside, no matter how impressive the surroundings.

I'm still admiring the patio set when a more troubling thought strikes. Whatever just happened to me, I shouldn't ignore it. Maybe once I've had something to eat, I should head over to A&E and get a check-up. I don't feel too bad now, but that's the second time in the last week I've experienced some kind of neurological head fuck.

I draw a deep breath and take a few cautious steps forward. Everything seems to be working okay and, as awful as it was, I don't think I'm suffering any ill-effects after the ... the episode.

By the time I reach the hallway, my mind has settled enough that I can focus on my surroundings a little more closely. The door to the lounge is ajar and a shard of bright light is stretched across the polished floorboards directly ahead of me.

I reach the lounge door and nudge it open.

The source of the light becomes immediately apparent — bright sunshine streaming in through the window at the front of the house. Whoever removed the shutters on the kitchen windows obviously removed all of them. When though? I'm sure they were all in situ when I first arrived, which is why the house was so dark.

I take a few slow steps towards the window, conscious that someone might still be outside, busying themselves on a ladder as they remove the shutters from the first-floor windows. If they want my advice, they'd be better off concentrating on the dilapidated roof.

I reach the window and immediately I notice that the jungle of weeds that occupied the front of the house is no more. It's been replaced by lush green turf and a couple of wooden tubs, both brimming with white and lilac flowers. The cracked, weed-ridden path has also gone — two lines of slate slabs now link the gate to the front door. Not that I can be certain, but I'd swear I only blacked out for a few seconds, a minute at the most. I certainly wasn't unconscious long enough for a team of landscape gardeners to transform the wilderness at the front of the house.

What I'm seeing makes no sense but it's at least consistent with everything else I've experienced since I first met Mrs Weller. Then I notice another feature of the view that's equally illogical but of greater concern — the Volvo isn't where I parked it.

Ordinarily, it would be fair to assume that some toerag has nicked my car but, in this instance, that seems an unlikely explanation. Thieves don't generally nick a car and then spend a few days upgrading a patch of rutted dirt and shingle to a perfectly appointed cobblestone parking area. Neither do they leave another car in place of the one they stole.

There's now an odd-looking white car parked in almost the exact same position as the Volvo. It's not a model I recognise but there is, ironically, a Volvo badge fixed in the centre of the front grill. I say front grill, but there are no vents to cool the engine. That in itself is puzzling, but not as puzzling as the registration plate: KR24 SJV. The format is out of kilter with most other cars on the road, including my own.

It then occurs that I'm wasting my already depleted mental resources on an odd-looking car when I should be focussing on the fact my own car isn't where I left it.

The Volvo is insured but it's a long walk back to Sefton Court. Then again, I've got a ton of cash in my pockets so I could walk to the nearest pub, have something to eat, and then order a taxi. I'll report the theft to the police when I get home.

After a parting glance out of the window, I traipse wearily back to the hallway. I get to the front door and reach for the doorknob.

"Ouch!" I yelp, snatching my hand away the second it makes contact with the cold metal.

Unlike everything else I've experienced in this house today, at least there's a rational explanation for the sudden jolt of pain across my hand — static electricity. I reach for the doorknob again, safe in the knowledge that I've already discharged my excess electrons, so a second shock is highly unlikely.

Not only is there another jolt of electricity the instant my fingers touch the doorknob, but the resulting shock is worse than the first time, as is the resulting pain.

I blow across my fingertips and then shake my hand a few times. What are the chances of receiving a second static shock from the same connection? Minimal, I'd bet, but that's been my luck this year.

Third time lucky.

I reach for the doorknob again.

"Don't!"

The order is so unexpected, I almost trip over my own feet as I attempt to spin around.

"You scared the shit out of me," I pant, holding a hand across my thumping chest.

"I'm so pleased to see you, Daniel," the dark silhouette standing in the kitchen doorway then says. "And I'm sorry. I didn't mean to startle you."

"Of all the things you need to apologise for ... and explain, startling me is way down the list."

Mrs Weller takes half-a-dozen measured steps into the hallway. "I know."

"Well, are you going to explain *this* ... whatever the hell *this* is?"

"Did you read my letter?"

"Yes."

"So, you know the truth."

"The truth?" I scoff. "That you're really Kim and you married Harrison in some alternate universe?"

"It's not quite as simple as that, but yes."

"Forgive me for having just a few tiny doubts about that, what with it being completely against all known laws of physics and, therefore, impossible."

She steps forward again until we're no more than four feet apart.

"I thought you might say that, and I understand your scepticism, which is why I invited you here."

"Here? The house I've visited four or five times before?"

"Not the house, the time."

"The time?"

"2024."

"8.24 pm?"

"No, the year 2024."

It's all I can do not to burst out laughing. Even so, I can't stop a bemused smirk reaching my mouth. "Are you on medication, Mrs Weller, because —"

"It's Kim," she interjects. "Please, call me Kim."

"You're not Kim. You can't be. And this can't be 2024."

"You looked out of the lounge window, didn't you? You saw how different the front looks, and you must have spotted my car on the driveway."

"Yes, I did, but that's hardly evidence that I've leapt forward in time by thirty-four years."

"What about the house itself? You saw the state of it in 1990, and this is how it looks today. Can you explain such a remarkable transformation?"

"Well, no, but ... with fear of repeating myself, it's impossible."

"I thought the same, until I bought this house and discovered what I presumed was a run-of-the-mill safe hidden behind a false wall in the kitchen. But, as you just discovered, it's not a run-of-the-mill safe, is it?"

I close my eyes for a moment and puff a long, tired sigh. I need to put a lid on this madness.

"If this really is the year 2024, let's go for a drive in your fancy car and you can show me what the town looks like thirty-four years into the future."

"That's not possible."

"Why not?"

"Because you can't leave the house today any more than I could leave the house in 1990. Don't ask me how or why, but if you try to leave ... well, you've just discovered yourself what happens."

"Brilliant," I snort. "So, my experience of time travel is a view of some fields and a nice patio set. I wonder why they never featured that storyline in *Back to The Future*?"

"Because that was a movie, Daniel — this isn't."

"That's true enough. No production company would entertain such a bullshit storyline."

"I get it, okay," Mrs Weller says, her tone erring towards frustration. "That's why I left the cufflinks."

"Ah, now everything makes sense," I respond, throwing my arms in the air in sheer exasperation. "The cufflinks. Of course!"

"You didn't read the inscription in the box, did you, or look closely at the cufflinks?"

"Eh? What inscription?"

"Unbelievable," Mrs Weller groans while rolling her eyes. "The one thing I needed you to look at, and you didn't bother."

"Excuse me for being a little preoccupied at the time."

I shake my head and then dip a hand into my jacket pocket. "I'll check now."

I flip open the box and do what I was apparently supposed to do before. There is indeed an inscription, etched in gold leaf on the inside of the lid: *To my darling husband on our 30th wedding anniversary.*

"Now, look at the cufflinks," Mrs Weller orders. "Closely."

I hold the box up so I can take a proper look. Only then do I notice the three letters engraved into each of the pearl discs.

"DTM?" I murmur.

"Yes. Daniel Thomas Monk."

"I don't get it?"

"They're *your* cufflinks, Daniel, or at least they will be if we can undo what went wrong."

I continue to stare at the cufflinks, struggling to work out the significance.

"If these cufflinks are mine," I eventually remark. "Who gave them to me?"

"I can't tell you that."

"Why not?"

"Because ... because you knowing who you'll marry could cause all manner of complications. The only way to fix this is for you to go back and set my life on the correct path."

"That makes no sense. What does your life have to do with me, or who I end up marrying?"

"Like it or not, our lives are now intertwined. That's my fault, because I set the wheels in motion the day I asked you to value the house. But it's also your fault ... in a way."

"How the hell is any of this my fault?"

"I told you in the letter. You should have shown Kim those photos."

"I couldn't. Partly because I didn't think it was my responsibility, but mainly because I knew it'd hurt her."

"Me. Hurt *me*."

"Yeah, yeah," I reply dismissively. "Anyway, I know how it feels when a partner cheats, and I wanted to save Kim from that pain."

"And that's admirable, but your kindness has complicated matters. Quite a lot, as it happens."

"I'm so terribly sorry," I retort with an exaggerated level of faux remorse. "But I never asked for any of this, did I? You asked me to help you out, and I did. It's not as though I even got what you promised, is it?"

"I appreciate that, but you can't deny that this experience has helped you."

Mrs Weller, or Kim, or whoever the hell she is, edges closer and gently places her hand on my arm.

"I know you've been through a lot this year, and I'm sure my involvement in your life hasn't helped, but you've come a long way in the last few weeks. I know, for example, that you've finally come to terms with the breakdown of your relationship."

"How do you know that?"

"How I know is unimportant. Have you come to terms with the breakdown of your relationship?"

"Well, yeah. I guess."

"And you've established a new career?"

"Kind of."

"You see, this has been as much about you as it has me."

"Great, but I'd have preferred a few sessions with a counsellor over this ... I don't even know what to call *this*."

"True, you could have spoken to a counsellor, but that wouldn't have been so much fun, would it?" she says with a knowing smile. "I mean, we had a good laugh that evening at The Malthouse, didn't we?"

"Eh?"

"Gavin saying he loved The Wurzels. That was so funny, bless him."

My mouth drops open, but the obvious question fails to materialise. How could she possibly know about that conversation?

"Alas, that evening didn't go the way I hoped," Mrs Weller continues. "Which is why, like it or not, our story is far from over, Daniel. In fact, it's only just begun."

The End
... for now

If you're reading these words before December 2024, I can only apologise for leaving Danny's story at this point. Rest assured, I'm beavering away on the next instalment of his adventure and *The Fourth Clause* will be available on Amazon before the end of 2024.

I'd also stress that I've grown to love both Danny's story and the cast of characters in this novel — I sincerely hope you have, too. And that brings me nicely to the subject of future stories involving Danny Monk, Kim Dolan, and the team at Gibley Smith.

When an author begins a new series of novels, they do so in the knowledge that the series will live or die with book one. If *No Easy Deeds* proves a commercial success, that will provide a solid foundation for me to add many more instalments to the story (and I've already planned five). Therefore, dear reader, the fate of this series lies entirely in your hands.

I cannot emphasise enough how grateful I am that you've paid good money for this book and given up many hours of your valuable time to read it. For that reason, it feels like a cheeky ask, but a positive five-star review on Amazon would certainly help build the foundations for this series.

As an indie author, I'm solely reliant on my readers to help spread the word about my books — there's no marketing department or PR guru working on my behalf. For that reason, every five-star review is so very important and massively appreciated.

Beyond that, I hope you've enjoyed *No Easy Deeds* enough that you might consider recommending it to friends, family, and colleagues. In fact, if you fancy approaching strangers on the street and waxing lyrical about it, that'd be amazing. Obviously, I take no responsibility if you're subsequently arrested for harassment and sent to an institute for the mentally unhinged, but do know that I'm grateful.

Until next time.

Keith

www.keithapearson.co.uk

Acknowledgments

Firstly, I'd like thank YOU. If you didn't buy my books, read them, and offer such encouragement, I wouldn't now be writing these words. It still amazes me that I can do this for a living, and never a day goes by when I don't thank my lucky stars that I have such fantastic support from my readers.

I'd also like to thank the following beta readers: Adam Eccles, Maf Sweet, Stuart Whyte, Alan Wood, and Chris Hewitt. I really appreciate your input, chaps.

Now, there is separate group of beta readers who went above and beyond, and they all deserve huge credit for not just their typo-spotting skills, but their invaluable feedback on several plot points. Therefore, my gratitude goes out to: Lisa Gresty, Tracy Fisher, Julie Turpin, and Evelyn Wagner-Leasley. Genuinely, your feedback made a massive difference to how Danny's story evolved, so thank you.

Last, but by no means least, I must thank my fabulous editor, Sian Phillips. There's nothing I can say about Sian's contribution that I haven't said before, so all I'll add is that a good slice of my modest success is down to Sian's hard work and professionalism. She's a true star.

Printed in Great Britain
by Amazon